Julie Anne Lindsey is an obsessive reader who was once torn between the love of her two favourite genres: toe-curling romance and chew-your-nails suspense. Now she gets to write both for Mills & Boon. When she's not creating new worlds, Julie can be found carpooling her three kids around northeastern Ohio and plotting with her shamelessly enabling friends. Winner of the Daphne du Maurier Award for Excellence in Mystery/Suspense, Julie is a member of International Thriller Writers, Romance Writers of America and Sisters in Crime. Learn more about Julie and her books at julieannelindsey.com

Danica Winters is a multiple-award-winning, bestselling author who writes books that grip readers with their ability to drive emotion through suspense and occasionally a touch of magic. When she's not working, she can be found in the wilds of Montana, testing her patience while she tries to hone her skills at various crafts—quilting, pottery and painting are not her areas of expertise. She believes the cup is neither half-full nor half-empty, but it better be filled with wine. Visit her website at danicawinters.net

Also by Julie Anne Lindsey

Deadly Cover-Up
Missing in the Mountains
Marine Protector
Dangerous Knowledge
Shadow Point Deputy
Marked by the Marshal
Federal Agent Under Fire
Impact Zone
The Sheriff's Secret

Also by Danica Winters

A Loaded Question
Hidden Truth
In His Sights
Her Assassin For Hire
Protective Operation
Ms Calculation
Mr Serious
Mr Taken
Ms Demeanour
Smoke and Ashes

Discover more at millsandboon.co.uk

SVU SURVEILLANCE

JULIE ANNE LINDSEY

RESCUE MISSION: SECRET CHILD

DANICA WINTERS

MILLS & BOON

First Published in Great Britain 2021
by Mills & Boon, an imprint of HarperCollins*Publishers* Ltd,
1 London Bridge Street, London, SE1 9GF

www.harpercollins.co.uk

HarperCollins*Publishers*
1st Floor, Watermarque Building,
Ringsend Road, Dublin 4, Ireland

SVU Surveillance © 2021 Julie Anne Lindsey
Rescue Mission: Secret Child © 2021 Danica Winters

ISBN: 978-0-263-28325-9

0221

SVU SURVEILLANCE

JULIE ANNE LINDSEY

For Alicia Wright.

Chapter One

Gwen Kind bent to stretch her hamstrings and catch her breath beside the busiest jogging path in New Plymouth, Kentucky. She'd hoped to shake the icky sensation of being watched off her sweaty skin before heading home, but that clearly wasn't going to happen.

She stood and twisted at the waist, pulling in deep lungfuls of crisp autumn air, then watching the little puffs of breath float away in frosty clouds. October was beautiful in New Plymouth, distractingly so. With the trees showing off their fanciest colors, the city planting endless bunches of gold, crimson and purple mums, and shop owners lining sidewalks in pumpkin-topped hay bales, what wasn't to love? Gwen particularly liked the fact that every downtown window seemed to advertise something flavored or scented in apple cinnamon and mulling spice.

In the park, folks had donned their cool-weather best. Zipped and tucked into brightly colored jackets and hats, they were a hundred dots of human confetti moving across the still green grass. A worn rubber trail ebbed and flowed through clusters of meticulously landscaped trees and around a lake continually packed with geese. Metro Park was never empty, so this was where Gwen would jog now. Even if that meant dodging moms with double strollers and dogs on long leashes, or being occasionally knocked into by folks on bikes, skateboards or Rollerblades.

She preferred her morning runs along the county's less-traveled hike-and-bike trail before work, but lately the solitary path had left her feeling uneasy and distinctly paranoid. She'd nearly sprinted back to her car on the last trip there, certain she wasn't alone, but unable to see anything besides a handful of squirrels and the occasional flock of birds among the trees. Still, instinct insisted she change her routine, and experience agreed. After all, it had only been six years since Gwen had been brutally attacked during her college's homecoming weekend. Raped, beaten and cut. Then left unconscious after a night out with friends.

She fished her car key from her pocket with a sigh. She missed the hike-and-bike trail, but she'd survive. She'd given up many more important things in the name of safety. Losing her favorite place to run was hardly a sacrifice in comparison. Even if Metro Park was a congested nightmare. She gave the area another visual sweep before making the final trek back to the large public parking area beside the busy downtown street.

She checked under the car on her approach, looked nearby men in their eyes, then peered into the back seat before unlocking and opening her door. She dropped immediately behind the wheel and locked up once more, then settled herself for the ride home. At least traffic wouldn't be bad with half the population already at the park.

The drive home was quick and easy, the day bright and pleasant with an unseasonably cold chill. The weatherman had thrown the word *snow* around this morning, making her wonder yet again why she'd relocated to New Plymouth, only one town away from her former college, when she could've stayed with her family in Florida. She'd told her parents she feared her attacker would expect her to go home, and starting over somewhere completely new made her feel safer. It wasn't a lie, but in hindsight she suspected her real motivation for staying in the area had more to do with being a stone's throw from her former fiancé than anything else. Silly, but knowing he was across the county instead of across the country had been a great comfort during the worst of times.

Gwen turned onto her street, then motored into her one-car attached garage and closed the door behind her before getting out. She unlocked the door to her home, then locked it behind her and pressed her code into the keypad beside the coatrack, silencing the alarm system.

She'd chosen the one-story open-floor-plan home for its small, manageable footprint and proximity to town. Just over a thousand square feet with postage-stamp front and back yards. The furnishings were minimal, but brightly colored and purchased locally to avoid the stark utilitarian look her mother continually complained about during her visits. Gwen liked that the place was easy to monitor and protect.

Forty minutes and a quick shower later, she was back in the car, hair clean but damp and wound into her usual tidy bun. She'd traded the running gear and shoes for a gray pantsuit and flats, then performed a speedy lip balm and mascara makeup routine.

The sensation of being watched struck again as her car hit the street beyond her driveway. She checked her mirrors, examining the empty lawns and silent homes around her before shifting into Drive and rolling slowly away. The paranoia grew as she traveled, despite her best efforts to will it away. She practiced controlled breathing and reminded herself that these feelings were normal for someone who'd been through what she had. That PTSD could linger for decades. And she was safe.

Gwen sighed in relief as her office came into view, then

waved at a familiar pair of women on the sidewalk. She hurried to park and catch up with them before they reached the front doors. "Good morning," she called, forcing a smile as she ran.

The women stopped outside a towering set of glass doors.

The historic brick building behind them had once been five stories of run-down apartments, but a recent conversion by her bosses had changed all that. Noble Architecture and Design had gutted the interior and created a phoenix from the rubble. Now the building's face was predominantly glass, and the inside was two soaring floors of design studios with spectacular downtown views.

"You look flushed," Marina, the older of the two women, said as Gwen hustled to reach them. She fastened another button on her white wool coat while she waited. "Or are you glowing? Is there a man?" She drew out the final word in a dramatic singsong way, as was her custom, and Gwen instinctively slowed her pace. The curvy mother of four never tired of trying to find Gwen a date, but Gwen had long ago tired of hearing about it.

"No man," Gwen answered, a hint of aggravation in her tone. She shook her head and smiled to soften the response. It wasn't Marina's fault she didn't understand Gwen's reluctance to date, or know the reasoning behind the decision. No one in New Plymouth did. "I've been running at Metro Park," she added in explanation of her flushed skin. "It was packed before work, so I'm a little behind schedule."

Marina's assistant, Debbie, gave Gwen a once-over. Her heavily lined eyes narrowed and her ruby lips pulled to one side. "I thought you jogged the hike-and-bike trail before work?"

"I do, but the Metro Park gets so much buzz, I thought I'd see what all the fuss was about," Gwen improvised.

"So?" Marina asked, her warm olive skin aglow. "How was it?"

"A definite hotspot from six thirty to seven fifteen a.m.," Gwen groused.

Marina grinned. "I'll bet that makes it a great place to meet people. Young, single people." She worked her eyebrows up and down.

Gwen laughed. "Enough about me. I'm waiting to hear how dinner went last night. Did the kids like the new casserole?" she asked, redirecting the conversation as she held the door for the other women.

Marina let her head drop forward as she crossed the threshold. "Don't get me started." She lifted her stricken face, then dove into a detailed play-by-play on her family's meal preferences and quirks. Debbie hung on every word, and Gwen was officially off the hook for discussion.

The ladies parted ways inside the design studios, and Gwen got lost in her administrative work. The day was a blur of invoicing and phone calls, testing Gwen's concentration and time management skills to the max. Then, just as quickly as it had begun, another day was over.

Her coworkers donned their coats and hats, then moved in a wave toward the elevator doors.

Gwen hustled to keep up. "Hold the elevator!" she called, pressing herself into the already-packed car. She didn't make a habit of being alone anywhere other than her home, and she had a bottle of wine waiting for her there. Plus a half slice of chocolate cake she couldn't wait to finish off.

The car's passengers shifted to make room as she pinned her body between Marina and a tall man in Armani. "Hey, Collin," she said, hoping to sound casual in the awkward position.

"Gwen," he said with a smile. "I stopped by to say hello earlier, but you seemed busy. I didn't want to bother you."

She pressed her lips together and nodded, trying not to think about his body pressed tightly to hers.

The doors parted a moment later, and the passengers spilled into the first-floor foyer.

Collin kept an easy pace at Gwen's side. They made their way back through the glass doors and into the chilly evening. She rolled her shoulders and breathed easier with the added space between them. "Already dark," she muttered, hating autumn for the singular inconvenience and heading for her car at a clip.

Marina and the other designers spoke in hushed tones a few feet behind, likely talking about Collin and his noteworthy physique.

"I think they're talking about me," Collin said with a grin.

"This is my car," Gwen announced, unwilling to bite. Her unremarkable sedan was bathed in a cone of lamplight. She couldn't see beneath the vehicle without bending down, but trusted her coworkers wouldn't let anyone drag her away without a fight.

Collin smiled.

"You already know that," she said. Just like she knew he drove the sleek black sports car parked a few rows away. "Sorry."

He shrugged. "Got any plans for the weekend?"

Netflix and chill crossed her mind, except in Gwen's world the phrase was extremely literal and done alone. "Maybe. You?"

"I'm thinking about dinner at La Maison Blanche. Any chance I can convince you to join me?"

She smiled, but shook her head. "I can't. I——"

"Say no more." He raised a hand and returned her smile. "Can't blame a guy for trying. Another night, then?"

"Maybe."

His expression brightened as he turned to walk backward, moving in the direction of his car. "That's not a no," he said. "And I'm nothing if not dedicated to a good cause. See you tomorrow, Kind."

She lifted one hand in a hip-high wave, then waited before turning around.

Marina and the other designers were blatantly eavesdropping from their nearby cars.

The older women waved innocently as Collin drove away.

Victoria Noble, owner of the design group, was the first to speak. "Are you crazy?" she asked. "Collin is smitten with you, and he's perfect. Have you seen his backside?"

Gwen snorted, suddenly absolutely certain of what the others had been whispering about behind them. Her humor faded, however, as the icy fingers of unease slid down her spine. The too-familiar sensation of being watched settled hot on her cheeks.

"She's blushing," Marina called. "We've embarrassed her. We're sorry, sweetie. We're just suckers for love."

"And that heinie," Victoria added.

Gwen's chest constricted, and the world began to tilt. She turned in search of an onlooker, but saw no one.

"We'll see you tomorrow, hon," Marina called.

Gwen raised a palm absently before dropping into her car and locking the doors.

A folded sheet of paper came immediately into view, flapping gently against her windshield where it was trapped beneath one wiper blade. For a moment, she debated leaving it there, driving away without accepting it, whatever it was. She didn't need another take-out menu. Didn't want to see a local band or run a 5K for charity. And she didn't want to get back out of her locked car, alone at night in the parking lot.

She stared at the offending flyer. If she left it stuck there, it would probably blow off in traffic, and Gwen wasn't a litterbug. She steeled her nerves, then jumped out to snatch the paper and return to her position behind the wheel. She tossed the page onto the passenger seat and locked the doors.

The dashboard vents piped hot air throughout the small space and rustled the paper, drawing her attention to the sheet once more.

A familiar logo registered with each flap of the folded sheet. She reached carefully across the car, as if the flyer might attack, then pressed the paper open. Air rushed from her lungs as she took the message in.

It wasn't a take-out menu, marketing for a band or a local 5K.

It was an invitation to the Bellemont College Homecoming.

Chapter Two

Lucas Winchester slammed the receiver of his desktop phone in frustration. Some days, being a West Liberty Special Victims Unit Detective was exactly what he'd signed up for. Most days it wasn't, and today was one of those. He scrubbed angry hands against his stubble-covered cheeks and swore. He'd hauled low-level street thug and repeat-rapist Tommy Black in three times in two years, and he'd hoped yesterday's arrest would be the last. Somehow the scumbag got off every time. A loophole or technicality. And unlike Lucas, Tommy was having a stellar day. According to the Bond Enforcement officer who'd dialed Lucas as a courtesy, someone had posted Tommy's bail. Now the creep was on the loose again. Bad news for his favorite victim, an on-again, off-again girlfriend he frequently beat, and also raped, from time to time.

Lucas stared at the silent phone. He had to tell Anise that her abuser was out again.

He should've been an architect. Should've listened to his folks and his professors, but the little voice in his head was too loud to be ignored. *Be a cop. Make a difference. Be someone's hero.* That was what he'd told himself before he knew how frequently the system let people down. When he'd been a peripheral victim of injustice, he'd blamed the terrible officers who'd obviously missed something and completely dropped the ball. These days he knew better. Lucas was a damn good cop, and criminals walked every day. One way or another.

He stretched his neck and gave himself a mental kick in the pants. Then he dialed Anise and gave her the news. The conversation went as poorly as expected. He encouraged her to make a statement, press charges and testify in court, but she refused. Rightfully afraid of Tommy, and certain Lucas would fail her again. He couldn't blame her for that. How could he? Anise swore vehemently at him before hanging up.

"Today sucks," he muttered, shaking a pair of aspirin into his palm. He kept a bottle the size of a football in his drawer, right beside a matching tub of antacids. *Thank you, Big Box Store.* He washed the pair of pills down with the dregs of his stone-cold coffee, thankful it was finally quitting time.

Based on the rumble of footfalls and familiar voices outside his office, Lucas wasn't the only one whose shift was over. His coworkers would get a drink together and blow off some steam before heading home to their families. Lucas had wild plans for uninterrupted solitude and maybe another self-loathing pass at the piles of worn-and-tattered files in his guest-room-turned-office. The five-year-old cold case had started him on his current path, though the case hadn't been cold at the time. Nowadays, Lucas was the terrible officer who couldn't name or apprehend the violent rapist.

"Winchester!" Bruce, a detective twenty years his senior, called before swinging through the open door with a small entourage at his back. "Beers and burgers. Let's go!"

Lucas kicked his open desk drawer shut and forced a tight smile. "Not tonight." He stretched onto his feet and threaded his arms into the worn leather jacket he'd had since college.

"Another hot date?" Bruce asked, sounding a little too impressed by the possibility.

Lucas tugged a knit cap over his shaggy hair and grinned. "Hey, don't worry, Bruce. Your wife always turns me down."

The group laughed.

Bruce scoffed. "Yeah, right. I don't believe that for a minute. Look at you, all *GQ*. I'm still wearing the loafers I wore when you were sworn in."

Lucas shouldered his bag and pocketed his keys, then led the way toward the exit.

"Who's the woman?" Bruce pressed, sticking close to his heels.

"You don't know her."

Bruce made a throaty noise behind him. "Of course I don't know her. I'm married thirty years. I got three kids in Catholic school. Who do I know besides them and the priest?"

"Then why ask?" Lucas challenged.

Bruce edged in beside him, shoulders raised to his ears. "I want to know more people. Where do you meet all these women? They aren't students at the college are they?"

Lucas groaned inwardly, certain the hallway was getting longer with each step. It was his fault really. He'd paraded a string of pointless dates through the local pub several years back and made a name for himself as a playboy among cops, which was saying something. It had been a failed attempt to move on with his new life, using women and booze as a distraction. Then, he'd made his first big arrest and everything changed. Suddenly the only distraction he needed was the thrill of the chase and the victory of seeing violent offenders get what they deserved. He'd cleaned himself up, stopped trying to replace the one woman who meant everything with a dozen who meant nothing and took up jogging to clear his head. Thankfully, his bad reputation still got him out of drinks with the boys whenever he wanted.

"Really," Bruce pushed. "Who is she this time?"

She, Lucas thought, was the smart, sassy, fun-loving woman he'd met on campus his junior year at Bellemont College. The same woman who'd promptly and irrevocably stolen his heart. Then broken it.

"You never bring your ladies out anymore," Bruce said. "Some of us are married, but we're not dead. We liked seeing your flavors of the month."

"Month?" Another detective laughed. "You mean week?"

Lucas glanced over his shoulder and shook his head. It was too easy to keep up the facade. These guys did all the work on their own.

A woman cleared her throat in front of them, and Lucas spun back. The group halted sharply, rocking collectively on their heels. "Pardon me, detectives," Officer Kim Lake said, looking wholly unimpressed by the conversation she'd clearly overheard. "Detective Winchester is needed in the conference room." She hooked a thumb over one shoulder, indicating the open door several feet away.

The group clapped him on the back as they strode past, probably thankful not to be the one held up at quitting time.

Lucas did his best not to seem disappointed. "What is it, Kim?"

"There's a woman asking to see you."

Lucas frowned back at her. "Someone's here to file a report?" He didn't normally take the reports. Cases were assigned to him.

"No, she's asking for you. By name." Kim crossed her

arms. "And I don't think she's here on a personal visit. She looks too smart to put up with any of your nonsense."

Lucas grinned. "Fair," he said. "Reporter?"

"Didn't say." Kim turned to stand beside him, staring in the direction of the open conference room door. "She seems shaken, so I wouldn't peg her for a reporter, but she wouldn't say more. Only that she needs to talk with you, Luke Winchester."

"Luke?" he asked, moving around Kim toward the open door.

"Yeah."

No one had called Lucas that in years. No one at the precinct ever had.

Instinct clawed at the back of his neck as he lengthened his strides. "Thanks."

He knocked on the door frame with a spear of anticipation, determined to look both professional and approachable. "Sorry to keep you waiting. I'm Detective—" The words clogged in his throat. His limbs froze, and his heart rate spiked at the sight of the barely recognizable woman before him.

But even six years later, her wild red curls tamed into a bun and wearing a high-end pantsuit instead of cutoffs and his old concert shirts, Lucas knew her instantly.

"Gwen."

Chapter Three

Lucas led Gwen into O'Grady's Pub, a place they'd frequented together in another lifetime, and one he'd avoided every day since. Still, O'Grady's had seemed like the best alternative when Gwen insisted on speaking privately, but not at the precinct. She hadn't said much more than that, and her silence had Lucas's nerves on edge. As if it wasn't enough that she'd shown up out of the blue like this, now she had a secret, too.

He scanned the multitude of faces as they threaded their way through the tightly packed space. Music thumped from overhead speakers and voices rose in waves, cheering at televised ball games and real-life rounds of darts. The beloved pub was only a few blocks from campus and downtown, making it a hotspot for civilians and especially unpopular with the cops who took too much interest in Lucas's personal life. For that reason alone, the place was perfect.

"Wow," Gwen muttered, taking in the static decor and general commotion. "This place hasn't changed."

"Not at all," he agreed. "The nostalgia is strong here." Thankfully, so were the drinks.

His thoughts, however, were erratic, confused and demanding. What had brought Gwen back to West Liberty after all this time? Why hadn't she told him yet? And why not just call?

Probably because she never called, he thought dryly. *Not in six years.*

She stopped at a small corner booth away from the crowd. "This okay?"

He dipped his chin, slightly aggravated by the secrecy and mild theatrics that had never been Gwen's way.

She dropped her purse on the heavily lacquered table, then slid onto the cracked red vinyl seat, facing the door and window.

Reluctantly, Lucas settled on the bench across from her with his back to the door. He clasped his hands on the tabletop and waited. Patience was a skill preached endlessly at the academy, one he wasn't any good at. "Ready to tell me what this is about yet?"

Her wide brown eyes snapped to his, and she matched his posture, twining her fingers on the table. "I'm sorry I didn't call first."

He shrugged. "It's no problem." He couldn't get a bead on her mood. Nervous, obviously, but why? Being back in this town? Being there with him? She'd marched into the precinct wanting to see him for something. It'd be great if she got around to explaining what that was. He clenched his jaw against the possibility she'd come to announce she was getting married and didn't want him to hear it from anyone else first.

"Do you need to call anyone?" she asked, projecting her voice against the din of rowdy patrons.

The question caught him off guard and drew him back to the moment, confused again. "Who?"

Gwen frowned. "From where I was sitting earlier, it sounded as if you might have a hot date."

Lucas fought the urge to laugh, opting instead to remove his jacket and toss it onto the bench beside him. Heat coursed up his neck at the memory of Bruce and the others teasing him in the hallway. "I don't need to call anyone."

She rolled her eyes. "How are your folks?"

"Good. Yours?"

"Fine."

"Gwen," he whispered, leaning across the table. "Whatever brought you here. Whatever you want to say. Just say it. I can't react until I know what this is about."

She shifted, pulling her hands into her lap. A flash of uncertainty crossed her pretty face, and she chewed her bottom lip. "Someone invited me to homecoming."

"Homecoming?" Lucas let the words circle, then settle, in his heart and head. After what had happened to her at homecoming six years back, it seemed a strange and senseless statement. Who would do that? And why had she made the trip to town to tell Lucas? "Do I know him?" he asked, hoping it wasn't one of his idiot college roommates. Should he care if it was? Did she want him to care?

"I don't know," she said softly, dragging the silver zipper open on her purse. She reached inside and removed a folded sheet of paper with trembling fingers. "It could be nothing," she said, her expression both apologetic and hopeful. "If it's nothing, then I don't want to talk about it, and I'll be on my way. But if it's something, I knew I couldn't talk to anyone other than you."

"Let me see." Lucas took the paper and fanned it open with unnecessary force, then smoothed it on the table between them. "Join Bellemont College staff and students for a week of homecoming fun," he read. He'd seen variations of the same flyer posted all over town, printed in the newspaper and splashed generously across local media all month. "I don't get it." He raised his eyes to hers once more, trying and failing to understand the reason one folded flyer had drawn her out of hiding and delivered her to his door.

A tear slid over the curve of her pink cheek, and she swiped it away with one shaky hand. "I know."

Her whisper gonged in the too-loud, overcrowded bar, pounding straight through Lucas's heart. He released the flyer to scrub a palm across his mouth. "Sorry." Coming back to West Liberty wasn't easy for her. The least he could do was be patient while she got to her point. Assuming she had one. "Who invited you to homecoming?"

Another tear fell, erased by a quick, determined hand. "I don't know."

Lucas straightened, eyes narrowing. "What do you mean, you don't know? Where'd you get the flyer?"

"I found it tucked under my windshield wiper after work." Gwen swallowed and wet her lips. "No one else's car had one."

Tension wound through his limbs. A hundred heinous thoughts presented in his brain. "When you said you were invited to homecoming. This is what you meant?" Suddenly things made more sense. Her visit. Her mood. "You think it was a message?" He bit his tongue against the thing neither of them would say. *A message from her rapist.* A man who had never been caught.

Her eyes misted, and she pressed her pink lips tight.

"Hey, y'all!" a perky blonde called upon approach. Her O'Grady's T-shirt and apron over blue jeans announced her as pub staff. "What can I get y'all started with?"

Gwen worked up a smile. "White wine. And fries."

The waitress grinned. "Gotcha." She flicked her gaze to Lucas. "For you?"

"House ale on tap," he said, not caring what she brought. The beer was officially a prop to put Gwen at ease. Her visit wasn't personal. It was business, which meant Lucas was on duty. Hopefully the glass of wine Gwen ordered would help her relax enough to tell the rest of her story in detail. The more he knew, the better chance he had at helping.

"Anything else?" the waitress asked.

Lucas trailed his gaze over Gwen's narrow jaw and frame. "Chips and salsa. Burger sliders. For the table."

Gwen waited for the waitress to leave before returning her attention to him. The tears were gone and fresh resolution burned in her eyes. "I started feeling as if I was being watched about three weeks ago. I wasn't sure at first, because I still get paranoid like that sometimes. Usually, it's a moment here or there. Nothing that sticks. Then a few weeks ago, the sensation never really left. Instead, it's gotten progressively worse, and today after work, there was a flyer for homecoming on my windshield. I understand it could be nothing, but I think it's time I get a second opinion."

Lucas ground his teeth at the possibility someone was following her, frightening her. "Any chance someone you know is messing with you?" he asked, trying to rule out the more likely and less dangerous possibilities first. "Maybe this person doesn't know the extent of what you've been through, only that you never visit your alma mater, and they wanted to tease you about it for some reason?"

"No." She kneaded her hands on the table. "I've never told anyone about what happened to me at Bellemont. No one even knows I went to college there. I didn't include the school on my résumé."

He frowned, wondering selfishly if she'd erased him from her revised history, as well. "What do you do for a living that didn't require your degree?" he asked, sticking to a safer subject. He didn't know a lot about fashion, but the suit, heels and handbag all seemed to scream corporate. And when he'd met her, she had been on track to be a very successful engineer.

"I'm an administrative assistant at the Noble Architecture and Design Firm in New Plymouth."

"New Plymouth." The town name nearly took him as off guard as her career choice. Gwen was living only one town away. "How long have you been back from Florida?"

Gwen lowered her eyes again, choosing to study her manicure, then their surroundings. "I only stayed with my parents for a few months. I told myself I had to come back and get on with living." She shrugged out of her coat and folded it on the bench beside her, then set her purse on top. "I got a job, eventually bought a home. But I couldn't bring myself to go back to Bellemont and finish those last few classes, so I didn't. What was one more change when my life was already topsy-turvy, right?"

"I suppose." Lucas took a moment to process the information and appreciate the subtle changes.

Gwen was beautiful as always, if thinner. Her formerly curvy figure was lean, almost willowy and her skin slightly sun-kissed despite the plummeting temperatures.

"You're still jogging."

She grimaced, as if he'd hit a sore spot. "It used to be the only time I felt completely unburdened, but that's different now, too."

The waitress returned with their drinks, and Gwen took a long sip of her wine. She traced a fingertip along the condensation of her glass, then told her story in full, filling Lucas in on the significant details of her last few weeks. How she felt unsafe at her usual jogging spot and hated the new one. How she felt watched outside her home and work. And worried she might be losing her mind.

"Have you considered getting a guard dog?" Lucas asked.

"I have," she said, "but I wouldn't want to leave him

home alone all day while I'm at work, and I wouldn't want to go out alone at night to walk him."

"How about a husband?" he asked, hoping to sound playful instead of jealous at the thought.

"No men," she said, her tone strangely sharp. "I don't date."

Lucas lifted his palms in apology, obviously hitting another nerve.

The waitress returned with their food and a second glass of wine for Gwen, then vanished into the crowd once more.

Lucas sipped his beer and processed all he'd learned. He pushed the chips and sliders into the table's center, indicating Gwen should help herself. His insides had tightened beyond the ability to eat the moment he'd realized she could be right. The son of a gun who'd left her for dead could be back and coming for her again. And what could Lucas do to stop him?

She snagged a fry and forced a tight smile. "Well, what do you think, Detective Winchester? Do I have reason to worry? Or am I being paranoid?"

Lucas flicked his attention to the flyer before leveling her with his most protective stare. "I don't like it," he said honestly. "And I don't believe in coincidences. But you can be sure I won't let anyone hurt you again. Not ever."

GWEN LET THE fervor of his words strengthen her. If anyone understood what she'd been through, it was Luke. He'd lost everything right alongside her. And when she'd asked him to, he'd had the grace to let her go, as well.

She dunked half a fry in the paper cup of ketchup at the edge of her plate and tried desperately to relax. But so much had changed. Her. Him. *Them.* He didn't even go by his nickname anymore. The female officer had nearly laughed when Gwen had requested to speak with Luke Winchester.

"Are you doing okay?" he asked, concern marring his handsome brow.

"Not really," she admitted. Being back in West Liberty was harder than she'd expected, and so was seeing him.

He'd aged unfairly well, of course, filled out in all the right places and seemed impossibly more fit than he had in college. He carried himself differently now, too, no longer the dorky future architect she'd fallen in love with. This Luke, *Lucas*, she corrected herself, had a coolness in his eyes and tension to his limbs she'd never known in him. "You've barely touched your beer."

"The night's young," he said, absently, his gaze searching the crowd.

"Is it? Or are you on duty right now?" she asked. "Because you seemed agitated when we sat down, now you're clearly on edge."

His lips curled into a cocky grin. "I don't know what you mean."

"Don't do that," Gwen snapped, the words coming more harshly than she'd intended. She pulled her shoulders back and pressed her lips together briefly before going on. "Don't pretend like I don't know you. You're scanning the crowd on a regular circuit, and you've angled yourself on the bench for a better look at the door and front window. You're obviously on alert, and if it's because of what I told you, I need to know. The fact that you're nursing that beer makes me think you want to keep a clear head, and I worry that it's because you think what I've told you is cause for concern and that I might be in danger."

He swiveled forward, eyes hot and jaw locked. "I don't know if you're in danger. I didn't even know you lived twenty minutes away until thirty minutes ago, but for what it's worth, yeah. I think you were smart to trust your instincts. And I don't believe in coincidences."

Gwen's stomach rolled. The wine and french fries revolted in her gut. As they should have. She wasn't twenty-two and carefree anymore. This night was too much. The whole day was too much. She rubbed her fingertips against a napkin and pushed the plate aside. "I should probably use the ladies' room then head home."

Lucas stood silently and waited at the end of the table while she gathered her things and slid out.

"What about your sliders?"

"I'll get a box." He stretched one arm toward the hallway in the back of the pub, then trailed her as she made her way to the ladies' room.

The protective gesture warmed her heart and stung her eyes.

He leaned against the wall outside the restroom while she hurried inside.

She splashed cold water on her face, then ripped the pins and elastic from her hair, letting her curls fall free. She plucked the creamy fabric of her silk blouse away from her heated skin a few times, then dabbed a wet paper towel along her neck and collarbone. "You are safe," she told the wide brown-eyed reflection staring back at her. Lucas was clearly still perfect, impossibly sexier than she'd remembered and on her side. If there was anything to fear, he would let her know. Until then, she'd finger-comb her crazy hair, wipe the drops of water from her face and go home for some much needed sleep.

She reopened the bathroom door and Lucas smiled.

"Hey." He reached for her with an apologetic look in his eyes, and she nearly leapt into him. "I should've done this earlier," he whispered into her wild and unruly hair. His protective arms wound around her, tucking her in tight. "It's nice to see you, Gwen. You look stunning as always, and I'm glad you're here." He released her too soon, gripping her shoulders gently and fixing her with a determined gaze. "I don't know what's going on back in New Plymouth, but I meant what I said about protecting you any way I can. A lot of things have changed between us, but not that. Never that."

"Thanks."

He motioned her ahead of him, back through the crowd toward the table. "So, what happened in that bathroom?" he asked. "It looks like your hair went crazy."

"Shut up." She shot him a sideways look as they reached the booth. "I thought you always liked my crazy hair."

"I do." He scooped a disposable container off the table. "I saw the waitress while I was waiting. She got the box ready."

"Great. Where's the bill?"

Lucas scanned the table and benches, then checked on the floor beneath. "I'll ask at the register."

Gwen led the way and stopped behind an older couple getting change. She slid her coat on as they waited, butterflies swooping in her core. Her nerves burned, hyperaware of Lucas's nearness and the way he made her feel when he looked at her like she wasn't permanently broken. She longed to reach for him again, hungry for the physical contact and proof she wasn't alone.

He smiled at the cashier as the older couple moved away, then explained where he'd been seated and requested the bill.

The younger woman smiled politely, then tapped on the register.

Gwen winced as the familiar tingles of paranoia lifted the fine hairs on her arms and neck. She scanned the room in search of someone looking her way, but the lively crowd was lost to itself, tuned in to a hundred different conversations that had nothing to do with her or her problems.

"It looks like your bill has been paid," the cashier said brightly.

"What?" Lucas asked. "By who?"

The uneasy sensation of being watched rode over Gwen's skin once more, and she clutched on to Lucas's sleeve for support.

"Are you sure you've got the right table?" Lucas asked, a clear measure of disbelief in his tone. "We were alone in the corner booth."

"Positive," the cashier said pertly. "There's even a note in the register's memo. Must've been a friend. It says, 'Welcome Home.'"

Chapter Four

Lucas felt his jaw lock and his senses heighten. He reached for Gwen on instinct, setting a protective palm over her hand, resting on his sleeve. "Can you remember what the person who paid this bill looked like?" he asked, reaching into his pocket for the badge he rarely went anywhere without. "This is important, so think carefully." He presented the badge, and the cashier's eyes widened.

"No. It wasn't me," she said.

"Then who?" Lucas demanded. If he had a chance at finding this alleged friend, time was of the essence, and the cashier was wasting his.

"Uhm." She stared nervously at the cash register's computer screen, her round cheeks going red under pressure. "It was Thomas. Server nineteen." She looked up proudly and clearly relieved. "We use our codes to access the register."

"Where's Thomas now?" Lucas asked. "I need to speak with him."

"Okay." The young woman backed away from the register and rose onto her toes. "He usually covers the back."

Gwen stepped closer, then sucked in a ragged breath, as if she'd temporarily forgotten to breathe.

"There!" the cashier said. "Tall. Black hair. Brown eyes." She thrust a hand over her head and waved. "Thomas!"

Lucas leaned his head closer to Gwen's while he tracked

Thomas visually through the room. "You're all right," he promised her. "I've got you."

She nodded quickly and seemed to struggle to swallow.

Lucas flashed his badge again as Thomas approached.

The server was lean and young, likely just old enough to handle the alcohol he served. He'd threaded his way through the crowd with ease and agility. An athlete, likely. And based on his posture and expression, a cocky one.

Thomas cast a wary gaze at the girl behind the counter. "What's up?" he asked, dragging his attention from her to Lucas. "I do something wrong?"

"No." Lucas motioned to the register. "I'd like a description of the person who paid our bill."

Thomas stepped around to the register and examined the screen. "Corner booth. Sliders and fries." He looked up with a frown. "Sorry, man. I barely looked at that guy."

Not surprising on a night as busy as this. "How long ago did he pay?" Lucas asked. "Was it in cash? Did he use a card?" Lucas nearly snorted at the absurdity. If the bill-payer was up to no good, as suspected, he wouldn't have used a credit card. Unless it was stolen, or the user was stupid. Lucas wasn't that lucky.

And if they were truly dealing with Gwen's attacker, he wasn't that stupid.

"He gave me cash," Thomas said, projecting his voice above the crowd. "Maybe ten minutes ago. Told me to keep the change. I wish I could tell you more, but I can't, and it's crazy busy. Now, if you'll—"

"No," Lucas said, widening his stance and pressing his palm onto the counter between them. "I need a description of the man who paid this bill. You can tell me here or at the station."

Thomas smacked his lips. "Man, I didn't do anything wrong, but I'm about to be fired if I—"

"Get arrested?" Lucas asked. "Please, check the time stamp. I want to know how long ago this man was here. Did you see him leave?"

Thomas shook his head, forcing his attention back to the register. "Says seven twelve, and no, I didn't see him leave. In case you haven't noticed, this place is packed. I'm barely keeping up, and leaving my area to come up here and pay your bill pulled me away from my tables. Now, I'm up here again, and I can't help you."

Lucas glanced at his watch. Thomas had handled the bill nearly twenty minutes ago. Long enough for the person to be out of town by now. "Take a look around," Lucas said, scanning the bar. "Do you see him? Was he with anyone when you spoke to him?"

Thomas looked slowly around, his agitation turning to defeat. "Nah, man. I don't see him. He was alone near the dartboard in back when he stopped me. I was rushing past with a big order. He put a wad of cash on my tray, told me what he wanted me to do and I agreed. That was it. I served the table, then came up here to pay your bill. After that, I got back to work. There's nothing else to tell."

"He stopped you," Lucas repeated, "gave you more work to do, a task that wasn't your job and paid with a large sum of cash, but you can't tell me what he looked like? You don't know if he was Black or white? Hispanic or Asian? Short? Tall? Young? Old?"

"He was old, all right?" Thomas said. "Probably thirty. He looked like all of you, decked out in our gear, coming back here for homecoming and trying to relive your college years."

Lucas sucked his teeth and forced himself not to argue that he was twenty-eight, not thirty, and neither age was old. *Unless you were twenty-one*, he supposed. He took another look at the crush of bodies in the popular pub.

Thomas was right. At least half were clearly over twenty-five and most were wearing Bellemont College colors or jerseys. They really did all look alike. He tipped his head to motion Thomas away from the register. "Got any security cameras in here?"

"Yeah." He lifted a finger to indicate a single unit above the cash register. A place the man who paid their bill had been careful not to go.

"Thanks," Lucas said, passing Thomas a few bucks for his time. Lucas had waited tables once, too, and he knew how important tips were to survival.

Gwen's grip on his arm loosened, and she backed away. "What now?" she asked, shoving her hands into her pockets.

"Now, we get you home," Lucas said, scanning the crowd for anyone who seemed especially interested in them. "There's no one else to talk to here. We know whoever paid our bill didn't go to the register. And I've got no description, other than old." He slid a sideways look in her direction, and her lips curved up on one side.

"I don't think you're old," she said.

"That's because I've only got a year on you." He left his card on the counter with the cashier, then led Gwen back onto the sidewalk. "I think you should stay at my place tonight," he said, once they were free of the music and gonging mashup of sounds.

"I don't think so," she said. "I have work tomorrow morning, and I never miss. The last thing I need is to alert anyone at the office that something might be wrong."

He stifled the urge to remind her that something was definitely wrong, and she had no reason to try to hide it. "Then you should consider letting me stay with you. Either way, I don't think you should be alone tonight. We've confirmed you're being followed, and I'm willing to bet this guy isn't overjoyed to see you with another man, or a cop. Since I check both of those boxes, there could be a problem."

Gwen shivered. "We can go to my house."

Lucas drove Gwen back to the police station parking lot, then followed her home at precisely the speed limit. Him in his new extended cab black pickup with a local PD sticker in the window. Her in her nondescript, plain as hell gray sedan. They turned off the main road through her town and into an older neighborhood with compact, nearly utilitarian homes lining each side of every street. Cookie-cutter boxes with postage-stamp yards and limited privacy, short of shutting all the blinds.

Gwen's home was sandwiched between two white single-story cottages on a cul-de-sac. Hers was a cheery yellow number with white shutters, a red door and security cameras everywhere.

She pulled into the attached one-car garage, then motioned him to follow once he'd parked in the drive.

She ducked her head shyly when he met her in the small space, then pressed a button on the wall, closing the garage door before unlocking the door to her home.

Gwen turned the lock on the knob behind them, then flipped two dead bolts and secured a chain before entering a code to stop the wailing security alarm. She waited, frozen, staring at the screen until a row of green numbers appeared beside the word *SECURE*.

With the alarm silenced, Gwen headed for the kitchen. "Can I get you something? Water or coffee?"

"Water is fine," he said, taking a turn around the home's living space.

The decor was simple and tidy. White everything, with an occasional blue-patterned pillow, strategically placed silver centerpiece or a leafy green plant to break up the monotony. The result was attractive, intentional and devoid of personality. Like a magazine cover. Staged, but not lived in.

Each room opened to the next in a typical, continuous plan. The kitchen flowed into an eating space that spilled left into a family room and right into a formal dining area, which Gwen had set up as an office. The living room and office were connected by a small foyer and hall which he assumed led to the bedrooms. "You have a nice place."

"Thank you."

The sounds of cupboard doors, clinking glasses and jostling ice cubes drifted through the space to his ears.

"Everything here is original," she called. "It's got good bones, and I knew I had to have it the moment the Realtor pulled into the drive. The place needed a lot of TLC back then, but I've been diligent. Refinishing woodwork, repairing crown molding, cabinets and floors. Pretty much anything the previous owners didn't get to. It's been a great experience, and I'm nearly done."

Lucas nodded to himself as he returned to her. Home restoration was a great way to pass a lot of time alone. "You were going to be an engineer," he said, watching as she approached, a glass in each hand.

"Life happened," she said, remorsefully. "I was going to be a lot of things."

Like his wife, he thought, uselessly angry again at what the actions of one monster had done to two futures. "Thanks." He accepted the water and sipped.

Gwen returned to the kitchen and stopped at an old landline telephone and answering machine combo. She pressed a blinking button on the answering machine, and a mechanical voice announced two new messages.

"Hello," a female voice greeted. "This is Dr. Maslow's office calling to confirm your appointment—"

Gwen pressed another button, moving quickly to the next message.

"Hey. Gwen. It's Collin," a friendly man's voice said. "I was thinking about that rain check and wondering what you think of dinner at—"

Gwen interrupted the second message like the first. She glanced at Lucas, looking suddenly as uncomfortable in her home as she had in the bar.

"You keep a landline?" Lucas asked. "Not a popular convention these days." Though he suspected he knew why it appealed to Gwen. Landlines were more reliable than cell phones when calling for emergency services, and a cell signal blocker couldn't stop a landline call. For someone still recovering emotionally from an attack, like Gwen clearly was, a secondary form of communication probably seemed wise. Comforting, at least.

Her cell phone hadn't helped her before.

"The landline came with the house." She shrugged. "It's convenient and always charged. Plus I never have to go hunting for it."

"All true," Lucas said, then watched as her smile faded, having never truly reached her eyes.

"And the security system uses it."

He set his water aside, thoughts running back to the messages that had been waiting for her. "You have a doctor's appointment. Are you feeling okay?"

"Therapist," she said softly. "I started seeing someone again a few weeks ago when the feelings of being watched grew unusually persistent. I thought I was relapsing. It was scary."

"Understandable," Lucas said. "You were smart to set up the appointments. Everyone needs someone to talk to." He tried not to wonder who her confidant was now, and if she talked to the man from the messages the way she used to talk to him.

Gwen climbed onto a stool at the kitchen island and cradled her glass between her palms. "Go on. Ask whatever you need to. I want to help you figure out what's going on here, however I can. It's been a while since I opened up about my life, but I'm going to do my best. I know it's important that you get all the facts, and that I'm as honest as possible with my answers. We need to know who's following me and why."

He took the seat beside her and tapped his thumbs against the table's edge. "How many people know where you live?" he began. "How many have been here? And how many of them have come inside with you after being away?"

"How many people have seen me disable my alarm?" she asked. "How many might have memorized the code as I typed it? None."

"Good," he said. "How many have been inside, seen your layout and the security measures in place?"

"Three," she said easily, releasing her glass in favor of crossing her arms. "My mother, my father and Marina from my office."

Lucas felt his brows raise. "In all the years since you moved in, only three people have come over to visit?"

"Yes."

"Okay. What about neighbors and friends? Anyone you've told about your attack or your recent feelings of being followed? Anyone your stalker might go to for information on you? Or someone he might use as a way to hurt you?"

Her eyes widened slightly, but she didn't flinch. "No. Everyone on my street keeps to themselves, and I'm not especially close to anyone. I don't talk about what I've been through outside of therapy. There's no reason to relive it more than I already do, and I don't want the pity that inevitably comes when people learn that I'm a victim."

"Were," Lucas said, feeling the familiar knot of regret and empathy in his core.

"What?"

"You were a victim. Once. Six years ago. You aren't a victim anymore," he assured her. He wouldn't allow her to be.

Gwen's lips tugged into a small, sad smile. "You're wrong."

"I'm not," he said, resolve rising in him. He hadn't been able to stop her from becoming a victim before, but that was a lifetime ago, in a world where they were getting married and he was going to be an architect. Her attacker had shattered those dreams, and Lucas was left alone to pick up the pieces. He made a damn good special victim's detective from the rubble, and he was going to make sure Gwen's stalker regretted ever targeting her.

Chapter Five

Gwen woke before dawn, eager to get outside for a run. She swung her feet out from beneath her covers, and the events of the previous day rushed back to her with a snap.

There wouldn't be a run in the park this morning. Not with someone following her, and Luke Winchester in her guest room. *Lucas*, she reminded herself once more. He went by Lucas now. A more grown-up name for the more grown-up man. One with all the heart and compassion she'd once loved, packed into a more-mature and slightly brooding, but equally attractive, package.

She rubbed her forehead to clear her thoughts, then shuffled toward her dresser in search of an outfit. Having Lucas in the next room, in her new life, was confusing and complicated enough without thinking about his handsome face or soulful eyes. Never mind the intense compassion he still had in spades. Her addled, sleepy mind thought that maybe being near him again was worth the tension of being followed for a little while.

A good sign she needed coffee. And a run.

Lucas had fallen in love with a whimsical young college student, and Gwen was officially an uptight, no-nonsense hermit. The attraction these days could only run one way. She was lucky he'd agreed to help at all after she'd shown up at his precinct, without invitation or notice.

Gwen dressed for a date with her treadmill, then headed to the kitchen for some much-needed caffeine.

"Morning," Luke said, startling her as she exited her bedroom. His smile was warm and his hair mussed. He was dressed nearly identical to her, in black running pants and matching long-sleeved top. "I keep a gym bag in my truck," he said, apparently noticing her staring. "Sometimes I work out at the precinct."

"Yeah, you do," she muttered, allowing herself a moment to appreciate his broad shoulders, flat stomach and long, lean legs. She easily imagined what his body must look like under those clothes, clinging in all the right places.

His lips kicked up on one side and he chuckled. "I thought we could have breakfast, then maybe go for a run."

"Okay," she said, unsure when he'd begun running, but liking the idea.

"I can drop you off at work afterward, then I'll head back to West Liberty and take care of things there. I can be back to your office in time to drive you home."

Gwen tensed, all the warm and fuzzy feelings going cold. "You can't drive me to work. People will see you. What am I supposed to say?"

"That a friend dropped you off? Your car is in the shop?" he suggested. "Everyone's ride needs maintenance eventually."

She considered the simple response. Car maintenance. It sounded completely logical coming from him, but no one had ever driven her to work, and she wasn't convinced she could so easily explain it away. "I want to think about it."

"Sure. How about some oatmeal and coffee before we go?" he motioned her toward the kitchen, and she led the way.

The scent of fresh-brewed coffee drifted out to greet

her. Two mugs waited beside a full pot and a bowl of mixed fruits.

"I hope you don't mind," Luke said. "I cut up some of your melon. The berries and grapes looked as if they needed to be eaten before they went bad. I thought the cantaloupe was a good addition."

"Not at all." Gwen smiled, recalling all the times he'd made her breakfast in another life. Usually burnt pancakes or hurried scrambled eggs before class. "Thank you." She poured coffee into both mugs, then spooned up two bowls of fresh fruit.

Lucas lifted a teakettle from her stove as it began to sing and added the steaming water to bowls of dried oats. He topped the mixture with brown sugar and drizzled it with maple syrup, then ferried the finished products to the island.

"Wow." Gwen took a seat. "This is fantastic," she said, popping a strawberry chunk into her mouth. It had been years since she'd had breakfast with someone, or eaten more than whatever she could grab on her way out the door. "You're really going to run with me?"

"If you don't mind," he said, sipping gingerly at his coffee. "I'll try to keep up."

She rolled her eyes and tried again not to think about his body or his incredible kindness. He'd made her breakfast and wanted to drive her to work. It was as if her past and present were colliding, and Gwen wasn't prepared to handle the emotions that came with that.

AN HOUR LATER, Lucas stood, winded, in Gwen's kitchen, having escorted her on a reconnaissance run through the neighborhood. She'd pointed out every home belonging to someone she knew, as well as those that had been recently purchased. Lucas made a note of those standing empty, either awaiting a renter or up for sale, but nothing had struck him as odd or problematic. Nothing had set off any text-book red flags or triggered his gut instinct, and that was the real problem. Because something *was* wrong. Gwen was being followed on her runs, to her office and almost assuredly to her home.

"When did you become a runner?" Gwen asked, swigging water from her bottle and wiping sweat from her brow.

Lucas shrugged, pulling himself back to the moment. "A few years ago." He'd had trouble sleeping after Gwen's attack. Hellacious nightmares. When she'd left, he struggled with internal rage and self-loathing. He'd needed a healthy outlet, one that didn't involve booze or women. "You always said it helped you think and get centered. I gave it a try and have to agree."

She nodded, then smiled. "I'm glad it helped."

The smile reached her eyes and did things to his heart rate. "You should probably catch that shower so you aren't late for work. I'd hate to make you late on my first drop-off mission."

Gwen glanced at the clock, then moved quickly away. "I won't be long," she called.

He laughed as she darted into the bathroom down the hall. "You always say that," he called back. "It's never true."

He gripped the back of his neck, hard. Reminding himself for the hundredth time to remember his place. Gwen didn't need a boyfriend or even a buddy. She needed protection. She was in danger, and he couldn't afford to let his guard down the way he had before. Never again. Last time, she'd nearly been killed.

He refilled his water bottle with the pitcher in her fridge, then paused to examine a set of snapshots he hadn't noticed before. A small collection of selfies was lined up like soldiers on a corkboard near the pantry. A shot of Gwen's parents. One of Gwen at her high school graduation. The family dog, Jeeves. And a photo of Gwen in Lucas's arms, taken at their engagement party.

His eyelids slid shut with the bittersweet memory of that moment, and pressure built in his chest. Their engagement had been the happiest moment of his life, and within forty-eight hours, his heart had been ripped from his chest. The smiling, youthful faces in that image had no idea how bad things were about to get, and he wished for the thousandth time that he could go back and warn them.

He'd proposed on Friday night, Homecoming Weekend, and they'd spent the next day or so in bed, celebrating. By Sunday, however, she couldn't wait to show the ring off and announce the news to all of her friends. When she was late coming home, Lucas hadn't worried. When she didn't answer her phone, he assumed it was loud wherever she was and she hadn't heard it ring. Or maybe she'd had an extra margarita and fallen asleep at a friend's place. When he'd gone to bed alone that night, she was being beaten and raped. When he'd fallen asleep under the covers, safe and content, she'd been naked and alone, fighting for her life and counting the moments, in and out of consciousness until dawn.

Lucas had never once worried for her safety.

No thanks to him, she'd lived, but she'd come through it into another life. One that hadn't included room for a man, and he couldn't blame her. But he also couldn't help finding hope in the single photo she'd kept of them. Maybe Gwen didn't blame him as completely for what happened to her as he did.

"I'm glad you're here," she said, high heels snapping against hard wood as she hurried back down the hall in his direction. She'd dressed in a cream blouse and black skirt with a string of pearls her mother had given her on her twenty-first birthday, the night he realized he wanted to marry her.

"Glad to be here," he said, feigning casualness and reminding himself not to reach for her as she approached. A habit he had to unlearn. "You look great."

"Thanks." She'd twisted her wild red curls into an updo again and had a pair of simple gold hoop earrings in her hand. "I'm sure it speaks volumes about my emotional state, but I'm glad you agree with me about someone following me. Knowing I'm right feels slightly better than thinking I'm losing my mind." She offered a small smile as she plugged a hoop into one ear, then another. "Being alone all the time is one thing. I'm not willing to let go of my sanity just yet, too."

"You're far from crazy," he said, meeting and holding her gaze. "You went through the unthinkable, and you created a new life for yourself afterward. A very carefully designed and executed life. To think the danger you've worked so hard to put behind you could be here and now?" He gave a short humorless laugh. "Let's just say I can appreciate how surreal it is when two timelines collide."

She blinked, then dipped her chin and turned away. "We should get going."

Lucas cringed, having clearly said the wrong thing. Unsure how to make it better instead of worse, he kept his mouth shut and followed her into the day. He waited while she set the alarm and locked her multitude of locks, then he walked her to his truck.

He opened her door and waited while she climbed inside. He admired her strength and will. She'd gotten through the most horrible thing he could imagine a person going through, and she'd done it on her own. Her terms. Her choices. Her success. She might not be in his life anymore, but he was still incredibly proud of her. And willing to do whatever he could to help her find peace again.

"We will figure this out," he promised, pausing before he closed her door. "And for whatever it's worth, you aren't alone, Gwen. Not anymore."

Chapter Six

Gwen climbed down from Lucas's truck with a promise not to leave her office building under any circumstances, and he vowed to be back for her at six sharp. It was a strange feeling, having another human in her immediate orbit again. Someone who made her breakfast, went running with her and drove her to work. It was something she hadn't experienced in a long time, and she was surprised how deeply she'd missed it.

He watched her walk inside before pulling away from the curb.

Marina waited silently inside the glass doors kneading her hands and nearly buzzing with excitement. "Who was that?" she asked, eyes wide as she followed Gwen across the foyer. "Did you meet him at the park?"

Gwen smiled as evenly as possible, ignoring the swarm of butterflies taking flight in her chest. "That was Lucas."

Debbie watched from her position at the elevators as they approached. She pressed the Up button and turned to Gwen with a cat-that-ate-the-canary grin on her face. "Morning," she said sweetly. "I didn't realize you were seeing anyone, Gwen. When did this begin? And does Collin know?"

Marina moved to Debbie's side, and the two of them waited for Gwen's answer.

"I'm not seeing him," Gwen answered. "We've known

one another a long time, and why would I tell Collin if I was seeing someone?"

The pair exchanged a look, then rolled their eyes in near unison.

"So, why the ride to work?" Marina asked. "Everything okay?"

The elevator doors parted, and Gwen rushed inside. "My car's in the shop. I'm getting some basic maintenance and needed a ride."

"Will he be taking you home tonight, too?" Debbie asked, their reflections staring back in the shiny elevator walls as they rose to their floor.

"Yep."

"Will we get to meet him?" she asked.

The doors opened, and Gwen made her escape. "Maybe. I'll see you guys soon. I've got to call the shop and make sure they know where I left the key," she said, speed-walking toward her office as the other women stopped to chat with the receptionist.

She ducked into her small sanctuary and shut the door, then did her best to keep her head down until her stomach demanded it was lunchtime.

At twelve thirty, she opened her bag and groaned. She forgot to pack a lunch, and she'd promised Lucas she wouldn't go out.

A small sound drew her attention to the window behind her. When the noise came again, she turned slowly in her chair to stare at the glass. Something small bounced off and she started. A pebble or maybe an acorn? Someone was throwing things at her window? Someone knew which window was hers?

Her muscles stiffened and her breath caught as she waited to see if it happened again.

Tink! Another pebble.

Tink! A pebble.

Thump!

A stone hit the window, and the glass rattled.

Gwen jumped in her chair. Her heart hammered as she pressed onto her feet and maneuvered in a wide arc through the room, coming up alongside of her window. She swallowed long and slow, then dared a peek outside.

"Gwen?" The receptionist's voice burst through the speaker on her desk phone.

Gwen yelped. She pressed her back to the wall and a palm against her aching chest. She stumbled forward and pressed the response button on her phone. "Yes?" she croaked, forcing the word past a massive lump in her throat.

"You have a delivery."

Ice slid through her veins and pooled in her stomach. "I didn't order anything."

She turned back to the window, fearful of who was below and what she might find if she looked. But she had to look. Had to know. If someone was really targeting her, trying to terrorize her, she had to help Lucas make the arrest. If she didn't, this might never end. And if she found some other reasonable explanation for the pebbles hitting her window, then she could relax and figure out what to do about lunch.

She squared her shoulders and crossed the room, determined to see something other than a stalker. She took a deep breath and peered into the lot below.

No one was there.

She fell back against the wall, breathing heavily and shaking slightly. No one was there, but someone had been. Hadn't they?

Was her stalker getting braver? Bolder? Angrier? Had he seen her with Lucas?

If her coworkers were this worked up about her ride to

work, what did her stalker think? Did he also know Lucas had spent the night? Realizing how bad that would look from the outside, she felt her empty stomach roll. Apprehension gripped her shoulders and tightened the muscles in her neck and core.

"Miss Kind?" An unfamiliar male voice spoke behind her and she squelched a scream.

A man in jeans and a leather jacket crossed the room to her desk with a large bag in one hand. The receptionist held the door open for him.

He unearthed a massive plastic container filled with salad from the bag and placed it on her desk, then added a baguette, bottle of water and an apple to the arrangement. "Enjoy." He shot her an uncomfortable look, then headed back the way he'd come.

"You okay?" the receptionist asked, lingering in the threshold and looking more than a little concerned.

"Mmm-hmm." Gwen forced her hand from her chest and nodded. "I didn't order lunch. That's all."

"There's a note," she said. "Let me know if you need anything." She closed the door on her way out, leaving Gwen alone once more.

She moved to the desk and tugged the note free from the container.

Now you don't need to go out.
See you at 6.
Lucas.

She collapsed into her chair with a smile and shook her head at the nonsense she'd put herself through. No one was throwing pebbles at her second-floor window. And even if someone was, they were gone now, and she wasn't alone anymore. She had Lucas, and she was going to count her blessing on that fact every minute until her personal nightmare was over.

THE OFFICE EMPTIED quickly at five o'clock. A few coworkers had joked about waiting for a look at Gwen's ride home, but thankfully no one had been willing to wait an extra hour. Gwen bit into her apple, having saved the sweet treat for exactly this moment. A nice reminder that even when Lucas wasn't physically with her, she still wasn't alone.

Collin appeared outside her open door and smiled, redirecting his path. "You've been busy," he said, stepping into the doorway and leaning casually against the jamb. "I was going to see if you were hungry at lunch today, but word around the office is that you got delivery."

"I did." She set the bitten apple on her desk and pressed her lips into a smile. "Rain check?" she asked, regretting the words immediately. She didn't want a rain check. Her neatly arranged world didn't have room for rain checks or plans of any sort. Especially now. The fewer people who were dragged into her mess, the better.

"Sure thing." Collin winked. "But I've got to tell you, those rain checks are adding up. Pretty soon you're going to have to cash them in for dinner. Or a pony."

Gwen laughed. "I've always wanted a pony."

Collin hung his head and mimed stabbing himself in the chest as he walked away.

Her smile lingered as she went back to her apple.

Almost five thirty, and Lucas would be back for her soon. Her bag was packed and waiting at her feet. Until then, she dared an internet search for recent attacks at Bellemont College. There were plenty of minor incidents and the usual reports of male-on-female crimes, but nothing like what she'd experienced.

She enjoyed the sweet crunch of her snack as she performed a wider search, broadening the parameters from the college to the community, then the city and county.

A door slammed somewhere in the quiet building, and she jolted upright.

A chorus of voices arrived with the elevator, blurring into gibberish before being drowned out by the sounds of vacuum cleaners.

The cleaning crew.

Gwen turned to her window, peering into the parking lot for confirmation.

The rear door to her building was propped open, and two uniformed women chatted while unloading trays of cleansers and carts of supplies.

She breathed easier, then returned to her desk as her phone buzzed with an incoming text.

On my way. Running late. See you soon.

She pushed the rest of her apple into the trash and rested her head in her hands for a long beat, regaining her composure and reminding herself she was safe.

Lucas's words returned to her from the night before. He'd said she wasn't a victim anymore, but the truth was that she'd never stopped being one. Her attack had changed her. Had altered her very being. And afterward, she'd built a nice, safe life around herself in an active attempt to keep the monster at bay.

And now, he was back.

The vacuums and voices fell silent at six o'clock.

Gwen wiped a tear she hadn't realized was forming. Her shaking hands were white-knuckled and curled into fists she hadn't meant to make.

Outside, an engine revved to life, and she breathed easier. The cleaning crew was leaving.

Her phone buzzed, and she nearly wept with relief when she saw it was Lucas.

I'm here. Building's locked. Have a good day?

Yep

She pried her body from the chair and collected her bag.

On my way.

She opened her office door and froze.

The dimmed space around her was charged with an uncomfortable energy. Her instincts rose to attention, reaching out, trying to place the source of the alarm.

Then she heard it. A continuous, muffled sound that scattered goose bumps across her skin and rooted her feet into place. She dialed Lucas.

"Hey," he answered. "Sorry I was running late. There was an accident on—"

"Shh," she whispered, feeling the panic twist and grind inside her. "Something's wrong. I think someone's here."

Lucas didn't respond for a long beat. "What's the security code for the building?" he asked.

She recited the numbers quickly, then stepped back into her office.

Images of sliding down the wall into a sobbing heap on the floor crossed her mind. Shoving her desk against the locked door. Even jumping from her window. Anything to stop her former attacker from getting his hands on her again. She'd die first.

No, she thought, suddenly, forcing the desperation from her head. *No.* She'd worked hard to vanquish those kinds of thoughts. To recover. To heal. Her lips trembled as she recalled the sleepless nights spent in a ball on her closet floor. Hiding. Crying. Praying he'd never find her. And how she'd finally vowed to stop letting him control her.

Gwen grabbed the large pewter Employee of the Year award from her credenza and gripped it like a baseball bat.

She was done running.

Done giving this psycho all the little pieces of herself one by one.

She marched toward the sounds. Down the narrow hall separating offices from conference rooms, the mail room and employee lounge. She stopped outside the only closed door in the office and steeled her waning resolve. Whatever was going on, it was happening in the mail room.

"Gwen!" Lucas called. His voice arriving with the ding of the elevator. "Gwen!"

"Here!" she called back.

He halted at her side a moment later, drawing his weapon and tucking her behind him as he opened the mail room door.

Inside, the massive corporate copy machine chugged and spewed its paper contents. Sheet by sheet across the floor.

A thousand photos of Gwen.

All recent and surveillance-style.

Chapter Seven

Thirty minutes later, Lucas paced through Gwen's office while she relayed the details of her situation to a local detective and a pair of officers processed the copier.

"And that's everything," Gwen said, having held her composure through a retelling of her past that made Lucas want to scream.

Special Victims Detective Heidi Anderson perched primly in a chair across from Gwen's desk. Her sleek blond hair hung neatly around her face, tucked behind her ears and barely reaching her shoulders. "And you believe the person who printed the photos tonight is the same man who attacked you six years ago?" she asked, sharp brown eyes narrowing behind dark-rimmed glasses.

"It's just a guess," Gwen answered. "Whoever it is, he knows where I work and jog, and that I went to Bellemont College. I suppose it's possible that someone else is doing this. Maybe someone on the periphery of my current life has become obsessed. I'd actually prefer that," she said with a sad smile. "Because I know what my attacker is capable of."

The detective dipped her chin in understanding. "I'm very sorry."

Gwen nodded back acceptance, then released a shuddered breath and pressed on. "Unfortunately, I can't link anything to my assailant. Aside from the location of the attack, all he left behind was an ugly aftermath."

Detective Anderson nodded. "I understand. And you reached out to Detective Winchester after you found the flyer on your windshield?" she clarified. "Because the attack was in his town and the college on the flyer is also in his jurisdiction?"

Gwen looked to Lucas before answering.

Detective Anderson arched a brow. "Was it something more?"

"Yes," Gwen said, and Lucas stilled. "We were engaged at the time of my attack."

The detective looked from Gwen to Lucas, then back. "I see. But you aren't together now."

"No."

"But you've remained close," she guessed.

Gwen shifted on her chair. "No." She folded her hands on the desk before her and stared at them. "I contacted Lucas when I found the flyer because he knows what happened to me, and until right now, I've never told anyone other than family, law enforcement and medical personnel. Anyone who read about it in the paper back then has surely forgotten about it, along with the first responders and medical staff who cared for me. I don't keep in touch with the friends I had then. So, aside from my parents, Lucas is the only one who would understand why I thought a simple homecoming invitation might be a threat."

The frank and emotionless assessment hit Lucas like a cold fist to his gut, and he reeled at the response. He'd known the words were true, but hearing her say them gave him an unexpected pause. Gwen had come to him last night because she had no one else to go to. Not because she trusted him to protect her and to get her through this. Not because she wanted to see him again. Or because they'd always made a phenomenal team. But because she'd been avoiding this very situation. She hadn't wanted to talk about what she'd been through, and with Lucas, she didn't have to.

Detective Anderson uncrossed, then recrossed her legs. "Any chance this has anything to do with you?" she asked, moving her gaze to Lucas. "SVU detective's fiancée goes through something like you described, and I've got to ask, could her attack have been motivated by an angry criminal you collared?"

"I was a student at the time," Lucas said, clearing his throat when the words came thick and gravelly. "I joined the academy after her attack, when the local PD came up empty-handed."

She cocked her head and frowned. "So, after going through something like that, you decided to make a career out of it?"

"No," Lucas said sharply. "Not like that."

"Well, it wasn't for the glory or the money," she said, a remorseful lilt to her tone.

"I wanted to find the man who did this," he said. "I wanted revenge and justice and some assurance that he'd never hurt anyone else or Gwen ever again."

Gwen covered her mouth, eyes glistening with unshed tears.

"He's still out there, but I've helped put plenty of others like him away," Lucas said. "And I'm not finished with this guy yet."

"Hmm." Detective Anderson looked from Lucas to Gwen. "I think I have everything I need." She closed the notebook she'd been making notes in. "I'll be in touch once the fingerprints from the mail room and copier are run and we've scanned the security feed from the parking lot cameras."

"The parking lot," Gwen whispered. She spun to face

Lucas, eyes wide. "Someone was outside my window before lunch. Throwing pebbles and acorns, then a rock. I
convinced myself I'd imagined it after looking and finding
no one out there, but maybe someone was here."

Lucas nodded.

"Detective Anderson?" A man's voice turned everyone
toward the door. One of the officers from the mail room
stepped inside. "We found a thumb drive in the copier's
USB port." He held a small evidence bag between his thumb
and first finger.

"Excellent," she said, rising to her feet. "Then maybe
we'll get some answers." She extended a hand to Gwen,
then Lucas. "Ms. Kind, Detective," she said. "I'll be in
touch. Please keep me posted if anything else comes up."

"Of course." Lucas shook her offered hand. "Thank
you."

GWEN WATCHED AS Lucas crossed the space from her kitchen
to her living room, delivering a steaming mug of tea to her
hands. She'd curled on her couch, tucked her feet beneath
her and pulled a pillow onto her lap, unable to do more than
stare. "Thanks," she whispered. Her feeble attempts to process the evening had failed repeatedly. Nothing made any
sense anymore. Least of all the fact that her carefully and
tightly constructed world was suddenly unraveling.

Lucas took a seat on the cushion beside her and watched
as she sipped her tea. "I think you should consider taking
the rest of the week off work," he said. "Your boss knows
what went on tonight. Detective Anderson spoke with her
earlier. I think you could use the time to focus on what's
happening."

"I know," Gwen said, instantly recalling the humiliation she'd felt listening to the detective's call. She'd been
discreet in her words, but had made it clear, nonetheless,

that the intended victim was Gwen. And there were no secrets in her office.

She had plenty of unused vacation time, and she wasn't
in any hurry to face Marina or Debbie. They'd seen Lucas's truck this morning when he'd dropped her off, and
likely noted the police shield sticker on the back window.
They'd make the connection between her trouble and her
protector. And there would be questions. "I'll call the office tomorrow," she agreed. "I'm sure they'll understand."

Lucas raised his brows. "Yeah?"

"Yeah."

He rubbed his palms against his thighs and a small smile
formed. "I'd expected a fight."

"Sorry." She sighed. "I'm fresh out of fight. At least
for tonight."

His expression turned soft, and he clasped his hands
on his lap.

"Don't," she warned, shooting him a look over the rim
of her mug. She'd seen that look before on a dozen people,
and she hated it. "Don't you dare pity me. I'm just tired,
and I'll be fine tomorrow."

"I don't pity you," he said, his tone gentle enough to
break her. "I meant what I said before. You aren't a victim
anymore, Gwen. I saw it the moment I set eyes on you in my
precinct. You're a fighter. And I'm here to fight with you."

"I'm not a fighter," she said, wishing he was right, but
feeling the defeat of exhaustion slipping over her.

"Really?" He laughed. "Because it wasn't two hours ago
I found you with some kind of silver vase on your shoulder,
ready to take out whoever was on the other side of your
mail room door."

Gwen laughed, surprised by his words and at herself in
the memory. "That was my Employee of the Year award,
not a vase."

Lucas grinned.

"I just want this to end," she said. Frustration and fatigue warred in her, but her mind wouldn't let her sleep, not yet, even if she tried. Her stomach growled, and she knew she'd have to deal with that first. "Are you hungry?" They'd missed dinner thanks to the lunatic trying to scare her.

"A little," Lucas said. "But there's something else I want to run by you." He inched closer and pierced her with a sincere and hopeful gaze. "I think we should stay at my place through the weekend. Get out of town. This guy is getting bolder, and it worries me. I can protect you here, if he manages to get to you, somehow, but if we're at my place, we might be able to avoid that scenario completely. Focus on figuring out who he is, then go after him instead of the other way around."

Gwen gripped the bunching muscles in her shoulders and along her neck. She hadn't spent the night anywhere else in years. Her home was safe and familiar. Her life was composed of closed-circuit routes and routines that were easy to monitor and guard. Or so she'd thought. "Can I take a shower and think about it?" she asked, smiling when he grinned. She'd made a similar request earlier, and thankfully, he'd agreed.

Her need to consider everything thoroughly probably seemed odd to someone whose career required him to make split-second decisions, but for Gwen, thinking things through provided a layer of assurance she needed. She could have and should have gotten a ride home, like her friends had, on the night of her attack, but she'd refused. She was so naively filled with joy and promise that she'd chosen to walk home on a whim. She wanted to enjoy the crisp fall air, distant sounds of parties and laughter, and bask in the fact that her life was utterly perfect, on a beautiful campus, under the stars. And she had for a while. If only she'd taken time to think about the potential consequences...

She pushed onto her feet without waiting for Lucas's response, then made her way down the hall, her eyes already on fire with the sting of rising tears.

GWEN STEPPED BACK into the hallway an hour later. Scents of rich, salty cheese and warm, buttery bread rose to meet her. She'd let herself have the breakdown she needed under the stream of hot water, and imagined the heartbreak, the fear and desperation circling the drain at her feet. She gave in to the feelings under her terms, and she let them go on her terms, as well. Down the drain beside her tears. She'd emerged from the shower with renewed resolve, with purpose and with hope.

Now, in her softest jeans and coziest sweater, wild curls swelling around her face as they dried, she padded toward her kitchen on socked feet. Toward the handsome man whistling at her stove. "Twice in one day?" she asked, sliding onto a stool at her island to admire the view.

Lucas cast an odd look over his shoulder. He flicked the knob on her stove, extinguishing the fire, then removed a perfect grilled cheese sandwich from the skillet. "Don't you normally eat more than once a day?"

"Yeah," she laughed, "but I make it myself."

He cut the sandwich into triangles and slid them onto a plate. "I was starting to worry about you in there. You were gone a while. I figured I'd keep myself busy while I waited."

Concern darkened his eyes as he delivered the plate to her.

"I'm fine," she lied. "Just taking my time."

He turned back to her stove, stirring the contents of a small pot. "You still like tomato soup," he said, before pouring the smooth scarlet mixture into a bowl. "You've got a shelfful in your pantry."

"It's warm food on cold nights," she said. Plus, it reminded her of home. "My mom still makes and cans her own. Once upon a time a grilled cheese and tomato soup combo was the cure for all that ailed me." In fact, the soup reminded her so much of her mother, and how badly she missed her, that she had a hard time leaving the grocery without buying a can. And an even harder time making it for the same reason. Tears did nothing to enhance the flavor.

"Do your folks get up this way much?" Lucas asked, slipping a spoon and bowl before her.

"A few times a year." She smiled at the food. "I visit them for Christmas. How's your family?"

"Crazy," he said, rolling his eyes. "Blaze is still pining away for the woman he helped put into witness protection. It would be comical if it wasn't so sad. Derek's cocky as ever. Isaac's trying to heal the world, one patient at a time, and Mom is still trying to marry us all off. So far, we're sorely disappointing her." His expression flattened. "Same old."

Gwen turned her attention to the soup, stroking a spoon through the bowl's creamy contents. "Thanks for taking care of me today," she said, the words coming more softly than intended. "Part of me wants to be sorry I dragged you into this, because honestly, I was hoping you'd look at that flyer and tell me I was being completely paranoid. But I'm glad I asked."

"Because I was already familiar with the case?" His keen blue eyes flicked to hers, something like hurt flashing in them.

"Because you're the only person I trust to not treat me as if I'm broken," she said. "Because you know what this monster has done to me and what he's taken from me.

You've seen the scars." She stopped, pressing her lips tight and forcing her hands into her lap. Her fingers ached to reach for the scars on instinct. To be sure they were still there. And that the wounds were healed. Because sometimes she was sure the memories and phantom pains would kill her yet.

She'd needed dozens of stitches where her attacker had dug a blade into her side, and where he'd curled his fingers into her hair then banged her head repeatedly against the ground. Where doctors had painstakingly removed pebbles from her punctured skin and lacerated scalp. "I came to you because you know," she repeated, her throat clamping down on the final word.

"I do," he said, looking ashamed and guilty. He set a hand on hers in her lap, and she flinched. "Sorry," he said, pulling quickly away, expression horrified. "I'm so sorry. I didn't mean to do that."

Shock turned to humiliation in her heart and soul as she realized her mistake and his. It had been so long since anyone had reached for her hand. Since anyone had touched her outside her parents' hugs. The move had startled her, and she'd flinched. That was on her.

He'd forgotten she was broken. That was on him.

Regardless of what she wanted, her attacker had taken something from her that she'd never get back, and Lucas deserved more than a few pieces of someone who'd never again be whole. Her stomach rolled, and her hunger vanished. "Um." She slid to her feet, emotions spiking and churning in her core. "I need to lie down. Do you mind if we stay here one more night?" she said, backing away. "We can go to your place tomorrow. I won't argue."

"Gwen." Lucas stood, eyes pleading and hands rising uselessly between them.

"I'll clean the kitchen tomorrow," she said. "Don't worry

about it. You've done too much already." A small sob burst
from her lips, and she pressed a palm to her mouth. "Good
night."

And she turned for her bed at a jog.

Chapter Eight

Early the next morning, Gwen watched the familiar streets pass by in a town she'd avoided for five long years. She'd foregone her run and eaten toast with her coffee, all in an attempt to leave home before the sun rose. Now, it was just after breakfast time for everyone else, and she was back in her old college town, West Liberty. Flags in the school's colors hung from streetlamps, and banners proclaiming Bellemont pride clung to shop windows and storefronts. The rolling green hills of campus ebbed and flowed in the distance, beyond quaint, historic neighborhoods and rows of rental homes filled with students

There was an undeniable energy in the air. Contagious and wild. Rosy-cheeked students with backpacks and steaming cups laughed on street corners and held hands on sidewalks. It was surreal and otherworldly. A movie set come to life. The picture of Midwestern collegiate perfection, where all days were good ones and monsters didn't lurk.

Nostalgia twitched and stretched in her core, calling on her good memories in this town. Of shared coffees and jokes between friends. But she shut it down, unable to recall the good without the bad, and unwilling to relive the bad.

"What did your boss say when you called in this morning?" Lucas asked, turning to her at a red light.

Gwen glanced his way, relieved for the distraction. "She understood. I asked for a week of vacation, but I don't see how that will be enough."

"I'll do everything I can to end this as soon as possible," he said. "If you need more time at the end of the week, we'll figure it out together. But let's take the days as they come for now."

The light changed, and they motored ahead, making turns down streets she remembered and others she couldn't recall.

Gwen didn't doubt his intent or motivation, but she suspected they needed more than a handful of days to find a man they hadn't been able to identify in six years. Assuming the current stalker was her old attacker, and she hadn't managed to attract a second lunatic.

Maybe it was time to put her home on the market and start over somewhere else. Farther away this time. Maybe Florida, near her folks. Though, she'd want to keep a little distance, just in case. She wouldn't want to put her parents in danger. Maybe she could buy a place a few towns over. Or not in Florida at all. A neighboring state.

"Gwen?" Lucas asked.

He'd been talking, she realized, and she'd missed whatever he'd said completely. "Sorry. What?"

He pressed his lips and shook his head. "You've barely spoken since we left this morning. I asked, what are you thinking?"

She'd been thinking about how much she'd hate having to sell her home and give up her life again. How had it come to this when she'd worked so hard and been so careful? "I knew something wasn't right," she said, the thought flying from her mouth the moment it entered her head. "My instincts told me something was wrong, and I ignored them. And he'd been there. Did you see all those photos? He'd

been everywhere. I was never alone. My carefully constructed life was all just a lie he'd allowed me to believe."

And she was a fool for having believed it.

"This is not your fault," Lucas said, pulling his truck into
a narrow driveway. "There's no accounting for psychopathy.
You're a sane person who made a sane decision based on a
logical review of the evidence. Intuition can't trump facts
when the facts were six years deep. No one this side of an
asylum would have believed a man who'd nearly killed you
once would be back now, quietly following you around."
He cut the engine with a curse and climbed out of the cab.

Gwen blinked, mildly stupefied by his uncharacteristic
loss of composure.

He opened her door looking chagrinned.

She slid onto her feet outside the truck. "Sorry. I guess
I was feeling sorry for myself."

"You were blaming yourself. That's different." He pulled
her bags onto his shoulders and shut her door. "The only
one at fault here is the one committing the crimes." He
smiled, dragging his gaze to the home beside them. "Welcome to my place. It's a work in progress."

Gwen turned to the house, finally seeing where he'd
brought her. She sucked in a sharp breath and stared. "You
bought the house?" she asked, nonsensically, the answer
immediately in front of her.

"Yeah."

Lucas had bought the house she'd fallen in love with
junior year. One they'd stood outside of a hundred times
on their ways to and from local events and admired. One
he'd vowed to buy her someday on the night he'd proposed.

"When?" she asked, thrilled for him and at the prospect
of finally stepping inside.

The 1870 Gothic-revival home had caught her eye the
first time she saw it. The stately brick structure was set back

from the road and circled by an aged wrought iron fence. The arched windows and doorways were lined in ornate details and scrolling woodwork that had called to her. It was always on the market, overpriced for the amount of work that had to be done, but worth it, she'd thought, to own such a beautiful piece of history. The realty site had claimed it to be more than four thousand square feet of living space with five large bedrooms and a study. She'd imagined her children growing up there, running wild down halls and corridors, where children had played for nearly one hundred and fifty years before them.

"Last year," he said, answering her question.

He carried her bags onto the wide front porch and slid a key into the lock. "It took me longer to save the money on a cop's salary than it would have on an architect's, but I got it done." He pressed the door open and motioned her inside.

"But why?" she asked, hurrying to gape at the perfection around her. If the Realtor's website was a decent resource, the home had likely set him back by five times his annual salary, and it would take one full-time cop a lifetime to restore.

The grand entryway boasted high ceilings, hardwood floors and a chandelier. The staircase began at the back of the space and climbed to the next floor, its lacquered handrail gleaming from a recent polish.

She turned to him, desperate to know his reasoning. Senselessly hoping she'd been some small part of the decision, or at least the memory of her.

"I guess I'm still an architect at heart," he said. "My life might've taken an unexpected turn, but my dreams have never changed."

Her heart swelled at the implication left floating between them, and her body warmed with need for his touch.

"Come on. I'll show you the guest room." He started up the steps, and she followed.

Gwen trailed her fingertips along the banister and over fifty-year-old wallpaper as they climbed, admiring the refinished tread under her feet. The upstairs hallway was decorated the same. Perfect restored wooden floors and elaborate gilded paper. Crown moldings lined the ceilings and thick trim-rimmed doors and windows.

She peeked into the rooms as they passed, awed by the doors' original white porcelain knobs and craftsmanship. One bedroom acted as a home gym with a treadmill, weight set and mirror in place. Another posed as storage. A third seemed to be a home office. There was a desk and chair, but the boxes were also plentiful.

"This is the only other room with a bed," he said, stopping at the final door on his right, just past a bathroom. "I'll make it up for you. No one's ever actually needed it." He latched a hand on his hip and rubbed his forehead with the other. "You know what? Why don't you take my room instead? I'll figure this one out later."

He moved across the hall and pushed the door wide before Gwen could respond.

The room was huge with a massive four-poster bed at the center and evidence of Lucas's busy life everywhere. Toppled boots by the closet. Cast-off clothing on a chair. The scent of him trapped in every scrap of fabric and carpeting.

He dropped her bags on the bed, his gaze darting. "It's a mess, but at least there are sheets on the bed."

"It's great," she said, nodding to punctuate the words. "Thank you."

"Well then, I'll leave you to it." He slipped past her in the doorway, then paused in the hall. "I'm going to check in at the station and return some calls this morning. I won't be long, and we can get some lunch when I get back."

"You're leaving?" She spun on him, ripped back to the moment. "Take me with you. I want to know what's going on, and I can help."

"Gwen," he started, fixing a perfectly blank cop expression on his face. "I'll fill you in on everything when I get back. I won't leave anything out. But I think you should stay inside as much as possible. I don't want you spotted, and honestly, there's no reason to drag you through the rehashing of details on this if we don't have to."

She crossed her arms, understanding his reasoning and hating it. "This is happening to me whether I want to deal with it or not, so I'm all in for the rehashing and whatever else it takes to catch him. I don't want to be left alone here, useless and idle. That'll only make me crazier." She stepped into the hall with him and leaned her head back for a look into his contemplative eyes. "Let me help you catch him this time."

Lucas clenched and released his jaw, the muscle flexing and jumping.

"Please?" she tried, taking another approach.

He groaned and rocked back on his heels, relenting. "All right. This way."

She followed him back toward the steps with an internal fist pump and a tiny kick in her step.

He stopped short at the room with a desk and chair, then flipped on the light. He waved a hand at the piles of boxes. "These are the details and findings from your original case, along with my personal research on the subject, not that I've ever gotten anywhere."

She inched into the room, surprised by his words. He'd told Detective Anderson that he'd put other monsters behind bars. It made sense for him to seek his justice however he could, and Gwen was glad he had. But knowing he'd kept hunting her attacker all these years was something else entirely. If he'd never given up on bringing her justice, then maybe he'd never given up on her. "Which boxes are the case files and research?" she asked. "Do you mind if I take a look?"

Lucas frowned. "These are all case files and research. Six years' worth."

"What?" Her heart pinched with appreciation and gratitude. While she'd been hiding, Lucas had been fighting. Her eyes stung, and she faked a yawn to cover the gathering tears.

She lifted the lid of the nearest box and peered inside. "I can't believe you have all these."

He leaned against the doorjamb, hands stuffed deep into the front pockets of his jeans. "I started bringing them home the day I made detective. I was photocopying pages and carrying them home in my bag before that." Emotion flickered in his eyes, and he peeled away from the wall, stepping closer, gaze fixed on her. "I go over them on the weekends or when I can't sleep. I keep thinking that one day something I've been missing will stand out."

Gwen moved, too, matching his stride, drawn to his goodness and strength. His compassion and perseverance. He'd done this for her. Gave up a future in architecture. Joined the force. Became a detective. And spent his free time in search of justice. For her.

The toes of their shoes bumped, and they stared at one another, a live wire of energy crackling between them.

She inhaled the warm, inviting scent of him, allowing it to envelope her. It would be so easy to reach for him. To stroke her hand up the length of his arm. To set a palm on his strong chest. To lean closer and fall into his embrace.

Lucas towered over her, his shoulders curving in and creating that nook where she'd always fit so perfectly. That place that had seemed carved just for her, where nothing bad could touch her. He lifted a hand slowly toward her cheek, watching carefully for signs the touch was unwanted. Another flinch, perhaps, like the one she'd accidentally given last night.

She wouldn't make that mistake again.

His phone buzzed, breaking the tension, and his hand fell back to his side. He retrieved the phone from his back pocket and pressed it to his ear without stepping away. "Winchester."

Gwen struggled to catch her breath, and her pulse beat between her ears.

His eyes caught hers once more, and he lowered the phone between them, giving the screen a tap with one thumb. "Gwen's here now, and you're on speaker. Go ahead."

"Miss Kind." Detective Anderson's voice rose from the phone. "We've had a chance to examine the full contents of the thumb drive recovered from your office. There were more than two thousand files."

Gwen's head lightened, and she stumbled back a step. How long had she been followed? How many photos had he taken of her each day? How had she not noticed?

"Two thousand?" Lucas repeated, anger coloring his tone. "How is that possible? Are we talking repeats? Like a photo shoot? Dozen or more photos of the same shot, from every session?"

"I'm afraid not," Detective Anderson said. "There were two thousand photos. Taken over the course of eight years."

Gwen's knees weakened, and her heart seized before breaking into a sprint. She was attacked six years ago.

"That's impossible," Lucas demanded, his tone defiant. "There must be some mistake."

"I'm sorry, but no," Detective Anderson answered. "Whoever left this thumb drive at Miss Kind's office last night has clearly been following her since two years before she was attacked. And leaving this behind suggests he wants her to know."

Chapter Nine

Lucas sat on the floor across from Gwen, take-out containers piled between them. He couldn't bring himself to leave her after the news Detective Anderson delivered, so he'd ordered her favorite takeout from a Chinese fusion restaurant they'd frequented in college. Then, he'd started sorting facts and photographs alongside her.

"Find anything?" she asked, a pot sticker captured between her chopsticks. She'd folded her legs into a pretzel and gone straight to work creating multiple piles from the photos Detective Anderson had sent him. Red curls hung over her shoulders, and there was deep concentration in her eyes.

"Nothing new," he said, shuffling through a mass of photos on his side of their makeshift picnic. All images of Gwen through the years. Some of the younger woman he'd known and loved. Others of this new Gwen, reborn and reinvented. On a jogging path. Outside her office. Lunching with friends. He'd yet to see a woman as beautiful as Gwen, and she still seemed completely unaware of that. He hated how much of her life he'd missed. "You?"

"Not really," she said, pushing a stack of images around with her free hand. "I'm trying desperately to look at this from someone else's perspective because when I let myself think about the fact that these are all photos of me, all taken by someone I didn't know was there, I want to move to Peoria." She bit into the pot sticker and chewed thoughtfully. "Maybe I could leave the country completely. I have some savings. Surely even this nut wouldn't follow me across the globe."

"If I thought moving would help, I'd help you pack myself," he said, "but you tried that once." He cast a pointed look at the photos around them. "I think we're going to have to see things through and catch this guy." He weighed his next words carefully. "Eight years is a long time."

She pressed her lips tight and set her chopsticks down. "More than a quarter of my life."

"It's a commitment. This guy is attached to you. He's bonded. In his mind, this is some kind of long-term relationship. And it's real."

Gwen wet her lips and averted her eyes. "I know."

Lucas felt a small sense of relief. It was important the victim understood the reality of the danger and situation fully. Gwen was smart and tough, but it was easy for anyone sitting at the eye of a storm not to see the full complexity of it. And that was paramount. "I've seen a lot of things since I started with the police force, but two thousand pictures over eight years? This is obsession, and it rarely ends well. My best guess is that something triggered him before, and something's set him off again. Whether that's something from his personal life or yours, I don't know." He trailed off, lifting then dropping a hand. He wasn't sure where or how to find this ghost, but if Gwen stayed with him, he could at least keep her safe while he tried.

"It's okay," she said. "I get it. It feels like we're starting over, but we're not. You've already done the research. We just have to reconsider everything you've collected with the new information in mind. Now we know he's a stalker first and foremost. A dedicated one, apparently." She huffed and rolled her eyes, then locked her gaze with his. "And I'm willing to fight this time. I ran before. As fast as I could, the moment the hospital discharged me. I did everything possible to avoid thinking about what I'd been through and what I'd lost. I'm not doing that again."

Lucas felt a fresh swell of pride at her determination. This woman was too much. And to be allowed into her new world, chosen as her partner in this? An honor.

"So." She picked up her chopsticks and forced a smile. "We can do this. Because we have to."

His lips twitched into a small smile. "I think I'm supposed to be the one giving the pep talks, but you're right. And that was pretty good."

"I'm pretty good at a lot of things," she said, blushing slightly as she lifted another bite to her mouth.

Lucas tried not to think about all the things she was good at. A few sordid images sprang to mind unbidden, and he shook his head to clear them. "Let's start from the beginning. What was your life like eight years ago?"

"Wow." She dug the fingers of one hand into her hair, pushing it behind her ear. "I've spent so long hyperfocused on the days immediately before my attack, I haven't given my freshman or sophomore year a single thought."

"At least we know when it started," he said. "You moved here from Florida for college, so this guy is someone you met at Bellemont or in town that year. What were your days like then? Your routines. Clubs or student organizations. Common hangouts?"

Gwen groaned. "Freshman year was tough. I was completely out of my element. I'd moved from a major city in Florida, where the ocean was everywhere I looked, to a small town in rural Kentucky where cows and cornfields outnumber cars and cabs. I stayed close to campus. Ate at the student center. Ran the campus track. I tried to show up and get involved with everything that happened on campus, sure that was how I'd find my groove and meet the friends I'd have for life." She sighed. "I was such a romantic. Everything was good in the world, and my future was full of endless possibilities."

"The world is good," Lucas said. Some people were absolute evil incarnate, sure, but the rest were good. "And your life is still full of endless possibilities."

Her lips parted, and hope flickered through the doubt in her eyes. "I suppose you think the best is yet to come and all that?"

"I'm certain of it," he said, willing her to believe him.

She returned her attention to the photos without comment or argument.

Lucas waited, watching as she considered the images before them. A chronicle of her adult life. From the lonely college freshman she'd described to the fierce twenty-seven-year-old with him today.

"There are a lot of photos from the hike-and-bike trail," she said. "Almost twice as many as those taken in other places this year. All the newest shots seem concentrated around my runs. It's where I first felt watched. The first time in years I realized someone was there."

Lucas finished his egg roll, then dusted his palms together. "Let's see."

She handed him a stack of photos. "I divided these into years, then again into locations. From there, I stacked them according to time. So, photos of me arriving at work are first. Going out to lunch are next, you get it. I wanted to see where and when he was most often. I thought we could check a calendar, too, see if he's only following me on certain days of the week. He can't work regular hours like me and most of the office employees I know, or he'd have to be at his office when I am. So, we know he's either unemployed, working part-time or on a flexible schedule."

Lucas marveled as he flipped through the stack she'd handed him. She was right. There were patterns. And the timeline of the photographer's availability was important. If matched to a suspect's work schedule, the timeline would be strong support for their case.

"How do you feel about another drive?" he asked, turning a photo in her direction. "We can go to the hike-and-bike trail. Try to find the place where he hid to take the photos based on the angles of the shots and landmarks captured in the images. Maybe he left a clue behind. Some kind of evidence, a nest or a blind."

"A nest?"

"A flattened area in the tall grass or excessive, centralized footprint among the trees. Maybe a clustering of trash, like wrappers from snacks or empty water bottles. Things that indicate someone spent a lot of time in that spot. If we're lucky, there'll be something we can use to track it back to one specific person." A jolt of adrenaline shot through him at the possibility.

Gwen leaned forward, a small smile creeping over her pretty face. "What are we waiting for?"

GWEN DIRECTED LUCAS to her preferred parking lot along the hike-and-bike trail. It was later in the day than she'd ever come, and the number of people was significantly higher. Still, the crowd here had nothing on the madhouse she'd jogged more recently.

Lucas swung his pickup into an empty spot and settled the engine, taking his time to observe the scene before climbing out.

She scanned the familiar area, hating the fear that pebbled her skin. She'd started most of her days here for years.

It was beautiful, always clean and well-maintained with benches and signs identifying indigenous flora and fauna every quarter mile or so for breaks and education. The parking lot was conveniently located at the end of a short winding road, easily accessed from a much busier one. A camp of trees separated the trail from the main road; the trail went on for miles, paralleling a set of old railroad tracks.

"Ready?" Lucas turned to her inside the warm cab, patient and assessing, as always.

If she said no, he'd start the truck and leave. No questions. No judgment or pressure. That was who Lucas was, but she had to stop running. So, she nodded. Unable to speak around a sudden knot in her throat and burst of nerves in her gut.

She'd promised herself she'd never go back on the trail, but she'd also asked Lucas for his help, then demanded he let her be involved. Now it was time to trust him to protect her, and get out of his way so he could work.

They climbed out and met at the truck's front bumper.

A couple on bikes pedaled past, and a man walking a dog stepped aside to give them space.

Lucas moved onto the trail behind the bikes, walking the dense tree line. "Do the trees grow along both sides of the trail like this for a long distance?" he asked, peering in each direction.

"Yes." She crossed her arms and hurried to catch up, feeling watched, even now. The trees she'd once loved for their beauty and solitude were actually the perfect hiding spot for a psychopath and his camera, she realized. Her stomach rocked with the thought.

"No good," Lucas muttered, waving from one side of the path to the other. "An attacker could drag a victim out of sight in seconds here."

Gwen shivered, wrapping her arms more tightly around her.

"I don't see any signs of a security patrol or cameras," Lucas said, squinting up at the telephone poles. "The hike-and-bike trail is maintained by local park services. Did you ever see park security or any other kind of patrol out here?"

"No." And how stupid was it that she'd continually come here believing she was alone?

She'd thought the danger was behind her. That she was a woman who'd been in the wrong place at the wrong time and suffered the consequences. Not the victim of a stalker.

She'd been concentrating on emotional healing and learning to let go of the trauma. All the while, she'd been putting herself in harm's way and thinking it was the right thing to do.

She groaned inwardly at all the times she'd gotten spooked and had forced herself to keep her chin up and finish her jog. She'd even congratulated herself on the days she'd persevered. Chanting internally that there was nothing to be afraid of.

Lucas whistled and slipped into the trees several yards ahead. "I think we've got something," he said. "Do you have the photos?"

Gwen hurried to meet him. She sorted through the photos, finding landmarks to orient herself. The telephone pole. A section of wooden fence. "Here." She passed the stack to Lucas. "This is the right place."

Lucas moved deeper into the trees, then bumped the toe of his shoe against the ground. A patch of earth was rubbed free of grass and littered in tiny debris. Gum foils and candy wrappers. Empty water bottles that had been smashed and tucked into the rotting stump of a tree. "I think this is it." He pulled a phone from his pocket and dialed. "You're dedicated to your routines, so he probably started coming early and waiting for you. Traffic noise this close to the road and parking lot would've masked his sounds."

He continued to toe the ground until his shoe caught on a string. "This is Detective Lucas Winchester for Detective Anderson," he said into the phone, then squatted to pull on the string.

Slowly, the red nylon rope came through the strategically arranged pile of leaves. Thicker than she'd originally thought, the durable outdoor line ran a dozen feet deeper into the woods. Lucas knocked away a heap of sticks and removed a small camouflaged bag. He tugged a set of Nitrile gloves from his coat pocket and slid them over his hands while relaying the situation to whoever listened on the other end of his call.

Gwen gripped the trunk of a tree for stability as she watched, openmouthed.

Lucas worked the drawstring on the bag and upturned it, dumping the contents onto a swath of dirt. A full bottle of water fell out, then a mass of freezer bags, each filled with a different snack or supply. Bandages. Over-the-counter painkillers. Beef jerky. Granola and nuts. Lucas gripped the bag with both hands and gave it another shake.

A large, oddly shaped item fell onto the pile. Its appearance elicited an immediate curse from Lucas while Gwen's mind struggled to understand.

He lifted the item carefully, pressing the phone to his shoulder with his ear and scowling deeply. "And an eight-inch hunting knife." He pulled the stiff sheath away, leaving a shiny silver blade in his opposite hand.

Gwen struggled for breath as images of her attack flashed through her mind. The scar along her side burned as she recalled the feeling of it plunged into her flesh. Desperation clawed at her throat and chest as she fell through time, suddenly present in the moments that had changed everything.

Lucas marched back onto the trail, indignant, describing their location to Detective Anderson while Gwen worked to stay conscious.

The psycho had packed a bag of snacks to pass the time while he watched her run.

And a massive knife to kill her.

She leaned forward at the waist and braced her palms against her knees, feeling the familiar wave of tension and fear take over. She pressed her eyelids shut, pulling herself into the present and forcing away the awful images. "Keep it together, Gwen," she whispered to herself.

Branches rumbled overhead as a mass of birds lifted from the treetops.

And a hand clamped hard across her mouth.

Another arm snaked around her center and hauled her back into the trees. The sharp point of a knife pressed strategically against her throat.

Chapter Ten

Lucas moved in long strides through the woods toward the hike-and-bike trail, trying to improve the cell signal and locate the nearest post with a mile marker to pinpoint their location. "We're at mile eighteen," he told Detective Anderson. "Send a crime scene team in an unmarked car. We want to get the job done without the fanfare of a lights and sirens parade. Especially if he's watching. Even if he's not, Gwen's struggling. I want to get her out of here as soon as possible."

The hair on Lucas's arms rose with a change in the air as he pivoted back in the direction he'd come. The trees rattled with a sudden mass exodus of birds, and his gut clenched.

His feet were in motion before he'd made the conscious effort to run. "Gwen?" he called, hoping his instincts were wrong, praying his nerves were just frayed. That she was safe where he'd left her, only a few yards away. "Gwen!"

"What's happening?" Detective Anderson demanded, her voice exploding from the phone he'd nearly forgotten he was holding.

He burst back through the trees and spotted Gwen immediately. A man in a ghillie suit stood behind her, one hand covering her mouth, the opposite arm snaked around her middle, just below her ribs, a large hunting knife in his fist. The fabric of his camouflage blended seamlessly with the surroundings, and Lucas couldn't help wondering just how close the man had been when Lucas had run off, distracted by a need to report his findings. How close had the attacker been when Lucas left her alone and in danger?

"Stop!" Lucas screamed, storming forward as he pressed the phone more tightly to his ear. "He's here. He's got her. I need backup. Now!" He plunged the phone into his jacket pocket, then unholstered his sidearm.

They were moving toward the road on the other side of the trees.

Gwen's eyes were wide with terror as the assailant dragged her backward. Her hands clutched at his arms, and she winced each time they stumbled over fallen saplings and branches.

A spot of blood spread through her jacket below the blade now glinting in the afternoon sunlight. The same blade that Lucas had just dumped from the bag and left on the forest floor to be used against her.

"Take another step, and I will shoot you," he promised, advancing steadily on the much slower pair. "I won't let you hurt her again."

The assailant looked over his shoulder, his face covered with layers of fringed camouflaged material and a thin black balaclava, revealing only his crazed eyes. The elaborate suit made him seem more like a ghost than a man. He was taller than Gwen by several inches, though hunched; it was difficult to guess with any precision. His shoulders were broader, arms and legs longer, and the boots he wore left an occasional imprint deep in the ground.

Lucas grinned. The man was armed, but he was no match for Lucas's marksmanship. All he needed was one clear shot.

Traffic sounds grew louder with each step, the busy road beyond the dense patch of forest drawing nearer.

"Stop!" Lucas called again, mind reeling, assessing, troubleshooting. Did this guy have a plan beyond snatch-and-grab? Did he leave a getaway car nearby? Parked along the winding road into the little lot, perhaps? Or parked along the busy street? Ready to help them vanish.

Lucas lengthened his strides, pushing forward, refusing to lose her again. "You're running out of forest," he warned, letting a sneer work over his deceptively cool face.

"Stay back," the would-be abductor called, his voice unnaturally low.

Disguised, Lucas realized.

"Stop moving or I'll gut her," he seethed, dragging the blade into position beneath her sternum.

Lucas's steps stuttered, and bile rose in his throat.

Gwen's eyes fluttered shut as they breached the wooded area and stepped into the blinding afternoon sunlight along the road.

Her attacker moved the knife again, seeking better purchase on her frame and turning them away from the streaming cars. The layers of the ghillie suit lifted and fluttered on the breeze. "Stay back!" he screamed, voice frantic as he looked in every direction. Exposed to a hundred commuters, some who were now slowing at the sight of him holding a captive at knifepoint. He whipped his face in the direction of distant sirens rising into the sky.

Gwen's eyes opened and locked with Lucas's once more.

"You can't get away this time," Lucas warned, stepping slowly forward and lining up a shot for the next time the assailant turned away. "Might as well let her go and take that suit off so we can see who we're dealing with."

The man shifted, releasing his grip on Gwen so quickly, Lucas barely perceived it before she was flying away from the man. Shoved hard. Into traffic.

The scream that ripped from her core nearly split Lucas in two. The blare of a horn pushed his heart into his throat.

The assailant broke right, sprinting back into the woods as Gwen crashed onto the asphalt and bounced slightly before becoming still.

Tires screeched, and Lucas launched himself after her. Cars careened out of their way, thankfully already somewhat slowed by the public abduction attempt. The sounds of multiple low speed collisions rocketed around them, spewing chunks of headlights and dropping portions of fenders, as one car clipped another vehicle, then another, only feet away from Gwen's prone body.

Lucas wrenched her off the ground, waving an arm at oncoming cars as she groaned and jerked to life. "Shh!" he soothed, guiding her back to the berm of grass outside the tree line.

Her legs fumbled to keep pace, and her hands gripped the material of his coat.

The scent of burning rubber from squealing tires mixed with angry voices and sirens in the air.

Her assailant was gone. Vanished back into the trees. But Lucas couldn't leave Gwen. He wouldn't let her bleed and suffer alone, not ever again.

She sobbed against his chest, fingers fiercely knotted into the fabric of his coat as emergency vehicles lined the busy road. "He came from the trees," she said, heartbroken. "He was there all along. Waiting."

Lucas gathered her closer, horrified by the afternoon's events and reverent for the outcome. "We'll find him. I promise. You're okay now. The ambulance is here."

An unmarked sedan took the turn toward the parking lot. Likely the low-key crime scene crew he'd requested. Followed by a set of cruisers, lights flashing, and a line of ambulances, probably dispatched for the fender benders. He swallowed a humorless chuckle at the irony.

He tugged Gwen back for a look at her side, the ambulances reminding him this wasn't over. She could still be seriously hurt. "How bad is the cut? Did you break anything when you fell?"

"I'm okay." She loosened her grip on him and stepped away slightly, forcing him to release her in turn. Far sooner than he was ready.

"You're really not okay," he said gently. "That's the shock talking. You're going to need to get checked out, and probably stitches." He turned to wave an arriving ambulance closer, and it wedged itself onto the berm at their side.

The passenger door flew open and a familiar man jumped down. "Lucas!" The paramedic raced to them, a look of confusion on his youthful face. "What are you doing here?"

"Is that Isaac?" Gwen whispered, eyes wide at the sight of him.

Lucas smiled at his younger cousin and close friend. "The one and only."

"What happened?" Isaac asked, still taking in the scene.

Isaac was the youngest of the Winchesters, though a cousin by blood, he'd practically been raised in Lucas's family home, making Isaac the unofficial little brother in most of their childhood memories. A brother he didn't see often enough these days.

Isaac reached gingerly for Gwen as he waited for Lucas to explain. His gaze ran quickly over her, assessing the work ahead of him. When his eyes met hers, he froze. "Gwen?"

She nodded, rubbing shaky hands across her face. "Hi, Isaac." She winced and pressed both palms against her side.

His gaze followed to the growing blood spot on her

jacket, then snapped back to Lucas. "Pick her up, let's get her into the bus. What the hell happened out here today?"

Lucas pulled one of Gwen's arms over his shoulders, then bent to sweep her off her feet before she could protest. He cradled her body to his as he jogged the short distance to the ambulance. "We think her attacker is back, and he got a hold of her today."

Isaac blanched. "You're going to be okay," he told her, his jaw setting with resolve. "How are you feeling?" He opened the bay doors and stood aside while Lucas carried her to the gurney inside. "Cold? Dizzy? Nauseous?"

"A little," she answered, her teeth beginning to chatter.

Isaac covered her with a white blanket, then fixed a stethoscope into his ears. Her tragedy had changed him, too.

Gwen set a palm against his cheek as he worked, listening to her heart and lungs. "Look at you." She sniffled, and a tear swiveled over her cheek. "You're all grown up. I'm sorry I missed it."

"Me, too," he said, checking her vitals before pulling a bag of IV fluids from a cabinet behind him. He hung the bag, then worked the line into her hand, smoothly inserting the needle without her seeming to notice. Satisfied, he turned cautious eyes back on hers. "I'm glad to see you again, too, but we could've just had lunch."

Gwen smiled, then winced once more.

Isaac pulled back with a patient grin. "I need to take a look at that." He cut the material of her shirt, exposing the wound in Gwen's side, then deftly cleaned and assessed. "You'll need a couple stitches, but this will heal. It's not deep." He applied a topical cream and bandage with skilled and confident hands. "We'll get the sutures at the hospital, and better evaluate that bump on your head."

Her hand rose to her forehead. She grimaced as her fingers found the rising knot.

"She hit her head on the road when he shoved her into traffic," Lucas said.

Isaac swore under his breath, then moved on to cleaning superficial wounds. First her palms, then cutting away the torn fabric of her pants to work on her knees. "He's really back?" he asked. "After all this time?" He looked up from his work, catching Lucas's eye.

"Turns out, he never left," Gwen said.

Isaac's gaze hardened. A silent order for Lucas to find this guy and put him away. As if that wasn't Lucas's new purpose in life.

"When did you decide to be a paramedic?" Gwen asked. "I thought you were going to study computer science."

"I decided I wanted to make a difference," he said, smoothing a bandage over the broken skin of her palm.

Isaac had spent every minute he was allowed in the hospital hallways and waiting rooms while Gwen had fought for her life. Then became a dedicated visitor during her recovery. He'd been crushed to learn she'd left for Florida without saying goodbye. Gwen had been his family, too. When he'd changed his choice of major freshman year of college, he'd told his mother there weren't any computer technicians involved in saving Gwen, but there had been countless medical professionals. He wanted to be like them.

"Hey!" A man in a local PD jacket waved a badge overhead, scowling and summoning Lucas from outside the open ambulance doors.

Isaac and the driver looked to Lucas.

"Are we okay here for another minute?" Lucas asked. "I'd like to talk to this guy, but I want to go with Gwen to the hospital."

Gwen reached for his hand. "Go. I'm okay here, and I want to know what he says."

"I'll be right back." Lucas hopped down to meet the man with the badge, hopeful the assailant had fallen on his own knife while running away.

"Lucas Winchester?" he asked.

"Yes, sir." Lucas extended a hand to the older officer. "West Liberty, SVU."

"Is our vic going to be okay?" The officer tipped his chin to the waiting ambulance. Sincere concern lined his brow.

"That's Gwen Kind," Lucas reported. "She's not a victim, and she's going to be just fine."

The officer seemed to consider that a moment as he watched Gwen on the gurney, then nodded. "Good. Detective Anderson wants to talk with you. She said not to let you leave until she did."

"I'm in a hurry," Lucas said, unwilling to be detained longer than necessary. "She can catch me at the local ER. Any news on the assailant?"

A sharp whistle drew their attention to the tree line. "I'll take it from here," Anderson reported, stepping onto the shoulder and taking in the scene.

An ambulance on the berm. A closed lane of traffic, courtesy of several crunched cars. A set of uniformed officers and an arriving tow truck, attempting to clear it all.

She excused the officer before Lucas with the flick of her head, then gave Lucas a cold stare. "What exactly were you doing out here? Investigating a crime in my jurisdiction?" she huffed the questions, cheeks pink with temper. "You only called to tell me what you were up to after the fact. Then by happenstance, I got to hear about that poor woman being abducted while you chased her and her assailant into traffic. Now, I have an injured woman, a crime scene, a pile of wrecked cars and a stalker who's both on the run and onto us. How the hell did he even find you here? Tell me a detective with a record as good as yours isn't being followed without knowing."

Lucas blinked. How *had* he found them there? In the middle of the day. Not at all according to Gwen's routine? What had she said when Lucas pulled her out of traffic? He'd come from the trees?

"If I had any chance of finding this guy before he knew I was looking," Anderson ranted on, "it went straight out the window the moment you decided to take on a New Plymouth case without any authority to do so. Do you understand what a loss that is? A disadvantage you gave me."

She worked her jaw and crossed her arms, turning her back to the ambulance. "I understand on a human level what you're doing here with her and why. I've read more about Ms. Kind's original attack over the past few days than I have ever read about any other cold case. Ever. And I get what this means to you, but this is my town, and I lead the investigations here. Whatever personal connection you have with the victim might be solid motivation for you, but it isn't doing you or your friend any favors. So, I suggest you take a big boy step back or the next time you cause chaos like this, I'll contact your supervisor and have you sent home."

Lucas narrowed his eyes, hating every word she'd said and the tone in which the message had been delivered. "With all due respect," he began, ready to explain a few things that weren't respectful at all, but he froze. Another thought pressed its way into mind, stunning him temporarily silent.

"Yes?" Detective Anderson demanded. "You've got something to say?"

"We came here today after reviewing the photo files you sent me. Did you include every photo from the thumb drive?"

She nodded, brows furrowed. "Everything. Why?"

Lucas shoved his hands through his hair and gritted his teeth. "We're here because there were twice as many photos of this place than any other location in the past year. It was the most obvious place to start looking for clues, so we came." He groaned and swallowed a thick line of curses. He'd been tricked. Manipulated. Beaten. "This guy knew we'd make that connection and come here to investigate. He set us up. He hid. And he waited."

Hunted, Lucas realized. They'd been lured like deer by poachers. "And he even left himself a knife for when we inevitably came waltzing into his trap."

Chapter Eleven

Gwen climbed into the bed in Lucas's room just after nine. They'd been trapped at the hospital in New Plymouth for hours, waiting for her to receive medical attention, then for the staff to observe and discharge her. They'd made their statements to the local police department, telling the story at length, and on repeat, to be sure nothing was missed or forgotten. Then Detective Anderson had laid into Lucas for inserting himself into her investigation and causing the pile of fender benders among other things. Gwen had done her best to settle the woman's temper, but she was beside herself, and Gwen hadn't had the energy to argue. She'd just wanted to go home.

"You don't have to do all this," she told Lucas for the dozenth time as he worked on stoking the fire.

"Temperatures are dropping tonight," he reminded her, shooting a sheepish look over his shoulder. "You'll be glad I did. The furnace in this place hasn't been updated since we were in middle school. Having a fireplace in the bedroom is practically a necessity."

"You've fussed too much already. It's been an awful day. Let's just call it and start again tomorrow." She rubbed her stinging eyes and yawned, pushed closer to sleep by the day's excitement and whatever had been in her IV, no doubt.

He stretched onto his feet, dusting his palms and surveying the room. He'd gathered his discarded clothing and closed the closet door while she'd showered and changed into pajamas. When she'd returned, the space was spotless, and there was a glass of water on the nightstand beside the prescribed pain medication she refused to take and the bottle of over-the-counter stuff she'd reluctantly said she might. The prescription would make her head foggy. She couldn't afford that now. The aspirin was a better option, once the medication from the hospital wore off.

He'd insisted they stay here tonight, when she'd wanted to go to her place, but that was a fight she'd be better equipped for tomorrow. For now, they were safe in his home. Back in his jurisdiction, where Detective Anderson couldn't complain about their investigation, which was nice. And hopefully, Gwen's attacker would be lying low tonight, recovering from his failure and allowing Gwen and Lucas to rest.

She tracked him with a tired, apologetic gaze as he crossed back to her. She'd come to him for an opinion and advice, now he'd inadvertently become her personal protector and caretaker.

"Hey," he said softly, sinking onto the bed at her side. His baggy sweatshirt and pants made him look younger and softer, like the man she'd fallen in love with in college. His hair was mussed from dragging his fingers through it and damp from a shower. His scent so familiar and enticing, she wanted to pull him against her and thank him properly for saving her life today.

More effects of that pesky IV, she assured herself.

She was too relaxed, and it was hard to corral her thoughts. Her mind circled around how good it felt to be with Lucas again, whatever else happened. How she felt more whole here, with a man she hadn't seen or spoken to in years, than she had any day in between. And her heart grew heavy, hating how hard it would be to leave again, and how empty her days would become without him. She couldn't stay with Lucas, and he couldn't come with her once this ended. They each had their own lives now, and no amount of wistful, IV-induced hope could change that.

"Tired?" he asked, a small grin on his handsome face. He caressed her forehead and cheeks before taking her hand.

Her restless heart leapt, and it took another long beat for her to realize he was checking her temperature and pulse.

She scooted up in bed, arranging the pillows behind her as a backrest. "I'm okay," she promised, then cringed slightly at the spear of pain along her newly sutured side. "Thank you for everything you're doing. And for saving my life."

Lucas's caring eyes searched hers. "There's an argument to be made that I'm the one who put you in danger by taking you with me today, and by not seeing his trap for what it was."

"Ridiculous," Gwen said, pushing herself up straighter against the pillows. "You're stuck in the middle of this because of me, and we went to the park together. As a team," she said. "I'm not here to hide out while you fix my problems. I'm here because I needed to know if you thought there was something to worry about. There clearly is, and you're helping me through it. Which is incredibly kind and gracious of you." Not to mention heroic, gallant and a dozen other wonderful things. "There was no way you could have predicted he'd be there today."

"Because I underestimated him," Lucas said. His cool blue eyes turning away, brooding again. Something he'd been making a profession out of since they'd ridden away from the crime scene in the ambulance. And it broke her heart.

"This isn't on you," she whispered, wondering where he went when he drifted away in one of those remorseful stares. A painful possibility occurred as she watched him draw into himself and noted the guilt and shame in his eyes. The way he was all-in with her from the moment someone had picked up their tab at the pub, and the way he mothered her now, trying to make every detail right. As if fresh bedding and the perfect fire would somehow heal her faster. Or make amends. "Luke," she whispered, forcing the word from her lips. "Do you blame yourself for what happened to me in college?"

His attention snapped back to her, a world of pain and hurt coursing behind hooded eyes. "Every day."

Her breath caught and her throat tightened. Unsure what to say, she reached for him, dragging him nearer by the sleeve of his shirt. He resisted a moment, confusion clouding his gaze. Then, he followed her lead and allowed her to hold him. A sea of emotions broke over her as she pressed him closer. It had been years since she'd touched or been touched by anyone other than her parents. And that had been polite and limited. She'd feared that being touched could send her into a spiral of memories she didn't want. Memories of the monster and all the ways he'd hurt her. But now, as Lucas belatedly wrapped his arms around her, the opposite was happening. It was as if she could finally breathe.

Her head fell easily into the crook of his neck, and she loved the feel of his heart beating against hers. "It's not your fault," she said. "Not what happened today and not what happened before. I promise you." He shuddered against her, and for a moment she wondered if he was crying. She wouldn't blame him if he was. Hers was the same message he'd repeated to her all those years ago, begging her to see her attack wasn't about some wrong choice she'd made, but about the attacker alone. She wasn't responsible for anyone else's behavior, and she had every right to walk home that night, or any night. No reason to think that choice would change her life. She couldn't shoulder any of that burden any longer, and neither should Lucas.

"I'm sorry I left you," she said gently, the truth flowing from her heart and through her lips without filter. The moment was too precious to ruin with veils and lies. Something had changed for her today, and she knew instinctually that this was the moment all the others had been leading to since that night. It was time to set Lucas free from any of the weight she'd unintentionally left on him when she'd walked away. "I ran away for a thousand really good reasons, but I should have handled our goodbye better."

Lucas pulled back, eyes tight with emotion. "You did what you needed to do. I never blamed or judged you for that. Not for a minute."

A smile tugged Gwen's trembling lips. "I was wrong, and I'm sorry. I loved you, and I owed you a proper goodbye."

His frown deepened. "Gwen, you've never owed me anything."

"I do." She worked to press back the painful lump in her throat. There was one more thing that needed to be said before she changed her mind. "I let a monster change me, but I didn't mean to let him change you, too."

Lucas shook his head slowly. "He didn't change me."

"No? So, you like being a Special Victims Unit detective?" she asked. "Dealing with this kind of brutality and horror every day. A constant reminder of what you went through?"

He turned stormy eyes on her without answering.

"You were going to be a great architect," she said, grieving the future he'd lost. "You had more brains and talent than anyone else in your class. And you gave that up. I think joining the force was noble, but this was never your dream."

"You were my dream," he said flatly. "You."

"But I was gone. And you quit school."

Lucas ground his teeth, eyes flooded with barely contained emotion. Anger, heartbreak and regret among others she couldn't name. "I didn't need my master's degree to join the force."

"You were never supposed to join the force."

"And I didn't quit school, I flunked out."

"What?" She pulled her chin back, stunned. "How?"

"I might've been a grad student at Bellemont, but I spent all my time looking for the man who hurt you. I looked for clues on my own, interviewing students and tracking leads. I blanketed the campus with flyers in search of anything that could further the case. My grades were in the trash by the end of the first semester. That was when I realized I didn't want to be an architect anymore. And what I really needed to find the man who hurt you was access to everything the police knew so far. There was only one way to do that. So, I joined the force. Not that it's gotten me any closer to my goal."

"Are you happy?" she asked. "As a detective?" That was the bottom line, she supposed. Even if she couldn't understand finding joy in being surrounded by people living her nightmare, if Lucas somehow could, then that was all that mattered.

"Yeah," he answered easily, and with a small laugh. "I am." He turned those intense blue eyes on her with a smile. "I like making a difference. I like seeing criminals punished, and I like seeing victims get the justice they deserve. When I get to be part of that delivery, all the better. I might've come to law enforcement by way of the unthinkable, but I've stayed for me. For them." He shrugged.

"Sitting where I am today, I'm not sure I'd be happy as an architect. So, no, that psychopath didn't change me, but he will regret he ever crossed me."

The words hit her like a punch to the chest. If Lucas hadn't changed, then she'd never really known him. He wasn't an alpha-male, gun-wielding lawman. He was a peacekeeper who loved numbers and old buildings. Wasn't he?

"What?" he asked. "Tell me what you're thinking. You look unhappy, and I don't know why. Was it something I said?"

"No. Not at all. I'm glad you're happy, and that you're being honest. I guess I'm just wondering how well I ever knew you." She glanced away, around the beautiful old room in a historic house he was renovating on a cop's salary and in his spare time. "You still love architecture."

"I still love a lot of things." He shifted on the bed to face her. "I'm the same man I've always been. I changed career paths, that's all, and our careers don't define us."

"Then why aren't you married?" she asked, cheeks heating with fatigue and frustration at her unintentional candor. "You date, but you haven't settled down. That's a big change from what I thought I knew. I always thought you wanted a wife and family. Carpool and Little League."

"I still do, and I don't date," he said, brows furrowed in confusion. "Why'd you say that?"

She frowned back at him, sorry to have pressed into his personal business, and certain she'd hate whatever he said next. "I heard the guys at the station talking while I was waiting to see you. They said you had flavors of the week." She huffed a sigh. "Don't answer that. It doesn't matter, and those guys weren't talking to me. I'm just cranky and tired. I should sleep." She punched the pillow at her side, leaning slightly forward with a wince to adjust them before she lay back.

Lucas pushed onto his feet, giving her room for the silent tantrum. "I lie to the guys about my dating life so I can be alone," he said. "I don't want to hang out with them after work because I have a ton to do here. I don't want to argue with them or offend them, so I tell them I have dates."

"But you don't?"

"Not in a long time, and it never felt quite right when I did." He gripped the back of his neck as he walked toward the door. "Truth is that there was only ever one woman for me. If I couldn't be with her, then what was the point?" He paused in the doorway. "I hope you're able to get some rest." He flipped out the light and walked away.

Lucas headed for his home office. He needed to check in at work. As suspected, Detective Anderson had already spoken with his superior, so Lucas had the pleasure of rehashing the awful day one more time. Thankfully, protocols aside, his supervisor had his back.

He disconnected the call feeling only slightly better than he had before making it. His neck and shoulder muscles were pinched and achy, his limbs and mind heavy with fatigue. Lucas was drained. Emotionally, physically and mentally. He needed a decent night's sleep and a fresh start tomorrow, when his head was clear and he wasn't saying whatever came to mind. He cringed internally at the memory of telling Gwen he didn't date, and that she was the only woman he'd ever wanted.

He listened to a long line of voice mail updates on his current caseload, then forced himself through some paperwork online. He didn't hear from Gwen again, and by the time the clock struck midnight, he was ready to call it a night.

Lucas locked the house down before setting his alarm and checking in on Gwen once more. She looked peaceful and perfect cuddled under his comforter, warmed by his fire. Maybe it was the influence of exhaustion on his clarity or the emotional impact of seeing her in a madman's clutches, but Lucas was certain losing her again, when this was over, would be more than his heart could bear.

Chapter Twelve

Gwen woke with a headache, likely from the goose egg on her forehead, dehydration and the knowledge that she'd said some overly revealing things to Lucas the night before. She scooted upright and winced at the pain in her side. Memories of the previous day's near-abduction raced back, images from the nightmare that had kept her stirring through the night.

She took inventory of her many aches and pains, then downed a pair of aspirins along with the glass of water on the nightstand. The house was silent outside her room, and she panicked, momentarily, afraid Lucas had left her alone. She pulled the covers higher under her arms, then dialed Lucas, hoping that if he had gone, he would be back soon.

The ring of her call echoed through the receiver of her phone, as well as in the hall outside her door.

Lucas appeared a moment later, wide awake and dressed for the day. His faded jeans hung low on his hips. A worn gray T-shirt peeked from beneath an unbuttoned flannel. The blue plaid pattern emphasized his brilliant eyes and the way he'd rolled the sleeves to his elbows highlighted the ropes of muscle along his forearm.

Gwen disconnected and forced her mouth shut.

"You're up?" he asked, rhetorically, slipping his cell phone into his jeans pocket. "How did you sleep?"

"Okay," she said. "All things considered."

"Restless?" he guessed, leaning against the jamb. The shift in position opened the flannel further, revealing the way his T-shirt stretched to accommodate his broad chest.

"Yeah. You?"

He shrugged, then crossed his arms. "How's your side? And your head? Are you in pain?"

"I've been through worse," she said wryly, hating how much that was true. "I've been thinking."

"Uh oh."

"Funny." She narrowed her eyes. "Do you need to go in to work today, or do you have time for a field trip? Something local this time, so Detective Anderson can't complain."

Lucas cocked his head and watched her carefully before nodding. "I talked to my sergeant last night. Filled him in on what's happening, and he assigned me to your case. It's officially reopened, and I can work in the field, checking in periodically."

Gwen's heart skipped, both at the idea of spending more uninterrupted time with Lucas, and at the idea her case was reopened. It had been closed when they'd had nothing more to go on. Opening the case meant there was new hope. Something she'd been without for far too long. "So, you're in for the field trip?"

He nodded.

"You didn't ask what I have in mind." She frowned. "I've been laying here for the last hour going over all your possible complaints and making watertight arguments against them."

Lucas let his arms fall to his sides, and a grin tugged lazily at his lips. "We can argue first, if you want, but since you're going to win anyway, I guess I'll just do what you say."

Her smile widened. "A lady could get used to that."

Ninety minutes later, Gwen climbed down from the cab of Lucas's truck and surveyed the college campus she'd once loved dearly. The aspirin, combined with a generous amount of water at breakfast, had taken the edge off, and she was ready to start at the beginning. At Bellemont.

"Ready?" he asked, eyes narrowed in scrutiny. Clearly, Lucas had reservations about her idea to retrace her freshman and sophomore year tracks, or as many tracks as she could remember anyway. It seemed logical that being back on campus would help her recall her early routines.

"Ready." She forced her shoulders back, certain he could see through her thinly veiled bravado, but determined to be strong. "We should head for the student center. My dorm was down that way, along with most of my classes. And we'll pass the computer lab on the way. We can make a loop, concentrate on the places I frequented. And visit the crime scene before we go."

"I don't think that's necessary," Lucas protested.

"It is," she assured him, then with a hard internal shove, she forced her feet to move.

Lucas fell into step at her side, tense and overly concerned, his two most common moods these days. He'd tugged on a knit beanie and pulled a black motorcycle jacket over his flannel. Between the ensemble and the scowl, he looked more like trouble than the law.

She'd settled for a jean jacket over her favorite cream turtleneck layered with a comfy tank top, jeans and brown leather boots. Her cream mittens and hat were speckled with gold, and her wild red curls lifted like a halo around her face with each fresh gust of wind.

They walked silently through the brisk day, past multiple parking lots, through common areas with meandering students, and around a group of prospective freshmen receiving a campus tour.

Sounds of the school's marching band rose into the day, punctuated by a cheering crowd and the mumbling of an emcee over the stadium speakers.

"Sounds like a pep rally," Lucas said, staring into the distance as the fight song blared.

Scents of hot dogs and popcorn peppered the air beside the ashy aroma of a bonfire. Was it even fall in Kentucky if no one had a bonfire?

"Spirit week," Gwen said. "I used to love these days." There was something about the camaraderie they provoked. The staff and student body came together with alumni to celebrate everything Bellemont. People were happy. The air was electric with anticipation of all that was to come.

Today was no different, and the nostalgia was palpable. It took immense self-control not to reach for Lucas's hand as they walked the familiar paths.

"Still doing okay?" he asked, slowing his pace when fear came bubbling back in her.

"Yeah." She nodded, then pushed her feet forward once more, refocused on the memories she needed, and forcing out those she didn't. "Let's make the library and computer lab a priority today, then the student center. I had most of my meals there freshman and sophomore year."

She rolled her shoulders back and forced her chin up. It was her idea to be here, and Lucas was letting her lead the charge. The least she could do was try not to look as apprehensive as she felt. She'd managed to lever her reluctant self from the truck, and get this far. There was no turning back now. It was time to explore and remember.

Lucas cleared his throat as they turned up the next path. "I was thinking about the fact that you were being followed for two years before we knew it." He shot a sideways look in her direction, then forced his hands into his pockets. "Then you were attacked on the weekend of our engagement. The night you went out with friends to celebrate."

Her steps faltered, and flashes of the attack rushed back to her. Angry hands in her hair. Cold eyes behind a black balaclava. A blow to her chest. Searing pain in her side.

"Hey," a man's voice called.

Gwen snapped back to the present, a sheen of sweat on her temple and brow.

The man nodded as he approached, pumping a fist in the air.

Lucas lifted a fist in reciprocation as they passed on the wide stone path.

Gwen angled to watch the group as they disappeared into the crowd behind them. "Who was that?"

"I have no idea," Lucas said with a laugh. "Other alumni, I'd guess."

She chuckled with him. That sounded right. "We're all friends now. At least for another two or three days."

There were people everywhere, plenty who were unfamiliar and others who weren't. Gwen had already spotted a former teacher and one or two classmates in the crowd. Everyone looked the same, if a little heavier and most with shorter hair.

Hope mixed with dread in her gut at the thought of seeing any of her friends while she was at Bellemont. She didn't want their pitying looks or to entertain polite but meaningless conversation. Gwen was on a mission. "Computer lab," she said, pointing to the next building on their right.

Lucas held the door for her as she slipped inside. The scent of burnt coffee assaulted her senses as she climbed the steps to the second floor. Balloon bouquets stood cheerfully outside key rooms, set up for guests and visitors.

She tugged off her mittens and stowed them in her pockets as they made their way down the hall.

The computer lab door had a "Welcome" sign.

Gwen peeked around the corner before taking a tentative step across the threshold. An empty room spread out before them, and a ripple of memories rushed through her. Same tables and chairs. Same whiteboards and motivational posters. She trailed her fingertips across the cool surfaces, feeling an unexpected smile grow. "I spent so much time here those first two years. I didn't understand the engineering software at all, among other things, and I still have a love-hate relationship with databases." She gave a soft laugh.

Lucas stopped at the large desk up front and surveyed the scene. Someone had decorated the whiteboard in school colors and made a pom-pom-and-confetti boarder with dry erase markers. A pile of flyers with the week's itinerary stood neatly at the corner of the teacher's desk. Lucas pressed a palm to the nearby mug. "Still warm. We must've just missed whoever was here. Do you want to wait?"

"No." Gwen completed her circle through the room, feeling lighter than she had since she'd first stepped onto campus. "We can come back."

He swung an arm wide, and she met him at the doorway.

Her long-guarded heart began to beat harder as he set a palm against her back. Being there with Lucas, old memories colliding with new ones and the tender way he still looked at her was almost too much. And she wondered again what life would have been like if she hadn't run away. If she'd come back to him instead of setting up some facsimile of a life, alone, in the next town. She'd fallen asleep thinking of the way he'd said his dreams never changed, and that there was only ever one woman for him.

If that was all true, when this was finally over, was there

a chance he'd ask her to stay? Could he still want her, broken pieces and all? Was it fair to hope he would?

LUCAS KEPT ONE eye on Gwen as they moved through knots and clusters of people along the walkways outside. She'd done well so far. Put on a brave face at first, then seemed genuinely at ease in more familiar spaces.

The path curved and forked ahead of them, part branching off to form a loop around the massive grounds while the rest continued on, through the center of it all. Gwen had been attacked, then discovered, on the perimeter loop.

All while Lucas was fast asleep.

Apparently feeling the tension, too, Gwen slipped her hand around his elbow as the fork in the path drew near.

"Look," he said, covering her hand with his. "You used to love this place." He urged her into the grass where a small coffee stand was surrounded by people. A chalkboard listed the daily specials, and garlands of pendants in crimson and gold hung in sweeps from the roof. "You lived on the hot cider and kettle corn for at least half the year," he said, leading her to the back of the line. Their tiny off-campus apartment had smelled of the mouthwatering combination every night when he came home from work. Gwen would be curled on the couch, or face down at her desk, having pressed on in her studies until no amount of sugar and cider could keep her going. Wherever he found her, he'd gather her into his arms, kiss her head and carry her to their bed, eager to slide in beside her.

They shuffled forward with the line, watching each customer walk away with something heavenly scented, a cup, a bag or both. Lucas ordered for them when they reached the counter, sensing Gwen was somewhere else completely. He tucked a tip in the jar, then stepped aside to wait on the drinks. Her gaze was distant and blank. Lost in a memory she likely wouldn't want to share.

"Maybe we can head over to the student center from here," he suggested, pretending not to notice her clear and growing distress. She'd only deny it if he brought it up.

They'd been moving in the direction of her attack site, but they didn't have to go there today, or ever, if she didn't want to. There was plenty of campus left to explore without it, and they had as much time as she needed to do it.

"No," she said softly, turning in his direction. "We should get back on the loop, take it around campus. I want to get that part over with. Then maybe I'll be able to relax, knowing the worst is behind me and I don't have to go back."

"We don't have to go at all," he said. "I have dozens of photos of the area at home. We can go over them together later."

"Photos aren't the same," she said with a sigh. "I can do this. I just have to get past the block in my mind that says it's still dangerous there when I know it's not. The path is safe. The man is dangerous, and he's not here. He's been in my head for years, keeping me from doing things I wanted, but not today. I can take a walk anywhere I want, in broad daylight, with a local lawman, and he can't stop me."

Brave words, he thought, though her expression wasn't selling the sentiment. Any clues that might've been found on the path were long gone, erased by time, weather and foot traffic, but she wanted to face her fears, and he was there to support her.

"You have your gun on you, right?" she asked, a small smile playing on her lips.

Lucas snorted. "Always."

"Good. I'm hoping the walk will trigger a memory we can use to name this guy," she said. "Right now, all I get are flashes of emotion, shocks of fear and single images or phantom pains. Nothing big picture. Nothing substantial." She swallowed hard, then started when the barista called their orders up.

Lucas passed her the cider, and she lifted it to her lips, a small quake in her arms.

Before he could suggest, again, that they go another direction for now, Gwen started down the path. Head high and cider pressed between both palms, she walked on, confident and determined.

He did his best to keep up while also keeping watch. With so many people on campus, it was hard to tell if anyone was looking their way and why. Maybe no one was watching, but he wouldn't be so naive as to assume that ever again.

Gwen's pace slowed as they drew nearer to the site of her attack, and the hairs on the back of Lucas's neck stood at attention. Frantic voices carried around the bend, where a grove of trees met the path and a shallow ravine was lined in river rock.

They both knew the spot too well.

Lucas set a palm against her back, and they hurried to meet the tiny crowd.

Six young faces looked to them as they approached. All women. All early twenties at most, and all with wide eyes and open mouths. When they turned away, their collective gazes fell to the ground before them.

"What's going on?" Lucas asked, stepping ahead and tucking Gwen protectively, instinctively behind him.

"We don't know," a petite brunette said. "It's really creepy. Right? Is it supposed to be a joke? Does it mean something?"

The group loosened their semicircle, revealing the outline of a body painted on the ground. A head drawn over the rocks, arms wide and legs splayed into the grass. A hunting knife stabbed into the heart of the outline pinned a flyer to the ground. The sides flapped, and edges curled in the hearty breeze.

Gwen gasped and stumbled backward. The brunette caught her and the others gathered tightly around, whispering words of comfort and sharing their own fears about what it might mean.

"We called campus security," someone said as Lucas inched over the small incline, snapping on a pair of gloves to avoid contaminating the scene. "SAVE THE DATE" was written across the top of the paper. Bellemont Homecoming across the bottom. Dates were inked in a series of pendants and balloons at the center.

"It doesn't make any sense, right?" a female voice asked from behind him.

"Homecoming is this week," someone else said. "The dates are wrong."

Lucas stretched back onto his feet and flashed his badge to the ladies, while a single tear fell from Gwen's eye. "That was the date of homecoming six years ago. And this is officially a crime scene."

Chapter Thirteen

Gwen perched on the edge of an uncomfortable chair inside Lucas's office at the West Liberty police station. It was nearly dinnertime, and she was feeling the weight of her day in the extreme. She was tired, hungry and the aspirin she'd taken that morning had long worn off. Add to that the stress of returning to Bellemont, only to see a threat had been laid out for her, and she wanted to scream. Somehow he'd known she would be there. Or maybe he'd planned for her to be there. After all, his invitation on her windshield was what had started her new nightmare. Was it possible the man stalking her knew her better than she knew herself? Because she'd only made the decision to go to Bellemont that morning, and it had taken some internal convincing.

Her knees bobbed wildly beneath her as she waited for Lucas to return once more. He'd been called away numerous times since their arrival, giving and receiving information on her case. Each consecutive disappearance seemed to wind her nerves more tightly. She chewed gingerly at the tender skin around her thumbnail, wrangling a mass of ping-ponging thoughts.

She wondered, for example, about the number of strange looks she'd received following Lucas into the station, after a crime scene crew had taken over on campus. The looks might not have been intentional, but there were definitely looks. Curious. Pointed. Looks. Did the lookers know who she was? Had they heard about everything that was going on around her? Or did they assume she was another in Lucas's long line of, allegedly fictional, dates. Not that any of that should matter now.

She freed her tortured thumb and clasped her hands, then released them again in favor of scrubbing her face. She winced when her fingertips hit her goose egg on her forehead. Maybe that was what they'd all been looking at. The entire day had been a train wreck of emotions. The whole week, really. From her suspicions of being followed, to the flyer confirming it, a near abduction, then all this. She leaned forward to wedge her forearms against her bobbing knees and hissed at the burn in her side where stitches closed her recent knife wound.

She closed her eyes and concentrated on her breathing. Deep inhalations. Slow exhalations. And she focused her thoughts on that night, six years ago. If she wanted to help stop her attacker, she needed to remember something useful.

She visualized her closest college friends. Recalled the restaurant where they'd met for dinner and drinks. The squeals and applause when she showed them her engagement ring. She saw the meal. The drinks. And the night's sky as she'd tipped her head back, admiring the endless stars on her walk home. In those precious moments, everything was right in her world.

Her eyes opened unintentionally, and her thoughts bounced back to the present. The way they always did when she got to this part of the memory.

She dropped her face into waiting palms, pressing her hands hard against closed eyes, and tried again. *Remember*, she ordered herself, falling back to the lost moments.

Her skin went cold, and the flashes began immediately.

Angry eyes. A black balaclava. Pain.

Grass. Trees. Rocks. Blood.

Her eyes opened once more. Protecting herself from what was to come. She struggled to steady her breaths, which were short and ragged. Her body shook with effort, as if remembering was physically exhausting, yet she hadn't managed to do that. Not really.

It had taken her weeks to recall anything at all about that night. She'd successfully, unintentionally, blocked every detail beyond the moment she'd kissed Lucas goodbye. He went to work. She went to meet friends. Her mind had buried everything else in mental concrete, which she'd slowly chipped away at for years. Only recently uncovering a few flashes of images and sounds.

Her therapist had called it progress.

Lucas's voice drew her attention to the door. He cruised inside with drinks. "Sorry that took so long." He set a cup of coffee on his desk, then offered her a bottle of water.

"Thanks."

"But wait," he said, digging into his pocket. "There's more." He produced a two-pack of aspirin and passed them her way.

"Bless." She accepted the offer greedily. "What's going on now?" she asked, popping the pills into her mouth, then washing them down. "You were gone awhile. Did they find something at the scene?" Something that led directly to the man who was ruining her life?

"No." Lucas rested his backside against his desk, stretching long legs between them. "This was something different." He grimaced and shook his head. "I've got a repeat offender I keep arresting, Tommy Black. He likes to get high and assault his girlfriend. I put him in jail again earlier this week, but he made bail. I called to warn his girl, because he sees her as the reason he gets arrested."

Gwen rolled her eyes. "She calls the police, so he says it's her fault?"

"Yep. Well, it's been more than seventy-two hours since he made bail, so I should've expected I'd see him again."

Heat rushed to Gwen's cheeks and her empty stomach heaved. "What does that mean? He hurt her again?"

"Like clockwork," Lucas said. His shoulders were slumped, his expression weary. "I hate this guy, deeply, and there's nothing I can do about him. I make the arrest. He gets off. Wash. Rinse. Repeat. It'd help if the girlfriend would testify against him, but she won't. She calls for help, but that's it. She says it's my job from there, and I just keep failing her."

"She's scared," Gwen said, her throat tightening with the words. "I can't imagine living like that. Face-to-face with a real and present danger every day." The fear of out-of-sight dangers was bad enough. What would it be like to know her monster was coming for her, in the flesh, at every turn? Hurting her again and again.

"Well, it is what it is," Lucas said. "Uniforms picked him up again, and they're hauling him in now. He's extra high, so he's extra obnoxious, aggressive and loud. A real trifecta of fun."

Gwen went back to chewing on her thumbnail. "At least he's been arrested. Is she okay?"

"Hospital." He sighed deeply, then peeled himself away from his desk. "I'm sure she'll be here to plead his case as soon as they release her. I'll have to leave you again for a few minutes when Tommy gets here. They'll rebook him, and I'll get a few minutes for another heart-to-heart. Maybe in his drugged-up state of mind he'll reveal something that leads to an arrest on some other count that won't need the girlfriend's testimony to make stick."

Gwen nodded, feeling the unknown woman's fear and turmoil as if it was her own. "Okay."

A sharp wolf whistle nearly launched her from her chair. The hearty laugh that followed drew a smile over her face.

She angled on her seat to watch the familiar man walk through the door.

Derek Winchester struck a cocky pose before her, all swagger and knockout good looks with a knee-buckling grin. "Well, if it isn't my baby brother's sexy ex. The fierce and formidable, Gorgeous Gwen Kind." He winked.

"Knock it off," Lucas complained, motioning his oldest brother to take a seat.

Derek obliged, lowering his lean body onto the chair beside hers. He slung a long arm across the back of her seat.

Her smile grew and her heart danced at the sight of him. "What are you doing here?" She loved Derek like a brother. A rebellious, sexy older brother. One who'd always taken her side when she and Lucas debated anything. Whatever Derek could do to ruffle his family's feathers, he was on it. Like becoming a private detective instead of just joining the force like his dad, granddad and great-granddad before him.

In hindsight, maybe it wasn't such a leap for Lucas to have traded architecture for law enforcement. Some might argue it was in his blood. Though, she'd never gotten the idea anyone expected him to do anything in life other than what he wanted. And Lucas had never said anything to make her think he was interested in carrying a badge.

Derek looked her over, long and slow. "I heard you were here, and I had to come and see for myself." His gaze lingered at the ugly purple-and-black knot on her head. "I heard you've had a rough couple of days." He cast a look in Lucas's direction.

"Who told?" she asked.

"Blaze."

"Ah," she said. That made perfect sense. Blaze was their middle brother, a homicide detective at the precinct. One she hoped she'd see again soon. The circumstances were awful, but being there with Lucas and Derek felt a bit like an odd family reunion, and she liked it.

Lucas pulled his phone into view and bobbed his head as he read the screen. "The guys are here with Tommy Black. I need to take care of that. You good?" he asked, flicking his gaze from Gwen to Derek, then back.

She nodded and smiled.

Lucas walked away slowly. "Don't listen to anything Derek says," he instructed.

And Derek's smile widened. "How are you holding up?" he asked, once Lucas had vanished.

"I'm getting through it," she said.

"You always do." He cocked his head and stretched back on his seat. "I wish I could say I'm sorry all this is happening."

"You're not?" she asked, frowning despite herself.

"Nah. If this guy wasn't at it again, and coming about things the way he is, he might never be arrested for what he did to you. Now, it's only a matter of time. Heck, Lucas might even let me help him now. Being a PI has its privileges you know. I don't have to abide by all the same rules and regulations my brothers do. I can go a little rogue, as needed. It's a perk of the trade."

"Uh-huh." Gwen's smile returned as she ran over his words with hope. "You really think he'll be caught this time?"

"I'm sure of it. He messed up when he made himself known. Whatever drove him to it is the same thing that's going to be his downfall." Derek's phone buzzed inside his pocket, and he took it out for a look at the screen. "Duty calls," he said. "I'm on the job, but I had to stop and say welcome back. You're in good hands with Lucas. No one loves you like my brother."

She stood to see Derek to the door, then fell easily into his embrace when he offered one. The second hug, from a man, in less than twenty-four hours, and once again she was surprised by how easy and natural it felt. Though, Derek was much more than some man. He'd nearly been her brother-in-law, and he'd always been her champion. "See you," she said, as he winked his goodbye.

She leaned against the doorjamb, watching him leave and wondering if it could really be so simple to fall back into her previous life. Would everyone be as accepting as Lucas, Isaac and Derek? Surely not, but wouldn't it be worth the meddlesome individuals who weren't if it meant she could be back here again…permanently?

Her ears perked at the sounds of distant shouts and commotion. Derek broke into a jog at the end of the hall, heading through the lobby door, toward whatever was happening.

Thumps, crashes and curses grew louder by the second, and Gwen leaned forward, senses on high alert and ready to run. She wasn't sure where she'd run, but the adrenaline was already building.

"Tommy Black!" Lucas's voice rose above the others, cut short as the door closed behind Derek.

Gwen stepped into the hall, a small measure of relief soothing the growing panic. The source of the problem was a conflict between Lucas and his criminal nemesis. Not her personal monster come to make good on his threat drawn in the campus grass.

A few steps from the door separating offices and interrogation rooms from the lobby, a thunderous boom erupted, and her muscles locked down.

Derek's face appeared outside the rectangular window in the door, eyes wide and expression hard. "Lucas!"

Gwen's world tilted. Her frozen muscles released, and she ran. Not away from the danger, but to it. The booming sound echoed in her heart and head. A gunshot? *No. Not that*, she thought. *Please, not that*. She couldn't lose Lucas again. Not now.

She burst into the lobby where a pack of officers had circled up, staring at the floor while a man in cuffs thrashed and kicked against his detaining officer. The thug landed a few kicks as others in uniform tried to still him. The mob shifted, and a large metal cabinet came into view, toppled onto the tile floor beside Lucas, glaring at the man in cuffs as blood rushed from his nose and lip.

Gwen nearly laughed in relief. Lucas was fine. He'd possibly been the recipient of one of Tommy Black's wild kicks, but he wasn't shot, and he would heal. She tugged on the door she'd exited, only to find it locked, of course. She'd have to wait until an officer headed back inside. So, she sidestepped a clutch of lawmen, attempting to stay out of everyone's way, and thankful the mess before her was something the police could handle.

"Tommy!" A woman wailed, pulling Gwen's attention toward the ladies' room door. The woman raced forward, into the mix of flailing feet and shouting officers. Tears streamed over bruised cheeks, falling from two black eyes. "Baby! I'm sorry," she cried, colliding with the man directly at Tommy's back and attempting to pry his arms off her man.

Tommy seemed to recognize her voice amid the chaos, and he jerked toward it, nearly tossing her and the man behind him off their feet.

She pleaded for Tommy's forgiveness as Derek caught her by the arms and pulled her back.

Tommy screamed every awful thing Gwen had ever heard at the woman, and then some more.

All the while, the station's front doors opened and closed with the arrival and departure of visitors and officers. Some in suits. Some in uniforms.

Gwen pressed herself to the wall, waiting for it all to end.

When another criminal was hauled in wearing cuffs, Tommy seemed to double down on his efforts for freedom, and gooseflesh rose over Gwen's arms.

The incoming criminal took Tommy's lead and began to buck and fight. His elbow landed in the doughy gut of his detaining officer, and the older man jackknifed forward, releasing his hold. The female officer manning the desk leaped into action, chasing the runaway man in cuffs, and the chaos doubled.

A scalding wet collision stole Gwen's breath, and for a moment, she thought she'd been attacked. A middle-aged man in a suit stared wide-eyed. His coffee cup now empty. Its contents thrown over Gwen's chest and face.

"I am so sorry," he said, genuinely horrified. "I was shoved." He looked behind him, but no one was there. "I'm sorry," he repeated, pulling a white linen handkerchief from his pocket.

"I'm okay," she said, plucking the material of her turtleneck away from her chest and waving off the handkerchief. For the first time in hours, she really was okay. "Excuse me." She ducked into the restroom Tommy's girlfriend had exited, then checked under every stall for good measure.

A smile bloomed over her face in another rush of relief. Lucas was fine. She was fine. And everything else would be fine very soon. Derek believed that, and she would believe him, too.

She tore a handful of paper towels from the dispenser then thrust them under cold water, prepared to do what she could for her cream turtleneck and jean jacket. And planning to take her time until the lobby quieted, and she could ask to be let back inside the main building.

She lifted her gaze to the mirror, wet towels pressed to her chest.

And saw the masked man's reflection in the mirror only a moment before his hands curved around her neck from behind, and he began to squeeze.

Chapter Fourteen

Lucas ambled back down the hall to his office. His nose throbbed, and if it wasn't broken, it'd be a miracle. A slow smile spread over his face at the thought. That would make two miracles, because his first was that Tommy Black officially assaulted an officer. Six officers, actually, while high, angry and extremely disorderly. He'd threatened to kill all the injured cops, blow up the station, murder his girlfriend and a slew of other vicious things while on camera. So, Anise would finally be safe, at least for a little while, because Tommy would definitely get some real jail time now. With or without her testimony.

He swung into his office with an apologetic grin. "Sorry that took so long."

The rest of the words stalled on his tongue. His office was empty.

He went back into the hall. "Gwen?" he called, looking in both directions before heading toward the officers' restrooms and vestibule with vending machines. He knocked on the bathroom door, then pressed it open an inch. "Gwen?"

"What are you doing?" Derek asked, dropping change into the vending machine.

"Looking for Gwen." He fought against a swell of panic, urging himself to be sensible. She hadn't been abducted inside a police station. "I thought you had work to do."

"I do, and what do you mean, looking for Gwen?" Derek asked, retrieving an ice-cold soda and handing it to his brother. "For your face."

Lucas held the can to his swollen nose. "She's not in my office or the ladies' room. Where was she when you left her?"

"In your office," Derek said, concern changing his usually smug expression.

"Check around back. Find someone who saw her leave my office. I'm heading to the lobby. If there's any chance she was taken outside during all that racket, it'll be caught on camera."

Derek broke left, heading toward the nearby desks and offices.

Lucas made a run for the lobby. He pushed through the automatically locking security door, then cut past the handful of people waiting to sign in. "Hey," he called, sliding in beside the next guest and drawing the young female officer's attention. "The woman I had in my office, Gwen Kind, have you seen her?"

Lanie frowned. She had an ice pack against her swollen cheek and a scowl on her face. "Your guy Black sure caused a hell of a lot of trouble out here. He kicked me in the face when I tried to keep Banister's guy from running out the front door."

Lucas straightened, raking frustrated hands through his hair. "Gwen's missing, and she's in danger," he said. "I need to know she wasn't taken during the chaos. Buzz me in to look at the security feed."

Lanie buzzed him through the door separating her from the lobby. Her scowl melted into something more like shock. "The redhead? You think that's possible?"

He froze, snapping his attention to her. "Why? Did you see her?" Heat crawled up his neck and over his face. If

Lanie had seen Gwen in the lobby, she'd been only a few yards from the front door.

"I think so. She was out here when I went to assist Banister."

"Then what?" he asked.

"I don't know. I subdued the guy, got kicked in the face on my way back. I didn't see much other than spots after that."

Lucas cursed. He turned in a small circle, then hunched over her desk, accessing the surveillance feed and rewinding by several minutes, to the start of the brawl.

"You think she's gone-gone?" she asked. "Taken during all the commotion?"

His chest constricted with rage and fear at the possibility. "Maybe."

"Pardon me." A shadow fell over the counter between them, and a middle-aged man in a suit smiled apologetically. "I'm sorry to bother you," he said. "I'm attorney David Neils, and I wonder if you're talking about the same redheaded woman I ran into? Midtwenties? Curly hair?"

"You saw her?" Lucas asked, fumbling for his phone. He accessed a photo he'd taken that morning and thrust the device in Neils's direction. Her red hair looked like fire, lifting and blowing alongside the colorful campus leaves.

"Yes. That's her." He looked sheepish again. "I spilled my coffee on her when someone shoved me during the brouhaha," he said. "She went into the restroom."

"Alone?" Lucas demanded, heading back through the security door to the lobby.

"Yes. I think so."

"Did you see her come out?" he asked, around the corner and darting for the public ladies' room. He swung the door wide without waiting for an answer. Intuition spiked in his chest, and he knew.

He'd failed her again.

AIR RUSHED INTO Gwen's lungs with a whoosh and a burn. Her body jolted upright on the cold floor, and tears flowed immediately from her eyes. Her heart raced with the knowledge something awful had happened, but it was several moments before the actual memories returned.

"Gwen?" The bathroom door swung open, banging against the wall and ricocheting off.

She started at the sound, but couldn't speak, still trapped in the horrific and detailed memory of her stalker's hands around her throat. His crazed eyes in the mirror's reflection. His breath in her hair.

He'd gotten to her in the police station bathroom with a half-dozen officers just outside the door.

Self-pity climbed to the forefront of emotions in her heart and took roost. The awful why-is-this-happening-to-me soundtrack began to play, and she let go as the desperation she'd barely kept under control all day broke free. She needed to get help. Needed to get up, but her body shook and her legs were weak and useless, as she tugged them tightly to her chest.

"Gwen?" Lucas fell to his knees before her, hands hovering, wanting to touch, but not daring. Extra careful because he saw through her pretenses and facades. Lucas saw what she worked so hard to hide from everyone else. He saw all her broken pieces.

She gasped, having forgotten to breathe, and her throat burned anew.

Derek appeared, barely a heartbeat behind Lucas, kicking open stalls and rising on tiptoes to peer through the undamaged glass block window high on the wall. "What happened?"

Her stalker had choked her. He'd watched her struggle in the mirror until spots had danced in her vision, and her frantic hands had fallen away from his arms. Then he'd changed his hold, offering her air while she was too fatigued and dizzy to fight. And as she'd gulped for breath, he'd applied pressure to her neck in a new way, winding an arm under her chin in a choke hold. He'd pressed the veins that carried blood away from her brain until her world had gone black. And she'd thought for sure he'd finally done it. After all she'd done to survive, he'd finally finished what he started and killed her.

Lucas leaned closer, palms up and expression flat. "Hey," he urged, fighting her thoughts back to the moment. "Can you hear me?"

She nodded, wiping hot tears from her cheeks. Tears would do no good now.

"Can I help you up? Are you able to stand?" he asked, keen eyes evaluating.

She wasn't sure, but she loosened her grip on her knees, willing to try. Anything to get out of that bathroom.

"Did you get a look at this guy?" Derek asked. "Did he say anything?"

Gwen clutched on to Lucas, forcing her trembling body to cooperate. A sob tore from her chest at the memory, ripping up her aching throat. "He said, go home. Go. Home. Go. Home," she whispered just as her attacker had while she'd slowly lost consciousness.

Lucas wrapped an arm around her back and held her tight as she worked to get her feet under her. "I'm so sorry," he whispered back.

Derek held the door for them as they shuffled away from the restroom.

Several sets of curious eyes watched as they emerged. She could only imagine what she looked like, and she didn't want to know. Blaze Winchester's narrow-eyed stare was among the onlookers. "Gwen?"

The three brothers exchanged a look, trading silent information in the curious way they always had, then they parted ways. Lucas hauled Gwen slowly toward the parking lot. Derek stayed behind, explaining the situation to Blaze.

The air was brisk outside, and she shivered in response. The sun had set on another awful day, spreading shades of twilight across the land. "Where are we going?" she asked. Her addled mind worked to make sense of leaving the station. "I need to make a report."

"You need medical attention." Lucas guided her to his truck, then helped her inside. "You can make a statement when we know you're okay," he said, eyes compassionate and jaw locked. "We're going to the hospital to get you checked out. Blaze will take over inside. He'll get the team to comb the ladies' room for anything left behind we can use to identify who did this to you. Lanie is probably already reviewing the video feeds. They've got that, and I've got you."

Lucas closed her door and rounded the hood to the driver's side. He started the engine and waited while she buckled up.

Every movement felt slow and complicated, like moving through molasses. Almost surreal. She blinked wet eyes as she trailed her fingertips along the tender skin of her neck. "He could have killed me," she whispered. "I thought he did. Why didn't he?"

Lucas shifted the truck into gear and motored away from the station. He stole a glance at her before pulling onto the road. "Have you ever seen a cat with a mouse? Everything they put them through? They lose interest once the mouse stops running."

Her throat tightened, and another tear fell unbidden as she heard her attacker's voice in her ear. *Go. Home. Go. Home.* He couldn't take her away, through a lobby filled with officers, and he couldn't stalk her properly with Lucas always at her side. So, he'd wanted her to go home.

She wouldn't be any fun to him if she was dead.

GWEN WOKE AGAIN late that night. With the hospital behind her once more, she'd fallen fast asleep in Lucas's bed. Fatigue had dragged her quickly under, and she'd slept soundly until the clattering of cups and plates had nudged her awake. A round of low voices rose through the old cavernous home. Four voices. And she recognized them all. Lucas. Derek. Blaze and Isaac Winchester.

She climbed out of bed and tugged a hooded sweatshirt over the T-shirt and yoga pants she'd chosen for pajamas, then headed downstairs.

The tangy scent of pizza sauce mixed with salty aromas of pepperoni and cheese in the air. Black coffee underscored it all.

The voices quieted as she padded across the foyer in socked feet, down the hall to the kitchen. The men turned her way as she took the final step into view.

Lucas was out of his chair in the next breath, meeting her where she was and ushering her to his empty seat at the table. "Here." He offered her a bottle of water from the collection of food and drinks on the table. Soda bottles, paper plates and napkins sat with pizza boxes and chips. "Coffee's on if you'd rather have that. Are you hungry?"

"Water's fine." She gave the food before her a regretful look, then frowned. She was hungry, but couldn't imagine attempting to swallow anything from the selection on the table. Not with her throat as badgered as it had been.

"I made soup," he said. "It's in the fridge. I can heat it when you're ready."

"Okay," she said. "Thank you." Her stomach gurgled at the promise of sustenance, and Lucas smiled.

"Give me two minutes."

The remaining Winchesters stared at her from their places around the table. Isaac with his evaluating eyes. Derek with his clenched fists. And Blaze with curiosity and regret, likely calculating how this had happened and what the next step would be.

She lifted a palm to them in a half-hearted wave.

"Hey," they mumbled back, each sounding a little guilty for something that was nowhere near their fault.

"Welcome back," Blaze said wryly. "Wondering why you ever left?"

Her lips tugged into a tiny smile. "Every minute. So, what were you all talking about before I interrupted?"

"You," he answered softly, honestly.

She'd expected as much. "Did the crime scene team find anything useful at the scene on campus or in the bathroom at the police station?" she asked. "Did you get him on camera entering or leaving the building?"

"Nothing from campus," Blaze said. "There are just too many people over there to isolate tracks or trace evidence for one individual. Bathroom was clean, too. Surveillance cameras cover all entrances and exits at the station, so we definitely got him. Problem is we don't know who we're looking for, and there were a lot of people coming and going while Tommy Black was causing trouble."

"No one noticed a man coming out of the ladies room?" she asked, heart falling with the question. Obviously not, or they would have told her already. "So, he got away again."

Derek drummed his thumbs along the table's edge. "Not completely and not forever. We have signatures from every visitor who signed in and out today. Once we compare the names to the faces caught on film, we can pare them down. Of those, one is likely linked to your past somehow."

"Okay," she said, breaking the word into halves. "So, he's definitely on video, but unlikely to have signed in. Maybe I can check the videos for familiar faces. Odds are I know him, right? We probably met before he started to follow me?"

Blaze and Derek exchanged a look.

"What?" Gwen pressed. "Tell me."

Blaze shifted, pulling her attention from Derek. "One of the officers wrestling with Tommy Black blocked the lobby camera that has a view of the restrooms in its scope. We can see someone leave, but can't see his face. We can guess his height, but little else. He seemed to be wearing a black coat, but nothing that stood out. Then, the crowd shifts and he goes out of frame. He becomes visible again outside, but he leaves with a group being asked to wait there while officers move Tommy Black and Banister's guy out of the lobby and over to processing. Our guy doesn't wait with the rest. He keeps walking until he's out of view again."

"So, he's familiar with your setup?" she guessed. An icy chill rolled through her core. "A cop?"

"No," Blaze and Derek answered together.

Isaac's kind eyes crinkled at the corners, clearly amused. "Lots of people visit the station. Cleaning crews, delivery people, maintenance, lawyers, visitors of detainees, criminals." He let the last word stick.

"Of course," she agreed sheepishly.

Lucas returned to her with a steaming bowl and settled it before her on the table. A spoon and napkin at its side.

The warm, buttery scents excited her stomach, which she realized had been empty for hours. "Thank you."

He dragged a stool into the space beside her and sat, watching as she managed the first hot spoonful. "We've been working with our profilers on this guy," he said. "Don't give up hope just yet. Even if we can't get a look at his face, we can generate a mold based on his behaviors this week that will help narrow the suspect pool."

Gwen had given her statement at the hospital, but it hadn't been much. Her attacker was tall. Same black balaclava as always. Same angry eyes and violent hands.

"We assume he's an outdoorsman," Lucas began. "He was comfortable spending hours on the ground among the trees at the hike-and-bike trail, watching for you. He owns a high-caliber ghillie suit and knew how to use it to his full advantage in the woods. Your original attack was outdoors, also. Some criminals would have followed you home that night, where there were walls to shield sound and view. He didn't do that. Maybe because he knew you spent most nights with me. Maybe because he prefers to be outside."

Blaze pointed to Lucas in agreement, but clearly with something to add. "This guy was patient in his stalking. Painfully so. Unrushed for at least two years before the first attack. And we know he kept watch for six years afterward. He has a job with a flexible schedule, and given the number of photos taken in public spaces, he moves through society unnoticed."

Gwen struggled to keep up, but her mind had hooked on the word *outdoorsman*. It was a polite way to summarize him, but her stalker was much more than that. Lucas just hadn't wanted to say the more accurate and on-the-nose word in his mind.

Hunter.

She thought back to the analogy he'd made in the truck

about the cat and its mouse. Her stalker was a hunter, and she was being hunted.

Lucas looked pained as he watched her processing the profile. "We think his patience only lasts as long as he feels in control. You never knew he was there until he wanted you to know. So, we can assume something changed to make him want to scare you this time. Something made him feel as if he was losing control of his fantasy. Based on timing, we can guess that our engagement was the catalyst before."

Gwen considered the notion of letting the punishment fit the crime. "You think his reaction was extreme because marrying you would have been permanent."

"Possibly," Lucas said. "He was younger. Newer at this. Age and maturity could have been a factor in him losing control, or there could have been another factor in his life that had him already on the edge."

His brothers grunted their agreement.

"Unfortunately, there's no real profile for rapists," Lucas went on, speaking gently, but factually. "These are all just guesses, but it would explain the extreme violence and timing of the first attack. Presumably his attempt to assert control and ownership over the object of his obsession. You."

Gwen abandoned the spoon in her soup. Her arms wound protectively around her center. "Ownership?"

Lucas nodded, emotion thick in his cool blue eyes. "The profilers at the precinct will have a more complete profile soon, but they say someone who's devoted so many years of his life to watching you probably believes he's part of yours. He's invested."

"He thinks he's part of my life," she echoed. "He's what? Delusional? Had a psychotic break?"

Lucas offered the saddest of smiles. "Extreme stalkers are often delusional in that regard. He probably imagines himself at the restaurant tables with you and your friends. Jogging beside you in the mornings. Curled on the couch with you at night. And in those moments, he's happy. And so are you. Together."

She pressed her lips tight, unable to stop the shudder rocking through her. "And when I accepted your proposal, I rejected him. A husband would have ruined his fantasy."

Blaze dipped his chin. "That's the working theory."

"Okay." She took a breath to center herself. "So, what upset him this time?"

"You tell us," Blaze said. "The infringements started small and in your town. Small punishments for a small infraction, likely. You came back to West Liberty, and the behaviors escalated."

Gwen's eyes fell slowly shut. "I came back to Lucas. The man I'd planned to marry." She peeled her eyes open with a groan. "But what did I do to deserve the small punishments back home? I haven't done anything unusual. I jog. Go to work. Go home. Same old. Everyday. Sometimes I get drinks or dinner with the ladies from the office, but not often, and I've been doing that for years."

The men didn't look convinced.

Derek kicked back in his chair. "Something changed."

"If not with you, then with him," Blaze agreed.

Gwen looked to Lucas. "Nothing. I swear."

Lucas heaved a sigh and raked his fingers through his hair. "We'll figure it out."

Gwen returned to her soup, running mentally over the past few weeks. Reviewing the days before the flyer arrived on her windshield. Had something changed?

She set the spoon down again. "Collin."

Lucas tensed beside her. Whatever he'd been saying to his brother was cut off at the sound of her voice. "Who?"

She covered her mouth, unsure how she hadn't thought

of him before, while wondering if she was completely off base. "There's a man at work," she began. "He's an architect at the firm. He walks me to my car at night." She grimaced, recalling the big deal her coworkers made of it. "He's asked me out a couple of times, as friends. For a drink or dinner after work, but I don't go," she assured him. She'd considered accepting his offer more than once, but she couldn't. Collin was a good guy, and he deserved a normal, uncomplicated person in his life. Gwen had stopped being normal the moment a psychopath had decided to hunt her.

Did her stalker know Collin? How else could he know about the flirting and invitations?

And then she remembered.

"I had dinner with him." Her eyes widened at the recollection. "We went for drinks as a group, but everyone else left before ordering any food. He and I had nowhere to be and were talking about ideas for a new client, so we stayed."

"How long ago was that?" Lucas asked.

"A few weeks." Right before she'd started feeling watched.

That accidental dinner had set her nightmare back in motion.

Chapter Fifteen

Lucas cleared the breakfast dishes, tired from a long night of rehashing ugly details with Gwen and his brothers. He'd barely slept afterward, and when he had, he'd woken to images of Gwen being choked out. In his dreams, she didn't wake up. And every time, he'd found his way to her bedroom to be sure she was still okay. He'd made the trip so many times before dawn, he'd considered sleeping in the hallway outside her door. Ultimately, he'd stuck it out in the guest room across the hall, door open and hypertuned to her every deep breath and rustle of blankets.

Now, on his fourth cup of coffee and her second mug of tea, they'd passed the morning in companionable silence, more lost in thoughts than conversation.

"Any luck?" he asked, moving to sit with her on his couch in the study. He should've known he'd find her curled up among the books. It was his favorite room in the house. He'd practically lived out of it while he'd renovated the rest of the home, undoing all the awful and occasionally unsound updates that had been made over the years. Thankfully no one had dared touch the study. It was architectural perfection without need of anything more. Grand built-in bookcases soared floor-to-ceiling on his left and right, flanking an expansive set of windows in the exterior wall. It was impossible not to marvel at the extensive detail and craftsmanship of everything in sight. He'd even salvaged the historic stained glass pendant chandelier hanging high above.

She shifted when she saw him, tucking her slender legs beneath her and setting her phone aside. "Not yet." Her bruised head was losing its knot, but the sickly shades of green and yellow made the healing mark look even worse. The dark marks on her neck were another story. "Collin hasn't responded to my texts from last night, and he didn't answer when I tried him again a few minutes ago. I'm starting to worry." She lifted the teapot from a tray on the coffee table before her and refilled her cup. "What if something's happened to him because of me?"

"Let's not worry until there's a reason to worry," Lucas said. "Remember. We're running on theories. Trying to troubleshoot and get ahead of this mess somehow." Not an easy task when they didn't know anything about the stalker's life or personality beyond his obsession with Gwen. Lucas took a long swig of coffee, then set the mug aside. "I have an idea." He turned his phone over and brought up the number to the design firm where Gwen and Collin worked, then dialed. "Maybe I can catch him at the office."

Gwen frowned. "I hate to bother him at work. Especially if we're wrong." She sighed, raising her teacup higher and inhaling deeply. "Honestly, I hate to tell him anything about this at all." She tucked wild red curls behind her ear a moment before they sprang free. She repeated the effort immediately, earning the same result. "He'll likely freak out and ask my coworkers if they know anything about my past or my absence beyond what you told my boss after the copier incident. No one knows anything, so they'll all go to the internet, if they haven't already, and just like that." She paused to snap her fingers. "All my carefully laid plans to keep the past and present from mixing are ruined."

Lucas shook his head. "I hate to break it to you, but your past and present have been mixing for years. You just didn't know it until recently. You haven't done anything wrong, so whoever finds out about what you've been through will just have to deal with it and get over it. However complicated that might feel to them, it doesn't hold a candle to what you've been through. What you're going through," he corrected.

The call finally connected, and a woman answered.

"This is Detective Winchester, West Liberty PD," he explained. "I'd like to speak with Collin..." He looked to Gwen, realizing too late that he didn't know her friend's last name.

"Weinstein," she said, filling in the missing name.

"Collin Weinstein," Lucas repeated.

The receptionist put him on hold, and he smiled at Gwen. "She's putting me through."

Ten minutes later, Lucas hung up, having provided Collin with an incredibly loose rundown on the situation. He'd left out the details of what happened to Gwen six years ago, because she was right, that was personal and irrelevant to Collin or anyone else. Instead, Lucas had concentrated on the possibility Collin's dinner with Gwen had provoked her stalker and launched him into action. Gwen had been targeted repeatedly this week, and Collin could possibly be next.

Gwen breathed easier when Lucas disconnected the call. "What did he say?" she asked, having hung visibly on every word from Lucas's mouth. "He's okay? Not hurt or abducted. So, why didn't he answer my calls?"

Lucas fought the pinch of rejection and jealousy her concern for Collin created. Gwen had only returned to Lucas's life out of necessity, he reminded himself. They weren't in love anymore, and it would do him good to remember that.

"He said it was late when you messaged him last night, and he's been busy at work this morning, but he planned to return your call during his lunch break." Lucas traded his phone for the cooling coffee and sipped to hide a frown. "He also said he dropped by your house to check on you after word got out about the copier incident. You weren't home. Does he stop by your place often?" Lucas asked, hoping she couldn't hear the intense curiosity in his words.

"No. Never. I didn't even know he knew where I lived," she said. "I guess he asked Marina." She touched a fingertip to her bruised forehead and frowned. "I hate being seen as a victim." Her wide brown eyes narrowed. "I know that's silly and petty in the face of everything else, but I really hate it." She sighed. "I'm trying to remind myself that everything is a matter of perspective. I'm still alive. That's good. And my attacker has gone from bold to flat-out reckless, which is strangely good, as well. He'll be caught for sure if he keeps that up. Right?"

The hope in her eyes nearly stole his breath. He couldn't keep letting her down. "Yes. And you did the right thing by making sure Collin had the facts he needed to stay safe. Even if nothing comes of it, it was good to let him know there was a possibility of danger out there. Now he can be more vigilant and let us know if anything strikes him as odd." Better to tell him the truth and nothing happen, than to tell him nothing and he's ambushed. "You'd never forgive yourself if he was hurt and you hadn't told him to be careful. You've got a big heart. This is just one more way it shows."

She sat straighter at the compliment, and an odd expression washed over her face. "I helped on a school hotline freshman year," she said. "I completely forgot. It didn't last, so it wasn't part of a lasting routine or anything, but for a few weeks, I tried helping strangers that way." Her gaze went distant with the memory. "The callers struggled with loneliness, homesickness and feelings of isolation. I thought I could help because I was going through something similar, so I signed up."

"Did any of the male callers you spoke with seem attached? Did you have repeat callers? Anyone who asked for you by name, perhaps?" Lucas asked, inspecting her beautiful face as it crumpled in thought.

"I don't think so, and we didn't exchange names. That was against the rules." She marveled a moment, lost in thought. "It feels like a lifetime ago. So much has happened since."

"I don't even remember a hotline," Lucas said. "Was it advertised campus-wide?"

"No. It wasn't a Bellemont-sponsored project, but there were flyers on the community boards in the student center, library and common areas."

"Did you take the calls at the counseling center?"

"No, in the psychology department. The hotline was a short-lived research project for a grad student's thesis on loneliness in highly populated spaces and small communities like college campuses. The lines were set up for temporary research, though some of the volunteers thought the school might implement the number permanently if there was a large enough response. There wasn't. The whole thing was done and over before the semester's end." She finished her tea, then set the cup aside once more. "I suppose it's possible that someone I helped on a call became attached. Being lonely is rough. It can play with your self-esteem, your emotions and your mind. Even one friendly person can make all the difference."

Lucas rubbed eager hands against the denim on his thighs. There was something to this worth looking into, but they needed a string to pull. "Was there a staff mem-

ber overseeing the project?" The grad student was likely
long gone by now, but maybe the teacher assigned to the
project was still around. "If we're lucky the teacher might
remember something worth knowing."

"I loved the teacher. She taught social psychology, I
think. She was the nicest woman. She might've even been
head of the department at the time," Gwen said.

Lucas brought up a search engine on his cell phone and
found the Bellemont staff directory. He scrolled to the list
of names in the psychology department, then handed the
phone to Gwen. "Any of those look familiar?"

"Bloomsbury," Gwen said, tapping the screen with her
fingertip. An image of an older woman in a black suit jacket
and white blouse smiled back. "That's her. She had longer
hair then, and it was darker, but that's her."

Lucas took the phone with a grin. "I'll give her a call."

He dialed, waited, then left a voice mail. "I'll follow up
with an email," he said, thinking out loud as he went. "And
I'll let her know we're coming in to see her during her office hours." He dared a look in Gwen's direction when he
finished. He probably should've asked her if she felt up to
another trip to the college before volunteering her appearance, but she always had the option of saying no. Or
changing her mind at any time. "Feel up to another trip to
Bellemont?" he asked, hoping she would agree.

Gwen had the relationship with this professor, not him,
and being back in the building might help Gwen recall
more details about her time on the hotline and the people
she spoke with while she was there. Not to mention the
fact that he refused to leave her alone anywhere again. So,
if he was going, she was going, and there wasn't a better
team for the job.

"Absolutely," she said. "I wouldn't miss it." She pushed
slowly to her feet, a small grimace tugging her lips. "I'm

going to get showered and dressed. I'll reheat the kettle for tea when I get back and maybe take a couple more aspirins."

"How about you just take your time and enjoy your shower," Lucas suggested. "The tea will be ready when you are."

Gwen smiled. "Thank you." She tipped carefully at the hips and pressed a light kiss to his head, then she was gone.

Lucas moved to the doorway, longing to call to her. To ask her what the kiss was for, and if she'd like to do it again. But he knew the kiss had cost her. After what she'd been through, every physical touch had a price. Lucas worked with rape survivors every day, and he knew how hard the simple gesture had been. He also knew it had taken serious thought and much motivation for her to do it.

He smiled as he crossed the room to his desk and powered up his laptop. He searched for information on the hotline project, hoping the grad student had published a paper on the topic. If he or she had, it wasn't available online. Lucas was sure, however, that if the published paper existed, it would be available in the Bellemont library. A special second-floor section of the library was dedicated to papers, studies and books published by faculty, alumni and staff. Until then, he'd have to wait and wonder.

He scrubbed a palm against his stubble-covered cheeks. He needed a list of people who'd used the hotline number while Gwen had been working there. A line like this would likely have been confidential, but it was also a research project, so there was a chance that some amount of information had been collected for the purpose of documentation. It'd take a warrant to get the details legally, if the teacher wasn't sharing, but that wouldn't be a problem. Finding information on a defunct temporary research project from six years ago was the problem.

Lucas pushed back in his chair, frustration growing.

When he thought of all that this lunatic had taken away from Gwen. From him. From the future they'd been planning. Every bit of rage he'd experienced over the years pressed hard against his nerves, willing him to act. He'd love nothing more than to lash out at Gwen's attacker, to let him feel what it was like to be overpowered and afraid, beaten unconscious by a practical stranger. Unfortunately for Lucas's rage and fortunately for her attacker, Lucas wasn't that guy.

He dropped the darker thoughts he'd entertained many times before, and pushed onto his feet instead. He was a good cop, a tenacious detective and an honorable man. Integrity was important to him, and it was what separated Lucas from the men he handcuffed. Gwen deserved more than another angry man in her life. She needed a protector, a partner and a friend.

Lucas was exactly that guy.

Chapter Sixteen

Gwen climbed down from the cab of Lucas's pickup, back on campus and determined to follow this new potential lead as far as possible. She'd do whatever it took to find the man who'd watched her gasp for air while he choked her. His eyes had been more cold than angry this time. His movements more intentional and calculated. Had he made her believe he'd kill her for the sick thrill of it? Had he enjoyed watching her fight frantically, helplessly, then lose, falling limp in his arms, defeated? Or maybe it was all just to prove a point. He was great and mighty and worthy of being feared. While she was a lamb waiting for slaughter. Whatever his motivation and ultimate goal had been, she was willing to bet he hadn't accounted for something else.

Like the fact that she'd reached her tipping point.

He'd taken his attempts to keep her afraid too far. He'd made her believe he'd killed her. And really, what was left to fear beyond death? That he'd really kill her next time? Well, it had felt pretty real this time. She'd already been through the scariest parts, and she was done being afraid of him.

Somewhere between the police station bathroom and Lucas's house, she'd become unnaturally numb. And it had started to seem as if the things happening around her weren't actually happening to her. A protective response from her psyche, no doubt, to keep her from losing her mind, but that was fine by her. The change made her feel brave again.

"You sure you're up to this?" Lucas asked, closing the passenger door for her and pressing the button on his key to lock up. "If you change your mind, we can leave anytime you want."

"I'm okay," she said, smiling for good measure. *Okay* wasn't exactly the right word, but she was ready.

Lucas moved in close, looking pained and unsure. His intensity had reached an all-time high, and it was fighting against her newfound calm.

The muscles in his jaw ticked, and lines raced across his handsome brow as he stared into her eyes. Debating. Scrutinizing. "I have a request," he said finally. "I'm not sure you're going to like it, but I want you to consider. If you say no, I won't ask again," he added.

Her core tensed and her fingers curled into fists inside her warm coat pockets.

Something had Lucas on edge, and he was rarely anything except calm.

She shifted from foot to foot as she waited for him to ask his question. Whatever he wanted, she could handle it. She was strong. And she trusted Lucas. So, how bad could the request be? Did he want to use her as stalker bait? To lure the lunatic out? Would Lucas suggest she let her attacker get his hands on her again so the police could make their arrest? Her stomach lurched at the thought of his touch. "Go on," she said finally, urging Lucas to spit it out.

A gust of sudden wind whipped past, spinning throngs of fallen leaves into a series of little tornadoes along the sidewalk. Lucas's overgrown hair lashed across his forehead, making him look wild and surprisingly youthful. "I think we should hold hands," he said. "As often as possible, while we're on campus or anywhere outside my truck or home."

Gwen barked a laugh, overcome with relief. "You want to hold hands?"

"Yeah," he nodded, looking baffled by her response. "I know it might be uncomfortable for you, but it will help me keep you within reach."

"It'll make you feel better?" she asked, her smile growing. "You've been trying to ask me if you can hold my hand?"

He shrugged, finally joining her in the smile.

Gwen pulled her hands from her pockets and offered them both to him. She'd lost her gloves since her last trip to campus, and was glad on a number of levels for the warmth of his touch.

"I only need one," he said, deliberating before making a choice. "Okay. This one." He made a show of interlocking their fingers before moving forward.

Gwen bit into her lower lip as the familiar jolt of electricity coursed through her at his touch. Then she kept pace thinking of nothing else.

They moved swiftly to the Garber building where the bulk of psychology classes were held, and the lab where the short-lived hotline had once existed. Campus was less crowded today, probably thanks to a heavy morning rain. The skies had cleared substantially, but Gwen suspected the showers had changed more than a few folks' overall plans for the day.

Lucas held the door at Garber Hall, and she hurried inside, pulling him along behind her.

They navigated the first floor to a set of closed office doors. Dr. Bloomsbury's door was the last on Gwen's left and standing open when they arrived.

"Come in," Dr. Bloomsbury said, spotting them immediately and stretching onto her feet behind her desk. She seemed to have aged by more than just six years. Her long salt-and-pepper hair was all white now and worn in a short bob around her cheeks instead of waves over her shoulders. She was thinner, too, and appeared more exhausted than Gwen recalled. Still, she had a ready smile as she pulled the tortoiseshell glasses from her nose. She let them fall against her chest, suspended by a delicate golden chain. Her gaze darted to their joined hands, then back to their faces. "Detective Winchester. Ms. Kind. It's lovely to see you both. Please take a seat." She waved a hand at the set of open chairs opposite her, then lowered onto her chair, as well.

Lucas released Gwen's hand and leaned forward in his seat, fixing Dr. Bloomsbury with his trademark cop stare. "Thank you for agreeing to see us. We have a few questions about the hotline project that took place approximately eight years ago. Do you recall it?"

Dr. Bloomsbury's gaze shifted curiously to Gwen. "Yes. It's where I met Ms. Kind."

"Gwen," Gwen interrupted with a cordial smile.

"Gwen," the older woman agreed. She turned her attention back to Lucas, then matched his no-nonsense expression with one of her own. "What's this about specifically? Your messages were brief and extremely vague."

Gwen cleared her throat and squared her shoulders. Then, she told her story.

Dr. Bloomsbury made appropriate expressions as the tale unfolded. She offered Gwen a box of tissues when she'd finished.

"I'm okay," Gwen assured her, "or I will be." She added a rundown of the last few days' events and how she suspected the hotline might've been where it all began, then waited for Dr. Bloomsbury's response.

The older woman sat back in her chair. "I see."

Lucas nodded approvingly at Gwen, and her insides fluttered.

Dr. Bloomsbury folded her hands on the desk between them. "Thank you for sharing your story with me. I'm sure it must be hard to go over it in detail like that. And given your timeline and experiences, I certainly understand why you'd come to me about this. But I don't have any information on the callers from the helpline. Those calls were all made anonymously."

"Maybe there's something else you can tell us then," Lucas suggested. "Anything will be more than we have to work with right now."

She raised and dropped her shoulders. "I don't even have details on the workers, thanks to the unexpected death of my laptop and a missing external memory device. I'd point you to Lewis, the grad student in charge back then, but he's out of town right now. Chicago, I believe. Designing social experiments with grant money earned from his continued work here at Bellemont. A very talented young man."

Gwen felt her knee begin to bob. "The student in charge of the hotline still works here?" she asked, wondering if maybe Lewis was the man who'd ruined her life.

"Several days a week," she said. "He's a teaching assistant, now pursuing his doctorate in psychology."

Gwen shot Lucas a look.

His chin dipped infinitesimally. "Did you say you have a missing thumb drive?" he asked, attention fixed on the woman in front of them.

"Yes, unfortunately. I lost a lot of work that week. I remember because I was writing my own research paper for publication at the time, and I lost both copies nearly simultaneously. When it rains it pours, I suppose."

Lucas patted the arms of his chair, expression thoughtful. "Maybe we aren't looking for a caller," he said. "Maybe we're looking for a volunteer, or Lewis."

Dr. Bloomsbury paled, but didn't speak.

Lucas turned to Gwen, an idea clearly taking shape in his mind. "What if her computer had help crashing, and the thumb drive had help disappearing, because a hotline volunteer, or its designer, knew his name and contact information would be on the drive, linking him to you?"

Gwen's bobbing knees froze briefly before taking off again, hard enough to shake her chair. "When were your things stolen?" she asked Dr. Bloomsbury.

"Not long after the hotline ended. Before the end of the same semester, if memory serves."

"Before my first attack." Gwen kneaded her hands on her lap, trying to recall the names and faces of men she'd worked with at the hotline.

Lucas straightened. "Can you make a list of all the male hotline volunteers? First name, last name, nicknames. Whatever you can recall. And we'll need Lewis's contact information, as well."

The professor's gaze narrowed in concentration. "I'll do my best to recall the male volunteers, but it's been a long while."

"We understand," he assured. "Anything you can remember will be a great help. We can always contact the men you remember and ask them for additional names if you forget any."

"I think that's a guarantee," she said, pulling a pen from a mug on her desk and beginning a list on a sticky note. "I haven't thought of that hotline in years, but there were only about two dozen helpers and most were women, so the list of men is short." She scribbled words on paper, looking away for a few seconds from time to time.

A few minutes later, she passed a note to Lucas, then

checked her watch. "These are the names I remember. I'm sorry it's not inclusive, and I hate to run off, but I have a class in a few minutes, and I need to set up my presentation before everyone arrives." She closed her laptop and loaded it into her bag while Gwen and Lucas rose from their chairs.

"Thank you for your time," Gwen said.

Lucas offered Dr. Bloomsbury his business card. "If you think of anything else, don't hesitate to call."

"Of course," she said, accepting the card, and trading him for one of her own. "Now you have mine, as well."

She turned to Gwen with an odd expression. "I hope you won't mind me saying this, but I'm proud of you."

"Me?" Gwen asked, wondering who the woman might actually be thinking of. Surely not Gwen, a college drop-out and virtual recluse being openly stalked.

"Yes, you," Dr. Bloomsbury said with a grin. "You are a strong and dedicated young woman. You've endured the unthinkable, yet here you stand, searching for justice. Not everyone can do that. Bounce back after a personal tragedy. Those sorts of experiences usually have a way of defining us, but it seems you've decided to define yourself."

Gwen smiled. "I have. Thank you."

Dr. Bloomsbury nodded and took a step before turning back. "If I remember correctly, you were great on that hotline. Maybe someday, when you're ready and this is behind you, you'll consider working with others who've been through tough things like you. Maybe you can help them define themselves, as well."

She checked her watch again, then hurried away.

Gwen turned toward the exit, cheeks warm with pride.

Lucas slipped his hand over hers and gave her fingers a gentle squeeze. "I'm proud of you, too, you know."

She smacked her lips, feeling lighter than she had in a while. "Don't try to copy."

He laughed.

At the end of the hall, Lucas held the door for Gwen to exit and an arriving professor to enter.

The man stopped short of the door and placed a hand on his hip beneath his dress coat. "Lucas Winchester?"

Lucas released the door, shaking the man's hand instead.

Gwen took the sticky note from his free hand and reviewed the names while the men talked.

"Someone told me you became a cop," the older man said. "I couldn't believe it. You loved architecture so much."

"Still do," Lucas said, and the conversation moved quickly between them while Gwen examined the list.

The paper felt infinitely heavier than it was, and terrifyingly fragile in the growing winds. The small, thin sheet of paper with its minimal strokes of ink could contain the name of the man who nearly killed her twice. Nearly abducted her once. And had followed her for eight years.

A low ache formed in her stomach and rose high into her chest. The familiar sensation of someone unseen climbed the back of her neck like witch fingers. She turned to search for signs of an onlooker. She scanned the faces of people nearby, on the paths and on the lawns. None of them were looking her way.

She returned her attention to the paper, pressing a cold palm to the back of her neck. Stopping the prickles. She read each name slowly, then tried to picture their faces. Had she even met them all?

Then another face came to mind, and she tried to match his image to one of the names on her page, but couldn't. None of these names were his, but something told her his name was important.

Chapter Seventeen

Gwen waited impatiently for the men to part ways, then explained to Lucas about the other male student she remembered from the hotline. "We only met a couple of times. He was there for training, and I worked with him once. Otherwise I only saw him around campus, and not often. I assumed he dropped out."

"Can you remember his name?"

"No, but he was tall with dark hair and glasses. Definitely the loner type. He said he joined the hotline to meet people, just like I did." She took a moment to consider that. "Is it strange that lonely students were the ones who responded to the ad to answer calls at a loneliness hotline?" Presumably the kids who weren't lonely had better things to do, but still.

Lucas snorted. "I'll bet Lewis the grad student had a great time analyzing that."

Gwen frowned. "I hope we weren't the experiment."

"The callers could have been other grad students," Lucas suggested, further exploring the notion.

"That'd be awful. And deceitful."

"It would be disconcerting," Lucas agreed, "but legal, depending on the wording of the contract participants signed. If you only agreed to take part in his project without specifics and qualifications, he could have done whatever he wanted within that context. It'd actually be better for us if the students answering calls were his subjects. At least then we'd have information on each of you."

That was true, Gwen supposed, but she couldn't help cringing over what she might've said on the questionnaire or during the interview. "Maybe we should contact Lewis in Chicago and ask him about it. He should have the name of the other guy I remember, too. If I describe him, it might jog his memory."

Lucas agreed, and they headed back inside. "I'll have my team run a background check on Lewis while we're at it."

She breathed easier. "Good."

After a full scan of the building, peeking in every door that wasn't locked, and finding a half dozen classes in session, but no signs of Dr. Bloomsbury, they admitted defeat.

Gwen's shoulders slumped as they moved back outside. "I guess when she said she had a class to get to, I assumed it would be inside Garber Hall. She could be presenting anywhere on campus. Or off campus for all we know."

"We'll call," Lucas said. "I'll leave a voice mail and send an email to follow up again. I live close enough to campus that we can get back here anytime she's available. Or honestly, if she can think of this guy's name, or wants to talk more about the hotline project, she can tell me by phone or email."

Gwen suppressed a sigh, disappointed to have to wait, yet again, before getting the information she wanted. She hated not knowing if something was a useful lead or just a random idea that went nowhere. "I could never be a detective. I have no patience, and everything feels so important. Not at all like things to be waited on."

"It's not for everyone," Lucas agreed. "Unlike food. Which is definitely for everyone. Hungry?"

She rolled her eyes. "Always."

"Good. Me, too." Lucas turned in the direction of the campus food court. "We never made it over to the student center last time we were here. Maybe we can do that now, and grab some lunch while we're there. Maybe a hot drink to keep us warm on the walk back to my truck."

"I like how you think, Detective Winchester." She smiled and offered him her hand.

He accepted.

They moved casually across campus, taking in the sights and sounds of homecoming week. Energy crackled in the air, despite the morning rain and reduced number of visitors. The Bellemont student body was unfazed. The school's spirit and pride were everywhere, from the banners and pendants to the occasional painted face and chest of a hooting male. Signs had been staked into the ground and erected at crossroads announcing the big game. Only two days away now.

Hopefully the nut terrorizing Gwen didn't have any grand attack planned to commemorate the fifth anniversary of their first violent encounter. The unexpected thought tightened every muscle in her body and caused her steps to stutter.

"You okay?" Lucas asked, noticing instantly.

"Fine." They could talk more about the gruesome possibility later. Her newfound bravery was waning, and she hoped some food and caffeine would give her the pick-me-up she needed.

Lucas traced lazy circles against her hand with his thumb as they moved deeper into campus and her timelines became more entangled. Her traitorous body responded immediately, confused and elated. He'd always done that. Made the circles. And they'd always excited her. She'd imagined the gentle caresses as tiny messages shared by only them. A secret code for *she was his*. And *he was hers*.

She gave herself a mental shake. That was another time, and these circles meant nothing. They were habit, or muscle memory, at best. Something he did with every woman whose hand he held at worst.

She dared a glance in his direction and found him looking her way. Her cheeks flared, certain he could read her mind.

"It's strange being on campus together again like this, huh?" he asked, lifting their joined hands slightly and smiling.

Yep. Reading her mind as suspected. "I promised myself I'd never come back here. Now, this is my second trip in three days. I never expected to see you again, and I'm sleeping in your bed." The heat in her cheeks spread to her neck and chest. "You know what I mean. Everything about this week has been unexpected and weird."

He turned away with a single nod.

"But it's nice," she said. "Being with you again. Not the other stuff."

"You don't like my bed," he asked, a teasing glimmer in his eye.

She smiled. "You know what I mean. Your bed is fine." *A little empty without you in it but…* The train of thought brought her mind to a full halt. Did she want him in bed with her? For what?

A parade of images began immediately. Lying with him, beneath the covers. His warm hand stroking hair from her face, his gentle lips pressing kisses to her cheeks, nose and eyelids, whispering sweet promises into her ear as he left a trail of caresses from her earlobe to her collarbone.

She sucked in a breath, feeling her body come alert with the fantasy. It'd been years since she'd considered anything so intimate. She'd avoided the thoughts, afraid they would bring memories of the attack with them. But they hadn't.

Now, on a campus she'd avoided, in broad daylight, a few tiny circles drawn on her hand had kick-started her sex drive? Okay, maybe those long-dormant feelings weren't exactly a revving engine, but Lucas had definitely turned the key. She knew the fantasies couldn't lead anywhere. Imagining a man's touch and receiving it were two very different things. Besides, she had scars. Inside and out. Too many for even someone as wonderful as Lucas Winchester to overlook. And he shouldn't have to.

He pulled the student center door open for her, then followed her inside. "You've gotten very quiet."

"Just thinking," she admitted with a smile, unsure how they'd crossed campus so quickly.

He gave her a curious look, but didn't press the issue.

She longed to hug him for what he was doing to her. For the first time in too long, she was beginning to feel alive. Maybe her fantasies would never be anything more, but they were still major progress in her overall healing, and she appreciated the breakthrough Lucas had brought her more than he would ever know.

They ate bad chow mein from the food court and watched students through nostalgic eyes. Had she and Lucas really been that carefree not so long ago? She'd asked herself the same question on a regular basis since starting over in New Plymouth. Everything about her life there had always felt surreal. She'd assumed it was a side effect from her trauma, that she simply hadn't engaged with her world in emotional ways. Looking back, however, she wondered if perhaps the carefully created facade had never really fooled her. And maybe somewhere deep down she'd known it couldn't last. That she'd have to face the ugliness eventually, if she wanted to truly be happy.

And she did.

Lucas ordered two coffees from the cart outside the student center, then passed her a cup. The temperatures were falling, and it was a long way back across campus. They skipped holding hands in favor of cradling their steamy cups against their palms as they moved.

He nudged her with his elbow a few minutes later. "You really think it's been nice being with me again?"

She smiled against the rim of her cup, pleased she wasn't the only one thinking about them as they strolled. "I do. I'm glad I came, and I'm glad you became a detective. I don't know who else I would've trusted with my fear, and I can see now it was important I got help. I suppose it all worked out kind of perfectly." She hoped the man stalking her could see that, and that he blamed himself. He'd kept her isolated and afraid for a long while, but in the end, he'd brought her full circle. Back to the man she'd started out with, on the campus where they'd fallen in love.

A car alarm sounded in the distance, and Gwen jumped. She pressed a palm to her chest and laughed. "Sorry."

"At least you saved your coffee," he said, eyeballing the cup in her raised hand. He smiled, but it didn't reach his eyes.

She scanned the world around them. No one paid the alarm any attention, and eventually it stopped. Hopefully, she hadn't said too much and inadvertently pushed Lucas away.

He set a hand against the small of her back as they walked, and she wasn't sure why. Did he miss touching her now that they'd stopped holding hands? Did he want to feel more connected to her? Or did he just want to keep her close, like he'd said when suggesting they hold hands?

She wouldn't know unless she asked, and she wasn't ready to do that.

They sidestepped a group listening to a speech on global

warming, then ducked carefully out of the way as crowd members attempted to snap photos of the speaker.

Lucas smiled over his shoulder as they passed. "You took more photos while we were dating than anyone I've ever known. Did you keep any of them?"

"A few." She turned away to hide her blush. She'd only kept a few if that parameter included hundreds.

His fingers bent and flexed against her back. "Me, too."

She dared a look at him. "You did?"

"All of them," he said. "I will find this guy," he added, changing the subject without warning. "The police forces in two towns are looking for him, watching and waiting for him to act out again. It's only a matter of time before he does, and he will be caught. That's a promise."

Gwen slowed, then stopped. She turned to him on the narrow cobblestone path between seas of green grass and bustling pedestrians. Then she took a step in his direction, and the noisy, windy, bonfire-scented world fell away. "I have never blamed you for what happened to me, Lucas Winchester. Not for a single second. Not then and not now. Do you hear me?"

He averted his eyes, casting his gaze over her head to scan the world around them.

"Hey." She poked a finger against his middle. "Look at me."

He glanced back at her before moving his gaze elsewhere.

She curled her fingers into the material of his jacket and hauled him closer, careful not to spill her coffee or his. "You need to believe what I'm saying to you. I don't blame you," she repeated, fiercely. "And you need to stop blaming yourself."

His eyes snapped back to hers, mournful and full of

regret. Emotion flickered over his face while he fought to maintain the careful blank expression.

"You said it wasn't my fault," she pushed. "Every time I woke up crying, convinced I was attacked because I knew better than to walk alone, even the short distance I was going, you told me it wasn't my fault. Now I'm telling you," she said, tugging again on his jacket. "It was never your fault, either."

LUCAS STARED INTO the most fierce and most loving eyes he'd ever known. "Okay," he answered softly, hoping he'd mean it one day. He couldn't imagine not blaming himself for what had happened to her and all she'd been through, but he could barely think of that now.

Right now, he was captivated. To say he'd missed her would be like saying he'd missed oxygen after being deprived of it for six years. Being with Gwen again was like unearthing the best parts of himself and realizing how much he'd truly missed them. He'd always known she'd taken a piece of him with her when she'd left, but he hadn't understood how much he'd needed them to feel whole. Standing with her now, in their tiny bubble made for two, her fingers curled into the material of his jacket, her warmth seeping into his long-dormant heart, he took his first real breath in years.

His free hand rose to carefully cup her narrow jaw.

Her eyes widened a moment, and he waited for her to step away or release him, but she leaned closer instead. The toes of their shoes already touching, she nuzzled her cheek against his palm.

Elation exploded inside him, and he ached to be closer still. He craved her kiss. To taste her sweetness, just once. He needed to know the heart-pummeling crush of emotion inside him wasn't one-sided. That some part of her had missed him, too. But he couldn't risk overstepping and accidentally pushing her away. Not now, when he still owed her the justice she deserved. He let his forehead fall to meet hers, wishing he knew how to help her heart find its way back to him.

His phone rang, breaking the spell and sending them each back a step.

Gwen looked bashfully away, setting her palm against her jaw, where his hand had been.

"Winchester," Lucas answered, hoping for good news.

"Hey, little brother," Derek said, his tone caught somewhere between mischief and regret.

Gwen slipped her hand into the crook of his arm, and they returned to walking. "What's up?"

"Oh, you know," he said. "Just swung by campus to check on you. Maybe give you a ride home."

Lucas frowned. "Give us a ride home?"

Gwen turned to look at him.

And the little lot where they'd left Lucas's truck came into view.

"Is that Derek?" Gwen asked, following Lucas's gaze into the distance.

Derek leaned against his Mustang, staring at a pile of broken glass, glinting on the pavement. Campus security guards held back a small crowd, and a uniformed officer snapped pictures of Lucas's truck.

"What happened?" he asked, towing Gwen forward, then breaking into a jog with her, as they neared the lot.

Derek greeted them, stuffing his phone back into his pocket and waving an open hand toward the mess, like a game show host.

Every one of Lucas's truck tires had been slashed. The side windows broken. And a brief but pointed message had been carved deep into the shiny black paint.

SHE IS MINE.

Chapter Eighteen

Lucas slid into the back seat of Derek's Mustang and moved to the center, hanging his arms over the edges of the seats in front of him.

Gwen took the passenger seat and shut the door. "Thanks for the ride, Derek."

He grinned, then cast a goofy look at Lucas. "I think your girl likes me."

"I've always liked you," she said, fastening her seat belt with a smile. She cast a regretful look through the window as they trundled past the tow truck hooking up his pickup for a trip to the body shop. "Sorry about your truck, Lucas."

Lucas grimaced. He was sorry about his truck, too, but more than that, he was infuriated to know he'd been followed again without knowing. Was he really so distracted with Gwen that he couldn't tell when he was being outright stalked? He was equally frustrated by the fact that there weren't any security cameras covering the small faculty lot where he'd parked, and that the son of a gun who'd ruined his paint job somehow believed that Gwen belonged to him. Like property. *Or a play thing*, he thought, recalling his own cat-and-mouse analogy. "Not your fault," he told Gwen, a little too late by the look on her face. "We know he's out there. It could be this beautiful Mustang next for all we know."

Derek frowned. "Watch it." He stroked her dashboard. "She'll hear you."

Gwen turned a bright smile on him. "You talk to your car?"

"Frequently," he answered. "I like to keep her happy, and you should, too. Since it sounds as if you're going to need a driver for a few days. Good thing I showed up when I did."

"Why did you show up?" Lucas asked, refusing to entertain the idea of Derek as his driver for a few days. "And how'd you know where we were?" Even if he'd heard somehow that they were on campus, it was a big place. How had he found the truck in a small faculty lot?

"I track your truck," Derek said, motoring into traffic outside the campus boundaries. "Your phone, too, but don't get cranky about it. I track everyone I love. You never know when someone might need help. Like now." He caught his eye in the rearview and smiled.

"You track my phone," Lucas repeated, misplaced anger boiling hotter in his chest. "What is wrong with you?"

"I care," Derek said. "I can't help it. I'm a caring guy."

Gwen laughed, and the sound drew both brothers' attention. She blushed in response. "I think what we want to know," she said to Derek, "is why you tracked us down. Did something happen? Do you have news?"

"Yes." Derek grinned. "I just got back from New Plymouth. I stopped by the design firm where you work and spoke with your coworkers."

"You questioned Gwen's coworkers?" Lucas asked, frustration mounting high and fast. "Should I even ask how you got them to talk to you? Because impersonating an officer is illegal. You know that, right?"

Derek made a get-serious face in the rearview mirror, then turned back to the road, splitting his attention between traffic and Gwen. "I told them the truth. I'm a friend of

Gwen's from years ago, and I wanted to ask a few questions. Everyone was extremely helpful."

"I'll bet," Gwen moaned. "I've never told them anything about my past. They know my folks live in Florida and I live in town. I don't date and like to jog. That's about all I was ever willing to share."

"That would explain the intensity of their interest," he said. "They loved that we were friends from way back. They're all big fans of yours. I think your boss wants you to marry me," he admitted. "She's got a good eye. I'm not a bad catch."

Gwen laughed again, and Lucas joined her. Derek wasn't a bad catch for a woman not looking to catch anyone. Derek was too busy pushing everyone's boundaries and looking for his next adrenaline rush to settle down, and Lucas couldn't imagine a point in the future when that might change.

"Go on," Lucas urged. "Out with it. I swear you are the worst storyteller."

Derek's lips curved down at the corners, unhappy about being called the worst at anything, no doubt. "I learned that Gwen's coworker, Marina, stopped by her place to check on her last night. She said it was a last-minute decision. She'd debated all day because everyone knows Gwen's a private person, but she wanted to let her know the office staff is thinking of her and wants to help if she needs anything at all."

"Derek," Lucas warned, already at the end of his patience. "What happened when she stopped by?"

"That's what I came to tell you," he said, lifting a pointer finger into the air. "She saw a man on the property who said he was upgrading your security system. She thought that was a smart move given your situation, but she didn't get a name for him or the company."

Lucas's pulse picked up. Gwen's coworker had seen the stalker. Spoken to him.

"I didn't order any upgrades," Gwen said. "I already have their most comprehensive system."

Derek took the next right onto the expressway. "That's why I came to get you." He stomped the pedal and launched every horse under the hood into action, catching up with traffic in seconds. "I thought we could all go check it out together."

GWEN UNLOCKED THE front door, then stopped the wailing alarm. It plucked at her nerves to silence the system before the door was closed and locked behind her, but two giant Winchesters were currently wedged in the doorway, looking for signs of a previous forced entry.

"No one broke in," she said, leading them to her office. "My security camera sends alerts when someone opens a door or window."

She powered up the desktop computer and accessed her account with the security company. "The cameras also record when anyone comes onto the property. We can watch the feeds from here and finally get a look at this guy. If I'm really lucky, he looks right at a camera, and I can get a good headshot for police and local media. When did Marina say she came by?"

Derek shared the details, and Gwen brought up the day and time in question. Then they waited to see Marina's car slide against the curb. "There she is."

Lucas shifted over her shoulder, moving in close enough to smell his cologne and feel his warmth. "Did she say the guy was already here when she arrived?" he asked Derek. "I don't see any other vehicles parked along the street or in the driveway."

Gwen gave the scene another look. Lucas was right.

There were vehicles parked in other homes' driveways, but none she didn't recognize, and definitely no commercial work vehicles. "He must come in a minute."

"Hopefully we can get a plate number when he arrives," Lucas said.

Derek hummed a little note of discord. "Actually, she said he was already here when she got here."

"Yeah, well no one's there," Lucas said.

Marina climbed out of her car, carrying a pair of shopping bags, presumably filled with wine and cake, then headed up the front walkway. She slowed before reaching the door, and looked to the left. "Hello?" she called. "Gwen? Is that you?"

Lucas pressed a palm to the desk, his body going rigid. "She hears something. Come on," he whispered. "Come around here and show yourself."

Marina turned back to the door and finished her approach. She rang the bell then knocked. Undeterred by the lack of an answer, she repeated the process. When that didn't work, she skirted around the shrubs at the front window and pressed her face to the glass, using a hand as a shield for a better view.

"Wow," Gwen groaned. "She's really dedicated to this excursion."

"She seemed like the determined sort," Derek said.

Marina stumbled out of the flower beds a moment later, catching her coat on the bushes. She yanked it free, then marched around the side of the house, chin held high. "Oh, hello," she said.

Gwen and the Winchesters stilled, silently willing the man into the frame with their minds.

Marina returned a moment later, got in her car and drove away.

Derek straightened with a huff. "That was underwhelming."

"Did you at least get a description from her?" Gwen asked, feeling let down, yet again, by something that had seemed so promising.

"Yeah," Derek said, dryly. "He was tall. She guessed him at my height, then said he was around six foot two or three."

Gwen blinked. "You're only six foot."

"Exactly."

Ridiculous. Gwen's hope deflated completely with that hit. When it came to Gwen's nonexistent love life, Marina remembered every minute detail, but when asked a simple, general question about a man's height, she had no idea what she was saying. "Figures."

Thinking of Marina and men in Gwen's life, something Derek said earlier came back to mind. "Did you happen to talk to an architect named Collin?"

He shook his head. "No. Just the handful of ladies in the front office and your boss."

Gwen chewed her lip, hoping Collin was still safe, and there wasn't a reason to worry.

Lucas shoved away from the desk. "We know this guy wasn't here to upgrade the security system, so let's figure out why he was here. We can start by making sure there aren't any signs of forced entry."

Derek moved toward the back of the house. "I'll check the patio doors."

Gwen went from window to window, checking locks while the men assessed the doors, then made a sweep of the perimeter. Everything was still locked up tight.

Unsure where to go next, Gwen made coffee while Lucas called Detective Anderson and brought her up to speed. Derek took a seat at the island and checked his email.

When Lucas made his way to the kitchen several minutes later, his expression was weary. "That woman hates me."

"Yeah," Gwen agreed, smiling over the rim of her mug.

Memories of the first time she'd met the female detective came to mind, bringing a new thought with them. She turned to Lucas. "Do you still have the email with the files from the copier?"

"Yes. Why?"

Gwen pursed her lips. "I'd like another look at those photos."

"What are you thinking?" Derek asked, setting his phone aside to watch her. "You've got that look. You used to look just like that before you took all my money in poker."

She laughed, surprised and pleased by the memory. "You let me win."

"Yeah, that's what happened."

"Here." Lucas handed her the phone. "What are you looking for?"

Gwen forwarded the email to herself, then hurried to her office. "Give me a minute."

The men followed her, impatient and eager.

She lowered into her teal, ergonomic chair, then accessed the file on her desktop computer. "I think we should look at all the photos taken at my place while we're here. Maybe we can use them to find his nest, just like we did at the hike-and-bike trail. Maybe comparing his two nests will give us a fresh lead."

"What kind of a nest?" Derek asked. "There's not too many places to hide around here."

"I don't know," she admitted. "Maybe a tree branch overlooking my yard or an empty home with a view into my bedroom." She could only hope the last suggestion wasn't a reality. "Lucas and I jogged the neighborhood a few days ago, but now that we have the photos, they can help us pinpoint where he stood to take the shots."

She brought up the images and began to sort them. It

took several minutes to work through all the photos, moving pictures of her home or property into a separate file.

Lucas hovered while she worked. Derek watched from a few feet away, arms crossed and leaning against a yellow credenza.

"This is it," she said. "Now let's see what we can learn." She flipped through the images slowly, looking for consistency and anything else that seemed relevant. "The angles are all odd," she said, clicking faster, and shocked she hadn't noticed the peculiarity before. The photos all seemed to have been taken from somewhere near her home's perimeter, not somewhere distant and looking in.

Derek cursed. His arms dropped loosely at his sides and he moved nearer, watching as she flipped through the images on her computer screen. "Is he somehow gaining access to your security cameras? Stealing freeze-frames from your feed?"

"I don't think so," Gwen said. "My only cameras are at the front and rear door." She flipped to the feeds from the cameras to show them what she meant. Though, once she looked, she wasn't sure that at least some of the pictures couldn't have been taken that way.

Lucas headed for the door, and Derek followed.

Gwen worked to steady her breaths. Apprehension weighed heavily on her heart, anchoring her temporarily in place. If her stalker had access to her security cameras, then she'd never really had any protection against him at all. She'd trusted her system. Believed in her cameras. Believed she'd been safe inside her home.

She forced herself upright, then willed her feet to move. Just like that first time back on campus. One foot in front of the other until she was outside.

Derek stood on a large rock near the garage and shined a pocket-size flashlight at the soffit. "The walkway, mailbox and street sign were all visible in a photo of you getting the mail," he explained upon her approach. He extended an arm in a diagonal, pointing across the yard, creating an invisible line that intersected those three things. "The photo had to be taken from here." He climbed down, dissatisfied, then trailed his hands along the downspout. "But anyone standing here would've been seen."

Lucas stood in the mulch outside her front window and beside the door, running his fingers over and behind the camera. Muttering to himself as he worked.

"Ha!" Derek cried, turning her back in his direction. "Got it."

"Got what?" she asked, hurrying to his side. "What is that?"

"Camera," he said, raising a small, white item on his palm.

Gwen stared, a shiver of dread and realization coursing through her.

Lucas whistled, turning her around once more. He, too, held something on his palm. "He's not using your cameras. He's planted his own."

The men traded a look, then jumped into action, pocketing the uncovered devices and pressing their hands to her house. They traced every inch of soffit, spouting and white vinyl trim they could find, searching for additional camouflaged cameras on the perimeter. In the end there were two more. Hidden in plain sight, but blended seamlessly into their surroundings. Just like their owner in his ghillie suit.

So, it was true. He'd been watching her from her own house. Probably conveniently receiving the feed through his cell phone like she did. Being alerted to her and anyone else coming or going. He'd known the moment she'd arrived home or left and with whom. He'd known when she received packages and what food she liked to have delivered. He knew everything. And the blow hit harder than any fist, because it shattered her last notion of safety.

Even in the one place she was sure no one could reach her without invitation. He'd been watching. And he was probably watching right now.

Chapter Nineteen

Gwen thanked Derek for his help and hugged him good-bye. Being in his brotherly embrace felt just as safe this time as it had before, and she smiled as she waved. Ironically, she'd seen more personal healing in the days since the new reign of terror had begun than she had in years. No thanks to her stalker, but big thanks to her willingness to step away from her self-imposed quarantine and back into the lives of people who knew and cared for her. She suspected her coworkers would accept her, too, violent past and all, if she gave them the opportunity. It was the kind of epiphany she wished she'd had years ago, but was thankful to have had at all.

She powered her garage door up and smiled at her little sedan. Not a big tough pickup truck, and not a fancy sports car, but the simple base-model four door had never let her down. Derek's chauffeuring services weren't needed after all.

She grinned as Lucas folded himself into the passenger seat. His long legs bent sharply between his torso and the dashboard. "You can move the seat back," she suggested.

He patted around and pulled a lever, and the seat rolled back two inches.

She laughed.

"What is this? An airplane seat?" He tried again and

managed a little more room, then adjusted the lumbar for comfort.

"You miss your truck already?" she guessed. "I'm sorry she was his latest casualty."

Lucas winced. "She's not a casualty. She just needs tires, a windshield and a paint job. That's like, new shoes and a makeover. She'll be just fine."

Gwen rolled her eyes at the analogy, then reversed out of her garage. She powered down the door. "I can't believe there was a camera right there and I never noticed it."

"I know," Lucas said. "Speaking of, I guess I'd better give Detective Anderson a call. We can drop these cameras off to her on our way out of town. If I had my truck I could've at least stored them in evidence bags."

"You don't think she'll like the freezer bags I had in the pantry?" Gwen teased. "They came with labels."

He shot her a flat expression as he worked the cell phone from his pocket, knees trapped against the dash. The phone rang in his hand. "That's weird," he said. "She's calling me."

"Perfect," Gwen said. "Maybe it's good news."

"It's never good news," he mumbled, then pressed the phone to his ear. "Winchester."

Gwen pulled onto her street then headed out of the neighborhood.

"I was just about to call you, Detective Anderson," he said. "We've got—" His words failed midsentence. "When?"

Gwen stopped at the next intersection and cast a curious look in Lucas's direction. Her heart pounded as the air thickened between them. Something else had happened. Something bad.

Lucas let his head drop forward, grunting occasionally as Gwen drove on.

Eventually, he disconnected the call and raised his head once more.

"What happened?" she asked. "Are we still going to the station, or should I go somewhere else?"

"We should probably head over to the county hospital," he said softly, pinching the bridge of his nose. "Anderson's there now. Collin Weinstein was attacked last night, and he hasn't woken up."

GWEN DRAGGED HERSELF into Lucas's house, after spending hours at the hospital waiting for Collin to open his eyes. He did, thankfully, but never for long, and because she wasn't family, she wasn't allowed to see him. According to Detective Anderson, and the details Gwen gleaned from the doctor providing updates to Collin's family, he was beaten in a way that mimicked her first run-in with the stalker, minus the rape. Detective Anderson suspected the similarities were meant to be a message to Gwen. Attacking Collin was direct retaliation for his perceived involvement with her, so the punishment had fit the crime.

She could only imagine what would happen to Lucas if the psychopath got ahold of him. She'd only had dinner with Collin. She'd been engaged to Lucas and was currently sleeping in his bed. Which she assumed her stalker knew, because he seemed to know everything.

It was after nine when Lucas pulled a bottle of wine from the refrigerator and looked at Gwen. "Do you still drink? And if not, do you mind if I do, because holy hell."

"Make mine a big pour," she said, sloughing off her coat and leaning heavily against the counter. "Wine has been one of my most cherished indulgences these last few years."

"Thank goodness." He poured two wineglasses nearly to the top, leaving only a small amount in the bottle. He tucked the bottle under his arm. "We'll take it with us so we don't have to come back. To the study?"

She turned without answering. She loved his study, and she was beginning to realize she still loved him. Wine would help her process that possibility, along with the three major disasters of the day. A vandalized truck. Discovery of surveillance cameras attached to her home. And poor Collin, who'd literally done nothing wrong, and his life was on the line anyway.

He hadn't spoken more than a few incoherent words before they left the hospital, but Gwen had faith for a full recovery. If she'd survived, Collin would, too, and she owed him everything when he did. His pain was on her. Like so many other things. Her silence about her past hadn't helped anyone.

Lucas flipped on the overhead light, then set the bottle on the coffee table. "When this place is done, I plan to have a wine cellar. I've even thought of planting grapes and erecting an arbor out back."

"I like that idea." She took a generous sip and sank onto the couch. "Wine is fascinating, delicious and it unwinds me. Something I need right now."

"Agreed," he said, taking the seat beside her. "I prefer mine with some food, but I haven't had much time to get to the grocery store lately. Feel like ordering in?"

Gwen tapped her glass to his. "Yes, and cheers."

Lucas took another sip of his wine before setting it aside and breathing deeply. "I'm really sorry about what happened to your friend." His expression turned tortured at the statement. "I was jealous of him when we spoke by phone, and now I feel like an enormous jerk."

"You were jealous?" she asked. "Why?" The notion didn't make any sense, and Lucas was always sensible.

More than that, he wasn't a jealous person. Two of her favorite things about him.

"He's an architect. Young. Successful. And he's in your life, a place you forced me out of." Lucas rubbed his palms together, clearly ashamed and heartbroken. "I wanted that life. Any life. With you."

Her heart gave a heavy thud at the possibility. Could she still have a life with him? "Lucas," she started, her mouth hanging open, then snapping shut, unsure what to say in response. What were the right words to express complete joy?

He groaned. "You know what? Let's put a pin in this and order that takeout." He grabbed his laptop and opened it on his legs. "How about something from O'Grady's? We can place the order online, then see if we can find the Bellemont social media pages with photos from your freshman year. If memory serves, the school newspaper keeps dedicated web pages with highlights from every year. Maybe you were caught in some of them."

"'Bellemont Bests,'" Gwen said. "I forgot about those. I don't think I've ever looked at them."

"Me neither, but they came to mind while we were waiting at the hospital." He opened the O'Grady's website. "What sounds good for a very late dinner?"

"Something simple," she said. "Salad and breadsticks?"

"How about salads and potato skins?"

"Perfect."

Lucas ordered two of O'Grady's grilled chicken salads and a family pack of loaded potato skins. "Now, we've got thirty minutes to kill. Let's see what's on the 'Bellemont Bests' pages from your first two years."

Gwen braced herself, unsure she wanted to travel back in time when the present was complicated enough, and wishing they'd finished the conversation about a possible future with Lucas. She sipped her wine and focused on the screen as images from her freshman year appeared. All candid, and a few with captions. According to the *About* section, students were encouraged to send in their photos throughout the year for inclusion. Photos were vetted for appropriateness and added to the collection until finals, then the year was wrapped and it was a few weeks before the next year opened for photos. Meaning there were hundreds of pictures to wade through and very possibly for nothing.

Lucas ran his cursor over a small navigation menu and dropped a list down. "We can search by event or department of study. Maybe the psychology department commemorates its grad students' projects." He scrolled quickly to the right selection and clicked. A group of familiar faces stared back at her.

"That's us," she said, astounded. She marveled at the youthfulness of the faces in the photo, then jolted into action. "We need the list Dr. Bloomsbury made." She dug in her pockets, searching for the small page she'd nearly forgotten. "Got it."

She moved through the list of names on the page, comparing them to the list of names on the screen below a photo of the hotline staff taken on training day. She didn't remember sitting for a group photo, yet there she was, smiling brightly at the camera, with no idea what was to come.

"That's the guy I remember talking to," she said, tapping the screen with her fingertip. He was exactly as she remembered. Tall, lanky, dark-rimmed glasses. Bushy hair. She dragged her finger to the names listed beneath. "Scott Tracey."

Lucas looked at the screen, then at the scrap of paper the professor had given them. "He's not on Bloomsbury's list," Lucas said. "I'll ask her about him tomorrow."

Gwen smiled. "Good." She inhaled deeply, then sipped her wine. "Hey." She held the list up to the screen. "There's a name on this list that's not included under the photo. What do you suppose that means?"

Lucas compared the two, then retrieved his wine for another sip. "Phillip Cranston." He frowned. "Where are you?" he asked the screen. He typed the name into the search engine under the year in question.

A photo of Phillip Cranston appeared in a group photo for the computer lab.

Gwen frowned. "He doesn't look familiar."

Lucas drew the laptop closer. "But he was part of the hotline and a volunteer in the computer lab, a place you frequented those years. I think it's worth digging into."

"Okay, and we still need to look more closely at Lewis, the grad student who organized this whole thing."

Lucas nodded, pulling his phone from his pocket.

She lifted her glass and smiled. "We make a good team."

"That we do."

She took a moment to enjoy the warmth spreading through her, courtesy of good wine and great company.

"I'll text my team and have someone run Lewis's, Scott's and Phillip's names. We should check their records, just in case." Lucas tapped the screen on his phone, getting the message out immediately.

Gwen sipped her wine and felt the knots of tension in her shoulders ease.

Lucas navigated to the "Bellemont Bests" page from her junior year. He stopped at a set of images from an impromptu party outside the auditorium where students had gathered after a concert. It was the night they'd met, and they were front and center for the photo. Smiling as if they already knew they'd soon be madly in love. "Look."

"I am," she said, marveling at the expressions on their faces. Complete happiness. "I remember that night." She'd thought of those moments repeatedly as she'd healed, physically, in the hospital. She loved Lucas so much, and she'd known it at first sight. "You made me feel so content," she said. "I'd felt sort of afloat until then. You anchored me. I shouldn't have taken it for granted."

Lucas curled his arm around her, bringing her closer on the small sofa and cuddling her against his side. "I will always be whatever you need," he vowed.

Gwen set her glass aside so that she could press a cheek to his chest and truly embrace him. She soaked in the peaceful vibes and let her heart accept how much she loved him. And the fact that she'd never really stopped.

Chapter Twenty

Lucas breathed deeply, inhaling the scent of her, and thanking his lucky stars that she was there. More than that, she was in his arms again and nothing had ever felt sweeter.

He tucked her tight against him with one arm, then set the laptop onto the coffee table with the other. Both hands free, Lucas cradled Gwen properly, protectively, and with both arms, the way he'd wanted to for so long. "I've missed you," he whispered, stroking her hair and holding tight to the moment.

"I've missed you, too," she said, her chest rising and falling with his.

"Should we watch a movie?" he suggested. "Something to take our minds off the night we've had? We can start fresh with new tragedies tomorrow."

She laughed, then groaned. "Definitely."

He forced his arms to release her so she could sit up, and he could choose a movie to stream. He decided on a small-town romance that she'd watched a hundred times while they were together. She'd jokingly called it her happy place when the stress of midterms or finals had grown too high.

He smiled as the movie began and recognition lit in her eyes.

She slid her arms back around him and squeezed, tucking her legs beneath her on the cushion and becoming a little ball of woman. "You remembered."

"Of course." He held her close as she nuzzled into him, and he let himself imagine that this could somehow last. That, maybe, ordering takeout and watching movies could be their new evening routine together.

She pushed away from him as the opening scene began, fixing a troubled expression on her pretty face. "I know this week has been an emotional train wreck, for me anyway," she added. Though she wasn't alone in that. "And I realize that all the bad things have served to enhance the good, but being here with you has felt a lot like being home. And that's a place I haven't been in a really long time."

She watched him with warmth and curiosity, taking in the surprise and pleasure on his face, no doubt. Then she set a palm on his chest, and let her gaze drop to his lips.

He covered her hand with his, and his heart beat against her palm.

Their gazes met, and desire seemed to break through her last remaining wall. She leaned closer, cautiously, then brushed her lips against his.

A fire lit in his core. The flames spread swiftly through him, urgent and needy. His hands ran up and down her back, savoring the feel of her as she took his mouth with hers. One kiss became two. Two became three. And with each fresh taste, Gwen's touch became less cautious and more fervent. More hungry.

She pulled back too soon, breathless and flushed.

Excitement danced across his skin at the sight of her like that. When she smiled, he let himself believe that she might stay when her monster was caught and her horror story was over.

He brushed the pad of his thumb across her lips, full and pink from his kisses. Already desperate to taste them again.

Gwen trailed her fingertips over his chest, then stroked her palm down the length of his arm, twining her fingers with his when they met. "I thought being near someone like this would be scary, so I've never let myself be close to anyone since you," she said. "Not after that night. And I told myself the reason was that I was broken by what happened to me. That I wouldn't be able to separate a man's intimate touch from memories of my attacker."

Lucas's heart broke. "Is that how you feel now?" he asked. "Are you...afraid?" He rubbed a hand across his mouth, hating himself for the possibility. Had he been adrift in pleasure while she'd been reliving her worst nightmare?

"No." Gwen shook her head and smiled. "Not at all." She pushed her fingers through his hair and traced the line of his jaw. "I can see now that I wasn't only avoiding other men because I was scared. Maybe at first," she conceded. "But I think the bigger reason is that I've only ever wanted you."

Lucas's lips parted in a smile. He nearly groaned in satisfaction. He'd never heard such perfect words. "Come here," he said, taking her hand and pulling her onto his lap. He stroked her crazy curls and stared at her perfect face, then brought his lips to hers once more.

Gwen took over easily, and he let her lead.

She sighed and moaned against his mouth as she shifted to straddle him, deepening their kisses and sending shock waves of desire through his body. Her warm, full breasts pressed against his chest. And her fingers ran over his shoulders, fisting in the hair at the back of his head.

He poured kisses over her neck and collarbone. She let her head fall back to grant him access.

Their lips met again, impassioned and easily parting. Tasting one another as their tongues moved sensually together.

He imagined rising to his feet with her, sweeping her

legs around his waist as he gripped her perfect backside and carried her upstairs. But upstairs was too far. And it was too soon for that.

Gwen shifted her position once more, spreading her thighs wider and aligning their bodies so perfectly he could feel the heat of her through their jeans.

He broke the kiss to swear, and she laughed.

"Yeah," she breathed. "Me, too. We can stop if you want."

Was she offering him an out? Was she insane? Lucas grinned and shook his head. "No, thank you."

Gwen was protecting him, by providing him the choice she'd once been denied.

He wrapped her in a hug and rested his head against her shoulder. "I will never not want you. And I'll never stop craving your touch. I'd keep you with me forever if I could." The words were out before he'd thought them through, and he felt her tense in response.

She sat back, and he raised his head to apologize for ruining the moment. He swore again when he saw her tears. "Gwen."

The doorbell rang, and she climbed quickly off him. "Food," she said, smiling politely and wiping tears with the backs of her hands.

He stood, shocked and confused at her response. His head still swimming from her kisses. "What's wrong? Was it something I said? Because the last thing I want to do is upset you or push you away."

She shook her head. "I'm okay. Happy, actually, and surprised. Did you mean that?" she asked, her voice small and cautious. "About me staying?"

The doorbell rang again.

Lucas growled. "Yes." He dug into his jeans for his wallet. "Very much. Why don't we talk about that over dinner?" When all the blood was back in his head, and he could make a solid case for her to stay.

She nodded, and he dashed to the door.

A man in the O'Grady's uniform stood outside, looking at the street, probably wondering if he had the wrong address.

Lucas felt his smile widen as he recalled the reason it had taken so long to answer the bell. "Sorry, man," he said, dragging the heavy wooden door open.

The delivery guy turned to him with a grin. "No problem." He handed over a box with hot potato skins and stacked a bag with chicken salads on top.

"Hang on," Lucas said, balancing the meal in one arm so he could pay the bill. "What do I owe you?"

"Everything," the man growled, pulling a Taser from his pocket.

The electrodes shot into Lucas's torso before he could drop the food or fight.

Fifty thousand volts coursed through him like a strike of lightning and his body went down with a thud.

Chapter Twenty-One

Gwen dried her hands on the small towel inside Lucas's first floor restroom. Her heart was light, and her mind full of hope as she smiled at her reflection in the mirror above the sink. He'd held her, kissed her and said he wanted her to stay with him. It was everything she'd hoped for, and they would soon discuss the details over dinner. She checked her face and hair, then took a steadying breath as she stepped out into the hall.

The anticipation dancing across her skin became an instinctual shiver as she absorbed the gonging silence.

"Lucas?" She'd heard him open the front door and greet the delivery guy. Heard him ask how much he owed. So, where was he now?

"Lucas?" she called again, more quietly this time, as instinct clawed at her chest and neck.

She brought Derek's number up on her cell phone, thankful again for being back in her old world, with her old circle of friends. Friends who would fight for her, and friends who would forgive her if she called them in a paranoid snit for no good reason at all. Like, hopefully, she was doing now.

"Lucas?" she tried a third time, peeking cautiously through each historic room.

Her call connected as she reached the foyer, and Lucas

came into view. His limbs sprawled out on the polished wood floor, their meal overturned beside him.

"Hello?" Derek's voice broke through her panic, pulsing into her ear from the speaker on her phone. "Gwen?"

Lucas groaned and grimaced. He waved an outstretched hand, trying and failing to form words.

"Lucas?" she whispered, shuffling closer, unable to identify the cause of his position or the reason he wasn't speaking.

He blinked pained, glossy eyes, and she knew.

Her stalker was in the house.

"Derek," she said softly. "Call 911. Lucas is hurt, and the stalker is here." Blood whooshed in her ears as she spun in a small circle, searching for the intruder. Could she hide? Should she run?

"Get out of the house," Derek demanded. "I'm calling this in on my work phone. You need to get to your car and go. Understand? Drive to the police station."

"Lucas," she whispered, a heavy round of shakes rattling through her body. "I don't know what's wrong with him."

"Leave him," Derek said. "He will never stop blaming himself if anything happens to you. Now, go."

She hesitated, hot tears falling fast across her cheeks. How could she leave him? What would her stalker do to him with unlimited time behind closed doors? "Derek," she pleaded. "Lucas would never leave me."

"Get. Out. Now," he demanded. He began to relay her situation and recite the address of Lucas's home. He must've made the call to 911. Thank goodness. Help was on the way.

"Gwen," Lucas slurred, his hand stretching in her direction. "Gwen."

She fell to her knees, prepared to clasp his hand, but he curled his fingers away, leaving only the pointer extended toward her.

"Run."

She heard the footfalls before she saw him. A tall, unfamiliar man stood behind her, a Taser in hand. "Phillip Cranston," she said, recognizing him from the photo they'd seen online. Phillip had been an assistant in the computer lab and a volunteer with the hotline. He was also the devil.

Lucas growled a series of animalistic sounds as he struggled to roll onto his side and get his legs beneath him. He made it onto his hands and knees.

Phillip swung his leg back, then kicked Lucas hard enough to make them both grunt. The force lifted Lucas's torso then flipped him onto his back once more.

Her blood ran cold at the sound of the impact. "Stop!" she screamed. "Please! Don't!"

Phillip pointed the Taser at Lucas, then pulled the trigger. Electrodes shot from the device, their metal hooks piercing Lucas's torso and sending his limbs into a frenzy. His back arched and his eyes rolled as Phillip held the trigger.

"Stop!" She lunged at the Taser, attempting to pull it from his grip. Ugly sobs raked up her throat as he moved it out of her reach. "You'll kill him!" she pleaded. "Please don't kill him!"

The worst of thoughts came then, towing a singular bright spot with it. This had always been the way her story would end, but it didn't have to be the way Lucas's ended, too.

"I'll come with you," she said. "Take me. Leave him. I'll do whatever you want. Whatever you say. Just please stop hurting him."

Phillip's wild eyes snapped to hers. He cocked his head like a puppy hearing a new word, then tossed the Taser onto Lucas's body. He grabbed Gwen's wrist and wrenched the phone from her grasp. It clattered to the floor with Lucas.

Derek's small voice rose up to meet her as he yelled her name. "All right then," Phillip said calmly. "Let's go home."

He slid his fingers into her hair, knotted them into a fist at the base of her skull, then bashed her head against the heavy wooden door.

GWEN ROCKED AND swayed in the trunk of an old car. Everything smelled of rot and motor oil. Her head ached, and her stomach churned with every bump and jostle. Her hands were bound. Her mouth gagged. The latter had come after she'd woken up, realized what was happening and began to scream. She'd hoped someone would hear her and call the police. So, she'd screamed herself delirious from lack of oxygen and extreme inhalation of motor oil fumes. Then the car had stopped. Her lungs burned from effort. Her head felt as if it had been hit with a mallet. Her throat was on fire. The sweet night air had rushed over her when the trunk popped open. She'd gasped and panted, desperate for full clean breaths, but Phillip had calmly shoved a rag into her mouth, one that tasted like the trunk smelled, and he'd closed the lid without a word.

She fought continual waves of nausea as the rot and oil seeped into her tongue. She'd made her situation worse, and there hadn't been anyone around to help her. Only the stars and moon had seen, and she had no idea where they were.

She didn't know how long she'd been unconscious before she woke. Didn't know how far they'd traveled or in which direction. She'd thought they were on the highway, based on the speed they were moving, until the trunk had opened and there was nothing else in sight. Phillip's angry eyes had bored into her, setting off a flood of miserable memories. Even without the black balaclava to feature them, his eyes were unforgettable.

Phillip, however, had been completely forgotten. She

squeezed her eyes tight and willed herself to find his face in a memory, any memory. Eventually, she did.

She hadn't met him in the computer lab or at the hotline. She'd met him in the library, her very first escape. He'd helped her get logged on to the online system for course information. He'd been the one to suggest the computer lab if she needed more help. They'd only spoken a short while, but she was sure that had been him. Except that Phillip had been kind and knowledgeable. Patient and shy. He'd told her he was from Kentucky, and he knew she wasn't. He'd said her lack of accent gave her away. But now, she couldn't help wondering if the first time she'd seen him was the first time he'd seen her.

The car turned and began rocking hard. The steady hum of tires on pavement had been replaced with the familiar crunch of tires on rocks. Gwen bounced and lurched inside the trunk, whacking her head against the carpeted floor until she was certain she would vomit or pass out from the pain. When she began to cry in misery and desperation, the vehicle jerked to a stop.

The engine went silent, and so did her world.

The trunk opened a moment later, and the stars were no longer visible.

Phillip had parked beneath some sort of makeshift carport. Instead of the night sky, there were old rotting boards and a rusty tin roof riddled with holes. He stared down at her, a vulnerable expression on his boyish face. "Sorry it took us so long to get here," he said, reaching slowly in her direction. "I had to be sure we weren't followed."

Gwen flinched, rolling deeper into the trunk, pulling away from his grasp.

He sighed, then grabbed her by her elbows and dragged her back to him. "You can't stay in the car all night. You'll get cold." He hefted her up and tossed her over his shoulder with some effort. As if she wasn't a grown woman, or even human. More like a sack of groceries or something to be hauled around. *Like a toy*, she thought. *A plaything under his control.*

Her head pounded with the sudden movement and slamming of the trunk. Her vision blurred and her stomach rolled until she was sure she'd be sick. She strained her muscles to minimize movement and combat the excruciating pain inside her head.

He crossed a wooden deck to some sort of outbuilding covered in limbs and leaves. Then he began the process of unfastening the padlocks.

She lifted her head slowly, turning it left, then right, searching for signs of life. Signs of people, homes or a road. Some way to signal she needed help. But there was none of that.

Silhouettes of trees were everywhere, backdropped by a deep velvet sky. The green eyes of night-things stared back at her from weeds and branches, watching as her life drew closer to its end.

HER ARMS SWAYED over her head, dangling past her ears, toward the ground. Her muscles ached from the clenching, a useless attempt to keep her still. She wanted to kick and fight, to get away and run, but she was useless like this, hurting and barely able to open her eyes.

He had her right where he wanted her, and they both knew it.

Inside the building, her world flipped and righted. Phillip flopped her off his shoulder and onto a couch that smelled of animals and dirt. She pressed her bound hands to her head, adding pressure to the pain and crying out when it only got worse.

Lights flashed on, blinding her and causing her to cry again. The wadded rag in her mouth stuck to her pasty tongue.

Phillip made a dismissive sound. He pulled the gag free and gave her a disappointed look. "You can scream all you want out here, but no one will hear you, and you'll just get yourself all worked up." He poked her bound hands with something hard and cool. "Here."

She pulled her hands back and squinted at the blurry water bottle in front of her.

"Take it," he said. "You need fluids to heal, and I bet that rag tasted terrible. You can wash that away."

"Where are we?" she croaked, her throat raw from screaming. She barely recognized her own voice.

He smiled, looking a bit apologetic. "Welcome home."

Gwen opened her mouth, and the extremely limited contents of her stomach poured out.

"You're going to have to clean that up," he said. "I'll let you wait until you're feeling better, but that's on you. Just like this place. I had a nice room set up for you at my house, but the cops are there now. Also thanks to you."

Gwen rolled onto her back on the couch, wiping sweat from her brow with the sleeve of her shirt. She forced her eyes open again and promptly wished she hadn't. The space around her was small and cramped, filthy and barely more than a shed. A card table in the corner held basic kitchen equipment. A coffee maker. A toaster. Canned foods and paper goods filled a clear-lidded container. Camouflaged gear and guns hung from pegs on the walls. And a collection of hunting knives was spread out on a toolbox beside his ghillie suit. "Hunting cabin?" she guessed, speaking more softly this time and hoping not to be sick again.

"Sometimes," he said. "This place is my secret, and it keeps my secrets. Unlike you." He pressed his hands to his hips, managing to look completely put out. "My dad always said you can't trust a woman. You're schemers, and a man's got to work hard to keep his woman in line or she'll step out on you."

"What are you talking about?" she snapped, the pain and anguish getting the best of her.

Rage flashed in Phillip's eyes. "I'm talking about how you were faithful for six years, and then you weren't. Now, I'm doing my part to fix that."

"I wasn't unfaithful," she argued.

He paced the small space between them in khaki pants and a polo shirt, as if he might be on his way to a nice office job instead of in the woods preparing to commit murder. Somewhere along their way, he'd removed the O'Grady's deliveryman shirt and hat. "Women always say that."

She moaned and closed her eyes against the pain.

"Drink," he said, pushing the bottle against her hands again. "You need to heal."

A new idea formed, and she opened her hands to accept the offer.

He uncapped the bottle with a satisfied smile. He wanted her to heal so they could live out his fantasy in the creepy shed.

She wanted to heal so she could get away.

"There. That's better." He helped her with the bottle, raising it gently, then wiping the dribble from her chin when she finished. "This would've been a lot easier if you hadn't talked to Dr. Bloomsbury," he said. "But you just kept pushing. Even after I'd warned you. And she gave you my name. Then you gave it to the police. Now I can't go home. And here we are."

"Cops are at your house?" she asked, a flame of new hope rising in her.

"Yep. They're at the office, too. Which is why I came for

you early and how we ended up here. If I have to be stuck in the woods day and night, at least we can be together."

Gwen's stomach revolted against the water, and a round of dry heaves sent bullets of pain through her head.

Phillip dug his fingers into his hair and pulled. "I wanted this to be perfect. Bloomsbury ruined it. You can blame her if you want. I do. She's always had a big mouth. Nosy, too. She only remembered my name because she caught me watching you one day. During our loneliness hotline training." He scoffed at the memory. "She suggested I talk to you and reminded me that the whole point of being there was to make friends and to help others do the same. I walked out, and I couldn't go back after that." He offered her another sip of water.

She accepted, going easier this time to appease her stomach.

"No one besides Bloomsbury would've connected me to that program or to you. Not even you," he said.

He was right about that. "Why are you following me?" she asked. "Why did you start? What did I do?"

"Do?" He frowned. "Nothing. You were just pretty, and I liked taking your picture. It became a game to guess where you would be. When I was right, I rewarded myself with a photo. When I saw you struggling with your computer in the library, I helped you, and you were so appreciative. You thanked me again and again. I liked that. And I could tell you liked me, too. I thought about talking to you again, but I liked watching more than talking. And I already knew you liked me. It worked out for a while. I even turned the other cheek when you met Lucas Winchester. I liked watching the things you did together, and I knew you were thinking of me when you did them, so that was okay. I was thinking of you, too." He stroked a finger over her cheek.

She recoiled.

He smiled. "I lost my temper once, when you said you'd marry him, but you got the message. We fought, but you saw that I'm the one in charge, and you let him go."

"You raped me," Gwen said, pain and anger lancing through her. "You hurt me. I almost died because of you."

"I was angry. You made me angry. I had to do something or you were going to leave me. I only planned to talk to you that night, but you wouldn't listen."

"You didn't talk to me," Gwen yelled. "You haven't talked to me in eight years!"

"Liar!" He threw his hands wide with a snarl. His knuckles collided with a nudie poster on the wall, and it fell to the floor. Behind it were photos of Gwen and Phillip in romantic and even compromising positions. None of them were real. All of them were disturbing.

"What are those?" she asked, feeling the panic build in her once more.

He'd photoshopped their faces onto a number of erotic images and placed himself in pictures he'd taken of her life. "Us," he said.

Bile rose in her throat. And the truth of his words hit like a punch to the gut. "You think we've been dating for eight years? And that I didn't marry Lucas because you raped me and left me for dead on campus?"

He grimaced. His fists closed tight before him. "That wasn't rape. We were together."

"We weren't together. We've never been together. And I begged you to stop. I said no, and that was rape," she assured him, her voice ratcheting higher and louder with every word. A torrent of emotion ripped through her chest. "I begged," she repeated. "And you beat my head on a rock."

"We were in love!" he screamed. "We are in love. And women always say no."

"You're crazy," she said, feeling the crowded room grow impossibly smaller. "No always means no." The word slurred and her tongue began to thicken.

Her frantic thoughts became slippery, and her vision dimmed.

How many women had he raped? How many times had he justified the attacks to himself and to his victim using this sick mindset?

She blinked heavy lids at him, her gaze sliding to the bottle in his hand. "What's in that water?"

"Rohypnol," he said, moving in close and stroking her cheek. "Just a little something to help you relax. Drink this every day, and you'll be happy for the rest of your life." His fingers drifted lower as her eyes finally closed.

And she wondered how long that life would be.

Chapter Twenty-Two

Lucas fought the waves of electricity that had temporarily short-circuited his body, willing his brain and limbs to work together once more. He swiped the cell phone off the floor beside him, then forced himself upright. "Derek," he croaked, lurching upright. He staggered forward, falling against the doorjamb where traces of Gwen's blood still clung.

How had he let this happen?

"Lucas?" Derek asked. His voice boomed over the roaring engine in the background. "Where is Gwen?"

Lucas stumbled through the open doorway and onto the porch, letting the cold night air smack his face and bite his skin. The street outside was dark and silent. No traffic. No pedestrians. No Gwen. "Gone."

Emergency vehicles screamed through the neighborhood, their lights already flooding his street. Cruisers and ambulances typically arrived in ten minutes or less. Often, less. Which meant that wherever Phillip had taken her, they hadn't had time to get far.

"We need a make, model and plate on all vehicles owned by Phillip Cranston," Lucas said, his training kicking in.

"Already on it," Derek said. "I called 911 right after she called me. I filled them in, then left. I stayed on the line in case she came back to it. I passed Phillip's name on to dispatch when she said it, but it sounded as if they were already working on him."

Lucas rolled that idea around, recalling slowly. "I sent a text to my team asking them to look into him before I ordered food from O'Grady's."

"I saw a cruiser at O'Grady's when I got off the highway. How much do you want to bet one of their deliverymen was robbed? Food, uniform and all?"

Two cruisers and an ambulance swung onto Lucas's block and cut the sirens. Derek's Mustang was only seconds behind.

Lucas bumbled back inside, careful not to touch anything he didn't have to as he grabbed his sidearm, jacket and badge. Then he reached for his keys and cursed. His truck was in the shop.

"Hey," Derek's voice boomed through the door behind him as a parade of medics and officers tramped inside. "What happened?"

The crew stopped, all awaiting the same answer. He recognized the lead officer as Brent Martin. One of the paramedics was Isaac.

Lucas swallowed his humiliation, stuffed his pride and emotions into a tightly sealed box, then relayed the events flatly. Just the facts.

Officer Martin looked up at the term *stun gun*. "You were tased?"

"Twice."

Isaac's jaw sank open. His hand was on Lucas's wrist in an instant, checking his pulse, before Martin had stopped speaking.

Lucas jerked free on instinct, but Derek's hands came down on his shoulders, holding him in place.

"Can you give me a physical description of the assailant?" Martin asked, fighting a smile as the Winchesters battled silently through a rudimentary exam.

"Yeah," Lucas said. "His name is Phillip Cranston."

"The man we're looking for," Martin said. "Good to know we're on the right track."

Lucas frowned. "We need to get out there and search the neighborhood. We might spot Phillip's car. He might've stopped for gas or supplies. Someone might've seen him traveling with an injured woman." His gaze jumped to the blood smear on his door.

"Be still," Isaac snapped, pressing a stethoscope to Lucas's chest. "You were tased twice tonight. Let me listen to your heart. Your guys are already going through the neighborhood."

"I want to go through the neighborhood," Lucas snapped back.

Isaac sighed. It wasn't a battle he'd win, and everyone in the room knew it. "Give me three minutes to finish evaluating you, then I'm coming along. My shift was up when I heard the call and recognized the address. I can go with you in Derek's car."

Defeated, and thankful for the support of his brothers, Lucas stopped fighting and let Isaac work.

Derek folded his arms and watched the police officers. He moved methodically through the room, gaze traveling slowly, sticking appropriately. To the cast-off stun gun. Dropped delivery food. Blood on the doorjamb. "He's good, but your girl won this one for you when she called me for help and gave me Phillip's name."

"We got the name from a professor," Lucas said, feeling the effects of the stun gun losing the last of their grip. "Then we found him online. I made the call to my team before we ordered the takeout."

"Blaze is at Phillip's place now," Officer Martin chimed

in. "He went with the team to look for this guy after they ran his name through the database. Turns out Phillip Cranston has a lifelong record, if you count all the times he's listed on his dad's arrests for domestic violence. Textbook hot mess family situation in my opinion."

Lucas stilled. He knew what Martin meant, and a violent upbringing too often led to an out-of-control adult. Some kids grew up and broke the pattern, but too many were stuck in the rut. Those kids grew up repeating the mistakes of their parents, madder for it all the time, and lashing out harder as a result. Creating a vicious, dangerous, deadly cycle. "Tell me about Cranston."

"Dad was an angry drunk," Martin said, painting the ugly picture. "Beat the mom regularly till she ran off, then he beat a bunch of other ladies who came in and out of his life. Phillip stayed with his dad until college. He turned eighteen before graduation and had a number of arrests. Vandalism. Fighting. Domestic disputes. Things were quiet for a while after he enrolled at Bellemont. He moved onto campus, and his dad settled down when his overall health took a turn for the worse. He died a few months later, and it wasn't long after that Phillip's dates started filing reports with campus security."

"What kind of reports?" Lucas asked.

Martin's expression turned grim. "Stalking behavior and accusations of rape. That's why there's a team at his place and looking for him now. Even if he hadn't shown up here tonight, we had enough to believe he was Gwen's attacker."

Lucas felt the lid on his tightly boxed emotions begin to rattle. "He raped others before Gwen? And the precinct knew it? What the hell happened here?" Rage pounded against the waning calm.

"Reports were filed, but the investigations never led to

any arrests. The women claimed to have been drugged. Their memories were unclear and inconsistent."

"Which is consistent with being drugged," Lucas growled.

Martin nodded again. "Phillip claimed to have dropped the women off after they had too much to drink. There were witnesses each time. He drove them home, then left. The rapes happened later that night. After Phillip was seen saying goodbye."

"He went back," Lucas said. "He planned ahead, set things up, then went back when there wouldn't be witnesses."

Martin released a defeated sigh, beginning to process the crime scene. "He could've unlocked a window or the back door while he was inside to pick them up for the date. Could've accessed their house key while gallantly taking them home, drugged. Lots of theories. No proof. As for the claims made about him following a woman his freshman year, they were in two of the same general studies courses. That put them in expected proximity on campus. Add in a communal student center, library and computer lab for all students, and two freshmen pursuing the same field of study are bound to run into one another frequently. She left Bellemont at the end of the semester."

Isaac stepped away, finished prodding and poking.

Derek spun his key ring around one finger. "Time to go. Officer Martin can lock up. I'll drive you and Isaac to meet Blaze at Phillip's place."

Lucas cast a look at Officer Martin.

He nodded. "Go on. We've got things under control here."

LUCAS CLIMBED OUT of Derek's Mustang twenty minutes later. Blaze's jeep and another unmarked precinct car were in the driveway. Every light in the house was on and the front door open. Neighbors watched blatantly from their windows and lawns.

The simple two-story home was in need of upkeep, and built in a neighborhood that had once belonged to the working class, but now belonged to landlords and the elderly.

Bruce, the senior detective on Lucas's team, met them at the door. He offered his hand to each brother. "Figured you'd be here soon. Blaze is already upstairs. He thinks he's running this show despite the fact that there hasn't been a murder or a single other reason for a homicide detective to be poking through our case." He craned his neck to shout the words up the steps behind him, then grinned. "All you Winchesters and your Boy Scout camaraderie."

Lucas clapped the older detective on his shoulder as he entered, thankful again for his family. Blood-related and otherwise.

Blaze appeared on the steps, headed their way. His expression was off. "There's something you should see," he said, skipping any measure of greeting and moving straight to the point. Something else Lucas was thankful for.

Lucas, Derek and Isaac followed Blaze through a first floor cluttered with officers and little else, to a back room lined with desks and monitors. The equipment was new and high-end, easily the most expensive things in the house. A tech officer was in position, scrolling through captured footage from outside Gwen's home.

Lucas's skin crawled at the sight of all the feeds. "So, this is where he watched her." When he couldn't be there in person.

Blaze crossed the room to a closet door and opened it. "There's more."

A collection of trinkets sat on a small table inside. A bracelet. A few hair ties. A handful of coins. Gel pens in pink and purple. Mismatched gloves and a pair of sunglasses. "We believe these are things Gwen has dropped, or he's flat-out stolen from her over the years," Blaze said. He tugged a string hanging over the items, and light erupted in the space. He pushed a line of hanging clothes aside. Behind them, the wall was papered in images of Gwen and Phillip in a number of false scenarios. "Looks like he used Photoshop to add himself into his surveillance shots of her alone and to impose their faces on the…other images."

Lucas moved closer, rage rattling that lockbox of emotions once more.

Phillip had pasted images of his face and Gwen's onto participants in a number of erotic encounters. She was never smiling. "He's demented. What kind of sick—"

"Freeze," Blaze said, cutting Lucas off and slapping his hand with an extra pair of blue gloves. "Don't touch anything without these."

Lucas's stomach pitched and rolled as he jammed his fingers into the gloves. He could only imagine what the psychopath was doing to her now, alone somewhere, knowing his time was nearly up.

Isaac moved into the space at his opposite side. "You okay?" he asked, hands hovering, ready to give medical advice or try to treat him somehow. But what ailed Lucas could only be treated one way. By putting Phillip Cranston behind bars for as long as possible and soon. "I'm okay," he told Isaac. "This guy's previous victims might not have had the evidence they needed to get him arrested, but I don't think there's a lawyer in existence who can get Phillip off now. Not when his creepy house speaks for him." He turned to Blaze, confused. "How'd you get a warrant to come in here like this?" The case had to be airtight, or Phillip would walk like so many others. "All I gave you was a name, and the officer at my place made it sound as if Phillip didn't have any related arrests. Only allegations."

Blaze's gaze jumped to Derek, then away. "We used photos taken inside the house to make our case."

Lucas tensed. "How'd you get inside his house without the warrant?"

Derek grinned his signature cocky grin. "I'm excellent at reconnaissance."

Blaze lifted a hand, stopping the conversation before it went too far. "Why don't we focus on finding something that will lead us to Gwen? I've got one more thing to show you."

"There's more?" Isaac asked, appalled. "I'm afraid to ask what it is. At least it can't get any creepier," he added more softly.

"Wrong," Blaze said, leading them through the kitchen to a door with two padlocks, already removed. He opened the door and flipped the light switch.

"The basement?" Lucas asked, a cold sweat breaking on his brow. Images from every awful case he'd ever worked flooded his mind with dark and twisted possibilities.

Blaze marched forward, leaving the obvious answer to lend itself.

The trio followed dutifully.

Phillip's basement was typical. Unfinished, musty and damp. Filled with old boxes and shelves of things no one really cared about.

But there were bars over the glass block windows. That part was not usual and definitely not good.

Blaze stopped at a doorway in a newly erected wall. Dust from the installation still littered the ground. A line of padlocks hung open on the doorjamb.

Lucas stepped forward, drawn by morbid curiosity to

whatever was on the other side of the wall. He pushed the door wide.

Thin vinyl flooring had been rolled out inside the space, covering the basement concrete. The walls were painted a serene and faded teal, like the accent color Gwen used inside her home. A small vanity and king-size bed had been placed against the walls. An armoire, rocking chair and two-seat dinette completed the furniture. The bed was dressed in white and piled high with lacy pillows. An old photo of Gwen and Lucas in a lovestruck embrace sat in a frame on the nightstand. Lucas's face had been replaced with Phillip's.

"There are cameras here, too," Blaze said. "They're monitored from upstairs, as well."

Lucas ghosted through the room, dumbfounded and sick. "He planned to keep her here? Indefinitely?" He'd never seen anything of this magnitude in real life. This was the kind of insanity saved for television dramas and horror movies.

Blaze rested a hand on the gun at his hip, his shoulders tense, expression blank. "Based on the amount of Rohypnol we found stashed inside an empty oatmeal box in the pantry, he planned to keep her drugged, and for a very long time."

"Detective?" A man's voice called down the basement steps.

"Yeah?" Blaze and Lucas answered in unison, then caught each other's eye and headed in the man's direction. The others followed.

Blaze cut in front of Lucas at the stairs, then took them two at a time. "What do you have?"

The tech officer from the makeshift office gave the line of Winchesters a look, then turned his eyes back to Blaze. "You'd better see for yourself."

They tracked him back to the row of desks and monitors where a small cabin in the woods centered a screen. Infrared gave the feed an eerie green glow.

"It's another surveillance feed," the officer said. "I came across it while I was going through the files on the computer."

"Where is this cabin?" Lucas asked, certain this was the answer they'd been looking for.

"We're trying to find out," the officer answered. He lowered into the chair once more and took control of the computer. He backed the video up ten minutes, then pressed Play. Headlights flashed over the cabin, then went out.

"Was that a car?" Lucas asked. "Tell me we get a look at the plate."

The officer didn't answer. Didn't look his way. He just stared at the screen, drawing Lucas's attention back there, as well.

An image of Phillip appeared. He had Gwen over his shoulder like a caveman, her arms dangling limp and bound beside her motionless head. He worked the padlocks, opened the door then carried her inside.

Lucas stumbled back. Pressing his palms against the cool surface of the wall to anchor himself. His head swam and the world tunneled.

Isaac clutched his arm and pulled him into an empty folding chair. "Breathe."

Lucas inhaled deep and slow, but there was only one thing on his mind.

Gwen's attacker had carried her, unconscious, into the woods, not to the creepy little room he'd made for her in his basement. He knew the cops were onto him. Knew he couldn't come home again. And that gave him no reason to keep Gwen alive.

Chapter Twenty-Three

Gwen opened her eyes to a blast of icy air.

Confusion became terror as the details of her night returned. Her pounding head and rolling stomach were the combination of a probable concussion and too much Rohypnol-laced water.

Her captor stretched a knit cap over his head, then stepped silently outside. He shut the door behind him, effectively cutting off the wind and delivering Gwen into comparative darkness.

Where was he going? And why?

She struggled to clear her vision and find a weapon she could use against him. She pushed into a seated position with a groan and a grimace, feeling a resurgence of pain in her still-healing side. Her still-bound wrists were sore and aching.

Through the filthy window, she could see the silhouette of him, standing frozen and staring into the distance. Down the path he'd driven the car in on last night.

She scanned the room again for a weapon she could manage and came up short.

His car keys, however, were laying peacefully on the table beside his wallet and an unopened box of condoms.

Gwen's mouth opened and bile poured out, mixing with the contents of her stomach spilled there the night before.

She wiped her eyes and mouth, biting back the tears. She couldn't fight like this. Couldn't run. And the things he would soon do to her were more than she could bear. He might not have assaulted her while she'd slept, but the ready box of condoms suggested it wouldn't be long now.

She steadied herself on the couch's edge, still struggling to gather her senses.

The white noise of a radio crackled nearby, and a voice barked out directions and coordinates. Orders and acronyms.

Outside the window, Phillip turned to face the cabin, anger painted across his face.

Gwen ducked. She surged forward, scraping the keys off the table, then diving back onto the nasty couch. A plume of dirt and animal hair rose around her as she pushed the keys between the cushions and closed her eyes. Her nose itched and eyes burned, but she couldn't gag, couldn't whimper or sneeze. Couldn't let him know she was awake. If he knew that, he'd also know she was the one who'd taken the keys.

The door swept open, filling the small space with another gust of icy air, and Phillip stormed inside. He slammed the door behind him, and her shoulders jumped involuntarily. He went to the table, listening intently to the rambling voice Gwen now recognized as a police dispatcher, delivering details of local law enforcement's hunt for him.

Phillip removed his phone from his pocket, then powered it down with a curse. He pulled the battery and SIM card, then threw the phone against the wall.

Gwen jumped again without intention, and her assailant looked her way. "Where am I?" she asked, not needing to fake the grogginess in her tone or expression. "What happened?"

He scowled. "They're coming. So, we're going. I'll take my car as far as I can, then swap it for something else." He looked her over, contemplating. "You look awful. I can't take you in public like that." He reached for her, roughly pulling her into a seated position. He tried to smooth her wild curls, then stuffed a ball cap over them instead.

She whimpered as the material scraped against her cut and aching forehead.

"Put this on," he said, grabbing a jacket from a hook near the door and tossing it in her lap.

"My hands," she said, raising her bound wrists and blinking to clear her vision.

Phillip cursed. His gaze swept over her, then around the cabin, presumably in search of a plan.

Gwen's plan was to stall. If she understood the situation correctly, help was closing in, and Phillip didn't plan to kill her and dispose of the evidence. He planned to take her with him. She could work with that. "I need to lie down," she said, swooning backward, pretending to go boneless from the drugs.

His expression lit. "That's perfect." He grabbed the water bottle from the table and forced it against her mouth. "Drink."

Her gut knotted at the idea of going under again. She let her eyes drift shut. She couldn't drink that water.

"If you drink this, I won't put you in the trunk again," he said. "You can sleep up front with me. I'll even remove your zip ties." He tapped a finger to the plastic bindings.

Untied and not in the trunk were two things she needed to be if she was going to escape.

She nodded slowly, then let him put the bottle to her lips. She sipped gingerly, making more noise than necessary and holding the small amount in her mouth.

He watched her swallow, then breathed a sigh of relief. "I'll get the knife for this," he said, touching the binding again.

When he turned away, Gwen buried her face in the disgusting cushion where her head lay and spilled the water from her mouth into the fabric. She pressed her cheek and hair against the wet spot before he turned back, wishing she hadn't swallowed any, but thankful for the amount she was able to reserve and spit out.

Phillip cut the ties with a pocketknife he pulled from a coat pocket, and she let her hands fall limply to her sides. "Okay," he said. "We have to go, and you need to keep drinking to stay hydrated." He set the bottle beside her, then pulled her up again. "Let's get your coat on and get out of here."

He fed her arms into the oversized sleeves of a black men's coat, then pulled her onto her feet.

She fell against him, overacting possibly, but he didn't seem to notice. His distraction grew with every new syllable from the police scanner in the corner.

"Where are my keys?" He patted his pockets and turned in a small circle, dragging her with him. "I put them on the table," he said.

Gwen bent her knees, sliding down his body and forcing him to set her back on the couch.

He crouched onto the floor, searching desperately for his missing keys.

Gwen slipped a hand up to the water bottle and loosened the cap until it spilled over the cushions near her face. She coughed and choked, as if she'd been trying to drink.

"Hey!" Phillip glared in her direction, clearly seeing the nearly empty bottle and furious about it. "What did you do? That's all the water I had for you. Now it's gone!"

She forced her expression to remain slack and her body still, but internally, she wanted to run. Adrenaline pumped hard in her veins, preparing her to take action, whatever that might be.

"Radio silence," the dispatcher called. "In three, two…" And the voice was gone. Only white noise remained.

Phillip jolted upright with a wail and a curse. He punched the wall in a rage, then slammed his fists on the table before kicking everything in sight, including the couch where Gwen lay. He whacked the water bottle off the cushion near her cheek, then spun suddenly away.

She pressed her eyelids shut, terrified he would rip one of the guns from the wall and kill them both rather than be caught or surrender.

The rustle of fabric pulled her eyes open a moment later, though her lids felt heavier than before.

Phillip had stepped into his ghillie suit and pulled on the balaclava. "They can't have you," he said coolly. "I won't allow it." He yanked a rifle with a scope off the rack near the door, and he walked outside.

LUCAS SECURED THE straps of his bulletproof vest and tucked a small communications device into his ear while members of the Jefferson County Sheriff's strike team made battle plans.

It was a bit of a shot in the dark, but the plot of tax-delinquent property in the middle of nowhere was the only hope Lucas had. Public records showed the property had belonged to Phillip's father and had been inherited by Phillip upon his father's death. There were no known structures or road frontage, but it was remote and familiar to Phillip. The perfect place for a psychopath under pressure to rest and regroup.

Lucas zipped his coat, tugged on his hat, then freed his sidearm from its holster. He nodded at the strike team captain who'd taken Lucas's call, and he'd mobilized a squad while Derek had raced Lucas across the county to join them.

Now, they moved in single file, up a rutted, leaf-covered lane into the wilderness, while the first fingers of dawn climbed the trees.

GWEN GRIPPED THE WINDOWSILL, steadying her body and wishing she hadn't swallowed any of the drugged water, but feeling the impact of the amount she had.

Phillip moved like a ghost through the trees beyond the window, looking completely at ease. As if he'd done the same thing a hundred times, *which he had*, she realized, while stalking her. He squatted in a thicket twenty-five yards away, then set the barrel of his gun in the deep V of a dying tree and pointed it down the muddy pitted path they'd taken to the cabin.

Gwen counted to ten, making sure he was staying put. Then she reached for the radio and turned up the volume. She needed the dispatcher's voice to come back. Needed to know what was happening out there, and needed to warn whoever was coming that Phillip was lying in wait.

She considered digging the car keys from the couch and attempting to drive away, but how far could she really get? Without being shot? Falling down? Or hitting a tree? The cabin slanted beneath her feet, as if confirming her inability to get far on her own. She stumbled toward the couch, woozy again and desperate to sit before she fell. Her toe connected with something small and hard on the way.

Phillip's cell phone skated across the floor, and Gwen nearly cried in response.

She dropped to the floor, chasing the device beneath the table and begging her eyes to stay open. She found the battery near the wall, then rushed to install it before Phillip shot someone or came back for her.

Adrenaline and panic made her clumsy. She dropped the

battery twice before getting it into place. And she powered up the device, praying for a signal.

That was when she heard the first gunshot.

THE BARK ON the tree beside Lucas's head burst into shreds, sending him skidding onto his knees behind it. His ears rang and his heart raced. He wasn't sure if that had been a warning shot, or if Phillip had missed. Neither seemed possible.

"Winchester?" The voice of the strike team captain sounded in his ear.

Lucas touched the communications device with one fingertip. "I'm okay," he said. "I wasn't hit."

"Did you see where the shot came from?" he asked.

"East," he huffed, trying desperately to slow his sprinting heart. "That's all I've got."

And it wasn't good news. At this time of day, a position in the east put Phillip between the lawmen and the sun. Phillip would have a clear view of them as day broke, and they would have a blinding view of the rising sun.

Still, a slow smile spread over Lucas's face as he pressed his back to the tree. The gunshot meant they'd found Phillip. And if they'd found Phillip, they'd also found Gwen.

GWEN WATCHED PHILLIP through the cabin window, nearly invisible in the trees. Her heart pounded harder than her head at the sound of the gunshot. "He's shooting," she told the emergency dispatcher on the other end of the line. "I think he just shot at someone." She hated herself for hoping it wasn't Lucas. Or Blaze. She knew neither of those lawmen would stay away from a rescue mission meant to save her. And she was sure Derek and Isaac would be there, too, if they could. Gwen's parents might live in Florida, but she had plenty of family, she realized, right here in Kentucky, and she loved them all.

So, she wouldn't let this psychopath sit out there and pick them off one by one.

"Can you communicate with whoever's here for me?" she asked the dispatcher. "Tell them I'm here in the cabin, and I'm okay. Tell them Phillip's in his ghillie suit and that he took a rifle with him. He's using a tree as cover and a gun rest. I can see him from here. Maybe twenty-five yards from the cabin. I'd run, but I don't think I can, and I'm sure he'll see me open the door."

"What if we can give you some cover?" a male voice asked in her ear.

"What?" she gasped, unsure what had happened to the female dispatcher's calming voice, or who she was hearing now.

"Ms. Kind," the dispatcher said. "I've got Jerry Horton, on the line. He's our strike team captain, and he's got men in place to bring you home."

Tears welled and fell from Gwen's eyes. Her chest heaved with a grateful sob, and the knot in her chest constricted impossibly tighter. She wasn't sure she could actually run, but she would make a break from the cabin if this man told her to. "I'll try," she croaked, "but I've been drugged."

There was a long beat of silence before Jerry spoke again. "Hold the line," he said finally.

Panic swept through her at the silence. What did that mean? Had he changed his mind? Had something bad happened outside? Why hadn't she asked about the gunshot?

"Ms. Kind?" the dispatcher said once more. "I won't leave you. Hang in there while he makes arrangements. Can you still see the shooter?"

Gwen jerked her gaze back through the window, terri-

fied he'd moved while she'd been distracted. "I don't know."
She stared hard into the woods, willing Phillip to move, if
he was there. Just enough for her to confirm. "The shot,"
she said, her voice shaky with fear. "Did he hurt anyone?"

"No, ma'am."

A fresh punch of tears blurred Gwen's vision, and she
blinked them away. "Good."

A moment later, wind rustled through the forest fluttering the material of Phillip's suit, and she nearly collapsed
with relief. "I see him," she said. "He hasn't moved."

"Excellent work," the dispatcher praised. "Now, we'll
stand by and wait for orders. You doing okay?"

"No," she whispered, her limbs beginning to shake severely. "I don't think I can do this."

"Ms. Kind," the woman on the other end of the line responded, patiently. "I'm sure you feel that way right now,
but from what I hear, you can do anything. I've been told
you're a fighter, a survivor and the reason those men are out
there. Reports coming through our office this morning say
you called someone when you suspected an intruder, and
you gave Phillip Cranston's name to the police before he
took you. You've been stabbed, choked and probably con-
cussed. You're currently drugged, yet you found a way to
call me. And it's because of you we now know the gunman's
position. So, whatever Jerry wants you to do, I am certain
enough for the both of us that you can and will get it done."

Gwen's knees buckled, and she cried. She didn't hold
back. Didn't have the strength left to fight the tidal wave
of emotions. And more than anything, she just wanted to
lie down and close her eyes. Just for a minute.

"Ms. Kind?" Jerry's voice boomed again in her ear.
"We're ready for you. I'm going to count to three, then in-
struct my men to open fire in the direction of the shooter.
Twenty-five yards to the east of the cabin. Right?"

She pulled her eyelids open, unsure when they'd shut. "Yes," she whispered, her limbs going slowly numb from the drugs.

"When you hear the first shots fired, you're going to open that cabin door, and you're going to run. One foot in front of the other. Northwest. That's behind the cabin and away from the shooter. We'll do the rest. Don't stop running until you reach us. We're moving into position for your recovery now."

The line went quiet.

"Phillip Cranston." The strike team captain's voice echoed strong and loud through the world outside, possibly through a bullhorn. "This is the Jefferson County Sheriff's department, and you're under arrest for the kidnapping of Gwen Kind. Lay your weapon down, and come out where I can see you, or we'll be forced to open fire."

Another shot rang out, and Gwen knew that was Phillip's response. He wouldn't give up or surrender, and someone was likely to die today.

It couldn't be her.

She pushed onto her feet once more and reached for the cabin door.

The forest exploded in a hail of gunfire.

And she ran.

Gwen's feet pounded loud and awkward against the wooden planks outside the cabin, shaking the platform beneath her. She gripped the wall at the corner as she leapt into the forest and bumbled quickly away, leaving the cabin door agape behind her.

Her legs were weak and noodle-y, her breaths coming loud and fast. And her head split with the continuous sound of gunfire.

Still, she stumbled forward, gripping trees for support,

then pushing off them for momentum. *One foot in front of the other*, she told herself. And then she saw him.

A blurry silhouette in black raced confidently through the trees before her, his presence instantly familiar and more comforting than anything she'd ever known. Her guardian angel, her personal protector, the only man she'd ever love. Lucas Winchester.

Epilogue

Gwen hurried to answer the door at Lucas's home for the fifth time in an hour. His brothers, parents and half the local police force were already gathered in the kitchen, laughing, chatting and generously splattered in paint. The party had been Lucas's idea. The painting part was Gwen's, though she'd yet to pick up a brush. "I've got it," she called, padding back across the layered sheets of plastic protecting restored hardwood floors.

It had been two months since her personal testimony, along with Lucas's professional one, had helped put her abductor, rapist and stalker away for twenty-six years. When something went that right in life, she had to agree, it was cause for celebration. So, she'd ordered eighty gallons of carefully selected custom paints, enough local takeout to feed an army and invited all their friends.

As for Phillip's testimony, it had been an unfortunate one. He was raised in a dark, twisted place by a dark, twisted man, and while Phillip had gotten some distance by moving out for college, the serious long-term damage had already been done. And it deeply tainted his every encounter with the women on campus. He wanted them to want him, but he also wanted to hurt them. And his frustrations became obsessions. Gwen had simply been in the wrong place at the wrong time when she asked for help in the library. When she'd taken his advice and visited the computer lab the next day, he'd seen it as their first date.

He'd testified that he regretted hurting her so badly back then. He didn't, however, regret that he'd done it, because for six years afterward, things had gone well in his mind. She'd broken the engagement like he'd wanted, and she'd stopped seeing anyone but him.

Gwen shook her head at the memory. Even on the stand, Phillip didn't fully accept that his relationship with her was totally in his mind. Or that hurting people wasn't the way to show them he cared.

She smiled at the sounds of laughter echoing through her home, then pulled herself back to the moment and opened the door.

"Surprise!" a chorus of female voices called.

Her coworkers stood on the doorstep, each with flowers or a bottle of wine. "Housewarming gifts," Marina said, passing a bottle of merlot from her hands to Gwen's.

Her boss, Victoria Noble, shot a knowing look at her, then handed over a bouquet of flowers. "I'm not here to paint, but you know I can't miss an opportunity to tour a home like this one."

"Come in!" Gwen said, pulling them all inside. Victoria had told Gwen not to hurry back to work after her abduction, but Gwen had been back in her place as quickly as possible. Eager to get it over with. Answer all the uncomfortable questions, field the rampant gossip and adjust to the pitying looks. Instead, her coworkers had been impressively understanding. No gossip. No pity. Just lots of warm hugs and a "Welcome Back" cake. "I'm glad you could all come."

"We wouldn't miss it," Victoria said, admiring the history all around her. "This home is stunning."

"Thank you," Gwen said, feeling immediately proud.

She and Lucas had made a thousand plans for the home over late-night glasses of wine and old movies they barely watched. She wanted to pinch herself every time she thought of how lucky she was to be here with him now.

Except, he wasn't there now. She checked the grandfather clock in the corner and frowned. Lucas had gone to run an errand more than an hour ago, and logical or not, she was beginning to worry.

Marina and Debbie hurried toward the kitchen, eager to join in on the chatter and laughter.

Victoria followed more slowly, her eye for design and love of history giving her pause at every glorious detail. "The two of you talked about living in this home together some day, back when you were in college?"

Gwen nodded, biting her lip and feeling impossibly blessed. "Yep. And even after all that had happened to me, to us," she corrected, "he bought the place as planned and began the renovations himself."

"Now, here you are together, as planned," she echoed Gwen's words. "Romantic." Victoria dragged a fingertip over the intricately detailed woodwork along the staircase. "And absolutely stunning."

Gwen's smile eased as something else came to mind. "Have you heard from Collin?" She posed the question every day and usually received the same response. He was recovering nicely, but not feeling like visitors. She couldn't help blaming herself for what he'd been through, and she knew firsthand what he might be feeling.

"I did," Victoria said, turning on her toes with a grin. "Collin called around dinner last night and caught me at the office. It seems he's fallen head over heels for his physical therapist and has officially resigned from his position at my company." She arched her brows. "He's moving to the therapist's town, about ninety minutes away, and he asked me for a letter of recommendation. I agreed, of course, but oh, to be young again," she mused.

Gwen laughed, and the doorbell rang. "I'll be right back," she said with a small sigh, eager to spend more than a few minutes with each guest and dying to actually paint something.

The music quieted behind her as she opened the door once more, hoping it would be Lucas and knowing he wouldn't have rung the bell.

She froze at the sight of two people she hadn't seen since the trial, then smiled immediately in response to their bright faces. "Mom? Dad?"

They engulfed her in a hug, pulling her into the house with them and closing the door.

"We missed you, sweet baby girl," her mother cried.

"I missed you, too." Gwen squeezed them tighter before letting go. She wished she could keep them with her forever. "What are you guys doing here? Is everything okay in Florida?"

Her dad stepped back with a huff. "Everything's hot in Florida. Lucas picked us up from the airport."

Gwen smiled. "So, that was where he went."

"He'll be right in," her mom assured her. "We were thrilled to get his call and invitation."

"Lucas invited you to our painting party?"

Her mom laughed and slid in close to her husband's side. "Not exactly. Lucas wanted to talk to us in person."

"About what?" she asked, mystified.

"About asking you to marry me," Lucas said, his voice breaking the sudden silence all around her.

Gwen spun to find him and all their previously chatty guests in a loose crowd behind her, silent and grinning from ear to ear.

Lucas lowered onto one knee, and the air left her lungs.

He started by telling her he loved her, and she picked up other words here and there. *Teammates. Soulmates. Lovers. Friends.* But louder than all his sentiments and promises was the look in his eye and the answering response of her heart.

She accepted the ring he presented with a kiss and plenty of tears. Because it wasn't just any ring. It was her ring. The one he'd given her six years ago. The one they'd found together at an estate sale. Probably as old, and definitely as beautiful, as their home. And she promised again that she would cherish it forever. The same way she cherished him, for all of the days of her life.

* * * * *

RESCUE MISSION: SECRET CHILD

DANICA WINTERS

To Jessica— You are an amazing friend and mother.
Thank you for all you do.

Chapter One

There was nothing that Mike hated more than a wedding. It didn't matter whose it was, the season, or the amount of love the happy couple professed to each other. He would still have rather ridden bareback on an angry bull than sit in some kind of mushy gushy feel fest.

Though, when push came to shove, it wasn't the love part that he despised. *Nah.* He had just found there were two events in people's lives that always brought out both the worst and the best from those around them—weddings and funerals.

The last nuptials he had attended had been so filled with poorly masked rancor that by the time the open bar hit, things had turned to verbal tongue-lashings and two brawls. If he hadn't interceded, he was sure a funeral would have soon followed. The last thing he had wanted was to attend two emotionally explosive events that close together.

He definitely would have preferred taking on the bull.

Thinking about bulls, a mechanical bull was exactly what this thing needed to kick it up a notch. He glanced in the direction of the reception hall, a ski lodge just beside the meadow that served as the bunny hill for new skiers in the winter months. Of course, the only thing he could spot through the windows of the A-framed building was a chocolate fountain and a tall, white wedding cake. Nothing gyrating, at least not until his cousin Savannah hit the bottle.

The pastor was talking about the meaning of life or something, but Mike wasn't really listening as he watched the crowd seated in front of him. Aunt Carlene had her signature beehive bun, now sprinkled with a few more gray hairs than when he had last seen her. She'd always been his favorite aunt, and as she and his uncle Bingo sat up at the front on the groom's side in what was traditionally the parents' seats, it made him miss his mom and dad.

Their dad had talked about being at their weddings, a conversation that had always made tears well up in his mother's eyes as she'd wistfully added how she hoped they would all find spouses who helped them be the best versions of themselves. At the time, Mike had teased her and accused her of clearly thinking they all had room for improvement. Of course, she had always waved him off and called him a stinker, but they'd both known what she'd really wanted for him and his five siblings was that they lived lives in which they were truly fulfilled and happy.

When he had gotten engaged to Summer, his mother had been over the moon. Within a week of finding out his news, she had called Summer and they had already decided on the location, colors and bridal parties. He had still been trying to come to terms with the fact their lives were about to change.

Summer had always been too good for him. She was the kind of woman who was strong and could weather any storm, but she was also the woman who understood that as a military contractor he was cut from a cloth that meant he would never be happy sitting still and would rarely be home. At the time, they had both thought they understood what their lives would entail and had naively believed their love was unlike any other, and that no matter how many horror stories they heard about contractors' relationships falling apart, theirs wouldn't. They had fully bought in to the idea that they, and their relationship, were different.

What idiots they had been.

Many times, like now, when he was forced to go to social functions without a date, his aunt would inevitably try to set him up with someone. He couldn't do it, though. He missed Summer. He missed the way they could just look at one another and know what the other was feeling and thinking.

What they had…it had been something special. But looking back, he wasn't sure they'd been an ideal fit. They were different. She liked hot and he liked cold. He wanted to conquer the world while she wanted to perfect her corner of it. And their biggest difference was their fatal flaw…he wanted all of her heart and she wanted every bit of his soul.

He'd never really get over losing her. Late at night, he would often have to console himself with the thought that, in the end, they had been too young for the kind of commitment they had made to one another. Who could promise forever when they weren't even sure where in the world they would be tomorrow?

She had deserved better. He should have answered her calls after they'd broken things off, but some things were just too damn hard.

In front of him at the altar, the bride, Kate Scot,

slipped the wedding band on his brother's finger as she smiled up at him and said her vows. There was no mention of her obeying his brother and Mike had to hold back his chuckle. Summer had always protested that particular vow, as well. He and his brother Troy had always had a similar taste for independent women.

He had to get his mind off Summer or he would only swirl further into madness, madness that would lead to far too much beer and he'd be the one who'd end up dancing with his gyrating cousin.

Nope. He couldn't get himself roped into any of that kind of nonsense. He had a stoic, lone-wolf reputation to uphold.

As soon as Kate and Troy kissed, he got up from his chair and moved steadily away from the crowd, not so fast to give his retreat away, but quickly enough to get out of the melee of family members who would try to rope him into a conversation. He'd dropped the gift off and watched the I do's, the rest he could hear about later.

He had parked at the far end of the lot, nose out in case he had to make a quick escape. But as he approached his truck, he noticed a woman standing near the tailgate. She had her back to him, looking toward the timber like there were answers in the pines. The only thing she would find by standing so close to his truck was a problem.

"Can I help you?" he asked, hoping the woman was just someone like him, trying to escape the ceremony, rather than a spook up to no good. In his business, he had to view everyone as a potential threat.

The woman turned around and, as she did, their eyes met. Those green eyes. Those eyes, the vibrant, down-to-earth color of spring moss, had always had the power to weave right into his soul. They, and the woman they belonged to, had an unspeakable gift to sparkle with contagious joy and instantly darken when danger beckoned. A thousand words were not enough to explain all the things her eyes had conveyed to him over the years; in fact, no words created could elicit the same feelings that she could with a simple glance.

A hint of a smile flickered over her features as she looked at him, her eyes lighting up, but just as quickly as the light had come, it disappeared and was replaced with pure unadulterated hate. Sadly, he understood why and how confused she must have been feeling, and a guilty sadness filled him. He had done this to her. He'd had a hand in the look she was sending him and the woman she had become.

"I'm sorry." It was the only thing he could think to say. As soon as it left his lips, he wished he'd led with something more innocuous, maybe a hello instead. Yet, the milk was spilled.

She chuckled. Blading her feet, she turned slightly away from him. He didn't blame her for not wanting to look at him a second longer than necessary. Then again, she knew this was his truck… She must have been waiting for him.

"I was hoping you would be here." He surprised himself with those words. If anything, he had feared seeing her—seeing her only made everything rise to the surface.

"We both know that's not true. I'm the last person you wanted to have be here."

Ouch.

Sighing, he tried to quell the ache that had suddenly filled his entire being. If he wasn't careful, this would only lead to a fight; they had one hell of a track record in bringing animosity out in one another.

"You were waiting for me?" he asked, trying to keep the question inquisitive instead of kindling for her rage.

She sat on the bumper of his truck, covering her chest with her arms and protecting her core. He'd seen her take this position a thousand times, and none had ever turned out well.

"I'm not here because I really want to be, let me start by saying that."

He had no doubt, but he wasn't about to say that aloud, so he simply nodded, waiting for her to continue.

"I was in the city for work. Ran into Kate and she invited me. I figured I needed to be here to show my support. Troy was always a good man." She paused, like she wanted him to respond, but he was far too gun-shy.

He had a number of things he wanted to ask her, starting with how her life was going. The last time he had spoken to her, she had been employed by a contracting company, running intel.

"Still working with STRIKE?" he asked.

She gave him a sidelong look, but she didn't answer at first, as if she was checking to see if he knew about the company; and if he did, what his opinion was. He gave her nothing, though he'd heard all about the company. They had made waves by controlling American gas reserves on military bases, gas that had lost thousands of barrels along the railways between bases and even more in the pipelines leading into the American strongholds. "Still working intel?" he asked, trying again.

She nodded. "Yes. By the way, I heard about you and your brother's run-in with Rockwood."

It had only been a couple of months since he had found his ass getting shot at in the streets of downtown Missoula—after the group had worked to take down Kate's family's company from the inside out—but it already felt like ancient history. "Yep, it's how Kate and Troy met. Never thought things would move this fast between them. You know Troy, he's typically about the speed of cold molasses."

"No," Summer said with a laugh, "that's you."

He felt the lash. "Slow is smooth and smooth is fast."

"You can try to feed me all that nonsense if you want, but you and I both know that you are never one to jump into or out of anything without a hell of a lot of thought— thoughts that you generally forget to express to others."

This time the whip struck faster, harder, and the lashes cut deeper with their truths.

"I'm sorry."

"You said that." She sounded almost glib. "It doesn't change the fact that you did what you did. And you are going to have to forgive the fact that I may never get over how badly you hurt me. Move on, sure. Move forward, you know it. But hurt…*forever.*"

"I know." He stared down at the toes of the wing tips his brother had asked him to wear for pictures, wishing he had stayed for the reception instead of trying to find any kind of refuge away from the crowds. They would have been a hell of a lot easier to deal with than this. "I hurt, too, Summer. It was never my intention to—"

She put a stop to his talking with the wave of her hand. "I didn't mean to take things this direction. The past is the past. Let's leave it there."

He didn't dare to believe she was done talking about their shared history, but he was glad for the parley. "Done. Now, what do you need?" If there was anything he could do to get back in her good graces, he would.

"Who said I needed anything?"

"I know you're friends with my brother and Kate, but we both know this kind of thing isn't your scene." He shrugged, making her smirk.

He had loved that guilty smile.

There was so much he missed about her and so many things he wished he could just tell her... Like the fact he would never stop loving her. He just hadn't been ready to walk down the aisle. Maybe he would never be ready for a real relationship. Marriage meant putting her in danger, and he was a protector at his core; a job that required he focus on things bigger than himself. The only way he could do that was by being selfless and giving up what he loved the most.

"I am here for them...and I don't hate weddings, even though..." She brushed the rest of the sentence away like it was some kind of pestering fly. "I did have something I wanted to talk to you about."

He didn't want to talk about work, but he had a feeling that was exactly where she was going to try to take things since she had brought up his and Troy's run-in with Rockwood. He was especially attuned to subtle snooping, and the fact that she'd asked about his recent job put him on edge. "STEALTH's work for ConFlux is strictly confidential. As much as I would like to help you out, you know how it is."

"Kate said your team would be who I needed to talk to about the security breach. That you could give me information."

"The way I see it, there are a few things wrong with this, Summer. First, I'm not the guy you want to be talking to if you want answers about this. And second, who is to say the people at STRIKE are people who can be trusted?"

She slid him a sly smile. She was hiding something, but he didn't know exactly what. "You know I'd never be a part of anything I hadn't vetted. My team is with the good guys gang, same as your teams at STEALTH. We work for the greater good."

She could do all the vetting she wanted, but that didn't mean she saw everything or had come to all the right conclusions. And when it came to the *greater good*, they both knew that was a load of nonsense.

"As far as I'm concerned, whatever was stolen from ConFlux is between them and the federal acronyms they are working for and with. If you stick your nose too deep into this kind of warfare, you will lose your face. Be careful, Summer." He turned as he moved to retreat.

"Stop," she called after him. "I have one more thing…"

He halted and faced her. "If this is about your work, as much as I want to, I can't help you. I'm out, Summer."

"I know, and that's fine. But my work isn't why I'm really here." She paused, chewing on her bottom lip as she clicked on her phone. "I have something—*someone* actually—you need to meet." She lifted her phone and he had to step closer to see the picture.

Smiling up at him was a baby. He had big blue eyes and appeared to be giggling at something off-screen.

"This is Joseph. I call him Joe." There was a soft cadence to her voice, an unmistakable tenderness that came when a mother looked upon her child. "Joe is our son."

Chapter Two

Summer really hadn't intended to tell Mike about the baby this way. There was such a deep, aching sadness in Mike's features, she wanted to wrap her arms around him. To bury her face in his chest and say how sorry she was. How she had wanted to give him the news for so long; how many times she had tried to call. She moved toward him, but stopped her advance.

Wait. No. She wasn't the one who needed to feel bad about how this had all played out. This was on him.

She had called. She had tried to contact him. *He* was the one who had refused to talk to her, to take her calls. And telling a man he was going to be a father wasn't something that anyone should do over a voice mail or a text. If he was upset, then he could only be upset with himself. He had been the weakling who couldn't face her after he had broken her heart.

Sucking in a long inhale, she collected herself.

Life had a dark sense of humor.

"You named him Joe?" Mike's voice cracked, breaking away some of her anger.

She nodded. "Joseph. After your dad. I thought it was only right."

Mike had never been one to cry, not even when he

had told her that he wasn't going to marry her…right in the middle of the makeshift bridal suite twenty minutes before their wedding was set to begin. The church had started to fill with their guests, and the caterers and florists had everything in place. When he'd spoken those words, those heartbreaking words, *I can't… I can't be your forever*, the string quartet had been playing "Ave Maria." Ever since, she had hated that song; before it had been one of her absolute favorites. But that day, there were many things she had thought she would love forever that had turned to ash in her mouth.

It was crazy how, in a single moment, everything in a life could change.

"Can I see the picture again?" He sounded plaintive, as if unsure she'd agree, his voice soft, even wavering.

She noted the way he didn't say *his* picture. It was *the* picture. As if the baby whom her whole life now revolved around was simply an image, nothing more. But then again, she had no doubt she was gunning for a fight. For the last few weeks, she had been trying to imagine every possible outcome of this meeting, but every scenario she had imagined had ended with a fight. No matter how badly she wanted things to be amicable between them, her pain was likely to stand in the way.

She pulled up Joe's picture and handed her phone over to Mike. He stared at the screen and there was a well of tears growing in his eyes. Would he let them fall?

Regardless of her personal feelings, they had a child together. A child who deserved to know his father and his entire family; even if that family wasn't really hers. Regardless of her feelings for him, Mike deserved to have a chance…a chance he didn't have to take, a chance he didn't have to grasp with both hands. More, he deserved to have a *choice*, one that didn't include her getting in his way or keeping his child from him.

Though she hated him for what he had done to her and the way he had made her feel, there was no doubt there was still a part of her that loved him, and would always love him. That part of her soul was deep, and she would have to keep it buried, but only love could make her feel this confused and so up in the air.

"He is so handsome. How old is he?"

"Seven months, yesterday. He has started to crawl and is starting to get into everything. He loves to be at my feet when I'm working in the kitchen." A smile took over her entire being as she thought about Joe's tiny fingers against her skin and the feel of picking him up and putting him on her hip, laughing as she moved. "He has a laugh that can light up the world. You'd love it." There was a bright timbre in her voice that made her wish she hadn't spoken the last bit aloud.

Mike nodded and there was a strained silence between them. She cleared her throat, knowing he could outwait her in any uncomfortable situation; it was basically one of his many superpowers.

"He is staying with my friend Jessica right now."

"Ah," he said, nodding as he looked down at Joe's picture. "So, you are still living in Great Falls?"

She wasn't really living anywhere, but she didn't want to admit to him that her new job was keeping her from being the mom she had always wanted to be. Yet, survival and putting food on the table were forcing her to make choices she'd never thought she would have to make.

"Right now, I'm staying in Missoula. Doing some training and certification courses, then I'm going to head back up to the high-line."

He nodded, but she could read the many thoughts flickering out and over his features, and yet, he still said nothing. His silence was going to be the death of her.

"Jess has been really good with him. She is such a good godmother."

"I bet," he said, his words filled with a pain that spilled over and poured straight to her core.

"If you want, you could come and meet him. You are welcome anytime."

A smile stretched over his lips, but there was a tiredness in his eyes. "I'd love that. To meet him, that is. When works for you?"

Oh, she had walked right into that. Of course, he would want to see their son this very minute. If she had been in his position, she would have wanted the same thing. Yet she couldn't drop everything and make the three-hour trip to Great Falls, spend the night, and then make the same trip back.

Her bosses wouldn't allow her to just arbitrarily take time off.

Then again, this could be turned into a positive. If anything, this was the perfect opportunity to bring her and Mike closer; and maybe she could get him to open up to her a little bit. She could see if she could mine some more information about Rockwood for her team at the DTRA—the Defense Threat Reduction Agency, a division of the Pentagon's Defense Advanced Research Projects Agency, also known as DARPA.

She would have to make a few phone calls, but maybe her boss would go along with this idea. Heck, she could even play it off like this had been her plan all along. Though she couldn't have predicted this any more than she could predict the nature of the wind. Just when she thought she understood the man she had once promised her future to, he would swirl away and carry her dreams off with him.

"If you wanted, I have to button a few things and then head up in a couple of days. You can follow me up, or whatever."

His brows rose, like he was surprised she would suggest they take separate cars for the long drive. He shouldn't have been. As much as she wanted to ply him for information about their teams' common enemy, the last thing she wanted was for them to be in such close proximity without a clearly defined exit. She needed to be careful around him; he always had a way of pulling her back in even when everything inside her shouted for her to stay away. Come hell or high water, this time she was going to listen to the little voice that told her to be wary when it came to any kind of relationship with this man—even a relationship of convenience.

"I have to work," he said, looking back in the direction of the chalet where the reception was now in full swing.

Okay, so maybe he didn't need to see his son just this minute. Work, once again, came first.

Even from where she stood, she could make out the sounds of someone making a speech and a round of applause.

That should have been their moment. And yet here they were, once again, standing so close to happiness that they could almost taste it, but still a world apart. She was fated to starve in a world filled with tasty morsels of happiness. Ah, the irony.

"If you wanted, I could go in there and talk to whomever I needed to talk to. Who's your team leader? I bet if I explain the circumstances, some allowances can be made."

He gave her a surprised look, like he thought she was calling his bluff in some way. "Do you really want to go in there?" He nudged his chin in the direction of the party.

Anywhere had to be better than standing there, alone with him and forced to face their uncomfortable reality.

"I could use some chicken or fish." She patted her belly. The action was oddly familiar and, as she moved, he smiled.

"When aren't you hungry?" Mike chuckled.

Right after a breakup, she thought, but she didn't dare say the words aloud. She simply walked past him and toward the reception.

There were two seats in the corner, and for once she had wished there'd been assigned tables so she wouldn't have been forced to sit next to him.

Guests enjoyed the buffet, and the entire simple and pioneer-style wedding spoke of Troy. Kate must have been just like the man she married, and the realization made her instantly like the woman. Summer had always loved the entire Spade family, even AJ, who, as the family patriarch, always seemed to have a spine welded out of steel.

AJ was sitting at Troy's side, the only groomsman in the wedding party. Kate's sister was sitting beside her, wearing a blue dress that looked as beautiful with its A-line waist as it was comfortable. Yep, Summer definitely liked her; this woman that could have been her sister-in-law if only Summer had played her cards right. Summer should have known that getting married was the one thing that Mike feared above anything else.

He had always talked about how much he hated the entire institution and the symbolic ownership that came with the arrangement. Ownership was slavery and, regardless of who owned whom, freedom was something he would forever lay down his life to protect.

And while he had remained free—thanks to his actions—her heart would never be freely given again. It would always be chained to the past.

They moved through the buffet line, putting together their plates of food, and they made small talk as they went to the table. Servers came around with drinks and after she'd had a beer and he'd had two, the conversation between them started to become a little looser, easier as they slipped back into their old ways.

As they talked, the world around them slowly began to disappear. More and more people moved to the dance floor as the DJ played the worst and best of all wedding songs. Right now, the chicken dance was blaring and even the older folks were out on the cedar floor, flapping their arms like makeshift wings.

"You want to dance?" Mike asked, motioning toward the craziness on display in front of them.

She didn't answer right away; instead she watched Troy, who was laughing as he waddled around his bride like a teetering bird. Oh, it was going to be a long, drunken night. Under no circumstances could she fall into some old habits…habits that led her toward the bedroom with Mike.

He was off-limits. He'd hurt her too bad.

And yet, as he slipped his hand around hers and helped her to her feet and then to the dance floor, his touch was like a salve on the burn of their past.

Chapter Three

In a million years, Mike would have never thought his life would make a complete about-face in just a matter of hours.

The morning after the wedding, he walked down the hallway that led to his bedroom at the Widow Maker Ranch, STEALTH's headquarters, and he peered through the crack in the door. Summer was stretched out across his bed as if she owned the place. Her dark hair was haloed around her head and her arms were up, giving her a look as if she was floating in a pool of water.

He had always loved to watch her sleep. She was serene and, for once in her life, she looked at peace with the world around her.

With Joe in the picture now, he couldn't help but wonder when was the last time she had actually had a good night's sleep.

Learning about Joe had been a gut punch. He wanted to be angry at her for not telling him sooner about the baby, but he couldn't be...not when he thought of all the phone calls he had gotten from her, phone calls he had sent straight to voice mail. This wasn't her fault. He was the jerk, the weaker one, because he couldn't face her.

This was on him. And now he was going to have to make things right. At the very least, he would try.

He had already missed seeing the ultrasound and hearing the baby's heartbeat for the first time. He had missed holding Summer's hand while she went to her prenatal appointments and learned about the sex of the baby. He had missed watching his son come into the world and take his first breath. More, he had missed supporting the woman he had once pledged his life.

Though things had gone well between them last night. They had spent the night dancing and laughing during wedding—his cousin Savannah had been even more wild than he'd anticipated, getting up on the wedding party's table at one point—but the night had ended with him pouring Summer into his bed and her whispering a series of simple words that he would never forget. "I'll never forgive you. You left me... *Us.*"

No doubt, she wouldn't recall what she had told him, but he would. Beer had been the truth serum that had unlocked what had been hidden in her heart.

If he had a choice, he would vow to never leave her adrift again. No matter what she or Joe needed, he would provide it; all while keeping his heart out of the mix. Old feelings would complicate things, open wounds. If he was going to be able to stay in their lives, he couldn't risk losing them for any reason—and especially one as selfish as love.

Summer shifted in the bed and looked over in his direction through a squinted eye. "How long have you been there?" she asked, her voice raspy from sleep.

So much for being stealthy. He opened up the door a tiny bit more. "I was just walking by, thought I'd check in on you. Need anything? Water? Pain meds?"

She groaned slightly as she stretched and must have done a mental inventory of what exactly had gone on last night. "I'd ask if we...*you know*...but—"

"You know my hard pass on any woman who isn't in control. And last night, you were well out of control." He sent her a soft, understanding smile. "Besides, you made it abundantly clear you were not interested in me—or any man *until the end of time*." He made air quotes as he recited her words back to her.

She shoved her face into the pillow, not bothering to deny her boycott of relationships.

Oddly enough, he found the idea of her not dating anyone—even him—reassuring. Though he didn't have a shot with her, ever, at least they could be alone together. Though, in all truth, she deserved to be happy and find love with a man who would treat her like the princess she was.

"See you in a few?" he asked, and when she nodded, he went downstairs for breakfast.

Twenty minutes later, she was fresh-faced after a shower. She walked into the kitchen, grabbed a cup of coffee and her keys and started outside. "Coming? It's a long drive to Great Falls," she said, not looking back at him.

"What?" he called after her. Last night she had said that it would take her a few days to get things lined up with her work, that she couldn't just drop everything and take him to see his son. And yet, she was now tearing out of the house like her feet were on fire.

Whatever, he wasn't going to look this gift horse in the mouth.

Luckily, his family and the rest of the crews were in the main house, or they would have had a ball ribbing him for Summer coming home with him. As it was, he was surprised he wasn't getting a slew of texts after the dancing and frivolity last night. Maybe they were all too hungover to be too full of snark this morning; regardless, it was only a matter of time until a few of them started asking questions. Especially after the conversation he'd had with Zoey Martin, their STEALTH boss, telling her that he was going to need a couple of weeks off so he could go meet his son.

Oh, that tidbit of information was going to sweep through the family like wildfire.

He really needed to stop going to weddings.

He stood and, grabbing his coat and a travel mug of coffee, he made his way outside after Summer. She was standing beside her car. "Do I want to know how we got home last night?" she asked, nudging her chin in the direction of his pickup.

"No worries, I went out this morning with AJ and we got your car. No drinking and driving." His hard pass on drunken anything ran the gamut.

"So, AJ knows I came back here…with you… And…" She gave a resigned sigh. "Crap."

"You know AJ, he isn't going to say anything to anyone," he said, walking over toward his truck.

"Where are you going?" Summer called after him.

"I thought you said we weren't going to drive together?" he asked, confused by her about-face.

"Saves gas if we just go together."

He had never known Summer to turn on a dime, but maybe she had changed more than even he could understand since the last time he had spoken with her. From what he'd been told, motherhood changed a person. In the few hours since he'd found out he was a father, he could feel himself changing too. Suddenly, his life had taken on a new meaning and a fight he hadn't known he'd had within him—he would do anything for this boy whom he had never met. He would give his life. He couldn't even begin to imagine the transformation in Summer, one she'd gone through alone because of his failure to respond to her. His chest ached.

He would understand if she never forgave him for his missteps in life. He doubted he would ever forgive himself.

As he got into her car, he peeked into the back seat. He expected to find a car seat base or something to give her role as a mother away, but it was conspicuously devoid of any whispers of a child. He could understand it, though, her need to keep her personal life out of any sort of public view. In their line of work, private lives were weak points. That was part of the reason he had told himself he couldn't get married. If they had…they would both have been weakened. Others could have used their love against them.

The first hour of the drive, they sat in silence as he waited for her to start talking. They careened through the mountains, the timber flashing by as they rolled past pristine rivers and blue skies. The snow was gone from the mountains, but there was still an icy chill in the air. When the peaks finally gave way to rolling plains, it was as if the mask of the mountains had lifted and so had Summer's mood.

Finally, she looked over at him. "I told Jess we were coming, she said she would be around with Joe anytime. I think she is looking forward to getting a bit of a break. She has had him for the last week."

"I'm excited to meet him. Seriously." He wanted to ask

her how often she left Joe in Jessica's care, but he didn't want to come off sounding judgmental in any way, so he remained quiet. Tension reverberated through the air as it was; he didn't need to add more. "And I'm glad Jess has been so great."

"I'm glad she is so willing to help me out. I have come to really understand the adage that it takes a village to raise a child."

"Well, I hope you know that I'm more than happy to help in any way I can. I want to be a part of your support system. Money, housing…whatever."

She gave him a sidelong glance, like she was looking for the truth in his words.

"I mean it," he repeated. "And I'm not going to say it again, but I want you to know that I will always be sorry for how things played out between us."

She raised her hand, silencing him. "Let's not talk about it. What happened… Not anymore… We have more pressing things to deal with and if we go there, ever… well, it's not good for either one of us."

He nodded, agreeing. There was no fixing the past. "Here's to moving forward." He raised his coffee mug in salute.

She smiled, and the simple action lifted the heaviness that had blanketed him. Maybe there was some kind of hope for a budding friendship, after all.

Twenty miles and a pit stop later, she let him take over driving. She stared out the window as he drove the straight, long road that led to the north. He'd always hated this drive. Many people thought of the rolling prairie as beautiful in its languid hills and lolling grains, but he found it monotonous. The only thing that changed was the crops. Though, maybe it wasn't the prairie that was at fault; maybe he had too many mountainous ridges and sharp crags around his soul.

Regardless of where he was in Montana, at least he was in the state he called home. These roads, these mountains, hills and valleys were where he wanted to be forever. He'd spent far too many days overseas and in foreign lands longing for this place to take it for granted.

"Do you miss it?" she asked.

"Huh? What?"

"Now that you are working in surveillance, do you miss your old job gunning down bad guys?" She was staring at him.

"I forgot how well you can read my thoughts." He chuckled, trying to dispel some of the pressure of her question.

"It's in your face. You always get that look when you're thinking about the Sandbox, it's like you're a million miles away."

He pinched his lips as he nodded. "I always thought I had a good poker face."

"Maybe you do, but you will never have one when it comes to me."

And that right there was one of the reasons he had forgotten—until now—that he had fallen in love with her. She seemed to see him in a way that no one else in the world ever would.

"Do you like the work you are doing with STEALTH?" she asked.

"Yeah, you know me. I'm happier working in the shadows, and the team lets me do that."

She laughed. "I hear you there. Lately, I've been working more in the open and I have to say that I miss the old days when I worked more behind a desk."

"So, you don't like your new job?"

She shrugged. "It's fine. But they are asking things of me that I'm not loving."

He didn't dare to question her about what in her job she didn't enjoy. Those kinds of conversations, in their lines of work, were places they could never go.

"I heard about the shooting at ConFlux. I'm glad you made it out unscathed. Did they ever find the shooter?"

He glanced over at her, surprised that she would press anything work-related. "We got as far as we could with the information we had. As far as I know, the feds are still digging into that one. And us talking about my job? I'm done. I told you before, this isn't something I'm going to open up about, especially when we don't even play for the same teams." He tried to ignore the way his hackles rose. Summer was someone he could trust and yet his professional instincts kept him silent on any details related to STEALTH jobs.

She huffed. "And I told you that we're playing for the same team."

He opened his mouth to challenge her, but she didn't pause long enough.

"But I respect your need for privacy. If I was your boss, I would be proud of you for your hard line on this. You are the kind of employee I strive to be."

Did that mean she had secrets she wanted to tell him? Was there something she needed help with, but was too afraid to ask?

"Are you okay, Summer? Safe?" Sometimes he hated the way they had to speak in the nuanced code that came with their lifestyle.

Her hands tightened into balls in her lap; he'd stumbled onto something. But what?

She chewed on her lip, but she didn't respond.

Silence rolled by along with the miles until the grain silos and hotels marking the Great Falls skyline came into view. Pointing to the upcoming exit, she gave him a few simple directions toward Jess's house. The home was a simple box-style, as if built in the 1950s when resources were limited and people only built exactly what they could pay for out of pocket and with little residual expense.

As he pulled to a stop, Summer finally turned to him. "Mike, I won't compromise you or your job, but I could use your help."

He would give her anything. There was so much he needed to make up for. But he could never compromise his teams—not even for her. And sometimes even letting out a small seemingly inconsequential bit of info could put a colleague in jeopardy.

Yet maybe there was something he could do to help, something he was sure wouldn't put a single life in peril. "What, exactly, do you need?"

"I need to find out what you know about Rockwood."

"Why?"

She shook her head, refusing to give him more. "If I tell you, I'm as good as dead."

His hackles rose even more. "If you don't tell me exactly what the hell is going on, there is nothing I can do to help you. You can't give me half-truths. It's all or nothing, Summer."

The front door of the little thrifty-looking house opened. Jessica stepped out, her blond hair whipping around her face as she lifted the little boy's chunky arm and helped him to wave at them.

He was upset with Summer, but as soon as he saw the

sweet, cherubic cheeks of the little blond boy in Jessica's arms, he forgot about everything but the baby. This boy, this little ball of chunk.

He stepped out of the car, slipping the keys in his pocket as he rushed toward the front steps. Summer exited the vehicle and he could make out the sound of her laughing softly behind him.

Walking up the sidewalk to his son, he could feel a single tear slip down his cheek.

As he approached, the little boy smiled and wiggled in Jessica's arms. He thrust out his arms, surprising Mike in the way he motioned for him, a stranger.

Jessica sent him a warm smile as she lifted Joe up and handed the baby over.

As he took him, he smiled through the tears that streaked his face.

This. This moment was what his entire life had led up to.

This angel was his now, and forever more, his everything.

Chapter Four

Watching him with their son drew memories to the front of Summer's mind, memories she had believed long forgotten. As Joe touched his face and giggled, then coyly tucked his face in Mike's neck, the simple innocent action reminded Summer of the first time Mike had made her laugh. She couldn't remember the exact joke—some dad joke about bees—but she could still remember the flames of love that had burned away her mask and exposed the real her.

She had thought herself capable of compartmentalizing love from work. And yet now, standing there and watching the two men who had brought so much joy to her life, she knew there was no such thing as compartmentalizing, not really. Sure, a person could shift attention and focus, stuffing away inconvenient feelings, but in life's quiet moments, those truths always returned... with more pain than any type of physical injury. Though she couldn't go back in time and make different choices, she could learn from them. And her greatest lesson to date? Love was a weakness.

Mike looked over his shoulder at her, his cheek damp. Had this man, this chiseled-from-granite man, really shed a tear?

Her weakness for him rippled through her like a piece had broken from his hard façade and dropped into the lake of her life.

Allergies. He had to be suffering from allergies.

"You didn't tell me he was so freaking cute." He glanced back at the boy. "He has your eyes."

"And your nose," she said, walking over and giving Joe a little bop to the round tip.

He giggled as she smiled down at him, making funny faces and blowing raspberries.

Mike looked up at Jessica. "It's nice to see you. Been a long time."

Even though she had warned her friend that Mike would be coming with her to Great Falls to meet his son, Jess looked at Summer like she wasn't entirely sure how she should respond to the interloper on her doorstep. Summer gave her a faint nod, hoping it would show her that this was all okay, this was what needed to happen for everything to fall into place.

Jess composed herself and plastered a smile on her lips as she moved her gaze to Mike. "I'm glad you are here. Joe has been waiting to meet you."

There was a pained expression on Mike's face, as though Jess's words were some sort of razor wire that had wrapped around him, piercing him with each syllabic burst.

"I would have come sooner, but…well, you know…" He cleared his throat.

"Let's not worry about the past," Summer said, walking by him and waving off his discomfort like it wasn't going to haunt him.

She didn't need a reminder of the pain that would always rest between them.

Jess followed her in, letting Mike stand alone with the boy for a moment before walking into the house behind them.

"Want some coffee? Tea?" Jess asked, giving Summer a pointed look.

Jess wanted to meet with her alone in the kitchen. Sometimes she hated having a friend who could speak through only a glance.

"I'd take a glass of water, you know me…nothing too fancy." Mike smiled, but he didn't look away from Joe.

There was no doubt Mike was just as much in love with his son as she was.

Jessica's living room looked like something off Pinterest with its cute farmhouse-chic décor and earthy tones. Everything was in its place, not even a speck of dust on a single surface. For a woman who spent her days working as an analyst for the FBI, Jessica always impressed Summer with her ability to keep things spotless as well as lend a helping hand with Joe. Summer could barely keep up with her job in intel, let alone be perfect in every other facet of her life.

The kitchen was an extension of the rest of the pristine house; even the flour container was perfectly centered and devoid of any residue.

One day, maybe, she would be able to keep a house like that of her friend. Then again, she could barely keep her car clean.

"Thanks for watching Joe. I hope he was good for you." Summer walked to the cupboard and pulled out a bottle and a can of formula. "Did you have enough of everything while I was gone?"

Jessica nodded. "You know Joe, all he wants to do is make everyone smile around him. And I had more than enough of everything, no worries. You done training? It go well?"

For a split second, Summer wondered what *it* Jessica was talking about—her meetings for work or her seeing Mike. Of all the possible meanings, she chose the one that would be the least uncomfortable to talk about.

"Work was good. We weren't buttoned up, but after I talked to the higher-ups, they decided I needed to handle things here and waved me through."

No doubt, given Jess's work in acronyms, she knew there was far more about Summer's work in Missoula than she was telling her—thankfully, Jess didn't press for answers.

Ah, it was great to have a friend who just *got it*.

Jess nodded, like she could hear all the things Summer wasn't saying. "So, we gonna talk about the big, burly elephant who is standing in the middle of my living room?"

"I would call him a jackass, but if you want to talk about him…ask away."

Jess laughed, grabbing the pitcher from the fridge and setting it out to get him a glass of water. "How did it go?"

"Fine. Better than expected."

Jessica nodded. "Did you guys discuss a parenting plan? Does he want to get back together?"

"Geez, Jess. He's only known about Joe for a matter of hours. Don't you think you're getting a little ahead of yourself?"

Jess turned and faced her. "You know you have thought through all of these things, probably a thousand times faster and more often than I have. You have to have some kind of idea how he is going to work through all of this. You know him."

Correction, she *had* known him. Or rather, she had

thought she had known him. And yet Mike always had a way of surprising her at the most inopportune times.

"I'm sure he is going to want to get some sort of parenting plan sorted out, but his life is generally even more all over the map than mine." Summer moved to the sink, filling the bottle with water and adding the powdered formula. Shaking it, she thought of his time in Syria, working with STEALTH. There were weeks in which she had not been able to hear his voice and had barely gotten more than a sentence or two in messages.

Though he was now working a different job for the company, it didn't mean he would be at home that much more. And how could a man who had no stability in his personal life be able to be a father?

It struck her that maybe that was the reason Mike had left her…maybe he had been right in his assessment of his life. Maybe he really wasn't able to be her everything—even if they loved one another. Hell, what if he had been right?

If that were true, perhaps it had been a mistake to tell him about Joe. This would put a whole hell of a lot more pressure on him—and her. He had crumpled under the possibility of being a husband. How would he respond when it came to feeling the burden of being a father?

There was a wail as Joe's cry filled the air.

What if she was making a huge mistake? This telling him about Joe and bringing him here without their thinking about all the potential consequences for both of them… All of it… She should have stayed silent, stayed home, stayed in the shadows.

Why did doing the right thing have to feel so wrong? It would have been so much easier to just let things remain as they had been, her blaming him for leaving her and their son, and then resenting him for the mistakes he hadn't known he had made.

Then again, telling him wasn't entirely about him.

She would be lying if she tried to say that it was all about Joe, either.

This was all too much about her and her needs, both personal and professional.

She needed answers for work and she needed to get the cloud of secrets out of her head. Now that the truth of Joe was out in the open, she didn't have to be caught up in the whirlwind of questions anymore. Now they could deal with the hurricane as it came.

Joe's crying intensified and, shaking the bottle, she walked out to the living room. "You want to feed him? I bet he is just hungry." Mike looked even more upset than Joe did, even with his little chubby red cheeks and tears. In fact, Mike's face was so pinched and tense that it made her wonder if he had somehow hurt himself in the few moments she had been in the kitchen.

"Are you okay?" she asked, not waiting for him to answer.

"I'm fine. Just hand me that bottle," he said, shoving out his hand like the bottle was the pin that could be put back into the grenade.

She bit back a chuckle as she gave him the bottle.

When Mike stuck it in Joe's mouth, the baby started to suckle so hard that there were audible gulps as he swallowed the milk. Though she was aware such a greedy feeding would lead to a gassy tummy, she still loved that sound. It was as if it thrummed some primal motherly chord, the music of fulfilling her baby's needs and helping him to grow. The timbre of success and pride. Making it even better was that it was coming from her baby in his father's arms.

Their family was whole. Their village was strong.

Instinct screamed that this, this was what Joe needed.

And yet, logically, that wasn't true. They had been doing fine on their own. She was a strong, independent woman.

She readjusted her footing, straightening her back with pride and consternation.

Mike loved this baby, but if he walked out and left them, she would be fine. *They* would be fine. The world would keep on going with or without him.

"Here, why don't you let me take him?" she asked, moving to take the baby.

"No, I got him. Really," Mike said, moving Joe away from her.

She had to check the anger that boiled up within her. Maybe she was being irrational and thinking too much; getting upset with him for this simple action would only lead to a fight. That wasn't what any of them needed. Not now, not ever. At least, not really.

What she needed was an ally, a friend, and a father. He could be all of those things; she would just need to check herself and allow him to be them.

This was going to be so much harder than she had ever imagined.

She dropped her arms to her sides.

Let him do this, she thought. *Let him be Joe's father.*

There was no going back on the choices either one of them had made; he had chosen to leave and she had chosen to bring him back into their lives. The only option was for them to move forward together in whatever way they needed to be for Joe to have the support systems and family that would bring him comfort and success as he grew up.

Joe needed this.

And truth be told, so did she. She *needed* them to be a family.

Chapter Five

Joe was nestled into the car seat in the back as they drove to Summer's apartment. The only sound was of the road and the occasional happy squeaks of the baby playing. Mike could get used to that.

"If you want, I can put you up in a hotel. We could both stay there." Summer shifted uncomfortably in her seat as she drove.

"You don't want me at your place?"

"Well… It's not that, it's just…well, it's not exactly put together right now." She sounded nervous, but he couldn't tell if it was because they were going to be staying another night so close to one another or if it was actually because of the state of her place.

"You know I've spent more than my fair share of nights in Connexes with dozens of other dudes. My standards for sleep and comfort are pretty low."

She laughed, releasing some of the tension. "You have me there."

"Besides," he continued, "I have no room to judge you for your accommodations. I'm the one holing up in my company's ranch. I don't even have an apartment to call my own."

"You were never one to be strapped down."

There was a needle in her voice and it made him wonder if she had meant for it to be there or if it had just been a convenient jab, one she couldn't miss the chance for taking.

"You know my world. Any day could be my last."

"Mmm-hmm," she said, a dark expression settling on her face like a shadow. "I always hated when you talked like that."

If he wasn't careful, this could lead to an argument. They had been down this road so many times. Yet he couldn't just let her comment go without some sort of response. If he did, she would get to the fight all by herself, anyway.

"You know how it can be." He paused. "Luckily, this new job with STEALTH has me mostly working in the States. For now, at the very least." Though he had meant it to assuage some of the anger and perhaps trepidation she was feeling, the look on her face didn't change. Her eyes were still dark and solidly focused on the road.

She was definitely gearing up for combat. He couldn't let things go in that direction.

"I think it's great that you are working with STRIKE. I've heard good things."

She chuffed, but *that* look disappeared. It was replaced by something more stoic, less readable. "They are a good company. They have good goals at heart, but I'm sure things are a bit different than they are at STEALTH. STRIKE was very much about the bottom line."

"It sounds like there is something there, something you are resenting."

She jerked, looking over at him. Clearly, he'd struck a nerve.

"That's not what I was saying at all. I'm just saying

they aren't a family-run company. STRIKE is all about measurable and marketable achievement."

"And they have you feeling pressured?" he pressed.

Her hands tightened on the steering wheel and her jaw clenched. "If you don't want to tell me anything about Rockwood, that's fine. But I'm not going to sit here and allow you to grill me."

Yep, she was definitely looking for a fight. But why? What was she hiding? What was she hoping to get him to do for her?

"Look, Summer, I don't want to argue with you. I want us to get along, especially now that Joe is in the picture," he said, glancing back at the baby, though all he could see was the back of the car seat.

She sucked in a long breath. "I wasn't looking for a fight."

"You and I both know how the other communicates, we've been together way too long to try to lie to one another. I mean, we *were* together." He cleared his throat, wishing he hadn't made the stupid misstep. "Something is wrong, and when there was something wrong, you always took it out on me. You made me jump through hoops in an attempt to break down your walls before you could just open up and tell me what it was that was bothering you in the first place. We've played this game a thousand times."

"Are you implying that I'm trying to manipulate you?" she countered.

He had to hold back the urge to roll his eyes. "That's not what I'm saying at all. I think you have just learned a way, albeit an unhealthy one, to get a man—me—to get you to open up. You obviously had to get to this point for a reason. Maybe it was my fault, or maybe it was something left over from something else in your life. All I'm saying is that I wish we could just openly talk to each other without fighting. It would save time and a whole hell of a lot of unnecessarily hurt feelings."

Her jaw clenched even tighter.

Sometimes he really needed to learn when to shut the hell up. "Don't be offended. That's not what I'm going for here, I just…"

What in the hell am I trying to say? Damn it. This was going so wrong.

"I just want to help you," he sighed.

"Mmm-hmm," she grumbled.

Say something. Give me a clue that I'm forgiven. That I wasn't wrong in saying what needed to be said, even if it sucked. It sucked for both of us. Tell me there is hope… hope for a friendship. I—no, we—need each other more than ever.

She pulled her car to a stop in front of an apartment complex. It was three floors, and people were coming and going around them. As he moved to unbuckle, she stopped him with the touch of her hand to his chest. "Wait." She stared out the window to her left. "Damn it."

"What? What's wrong?"

"Er," she said, biting her cheek, "my ex is here."

"*Here?* As in the parking lot? In the building? In your apartment? Explain." His fingers twitched toward the Glock always tucked into his waistband.

"Whoa there, Quick Draw McGraw, I said it was my ex, not the lead terrorist on an international watch list." She sent him a sexy half smile, one that had the power to make him almost forget his damned name.

Ex, terrorist, what difference was there when it came to people screwing with his personal life? He should have assumed she'd dated, but somehow, especially after learning about Joe, he'd figured she'd been alone. That was crazy, though. She was a beautiful, smart woman. Even if she'd not been interested in being a fish in the dating sea, some eager man would have tried to reel her in.

He had so many questions about the man, but he barely knew where or how to start asking about everything he wanted to know. So he went with the most obvious. "Are you guys still seeing one another? You know, late-night hookups or whatever?"

"No." She laughed, the sound high and scoffing. "Besides, would you really want to know?"

So he was yet to be forgiven for his saying the truth. Some things between them would never change. As it was, there was no chance they were ever going to be anything other than two single parents working to raise one single child.

How had his life gotten so screwed up in just a matter of hours?

"His name is Ben." She paused, waiting to be barraged by questions.

Mike remained silent out of fear that whatever he said would later be used against him in the Summer Daniels court. He had never liked a single dude named Ben, and apparently that trend wasn't going to come to an end anytime soon.

"He says he's an engineer for a petroleum company out of the North Dakota oil fields."

So, this Ben was rich, probably hot, and probably a total ass.

Then again, what should it have mattered to him? So what if she had moved on and started dating again? Just because Mike hadn't, it didn't mean that she would follow the same trajectory. Besides, it wasn't like they would be getting back together. He and Summer could barely have a civil conversation, let alone attempt to build a future together.

"If you guys aren't still hooking up, why would your ex be here unannounced?"

She chewed at the inside of her cheek. "He isn't exactly a nice guy. I thought he was great at first, he was so helpful and kind about Joe, and then… I don't know. Something shifted and he became this possessive mandemon. I made him leave."

"Is he harassing you?"

She sighed. "I wouldn't call it harassment exactly. He is definitely not taking the breakup well, and he doesn't want to let things go between us, but he usually respects my boundaries. And then sometimes he just shows up like this. Usually, he is making some kind of grand gesture in hopes that I will take him back."

"Then that is not him respecting your boundaries. If anything, it's him pressing against them and hoping you will relent, loosen up what lines you've drawn with him. He is trying to wear you down."

She rolled her eyes, the motion somewhat juvenile and in direct contrast to the woman he knew. That meant one thing: she knew he was right and didn't want to admit it aloud in front of him. Of course she was smart enough to know exactly what was happening in her personal life, even if she didn't want to face the truth.

"No matter what Ben thinks, he is not going to be allowed back into my life. At least, not in any kind of meaningful way." She paused. "And you're wrong. I don't think he wants me back, well, at least not *just* me. I think he liked the little family unit we had going for a while.

He loved Joe and the patriarchal role he got to have in our lives."

Though Mike knew it wasn't her intention to stab him square in his heart, her words still landed a blow. Here was a man, Ben, who was fighting to have what Mike himself should have been fighting for...what he *was* trying to fight for.

But which battle was harder—the one to garner a place in Joe's and Summer's lives, or the one in his heart?

All he wanted to do right now was to get Ben out of the picture. If that meant him charging over to Ben's car and giving him a piece of his mind, and likely a quick kick to the ass, so be it. As long as it meant he was out of his way. There were a lot of battles he could fight, some of which he could win, but he didn't think he could also take on this fight and come out of this looking like a superhero.

He'd have to be careful. He didn't want to step on Summer's toes, but at the same time he wanted her to know he would do whatever it took to make her happy.

"If you want, I'd be more than willing to have a chat with him. I could make it clear to him that you no longer want him showing up at your place."

She sent him a look that made Mike question the validity of his offer. Maybe he'd already overstepped his bounds when it came to the other dude. He was never going to get anything right when it came to Summer.

"I appreciate the offer, but in case you forgot, I have never been one of those women who want others to fight their battles for them." She put her hand down on the door handle, readying to step out.

He raised his hands in surrender. "I...just... Fine. Whatever."

This whole thing? It was going to be impossible.

There was a knock on the trunk of her car and, looking back, Mike saw that there was a tall, Mack-truck-size guy staring daggers at him.

If this was her ex, it was no wonder she hadn't wanted him to go have a talk. Mike wasn't a small man by any means; he had even prided himself on being thick with muscle…not bodybuilder thick, but still stacked. And yet, if this thing came to blows, not even Mike was sure that he would win. This dude must have been the kind who lifted at least twice a day, seven days a week.

Yep. He had been right. The guy was an ass.

Or maybe, if Mike was being completely honest with himself, maybe there was a dash of inadequacy peppered through his psyche.

The man walked up to Summer's side of the car. She opened the door in a hurry and jumped out, slamming the door behind her. Maybe she was afraid Mike would lose the fight too.

The guy kept moving, so Summer couldn't block him from seeing him, calculated actions that indicated the dude wasn't as stupid as Mike had initially assumed. Though he probably couldn't take him at fists, he did have enough street skills to bring the man to his knees.

Though Summer had closed the car door behind her, Mike tried not to listen to their conversation, though it was barely muffled through the thin glass of the car's windows. He turned around and faced the back of the car seat where Joe was sucking away on a pacifier.

"Hi, little guy," he said, smiling at him in the mirror attached to the headrest of the back seat.

Joe smiled up at him, the pacifier teetering at the edge of his mouth.

"We are going to play football when you get bigger. Would you like that?" he asked, his voice high and pleasing.

Joe gurgled in response. The sound made him chuckle. But as the noise escaped him, Summer yelled, "No! That is crap. You have no business. How dare you!"

The teetering blue pacifier dropped from Joe's lips and, at the sound of his mother's angry voice, tears started to well in the baby's eyes. His lip quivered. A piercing wail filled the air.

Mike unbuckled his seat belt, turned fully around and unstrapped the baby. "It's okay, little guy. They are just doing adult stuff. I don't like it, either," he cooed, trying to comfort his son.

If this was how Summer and her ex communicated with one another, it was no wonder they hadn't lasted. Though she and Mike had had their fair share of problems when they had been together, they had never fought like that. They had both respected each other enough not to let their disagreements turn into screaming matches.

He scooped Joe into his arms and started to gently rock back and forth with him as he hummed "Two Little Blackbirds." Joe's cries started to subside, but he still whimpered as his mother and Ben stood outside the car and yelled.

Mike'd never seen Summer like that before, that angry or that loud. Even when she had been royally pissed with him, she had stormed away. Had she changed since they had broken up? Had he turned her into this raging woman?

Ben called Summer a word that didn't bear repeating. That was it. That was the final straw.

He stepped out of the car, Joe perched on his hip as he walked around to the driver's side. "Look, I know there is something going on here, and frankly I don't care. But what I do care about is that you are having a screaming match out in the middle of the parking lot in front of your neighbors and my son. If you guys can't control yourselves, then you need to go inside or put a pin in this until you both come to your senses and decide to act like adults."

Ben stared daggers at him. "And who the hell do you think you are that you think you can come out here and talk to me like this?"

Mike handed Joe off to Summer. "First of all, I'm Joe's father. The name's Mike. And, second of all, if you are looking for a fight, I'm more than happy to oblige. At least you would be picking one with someone who stands a chance. Or do you just face off with women?"

Ben moved his head side to side as though popping his neck in preparation for a rumble.

Oh yeah, Mike was definitely going to get his butt kicked, but if it meant taking the pressure off of Summer, at least it was for a good reason.

"Look, Ben, I've heard all about you and what a crappy dude you were to Summer. So, I don't know how you think you can stand there and talk to me like you have some kind of moral high ground. You are the lowest piece of garbage—"

Summer stepped between them. "Stop. You two need to stop."

Two apartments down, a man opened his front door and stepped outside.

They were definitely drawing all kinds of the wrong attention.

"Look, let's go to my place. We can all talk and—"

"There is no way that I'm going to walk into an apartment with this jerk," Ben said, thrusting his thumb in Mike's direction.

Yeah, he certainly felt like a jerk right now for stepping into the middle of Summer's personal relationship, but then again, he wasn't the one using expletives to talk about Summer. The man didn't have any kind of room to judge him; at least he knew how to treat women.

"Yeah, you're right, Ben, if we both walk into that apartment, only one of us will walk out."

Ben laughed, the sound low and dangerous. "I know you think you are some kind of badass, that you kill people for a living and get away with it. But I've got your number. I know exactly who you are and what you are actually capable of."

Summer talking about Mike to anyone, especially another one of her lovers, felt like a huge slap in his face. He had always thought that, given the nature of his work and the promises they had made to one another, she would never divulge any of the information that he had shared with her about him or what he did. He was supposed to be nothing more than a shadow in her life, a faceless someone from her past—as far as other men were concerned. And yet it seemed as though she had compromised his safety. But that was a fight he was going to have to shelve for now.

Mike smiled, matching Ben's malice. "That's good. Then I don't need to tell you how serious I am, and how much I mean that if I ever see you again, or if you are ever around my son or Summer, I will hunt you down."

"I sure as hell know you don't know who I am, but I hope to hell you do know the woman you are trying to stick up for." Ben looked over at her and smirked. "She isn't the pristine little angel she pretends to be. She might as well be called Black Widow with as many men as she has killed when they walked out of her bed… It's a wonder you and I are even still alive."

Summer pulled a gun from behind her waistband and pointed it square at Ben's center mass. "Get the hell out of here, Ben, or you will be the next one I kill."

Chapter Six

Summer had not anticipated things going as they had, or she would have just kept on driving until they were back in Missoula. Now, she had a whole hell of a lot of explaining to do.

They watched as Ben got into his car and squealed his tires as he pulled out of the apartment complex's parking lot.

She couldn't blame him for being pissed off with her; she hadn't wanted to get into a yelling match, either. That was always the last tool in her arsenal…well, that and her Glock. She slipped the subcompact back into the holster nestled into the crook of her stomach just over her appendix.

"Please tell me that was the one and only time you have ever pulled a gun on someone you didn't intend on shooting." Mike took Joe back from her, like her pulling a gun on the man who had threatened to do her harm in some way made her a delinquent parent.

"If he didn't leave, who said I wasn't going to shoot him? You don't know what Ben is capable of."

"No, but he seemed to know exactly what you are capable of…and *me* for that matter." Mike hesitated, but she had already heard the hurt in his voice. "How does he know about me? About my past? Does he know who I work for? What I do?"

She stared at her feet. "I never told Ben what you did. He just sort of figured it out over time. He doesn't know who you work for or what you do…at least not really. He just assumed."

"And you didn't bother to tell him not to assume certain things?" Mike countered. "You know that his knowing severely compromises me. Who in the hell else knows who I am and what I do?" As he spoke, his words came faster and faster as the rage burned through him. "And now he knows what I look like, he could pick me out of a lineup. Do you want him…do you want *me*…to end up dead?"

"You know I would never intentionally put you in danger, ever. Your secrets have always been and will always be safe with me. I didn't tell him anything. He just wanted to get a rise out of you. Please. Mike, believe me." Her chest clenched as she thought about the times she should have stopped Ben from ever even broaching the subject about her exes. Yet, Ben had always been adamant in comparing himself to all the others she had once had in her life.

Keeping him at arm's length while she had been investigating him and his job at Rockwood had forced her to make far too many compromises when it came to her own well-being. Being a spy and infiltrating the Rockwood network to find out who had been stealing secrets had been more of a challenge than she could have ever expected. It was why she had broken things off with Ben and then requested more training before she was thrown too deeply back into the Rockwood—or any—clandestine investigation.

It was hard to believe her past, present and future were all colliding into this one epic mess.

She didn't know what to say or to do to make things right; avoidance seemed like her only option. So she smiled, the action forced, but it was the only appeasement she knew would work in a moment like this. "You want to come in and see my place? It's not much, but it is mine." There was a touch of sultry familiarity in her voice.

Mike sighed, as though he knew exactly what she was doing to get him to ignore the awkwardness between them.

Without waiting for him to speak, she walked to her door and let them in. As he made his way into her box-filled den with its one leather recliner and a baby swing, she was overcome with embarrassment. This place was a far cry from her Barbie dream house, but after the breakup it was all she could find. Great Falls had some nice apartments, but mostly they had military families and officers from nearby Malmstrom Air Force Base as their long-term tenants.

Mike put Joe down and he sat upright for a moment, then he broke in to a mad-dash crawl toward a stuffed octopus near the swing.

"Dang. That kid is fast," Mike said with a laugh.

He could pretend not to notice the stains on the carpet and the dog scratches at the corner of the entryway all he wanted, but she knew what he had to be thinking.

"I don't plan on being here for long. I just need to figure things out at work and then we will get a real place. Ya know?"

"You don't need to worry about what I think about your place. I told you, I get it."

"Do you want something to drink?" she asked, pointing to the only chair in the place. "I'll go get you something. I think I have some…" She did a quick inventory of what she could possibly have in her fridge. If she remembered correctly, there may have been a beer, but only one.

"Water is fine." He looked toward her kitchen and had to have been noticing that the only thing on the counters was a bargain-basement toaster.

It was a harsh reality to see a person's makeshift life through the eyes of another. "You can tell I've become a bit of a minimalist." She laughed nervously as she walked to the kitchen, grabbed a glass and filled it from the tap.

"How long have you been living here?" Mike asked, sitting next to Joe on the floor and picking up the octopus. He tapped Joe's nose with one of the octopus's tentacles, making Joe gurgle and smile.

"Just a few months." Well, if a *few* meant about six.

"How long did you and Ben date after we broke up?"

She didn't know that exact date, either. Ever since the wedding had been called off and she had given birth to Joe, everything had been a whirl of well-baby checkups and trips to the store for baby supplies added into the jumble of trying to get her career moving in the right direction. Ben had been a stepping stone for her career, but she could hardly tell that to Mike.

"I don't know how long we were together, to be honest. I mean we were friends, then stayed together a lot, and he was great with Joe for the most part…"

"Does he really work for a petroleum company?" Mike prodded, the question coming from out of nowhere.

She gave him a befuddled look as her body clenched. "Why do you ask?"

"Don't you think it a bit odd that your boyfriend was

working out of North Dakota, but living dozens of hours away in a nowhere town at the edge of a military base best known for nuclear weapons?"

She had contemplated Ben's inane cover story more times than she had wanted to, but it was how he had always asked her to introduce him. "What about it? You know just as well as I do that most people can telecommute now."

"I agree. But you can't tell me that he moved to Great Falls because of the beauty of the place."

Great Falls was as nasty as Medusa's stare in the winter and hot, dry and unforgiving in the summer. It was flat and desolate, and the winds ripped through the plains all year 'round, but there was an austere, understated beauty to the place. It definitely wasn't a tropical paradise that drew in nature lovers, though. Problem number two with Ben's story. But it had been *his* story.

"You and I both know that, given the nature of our jobs, we tend to respect secrets." She wanted to tell him the truth, tell him who Ben really was, but now wasn't the time. It would only make this fight worse and threaten their safety.

"And yet you told him what I did."

So, he wasn't going to let it go. Odd that her palace didn't make him so gobsmacked that he forgot about their fight. She chuckled, the sound admittedly out of place and wrong in the tense world that rested between them. "I already told you, I didn't tell him anything."

"Have you lost your damned mind?"

Oh no, you don't. Her hackles rose as his inflammatory accusation drifted down like a spent ember.

"Excuse me?" she challenged, letting his words flitter

through his psyche so he could hear exactly how wrong they were before she chose to answer.

"I…" he started then said, "I didn't mean it like that. I just mean, I am surprised that you would let a man like Ben, one whose story doesn't quite fit, this close to Joe. You have always been the kind to ask too many questions, to make sure that everything lines up and is triple-checked. What happened?"

Again, did he really want to ask her that question? It seemed like he was asking her to rain fury down. And yet his words struck home. She *had* made a mistake, a huge mistake in letting Ben in their lives. But she had been doing her job, and sometimes the lines between personal and professional had to be blurred because of Joe's age and his intense needs.

"First, things between Ben and me were never what I would call serious." She took a quick breath, trying to check her anger before it flew from her lips. "You. Joe. Life. That is what happened to me. I don't know if you can tell or not," she said, motioning all around her apartment, "but I'm struggling a bit right now. I'm trying my hardest to do all the things and do them well, and when a man came into my life wanting virtually nothing but to be a source of love and kindness, I let down my guard and let him in. Can you blame me after all you put me through?"

The silence between them was broken only with the sounds of Joe talking gibberish to his toy.

"I think it's ridiculous that you think you can come in here and start judging me for the way I've conducted my life," she raged. "I had a plan. I had a man I loved in my life. I had my world figured out and I was preparing to run, to make this life everything I had ever dreamed of, and you pulled it all out from under my feet. You are the one who needs to answer for what life has become. Not me."

She was pretty sure she could see a red welt rising on his face where she had just slapped him with her words.

"I'm so, so sorry," Mike said, moving near enough that he could wipe a tear from the corner of her eye.

Damn it, why did she have to cry when she was angry?

She moved away from his touch, not letting him console her.

He had done this. He deserved to watch her fall apart in front of him. To bear witness to the ravaging effects of one decision…a decision she had not been able to make with him and yet that had had the power to strip her future away.

Screw him.

From the way he moved into her, she could tell that he wanted to pull her into his arms and console her. He'd always been so damned good at making her forget the pain, and yet she doubted his touch would work like it once had. After a person crushed a soul, they no longer held the power or tools to rebuild it.

She was the only one who could rebuild her life. And right now, that meant boxes where there should have been chairs and questions where there should have been answers. Mike was just going to have to deal with what she had done with her life, whether he liked it or not.

"I never thought—"

"Yeah, that's one of the truest statements you've ever made," she said, her words laced with venom.

His shoulders fell and he looked crestfallen. "You're right. I didn't think. I would have never asked you to marry me, I would have never dated you, if this is what

I thought would happen. I have only ever wanted what was best for you."

Though she was fuming with anger, she believed him. Mike wasn't a bad man. There was no way that he could have ever wanted to hurt her as he had, but that didn't make the pain any less real. It only meant that he was as clumsy and as ill suited to love as she was.

"You weren't the only person in the relationship. I chose you and wanted the best too."

And though this was a low point, she couldn't say she actually regretted falling in love with Mike. He had given her a beautiful baby boy and many hours of happy and blissful memories. And, oh, the way he had once been able to make her laugh.

"You were proof to me that I could really love," Mike said, sending her a soft look that made all the anger still pulsing through her seep through the tips of her toes and disappear into the ground.

It was that look and his unexpected moments of sweetness that had made her fall in love with him in the first place. He had so many facets to him and, standing here, looking at him, she was reminded of what a great man he was…and how much she missed having him in her life. And yet she couldn't let herself be swept up by him again. As sweet as Mike could be, he could become equally cold and hard.

He moved in closer to her, so close she could feel his breath against the skin of her face. Her heart thrashed in her chest, just as confused by all the emotions it was feeling as she was. The ancient Egyptians had believed the center of all thought was the heart; and in this moment, she could understand how an entire culture could believe such a thing. Her heart definitely had a mind of its own, one totally independent of the logical and rational thoughts that filled her brain.

He didn't love her and she didn't love him. At least, not like that, not like this moment, this closeness, seemed to indicate. Sure, she would love him as the father of her son and the man she had once promised her life to, but now it couldn't be that way. They could only love one another for the people they had become, people who were strangers to one another. He only knew her before the pain.

And yet, when he leaned in close and his lips brushed against hers, she didn't back away. The kiss started slow, gentle as a butterfly's wings' caress against her skin. Perhaps he was just as afraid of what was about to happen as she was, but yearning for her as she was for him.

Yearning. That was it. This wasn't love. This wasn't something so stupid. This was just her body needing his body. Nothing more. It was the familiar. *He* was the familiar.

She wrapped her arms around his neck and ran her fingers through the back of his shaggy hair. It was odd how, in a moment like this, she was reminded of how much she had loved his soft hair and the way it felt in her fingers while his lips pressed against hers. It was the conglomeration of sensations—the soft and the firm, the hot and the cold, and the push and the pull—that had always made this man so… So right.

She moaned into his mouth as his hungry kiss grew more voracious. He felt so good pressed against her, his body telling hers that he had missed her just as much as she had missed him.

Maybe they weren't really strangers, after all.

Maybe his leaving her had just been a stupid mistake.

She had made mistakes.

She could forgive him.

Yes.

Especially if he kept kissing her. His lips moved down her neck and his hand moved up beneath her shirt, finding its way under the cloth of her bra. He thumbed her nipple, making it harden and ache for the warm softness of his mouth.

And then Joe laughed, the sound bright and cheery.

The sound stopped the advance.

Mike pulled back and Summer readjusted her shirt, suddenly feeling like a teenager who had just been caught making out by a wayward parent.

Running her hand over her hair, it came to rest on her neck in the place where Mike had just been kissing her. Oh, and had he been kissing her.

Mike did a little sidestep and turned away from her to face Joe. He scooped him up in his arms and lifted him toward the ceiling, laughing as he moved. "You! You know how to ruin a moment, don't you?" He laughed. "You are definitely my kiddo, Mr. Man."

Joe giggled, arching his back like he was doing a baby version of Superman as Mike walked him around up in the air. "'It's a bird. It's a plane…'"

"It's mother nature's best form of birth control," she finished, laughing.

Mike lowered Joe onto his hip. He came over and gave her a long, soft kiss on the cheek. "Maybe we should have had a kid together a long time ago."

His words came as a surprise. So much so, she didn't know what to say.

Just yesterday she had thought that Mike was going to be furious with her, that he was never going to speak to her again after she told him about Joe. And now, here they were almost falling into the trap of being a happy family.

This…this was far too good to last. She had to tell him the truth before things went any further and she hurt him. If she told him now, he might still forgive her.

"Mike, I have to tell you something."

The joy that filled his face drifted away as he must have recognized the reserve in her tone. "What?"

"Promise me that you won't be angry with me if I tell you," she countered.

He frowned. "That is like asking someone to forgive you for a mistake you know you are about to make, and yet you don't stop."

Oh, this was going to be a mistake, no doubt. But some things had to be said, some truths had to be known. Without them, there were only false starts and empty promises.

If he was going to come back into their lives, he needed to come back fully aware of what that would mean for them all.

"You know I worked for STRIKE…" She paused.

"Yeah."

She hadn't meant that as a question, but she was glad for the moment to collect her thoughts. "Well, things go a little deeper than that." She looked down at her hands.

But did she really need to feel as sullen as she did? She'd not known this would be where things would head with them; if anything, she had just been looking for the right moment to really open up to him and tell him the truth. She needed to know, regardless of their past, that she could still trust him.

And though she wasn't entirely sure she could, she

had to try. She had to tell him the truth about Ben, and what he had come here for, and then let the chips fall.

She wanted Mike to say something, but he just stood there looking at her, studying her and waiting for her. The silence was more painful than she could have expected.

"You were right about Ben. He doesn't just work for a petroleum company—it's a little more complicated than that."

He scoffed, stepping back from her. "No crap. I called that."

She chewed at her bottom lip, wishing she had allowed the kiss to keep going instead of standing there and exposing her weak points.

"He wasn't here to get back together, was he?" Mike continued.

She shook her head.

"What *did* he want from you?"

She swallowed back the fear that had pooled in her throat. "He and I...we both worked for the same team at a certain point. We don't anymore. And when I quit, apparently they came to suspect some things about me, thanks to Ben. Things I can't tell you about. But if they find out that there is any validity to the rumors, they are going to take Joe and kill me. Mike, I'm afraid."

Mike's eyes widened and she was sure she saw flames at their centers. "And here I thought I needed to be a gentleman. If I ever see Ben again, he's as good as dead."

Chapter Seven

Mike wanted to go back in time and take Ben out. One little tap of the trigger and Summer's problem would be handled for good. He really should have trusted his gut about the guy, but it was hard to look at any situation objectively when it involved an ex and their newest fling.

He just couldn't get over the fact that Summer had let this man into her life. Seeing Ben as merely a jerk of an ex, a man who didn't know how to treat women, was bad enough, but then add a death threat and it took his hate toward the guy impossibly deeper.

Ben had to go.

"I'll take care of him. Where does he live? He can't be that far ahead of me. I bet I can still get the drop on him." Mike's thoughts were a flurry of whats, buts and whys. He needed to be logical. Stop his mouth and click on his brain. But first he needed some answers. "Does he think you will tell me who he is? The threat I pose to him?"

If the guy was smart, he would already be heading for the hills in anticipation that Mike would be just about to come bearing down on him. No matter the status of Mike and Summer's relationship, she was the mother of his son and if anyone dared threaten them, hell would have no greater fury.

The man had to know his ass was on the line. That meant any sort of element of surprise was well out of the question.

If only he had taken the lead when he had first heard about this dude, maybe it wouldn't have played out like this. Mike could have lied about who he was, what he was doing there…if only Summer had told him the truth earlier. If only she had been honest about her ex with him well before their confrontation.

Summer opened her mouth, about to answer, but Mike waved her off. "Never mind. I answered my own damned question."

He paced around the apartment, thinking about the resources he had on hand and what he could quickly access if he was in a pinch. STEALTH had operatives all around the world and if he needed… No, this was a personal matter. He didn't want to bring in his siblings or any other members of the team to handle this. He could kill the bastard himself.

"Wait. Ben isn't the bad guy here," Summer said, raising her hands in surrender. "I mean he isn't a good guy, but *he* isn't the one threatening my life—he was only the messenger. Don't get ahead of yourself."

The anger seeped from his pores, but instead of diminishing, it changed direction. "What in the hell are you talking about? I thought you just said that he came here and threatened you and Joe, that you were in danger."

"Yes, but it's the entire group I'm worried about. Even if we take Ben out, they could be coming for me."

He was so confused. What all had she gotten herself into? And how had she fallen prey to this group who threatened her life?

"You need to explain to me what the hell is going on. If not, I can't... I'll take care of Joe, but..."

She looked at him like he had just asked her to tell him the location of the last unicorn so he could go and murder it.

"I know this is uncomfortable. I know you don't want to tell me. And I'm not going to judge you for whatever the hell happened to wrap you up in this mess. But I need to know what I'm going to face. We need to be prepared in order to keep you and Joe safe."

She chewed on her lip. "If I tell you the truth, you have to promise that you won't tell anyone... Ever. And you can't judge me for this. I... I have been struggling."

He nodded, but fear rattled through him. What had he done to her that she'd felt compelled to get involved with Rockwood—and maybe worse—to provide for herself and her son? If only he had followed through on their wedding, none of this would have ever happened. Instead, they could have been living in a house of their own, maybe something along the river like they had always dreamed about, and he could be playing out in the yard with Joe. Instead, here they were, needing to run for their lives, and it was all his fault.

He had tried to do the right thing, and it had come back to bite not only him but all of them square in the ass.

"I have no room to judge," he said, trying to not self-flagellate when he'd have years to think about all the things he had done wrong. "I'm here to listen and help, nothing more." It felt strange saying that, but he absolutely meant it.

"After our breakup, STRIKE and I had a bit of a falling out. They weren't using me much, I'm sure it was because I was a massive train wreck." She sucked in a long breath and, as she paused, he could almost hear what she was going to tell him next. "Another company approached me, asked if I would like to be involved with their cyber team working on government-issued contracts. They had me working undercover."

He chomped on his lip, trying to stop himself from saying anything that would upset her and stall her confession.

She looked away, guilty. "I was doing really well as a double agent, and after Solomon Scot—Kate's father— was killed, the group I was working for with Ben had me doing industrial espionage, spying on ConFlux, trying to get military engineering secrets. I got them and handed them off to Ben. Before Ben and his colleagues could use them, the codes were changed, access denied. I came out okay, and ConFlux didn't lose anything."

"Were you gathering and selling state secrets, Summer?" He took his phone out of his pocket, thinking about Zoey. Maybe she could help them, maybe she knew someone in the higher-ups who could pull some strings and get Summer out of this jam. Treason was serious business.

But he put his phone down on a nearby box. No. If he told Zoey, she would want to know everything. She would ask far too many questions he didn't know the answers to. He had to play this smart. *They* had to.

"It appeared like I was—at least to the people whose group I was infiltrating. But all I knew at the time was that I was to find a way into the ConFlux network, grab a specific set of codes for my main team, and then leave the door open for the rest of the teams. Kate was in on it. She knew that we were trying to bait a trap and pull out anyone who was trying to steal American military secrets."

Mike didn't know what to think about all of this. There

was so much information, so many secrets and so many twists. Summer had gotten herself much deeper into the world of spies and counterspies than he could have imagined.

"It was then, when I met up with Kate, that Ben might have seen me. Maybe he connected the dots, or someone did... I think I may have compromised my work."

"This is crazy," he grumbled. "You. Me. This is crap. You were *stealing* military-grade secrets."

She raised her hands in supplication. "That's not it... I was just doing my job. I am working for and loyal to the good guys. I swear."

Mike opened his mouth. She hadn't told him enough so that he could really believe her, and he wasn't sure that he wanted her to bring him any deeper into her blurry-lined world than she already had. She was a spy. What if she was using him to spy on STEALTH? She had been asking questions about Rockwood, too.

He struggled to connect the dots based on everything she had told him so far.

Joe crawled toward the couch, and after bonking his head on the corner of a box, he started to cry. Mike swooped in and picked him up just as Summer moved to get him. "He'll be okay," she said, her tone soft and cooing as she gently cupped her son's head and nodded. "He's a tough boy. Aren't you, baby?"

Joe rubbed his eyes as he sniffled and then took hold of Summer's finger.

The simple action threatened to rip out Mike's heart and trample it on the ground. This was his family; he had unintentionally made this family and, as angry and upset as he was, he would do whatever it took to make sure they were all safe.

He rocked him, trying to comfort his son. As he swayed side to side, it occurred to Mike that this little man in his arms was perhaps a sponge for all the emotions swirling around him. If that was the case, even though he didn't understand the conversation, it was still doing the child no good.

Joe stuck his thumb in his mouth and looked up at him, his blinks starting to get slower and slower.

"Do you have somewhere we can put him down for a little nap? I think our boy is getting sleepy," he said.

"As soon as you put him down in the crib, he will wake right up. He hates being alone. But you're right, our little guy looks sleepy. Most of the time, when he fights it, I take him for a little drive in the car." Summer looked toward the window. "We left his seat out there in the car. We can take him for a short ride. You know, drive around a bit until he's fast asleep."

The last thing he wanted to do was to put the kiddo down and upset him.

He chuckled as he realized what he had been thinking. Here he had only known he was a dad for a day and yet this little being already had him wrapped around the tiniest of his fingers. It was only too easy to fall so desperately in love with a child.

It was strange, but once upon a time, he had fallen in love with Summer almost as quickly.

"I'm going to freshen up and grab some things for his diaper bag. I will meet you out there in a few minutes," she said.

"I'll go put him in the car seat. Sound good?"

"Great." She headed toward the back bedrooms. "The car's unlocked, but the keys are beside the door." She motioned to the peg where her keys were hanging.

He looked down at Joe, who was sucking away on his thumb, still fighting the sandman. "It's okay, little man, you can give up the ghost. Papa has you, you're safe."

As she disappeared down the hall, Mike made his way outside. Ben was nowhere to be seen and the apartment complex had slipped into the midday sleepiness that came when it was a warm late-fall day. It was cooler outside than it had been in the apartment. No wonder Joe liked sleeping in the air-conditioned car far more than sitting in the muggy crib.

Truth be told, Mike could have gone for a nap too. His mind wandered to Kate and Summer working together. Had Summer told Kate about Joe? Had Kate told his brother? Did people in his family know that he had a child and yet no one had told him?

He was furious, but he was also so freaking confused. Could he be mad at his teams for keeping a secret from him when they were all members of a shadow team? Everything they did was for a reason. No doubt, no one wanted to be the person to tell him about a son he didn't know he'd had when that was Summer's decision to make.

And who knew, maybe Summer hadn't told them about Joe. She hadn't given any clues outwardly that she had a kid when he had first seen her. It was more than plausible she hadn't wanted to put any of his family or team in such a compromising position by telling Kate about the baby.

She hadn't wanted to leave the news on his voice mail, so there was no way she would put the power of this revelation in the hands of anyone else.

He opened the back door of the car and put Joe into his car seat. As he pulled the straps over Joe's arms, the thumb went right back into his mouth and he turned his head to the side as though the little guy knew exactly what was going to happen next and he was just readying himself to fall asleep.

Mike couldn't be angry. Not really. Not when he had been given such a tremendous gift. Summer had tried to talk to him. He hadn't listened. By her stepping forward at the wedding, she had granted him access to their baby. She hadn't had to do what she had done. There had been other options.

He couldn't even imagine how it would have felt only to learn in twenty years that he'd had a child, after Joe was grown and likely starting to think about having a family of his own. She could have held out. She could have been so angry with him that she could have denied him the opportunity to be involved in their child's infancy. And yet she had forgiven him enough to let him in.

She had mucked up her life and she had gotten herself into trouble, but if they worked together, this potential compromising position was something they could get her out of. It would be hard, sure, but maybe with a few of the right phone calls to the right people, she could be safe.

But that didn't mean he didn't need some answers both from her and from his team.

He reached down and moved to pull his phone from his pocket, but realized he'd left it sitting on top of the box in the living room. And, he'd left the keys hanging beside the door. He needed to run back inside.

Joe had his eyes closed and his head was resting comfortably on the gray polka dots of the car seat's lining. Mike glanced around, looking for a button or something that would unlatch the car seat from its base, but there were a million little red buttons and tabs and he wasn't sure which was the self-destruct button. Joe looked so at ease that Mike didn't want to go through the motions of trying to unbuckle him.

There was no one around, no cars coming or going, and he would only be inside for a second… But every part of his being told him not to leave the child alone. He looked down at Joe, whose eyes were now closed. His head dipped in sleep but jerked back up, eyes still closed.

His son was definitely a fighter. Hopefully he would remain that way for the rest of his life—it was the only way to come out the other side of it in a way that was true to a person's soul.

How had Summer been able to be a single parent? This was such a simple thing and yet, by himself, it was immeasurably hard. He couldn't imagine going through these seemingly easy, inconsequential moments where a person was stuck between a rock and hard place. She really was deserving of some kind of an award.

He wouldn't let her be on her own with his kiddo ever again. Joe needed a father and Summer needed a teammate, someone she could call whenever she needed anything.

He held his breath as he pushed the red button near the top of the car seat and it unlatched from the base. Thankfully, Joe didn't stir.

He walked to the apartment and set the car seat down just inside the door. He pushed the door gently, barely closing it behind him as he made his way into the living room to grab his phone.

Dude, seriously, this was rough. This back-and-forth thing. How did a parent get anything done?

He'd heard many new parents complain about the inability to even do something as simple as take a shower when they had a new baby, and now he finally under-stood it. It wasn't that they were incapable of showering, it was the anxiety that kept them needing to see where their child was and what they were doing at every sec-ond of every day.

He suddenly felt sorry for his own parents. The hell he and his siblings must have put them through. At what point had they started to loosen the reins on their kids and started trusting that they would be safe? Or did they ever really assume they were safe? What if this fear never went away? He doubted that it did. Rather, it had likely only been dampened by the ravages of time and the need to keep moving forward and through the crippling anxiety.

How did parents live like this, regardless of the age of their children?

He grabbed his phone and glanced down the L-shaped hallway in the direction of what he assumed was Sum-mer's bedroom. "I don't know how you do it," he yelled toward her.

"What?" she asked, her voice muffled behind the door.

"I said, I don't know how you do it."

"Huh?"

He walked down the hall and to the left until he was standing outside the closed door. "I said, I don't know how you do it."

"Do what?" she asked, moving closer to the other side of the door.

"This. Be a single parent. It seems like it's a real jug-gling act."

She gave a sarcastic laugh. "You don't even know. You've only been at this for a day. And, honestly, I don't know how I'm doing it. I have to admit that I feel like I'm literally figuring this out minute by minute."

That, he totally understood.

He rested his forehead on the door for a moment. "Thank you, Summer."

"Huh? For what?"

He put his hand on the white paint of the paneled door, it was cool under his fingertips. "For letting me into your guys' life. I know things must have been so hard for you. But you don't have to go through any of this by yourself anymore. I'm here for you. I don't expect that we will always see eye to eye, and we will probably fight about a lot of things, but whenever you need anything you know I have your and Joe's back."

There was a long silence from inside the room. "Thanks, Mike. And hey, you know I'm sorry."

"What do you have to be sorry about?" He had been the one to put all this chaos into motion.

"I'm sorry for not telling you sooner. I hope you know I tried."

"I know… I know you tried." He paused, still angry with himself. "I am the one who needs to be sorry. I *am* sorry."

He could hear her breathing right on the other side of the door, like she was standing parallel to him, sharing this moment of pain. He wanted to open the door and pull her into his arms, but if he was touching her or even just seeing her, he wasn't sure that he had the power it would take to say all the things he needed to say.

"I think we need to go to the feds with all this."

There was a long pause. "No, not yet." Her voice was high, the sound false. She was still not telling him something. He could hear the hesitation and the lies in her tone.

"What company was it that you were working for— the one that is threatening you?" he asked, questioning his judgment in asking. If she told him, he might come under fire, as well. But if she didn't, he wouldn't know exactly who he was fighting.

Her breathing quickened. "Er, Ben and I...were working for a company."

"What company?" he asked, not understanding.

"Rockwood—the group that tried to have you and your brother gunned down." She paused as if to let her words sink in for a moment. In interrogation, he would have called that tactical silence. He hated it, but not as much as he hated Rockwood.

He ran his hand over his face, trying to stave off the start of a headache. "I've got to run. I left Joe alone in the hall. We can continue this conversation when you get out to the car. Hurry up."

When this woman screwed up, she screwed up royally. At least they had that one thing in common—they could both wreak havoc on their personal lives.

He hummed as he made his way back out to the hall to fetch the keys, the song just a little ditty, a reflection of the hope he was feeling even during these dark times. It was crazy, but the fact that she had been working for his enemy—or rather, had been spying on Rockwood— made him feel better. Something about this entire scenario made him feel like they were approaching even ground. Maybe this, being here with Summer and Joe, was an opportunity to put all of their lives back in order and he could be her hero and show her how much he was willing to sacrifice to be with them.

"All right, little guy, Mom is just about done. She'll be out in a minute," he said, walking toward the front door where the car seat had been sitting on the floor. However, the spot where he had put Joe was now empty and the door was ajar.

He rushed to the door, jerking it wide open and looking outside as if Joe could have gotten up and somehow moved himself. But the baby and the car seat were nowhere in sight. Someone must have been watching, reached inside the moment his back was turned and taken his son.

His heart shuddered, threatening to stop beating with the pain. Joe was gone.

Chapter Eight

His scream was something unlike anything she had ever heard before, a blood-curdling sound like a dying animal—and something that she never wanted to hear again. Summer rushed out, expecting to find Mike lying on the floor in a pool of his own blood or maybe being bludgeoned by a house bandit. Instead, he was standing beside the front door, his hand on the top of his head, staring at nothing.

"What's the matter? What happened to Joe? Is he okay?" She found herself beside him, but she had no idea how her body had gotten her there. "Where is he? Did you put him in the car?" she asked.

Not waiting for Mike to respond, she rushed outside to the car, but it sat empty.

Mike stared at the car, saying nothing for a long moment. "He's…he's gone. They must have just opened the front door and reached in. I didn't lock it. I wasn't planning on leaving him alone… I-I just…" His voice cracked as his breath seeped from his lips.

Summer couldn't hear anything over the din of terror ringing through her. Someone had taken their son. Someone had taken him. It had to have been Ben. But he had only threatened her. He hadn't said Rockwood had concrete evidence about her being a double agent. If anything, he'd just seemed pissed about the breakup. And as much as he had scared her, part of her hadn't really taken him seriously.

If Ben had wanted her dead or to kidnap Joe, why would he have done it now?

No. It didn't make sense. Ben had always come at her head-on, he wouldn't have just taken Joe and slipped away. It wasn't his way of working. He would have wanted her to see him with Joe, to witness in horror as he took him away. He would have made a show of it, making her watch what she had caused.

Besides, when they had been dating, Ben had always said he loved Joe. He had even gone so far as to talk about adopting him—not that she would have ever let that happen.

But then there were times when Ben had made it no secret that he'd thought she was a terrible mother—especially when she had gone away for days without telling him where she was going. Little had he known at the time, but she had been meeting with her boss, Kevin, at the DTRA and reporting what she had learned about Rockwood.

Maybe Ben had been pushed over the edge by seeing her with Mike. Maybe this was all some terrible and warped way for Ben to get his revenge.

Her breathing started to quicken as panic wormed through her. She pressed her forehead against the cold steel of the car door as reality hit. This was her fault.

What made it worse was that it was all because she had once again put her faith in Mike Spade. She had trusted him to watch her son. To keep him safe.

This was Mike's doing. He had left their son alone.

She had told him that Rockwood was threatening to take Joe and yet he had not put her baby's safety first. Then again, Joe had been *in her apartment*. She could have made the same mistake. And yet, she had to be angry at someone other than herself.

She turned to Mike, hate filling her as she looked at his terror-stricken face. "You did this."

He didn't speak. He didn't bother to deny.

He had to have known that what she said was true—they had lost Joe because of him.

"We will get him back. *I* will get him back." Mike sounded breathless, as if the vastness of loss had stripped him of his voice.

"If you don't, I will spend the rest of my life hating you." She didn't like the words that spilled from her like blood, but she couldn't help it, she couldn't control anything anymore, least of all what she was feeling.

Her son… Her son was gone.

"I'm so sorry," he whispered. "I just put him down for a split second. I didn't think—"

"I already know that much," she seethed.

Mike ran his hands over his face and held them there, covering his eyes for a long moment as though he could strip away the reality of what he had caused. "You have every right to be upset. I screwed up. But I will get Joe back. I will set things right. I will fix this. All of this."

She opened her mouth, ready to spit more fire at him, but he stopped her when he glanced over at her. He looked like he was in physical pain, like someone had slashed through his chest and removed his heart. She knew the look because she was feeling it too.

"You can hate me all you want, but we have to work together to get Joe back. We are in this together." Mike paused. "We have to be strategic about this. We have to think. We can't let our emotions cloud our judgment. Not when Joe's life, all our lives, are on the line."

"Since when has it been *our* lives? No one is trying to gun you down." She was indignant in her pain, but she couldn't stop herself. He couldn't possibly be hurting as much as she was right now.

Mike stepped closer to her and she backed away. He couldn't fix this like he normally did, when he'd let her fall into his embrace. No. That wouldn't work anymore. Her weakness for his touch had gotten them into this mess in the first place.

"We need to call in backup. We need to get law enforcement involved. They need to know that Joe is missing."

"No." The word was a knee-jerk response, but she meant it. "Bringing them in would be a slippery slope." She stopped as she thought about all the different facets of what it would mean to bring in the locals—few of the advantages would outweigh the profusion of potential negatives. "Your team has just about the same level of resources at their disposal. Do you think they would be willing to help me out? I can pay."

"You know if this thing goes even more haywire, the police will end up getting involved. I mean what if someone gets killed? How will we come out of this looking like the good guys if we work behind the police's backs and they find out about it?"

"I hear what you are saying, but I can't expose what I've done."

"Not even if that leads to our son being returned safely?" Mike challenged.

"How dare you. That was low, even for you." She tried

to control her rage. "I can't expose what I've done because it might lead to worse things happening…to Joe."

"I'm sorry," Mike huffed. "I didn't mean it like that… I mean I did, I want Joe home, but I didn't mean to attack you. I'm just as scared and upset as you are."

How could he be when he'd only just entered their lives? He didn't know the feeling of holding Joe in the hospital when he had taken his first breath. He didn't know what it was like taking care of a baby with a cold, worrying if he was going to make it through the night.

As hurt as she felt, Summer didn't voice her thoughts. He didn't deserve to be lashed with them. He loved Joe. He loved their son just as much as she did.

Love had the power to overwhelm a person in less than a second—and she had seen it engulf Mike when he'd first held their son. Their love for their son was different, though. Hers had had more time to grow and blossom. But love, she knew, wasn't something tangible that could be measured by such feeble metrics like time. Love could only be measured by sacrifice. And here Mike was, willing to sacrifice his life for their son. No matter what she was feeling, the power of his love was undeniable.

But she wasn't ready to forgive him for everything he had put them through.

"Do you think it was Ben who took him?" Mike asked.

She shook her head, violently. "He would have made a show of it. But it very well could have been someone from Rockwood."

Mike scowled, and she could see the terror in his eyes at the possibility that just about anyone could have taken their boy.

"Did you see anyone when you came outside?" she

asked, trying to shift her focus to what needed to happen next to bring Joe back.

"I didn't," he said, shaking his head. "Whoever did this had to be watching. Either they followed us or were staked out here and just waiting for an opening to get their hands on Joe."

Whichever it was, it didn't matter. They needed to assume they'd been followed and that there probably had been someone staked out and watching her. The people she was working for, or had been working for, weren't stupid, but they were dangerous and angry.

She had been part of kidnapping cases before, not on the frontlines or in the role as a negotiator, but she had seen enough of these things to know that people—and kids, specifically—were usually used to barter for ransom. She doubted Rockwood would use Joe for ransom, but why else would they have taken him instead of killing him outright? They had to have wanted something.

"They are going to reach out to us. Right now, I think all we can do is wait." She couldn't believe what she was saying. To wait went against every particle of her being as a mother, but it didn't change the reality of what was happening.

"Are you absolutely, one-hundred-percent sure that it's Rockwood behind Joe's kidnapping? You are *sure* that Ben wouldn't have done this?" Mike countered. "You know I've always said that usually the most obvious suspect is the perp."

"I know you don't like Ben, neither do I. But he loves Joe and I truly believe he wants me to be cleared of being a double agent. He wants me to come back to him. He is volatile, and he is angry, but he wouldn't compromise

Joe like this. And he wouldn't compromise any possible future the three of us could have together. He loves us."

Mike nodded, but she could tell he didn't really believe her. Or maybe it was that he just didn't like what she was saying.

"Ben is a lot of things, but I really don't think he's behind this. I don't think he's the bad guy here."

Mike shook his head. "I am not trying to make Ben the bad guy. I just want to make sure that we don't waste time chasing the wrong people. But you seem to want to defend him all the time... If you still love him, that's fine. Just admit it and then we can move forward with that awareness in place."

"I don't love Ben." She could feel the truth of her words, but she wasn't sure Mike could feel them as well. "Ben was just a space filler, a soft landing, if you want to call it that. I needed someone who could staunch the loneliness in my heart after losing you, and he seemed to love me. Having him as my boyfriend made it easy to spy on Rockwood. Things with him checked a lot of the boxes for what I needed in my life." It ached to admit her folly.

"Summer..." Mike slipped his hand into hers.

There was that touch. That damned touch. He was a master of making her forget herself with that simple thing. And he would always have that power over her, no matter how much she knew she shouldn't let him.

"Let's just get Joe back, then we can think about everything else. As it stands, let's just call a truce. Fair?"

From where she stood, it was more than fair, it was a million miles past fair, given the circumstances. It was better to be a team than to fight with the one man she had always loved and always would.

Mike could never know, but it was so easy for him

to see if he wanted to—her love for him would always mean sacrifices. Sacrifices she would gladly make if it meant having him in her life.

Chapter Nine

Women made no sense at all.

He'd always hated when other men had said things like that to him, but now that he was standing there and forced to see everything that was Summer, Mike really understood it. She was just a little bit, albeit justifiably, crazy. Luckily, she was the right kind of crazy for him.

"Let's go inside. I can make some phone calls to see if we can get my team on this and then we will go from there. How does that sound?" he asked, trying to help.

She nodded. "I think we need to talk to the neighbors to see if anyone saw anything."

They could work on securing the scene all they wanted and collecting eyewitnesses, acting like this was a regular investigation that didn't personally impact them. But this was their child and they needed to fly under the radar. The second they started going around and knocking on doors, their ordeal would be out in the open, and that could trigger police involvement. Whatever anonymity they'd been hoping for would be gone.

There was a certain amount of power that came into play outside the rules and regulations of the legal system. And they would need all the leeway they could get when he got his hands on whomever had thought it acceptable to steal a baby out from under their noses. There was a certain level of hell reserved for people like that, and he would make sure they had the chance to experience the heat.

Mike shook his head. "There wasn't anyone around that I noticed. Whoever did this wouldn't have been stupid enough to be seen and, as much as I want to ask around, I doubt we'll get anything—the kidnapper seemed smart enough to watch for nosy neighbors. Plus, I think it's best if we are just quiet and lay low a little bit. Like you said, we just need to wait for the call."

As if on cue, Mike's phone pinged. The number, from Montana, was the generic type likely generated by some kind of app. He would have his team look into it, but he'd done this enough to know a spoof when he saw it.

He clicked on the message; it was simple and yet terrifying.

Baby safe. For now. You have 46 hours. Anything more and baby loses toes.

Summer gasped audibly when he showed her the text.

Yep. Someone was going to die for this. Actually, there would probably be several before he was done.

He dialed the number, wanting to hear the voice of the person responsible for the hell he was going through. A man picked up, but Mike didn't recognize the voice. "I assume you got our message and that your little girlfriend told you about what was going on and how she appears to have been playing on both sides of the fence. As it is, she is lucky to be alive."

"If you don't return Joe in the next ten minutes, it is

not us who need to be worried. It will be you and your damned crew. We will hunt you down—"

"Hold it," the man said, cutting him off. "Do you think it's a good idea to threaten the person who has your girlfriend's baby?"

Damn it.

Rational. He needed to be rational.

First, he'd called Summer his "girlfriend," which meant that he was either downplaying Mike and Summer's past and using it to demoralize and deride him or that he had just been watching them for a finite period of time and had made incorrect assumptions.

Second, the guy had called Joe *her* baby and not his son, which had to mean he didn't know the truth. Together, this was good. Whoever it was didn't have all the answers, which meant he hadn't infiltrated Summer's life too deeply. He was still only at surface level, which meant Mike and Summer had some degree of autonomy and leverage.

Third, Summer had been right: the kidnapping couldn't have been perpetrated by Ben. Mike had introduced himself to Ben as Joe's father. Therefore, someone else was behind the kidnapping.

The only good news was that their enemy didn't know he could use Joe against him; as it was, he was looking at Mike like he was just a passive outsider—a mere boyfriend with little skin in the game. Well, he could play off their ill-conceived and poorly executed strategy.

"Before you make any more demands, I need to know Joe is alive and doing well. What can you do to prove that he is safe?" He forced himself into negotiation mode.

"We don't wanna hurt the baby. Our primary objective here is to get the information we need and that's it.

Summer is lucky. We need the information she stole from ConFlux or she and the baby would already be dead."

"Who are you?" Mike asked, though he was more than aware these people were likely from Rockwood.

The man grunted. "Don't interrupt me again, or the baby will pay."

He shut his mouth.

"Now, your little girlfriend has come into some information. Codes..." The man paused. "If she gives us those codes, we will keep your baby alive. If she doesn't, we will make you all pay."

"Before we agree to do anything, you need to prove to me that Joe is okay." He was careful to use calculated statements, ones all about the man he was negotiating with.

The most crucial key in successful negotiation was for the negotiator to solve the problems and to always push for additional time. But this kind of crisis response was difficult in even the best of times, times when there wasn't such a deeply personal tie. Negotiating was going to be nearly impossible if Mike kept putting things in terms of this being his own child.

"What do you want with the baby?" he asked, trying to find a baseline on their hostage taker.

"Well, the last damned thing I want is to wake his ass up to prove he is unharmed and then have to deal with a crying baby for the next few hours."

Interesting, so the guy didn't want to hurt Joe or, at least, to cause himself too much unnecessary stress. This was good.

He opened his mouth to speak, but then thought about his many hours of training. One of the first practices for negotiating in this type of circumstance was to follow the 80/20 rule. A negotiator had to keep the hostage taker talking eighty percent of the time; he should only do twenty. Next, he had to be a strong, active listener and hear the things not being said in addition to what was.

The man on the other end of the line huffed. He sounded annoyed, as if having to wait for Mike to speak and give him feedback was more than he could handle. "Look, I can send a picture of the baby. But there are conditions."

"What are the conditions?" he asked, carefully mirroring the man's language so he would feel validated.

"We want to make this as simple as possible. If you give us what we want, you can have the kid back in a matter of hours." The man halted, but Mike didn't say anything. Instead he let him continue with his demands. "We need all the codes that were taken from the Con-Flux system."

"You need all the codes." Mike pushed the speaker button on his phone so Summer could listen in; the more ears he had on this, the better. Maybe she could pick up something he missed and make sense of this in a way that he was unable. "What are you planning to do with these codes?"

"That's none of your damned business, Mike."

The man had used his name. It didn't come as a huge surprise, but it was jarring, like this guy had somehow just made things a degree more personal and threatening. More, the man had used his name on purpose. Mike had clearly stumbled onto something that had caused the guy to lash out and get emotional.

"How do you think we should get these codes?" he continued, trying hard to restrain his own emotions. He couldn't backslide, they were making progress, but he needed more time and more information to safely get Joe back.

"That isn't my damned problem. My problem is that you are apparently a freaking idiot."

Okay, he needed to dial it back a bit and deescalate. "I'm not trying to be stupid, just trying to get all the facts and to fully understand your demand. This is about you, what you need."

"No, this is about the kid." The man sounded frantic, and Mike didn't try to dissuade him. Some amount of stress on the other end of the phone was good, as long as it didn't lead to Joe's being hurt. Stress led to poor negotiation skills, which could definitely be to Mike's benefit just as long as he was careful.

Summer moved closer, as if to say something, but he stopped her with a shake of his head. She was far too angry and far too close to the situation. He pushed Mute on his phone so the man on the other end couldn't hear what he was saying.

"Summer, you need to just listen. Please. I'm going to see if we can get this guy to fold without having to play into his demand. We need Joe to be safe. If you get involved, get emotional, these guys will have us at their mercy."

She nodded. "If they hurt Joe…"

"They don't want to hurt Joe. But you and I are both going to have to be patient. This is a dance marathon, not a sprint. The longer it takes, the better. We can wear them down and keep Joe safe."

"How do you know they aren't going to hurt him?"

"They didn't even want to wake him up."

"That was more about them than it was for Joe."

She wasn't wrong, but she did give him an idea.

"We need to make them feel something for him," Mike said with a subversive laugh.

"You think that will work? That they will be that easily coerced?"

Love always had a way of making a person do things that went against reason. He'd once heard that feelings were thoughts of their own and to negate and devalue feelings would only limit a person's intellectual abilities. In essence, to avoid feelings stunted a person.

He wasn't sure if he bought into the philosophy in its entirety—whenever he had been able to avoid feelings, it had been an asset rather than a hindrance—but then he could hardly be thought of as the perfect specimen of man. Regardless of his personal introspection, love could be the answer to most of life's problems.

"Helloooo? What in the hell! Did you hang up?" The man on the other end of the line spiraled into a full meltdown. "Rico, they effing hung up, man. How in the hell are we supposed to work with these people?"

Rico. The man had a partner named Rico.

Mike clicked off the Mute. "I'm right here. I was just trying to think of a solution to the problem with Joe." He paused.

"What problem?" the man answered, too quickly.

"Well, he is going to require a lot of care," he said, thinking about all the baby-related items he'd seen around Summer's house. "He is going to need a bottle, diapers, and someone to take dedicated care of him. Can you provide him with those basic necessities?"

There was a long pause. "You think I care if the baby eats?"

"You may or may not, but I think you are going to

care when he is crying because he's hungry." He turned to Summer. "What kind of formula does he drink?"

There was so much he didn't know about his son.

She nodded. "He has a sensitive stomach, so I can only use the formula from Costco, the one with the yellow lid."

Oh, this was going to be good. These guys clearly hadn't put a lot of thought into the actual logistical needs of taking care of a baby as young as Joe. And yet, that added level of need and dependence was going to also be what put Joe into additional danger. It took a lot to raise and care for a baby, and these guys knew maybe slightly less than Mike did.

"Did you hear Summer? The baby has special dietary needs. What can we do to get you the food Joe is going to need?"

"We don't need jack squat. If the baby cries, he goes outside. Plain as that." The man's voice sounded strained, as though even he knew that what he was saying was a bad idea. If someone heard a strange baby crying outside, that would pull in all kinds of attention. The only humans who would be pushed outside would be the kidnappers.

Mike paused, letting the lie sink into the man's psyche as he thought about the reality in which he had just placed himself. The expression "bit off more than they could chew" came to Mike's mind. But this was all good, all things he and Summer could use to buy time and even maybe to get to Joe all without giving the kidnappers the ransom they were asking for.

There was a rattle and the sound of a hand being placed over the phone as the kidnapper must have turned to his cohort, Rico. "Dude, do we have diapers? You know anything about where we can get some?"

Mike nearly laughed out loud as the bumbling kidnappers argued with one another about buying diapers at a gas station.

Summer covered her mouth as she nodded excitedly.

They had found the weak point in the other party's negotiation that would clear the barriers and give them the *in* that they needed.

"Look. I know you don't want to hurt the baby. That would land you in more trouble than I think you care to take on. So let us help you with him. We can bring you everything you need for Joe for the next two days, while we also work on getting you the codes. What do you think?" Mike hoped these idiots would see the advantage of keeping Joe well fed and looked after.

The man mumbled something Mike couldn't understand. "We are going to need some time. Let me talk to my people. We'll be in touch."

The phone line went dead.

Damn it. He hadn't meant to run the kidnapper off; all he had wanted to do was to get him to give them a little wiggle room.

He stared at the lit screen until it went dark.

There had to be something they could do, something that would help them take back control.

Chapter Ten

Hours later, Summer's phone rang and she hesitated to look at the Caller ID. Her only hope was that it was the kidnappers and they were coming back with a list of demands—demands that would bring Summer and Mike closer to getting their son back.

And yet, as she looked, she saw that it was her boss, Kevin Warble, from the DTRA. Luckily, as Mike glanced over at her phone from his seat next to her on her couch, all the screen said was Kevin. Mike couldn't know everything, not yet and maybe not ever. She had been doing the best she could, right up until her enemies had taken Joe. Now everything she had been trying to do, every safety precaution she had thought she'd had in place, was out the window.

She stood. "I'll be right back," she said to Mike, quickly making her way down the hall to her bedroom where she could find a little bit of privacy for the call that would now have to take place.

This one was going to hurt. She'd reached out to Kevin earlier when Mike was doing a perimeter check of the apartment complex after they'd received the ransom call.

Closing the door, she answered the phone. "Hey, thanks for getting back to me. I know you said you couldn't get me the codes, but there has to be something you can do. Something we can trade with these guys in order to get Joe back. Some innocuous codes. Anything…"

"Whoa. Let's not get ahead of ourselves. You know that isn't a possibility. Can you imagine if the code used by high-level, security clearance military engineers got into the hands of America's enemies? It would be a nightmare." Kevin sighed as though just the question of him getting her the codes exhausted him. "Have you had any other contact with the kidnappers?"

"No. Not yet. Have you had any luck tracking down the phone number or location of the device Rico and his buddy used to call?"

Kevin groaned. "Like we had assumed, it wasn't a number registered to any known phone. However, we have figured out the source app and have contacted the designers. They are looking into things to see if they can identify the phone assigned the number. But unfortunately, you know how all this goes. It's a waiting game."

"Did you guys manage to pull anything from any of the local cameras? Have you gotten any definitive answers?" she asked, begging for information about her son.

Kevin sighed. "I'm so sorry, Summer. All I can tell you is that we're doing our best and we are trying to work as fast as we can. Just know that we are using every single thing we can to get Joe back."

She held no doubts he was telling her the truth, but it did nothing for the panic and terror she was feeling. Nothing would help calm her until she had Joe in the safety of her arms. She swallowed back the lump in her throat.

"I assume Mike is working on things from his side, correct?" Kevin continued.

"Yeah."

"Keep us apprised of any *issues* that may arise from his digging. We need to keep your role in the DTRA concealed—even from him. If not…well, you know how these things work. If you are exposed or your cover is blown, we are going to have to deny everything. You know what's at stake here, I hope."

Apparently, he meant beyond the scope of losing her son—the most important person in her life—she was also quite possibly going to lose her job and her freedom if her truth was uncovered.

Swell. Just swell.

Everything was falling down around her.

"I don't need you to tell me what else I have to lose. I'm more than aware. But right now, my main concern is the welfare of my son." Her anger pulsed within her and, for a moment, she wondered if it was misplaced and ill-advised for her to speak up, but at the same time she didn't care. "I think you calling me to tell me this is reprehensible. You promised to keep me and my son safe—and yet here we are and now you are threatening to throw me under the bus."

"I didn't mean it like that, Summer," Kevin said, contrite. "I just mean that you need to be careful with Mike. This is a tough situation, but know we are all working to fulfill our promises to you. However, you need to focus on doing your job."

Summer sighed. Maybe she was lashing out in the wrong direction. It was just…well, it was this inability to take direct action that was really killing her. All she wanted to do was to rush out, cut down the bad guys, and get her son back into her arms. And yet, all she could do was to sit in her apartment, make phone calls and wait for them to come to her. This powerlessness was unlike anything she'd ever felt before.

Not even being left at the altar compared.

And then there was that.

Here she was, forced to trust a man who had broken her heart and ripped out a piece of her soul once before. And already, he had allowed kidnappers to get to Joe. He'd only been back in her life for a matter of hours and he was destroying it all over again.

Logically, she wasn't angry with Mike. She couldn't be. Not really. The kidnappers had been targeting her; she had brought them to her doorstep. But she couldn't help the anger she was feeling from spilling over and tainting everything in her life.

Bottom line, she was angry with the world.

"Is there anything I can do beyond sit here and wait?" she asked, hoping Kevin would have something that could help staunch the roiling emotions threatening to destroy her.

"Like I told you earlier, the best thing you can do is stay exactly where you are. Get as much information about Rockwood as you can."

When she had been a child, she had been taught that if she was ever truly lost in a forest, the best thing she could do was just sit still—to stay where she was. Others would find her. And yet, this tore at the very cloth of her being. She wasn't a sit-and-wait kind of woman, especially in situations like this. She *had* to do something.

"Mike won't tell me anything. I need to start moving, to do something that will bring me closer to getting Joe back."

"Stop, Summer." Kevin's voice was rife with pity, and she hated it. "Let us take care of you. We have teams in place who are doing more than even I can tell you. Just give us time."

When she had signed her Department of Defense contract with the DTRA and taken the oath of office, there had never been anything about putting herself first. This was about her team and keeping them safe even if that meant putting the needs of her son and herself second. She didn't have to like it, but she had made the deal when she had taken the job.

She had known there would be sacrifices she would need to make when it came to being a DTRA agent, but she had never assumed her sacrifices would come in the form of her son's life.

She had been a fool to take this job on. She should have just stuck it out with STRIKE and made it work. She'd loved her contracting world, but when things had gone haywire, she'd thought it had been the impetus she had needed to work full-time for the DTRA, which had led to her taking a position at Rockwood as a spy.

She'd thought she'd been making the right choice, making the best out of a bad situation and getting her life set up so that she could be a good mother while also being able to stand on her own two feet. But all she had done was make everything so much worse. She had fallen for the trap of greener grass in the hope of being a better provider. Guilt flooded through her. She should have just shut her mouth and done the job she had been paid to do for STRIKE, taken the money and gone home to her son. But no, and look where being a good person and doing the right thing had gotten her.

Why did being a good person, a good employee, and a good mother have to be such a juggling act? There was always one ball being dropped.

"You okay, Summer? Do you need anything from us, something I can have someone deliver? Maybe some dinner?" Kevin continued, breaking her train of thought.

"That's kind of you, but we'll be okay." She wasn't hungry and until now she hadn't even bothered to think about food.

"Okay, but let me know if you want or need anything. And I'll be in touch if we get any more leads."

"Thanks, Kevin. And hey, I appreciate all you're doing." She sounded resigned, even to herself, as she ended the call.

When she walked out, Mike was holding a pizza box. "I hope you don't mind, but I thought you might be hungry."

What was it with everyone thinking that she needed to eat?

Summer nodded, giving him a weak smile as she forced herself to remember he didn't deserve to be the target of her rage. She followed him into the kitchen, where he set the pizza down and grabbed a couple of paper towels, handing her one. "Only the finest china for you, m'lady." He gave a little bow as she took the towel.

"Thank you, kind sir." She forced herself to curtsy as she played along, the small exchange reminding her of the dorkiness and quaint familiarity they used to have.

"And it is plain, just as you like it—thick crust and extra cheesy." He pulled out a chair at the island and helped her to sit before sitting next to her.

He remembered. The thought made some of the heaviness in her chest lift. He had made his mistakes and she had made hers, but there was such deep love between them. No matter what, they would always share an inexplicable bond; one filled with the nuances that came with familiarity and time.

This man still loved her, though it would never be the same love he had once felt for her—or the love she had once felt for him. They had now entered the world of love reserved only for those with the most broken of hearts.

He opened the box, the greasy scent of dough and butter filling the air and, doing so, making her stomach pang. She chuckled at the thought of how funny it was that others could sense things in her that she denied noticing in herself. Or maybe it was just that what she was really hungry for was the act of caring, a hunger Mike had filled, even without her so much as asking.

Mike was a good man.

She took a bite of the pizza as he made his way to the fridge and looked inside. It was exactly as she had remembered it, empty except for a few old beers, a bottle of mustard and some banana baby food she had forgotten to use up. He grabbed one of the beers, twisted off the cap and handed it over to her.

"No, I don't think I should." Summer shook her head slightly. In truth, she wanted the beer and the relaxation that it whispered of, but what if someone called about Joe?

She looked over at the clock. He should have been in bed right now.

Had they changed his diaper? Given him a bath?

At night, he loved to be rocked to sleep after a warm bottle. If they didn't do it, Joe would pitch a fit and, once he got started, and if he was overly tired, there was little anyone could do to calm him except to let him cry it out until he wore himself down and went to sleep on his own.

Anxiety pierced through her. What if they weren't

taking care of him at all? What if Joe was alone, un-changed and unfed?

Her breathing started to quicken as all the fears she held for Joe's safety filled her mind.

This wasn't going to be okay. Nothing was going to be okay. Things would never get back to where they had once been. And what was she doing about it all? Eating pizza. She was the worst mother ever.

"He is going to be okay, Summer." Mike spoke as though he could read her mind, or maybe it was that all of her thoughts were streaming on her face like it was a wide-screen television.

"How do you know, Mike? What if—"

"Stop. Don't swirl the drain of what-ifs. It does you and Joe no good."

He was right, but she hated to admit it. Without the what-ifs, she was left with only the reality of the situation—her son was in the hands of potential killers.

She took the beer Mike offered and took a sip.

"This is all going to be okay. We will get him back and they will take good care of him. A baby has a way of making everyone around them love them. I mean look at me," Mike said, sending her a wilting smile. "I love him. I loved him the moment you told me about him. That's all it took. And when I saw him, man…put a fork in me."

She smiled. "He is a handsome boy. And when he laughs, he laughs with his whole body in a way that makes you laugh too. I never thought I could love some-thing as much as I love him."

"See what I mean? No one can walk by that boy and not fall for him. He is going to be safe if these men are at all partial to his charms; which, after our conversation with them, I think they are."

"We will see if they say the same thing in the morning; after he keeps them up all night. He likes to fall asleep with me, in my bed." Her eyes welled up with tears as she thought about the week after she had brought Joe home from the hospital. How hard she had tried to follow the rules she had read in the parenting books, chapters of which discussed the pitfalls of co-sleeping. In the end, instinct had taken over and she had given in to the needs of her baby over the opinions of a few.

Snuggling with Joe had become one of her favorite moments in her life. It was an incredible feeling to fall asleep with a baby, flesh of her flesh and bone of her bone. This little being who trusted her so much.

She had let him down.

Taking a long pull off the bottle, she thought about her mistakes. There had been so many in her life already, so many wounds, bruises, scrapes and scabs. It was really no wonder no one made it out alive.

"Mike, what did I do wrong with us? How did I push you away?" She put her beer down on the counter and started to play with the paper ring around the bottle's neck, pulling at the corners like behind it were the answers to life's questions.

He reached over and took her hand, interlacing their fingers. "Summer. Babe." He spoke the word like it was even more tender than his touch. "My problems that day... They really had nothing to do with you."

"Ah," she said with a forced laugh, hoping to diffuse some of the tension, "the old 'it's not you, it's me' line."

"You didn't do anything wrong. It wasn't you. It was me. I saw the future. I'd overheard Troy talking about a threat STEALTH had neutralized. A threat to us. To you. And I thought, *I can't do this*. I couldn't live a life with you, knowing I put you in danger. It was the hardest thing I ever did, walking away from that altar."

"You never told me…"

"I didn't think you would understand. You would have told me to push aside my fears and just follow through with the wedding. But I couldn't… I couldn't risk having you hurt or killed because of me."

He was right. She would have tried to convince him not to leave. But it wasn't him. It was her. What she had needed was a real, concrete answer…an aspect she could change in herself that would help her become stronger, better, and then never find herself in the same position again—and especially not with him.

"Do you think you will ever want to get married again?" he asked.

"To you?" She jerked, stunned by his question.

He let out a tight, surprised laugh. "Sure, or to whomever you love. Man, woman, alien…" he teased.

He had said "sure." Did that mean he was thinking about *them* becoming an *us* again? Could she handle something like that? Could she trust him with her heart after all the pain, confusion and misery he had put her through the last time?

If she said no, would she be doing a disservice to Joe? Probably. But if she said yes, would she be doing a disservice to herself?

"I don't know," she said, striking down the middle. This was one question better unanswered. "I guess I haven't really thought about it too much. I've been really busy for the last year or so." She sent him a smile to let him know that her words weren't meant as some kind of jab, but rather a truth masked in cotton. "And I've loved every second of it," she added.

"After we get Joe back, do you think I can get involved? I mean maybe we can figure out some sort of parenting plan or something. I don't want to step on your toes, but I can't imagine knowing that I have him and yet not having time with him. You know?" He looked slightly stricken at the thought.

Was his question about marriage directly related to his concern for being or not being in Joe's life? "If I get married, don't worry. You will always have a place. You are Joe's dad, and I want to give you every opportunity to be a part of his life as much or as little as you want. I will never stand in your way."

Even if they weren't destined to be together as a married couple, it didn't mean they weren't supposed to be together as parents. Raising Joe would require a collaborative effort and they would both have to give a little to make things work, but she was willing to do the work if he was.

"I just want what is best for Joe," he said.

"I agree. But I also think you coming and going in Joe's life will be hard." She paused. "So, if you are going to be in and out of his life when it's convenient for you, it's not going to be good for him. Before you commit to anything, I want you to really think about your options. With this, you are either all in or all out. No in-betweens."

He squeezed her hand as he listened, like he was already agreeing to her terms.

"Mike, this isn't going to be easy. I don't think you can possibly understand how hard parenting is going to be."

He smiled softly at her. "You know, I have always found the things in my life most worth having are never easy. Far from it." He moved her closer to him and lifted her hand to his mouth, softly kissing the back of her knuckles. "Those things that I have to struggle to attain are what I respect, love and cherish the most."

Ummmm... What? Did he just tell me that he loved me? That he cherished *me? I didn't even know he knew that word. What in the hell?*

She couldn't read too much into his words or his actions. Nope. This had to be one of those times her imagination was playing tricks on her. Mike was the silent type. The type who rarely spoke the truths that lay in his heart. Then again, since they had reconnected, he had been more candid with her than he had been in nearly their entire previous relationship. Had he changed? Had he realized their communication was one aspect of their relationship that had been lacking, by both of them?

"Mike..." She said his name, the sound barely above a whisper. It instantly took her back to the many nights they had spent making love until they were exhausted and only sated when they found themselves engulfed in one another's arms.

Was that where this was headed? Was he making his move? Was he hoping she would take him to the bedroom? That they would make love?

She panicked and yet she didn't pull her hand away from his; she needed his touch. Tonight, of all nights, she wanted the support and love his being there provided. And, well, she wanted *all* of it, and him.

He helped her to stand and she took the lead, walking him slowly toward her bedroom. He had to have known what was coming next, just as much as she did, but he didn't seem to hesitate, though he also wasn't taking the lead. She liked that. He had normally always been the one to be the commander in the bedroom, taking what he wanted from her and leaving her so well pleased that she would collapse into a comatose-like sleep. Yet now he seemed almost passive, demure, in his want of her.

Or maybe he didn't want her?

No. She couldn't think about that—about being rejected by him for a second time, albeit maybe in a slightly less painful way.

Though, come to think of it, which was worse—having a heart or a body turned away?

Either way, it hurt.

She stopped outside her bedroom door. Questioning the step they were both about to take. "Mike—"

He stopped her by taking her lips with his, unexpectedly hurried but tender as he stole her words.

His tongue found the center of the bottom of her lip and she met him there. He pulled her close against his body and her hands moved down his sides. She could feel the bulge of his muscles underneath the fabric of his shirt. He still worked out. So many push-ups.

She grew weak at the knees, but she wasn't sure if it was because of his kiss or his body pressed against hers. It had been so long since she had been properly made love to.

Ben had been great, but he was nowhere near as good or as attentive as Mike had been to her when it came to between-the-sheets time.

She needed to feel Mike inside her, making love to her in the way only he could.

If they just had tonight and then things went back to the way they were, then fine. Whatever. But at least tonight they could forget about the reality that surrounded them, pushing in from all sides, and they could both just concentrate on the pleasure they could bring to one another.

For tonight, he could be hers and she could be his.

She melted into his kiss, letting him consume her soul as he took her lips. That feeling…that feeling of deep carnal bliss, oh…how she had missed that.

As he kissed her, it was easy to remember why and how easily she had first fallen in love with this man. There was nothing as good or as satisfying as what he was making her feel right now.

She moaned and he opened his mouth slightly, letting her breath fill him as she hoped that he wanted to fill her.

"I want you." She slid her hands up, running her fingers through his thick hair and pulling his mouth hard against hers as he took in her words.

She moved them toward her bed, pushing away a box that was in the center of the room with her foot but still not breaking their kiss.

It had been so long since she had felt this way in his arms. And even in her wildest fantasies, she had never thought she would be back falling into bed with him.

He broke away. "You know I want you. This." He pressed himself against her. "You do things to my body…" He growled. "But I want to take care of you. And the last thing I want to do is screw up whatever is starting between us."

Logically, everything he was saying was sweet and thoughtful. She could even argue he was right, but it didn't staunch the way she felt or the need she had to feel him.

"Let's just see where tonight takes us." She tried to sound sultry, unconcerned, and far from the woman she really was—the mother who had a million worries on her mind.

Right now, all she wanted to do was to run away from

the truths of her reality with a man who had often taken center stage in her dreams.

Mike looked up at the ceiling, like the answers he was looking for were posted there. He should have known by now that when it came to their relationship—or whatever it was they were trying for here—there were no easy answers. They were both only left with questions.

He took her by the hand and led her to the bed. "Here, lie down."

Yes.

She did as he instructed, letting go of his hand as she scooted over to the other side of the bed—the side that had always been hers when they had been together.

He smiled as though he was thinking about the same things. He got into bed behind her and perched on his elbow as he looked at her. "Now, roll over."

She frowned at him, but he made a spinning motion with his hand.

"For now, I'm only going to rub your back. You need to get some rest. If this…this step in our relationship is something that you seriously want, it can wait. I am not going anywhere."

Chapter Eleven

He'd always had a special place in his heart for Summer, but damn if this woman wasn't going to kill him—she could be hard on a man. All he had wanted to do was to throw her down on that bed and make love to her until the morning sun broke into their reality. But those kinds of decisions led to ramifications he wasn't sure either of them was ready to face.

She was confused right now, hurting. As was he. But he hadn't been about to take advantage of her vulnerability, even if she had initiated the physical closeness, so he'd rubbed her back until she'd dozed off last night and then slept on the sofa. Or tried to. He'd spent most of the night tossing and turning, waiting for a call from the kidnappers. And he'd risen early to head out for breakfast, so she wouldn't have to make it or fret about not having much to offer.

Yes, he would have loved to have had a relationship with her, but if something went wrong—as things so often did in life, especially when she still had a chip on her shoulder about their past—he couldn't risk losing what he was hoping to have.

Wait. What was he hoping for, really?

He had told her all he wanted was for a functional,

even good, parenting arrangement between them. But was that all he wanted? If they could go back to where they were and things went toward marriage again, he wasn't sure how he would react.

After last night and him putting a pin in her advances, he couldn't help but wonder if Summer would see his actions as just another rejection. He wouldn't blame her if she did. But she had to know that when it came to matters of the heart, he was a man who had to take things slowly. Sex was easy. Love was incredibly hard. And he had an awful habit of having sex turn into love and a need for a relationship.

They both couldn't give a relationship the attention it needed. Joe had to come first. Finding him had to come first. And God forbid something worse actually happened to Joe—and things didn't turn out like he wanted them to and he didn't make it out of this alive—they would never get over it. She would hate him. No. Before anything happened between them, he needed to get Joe back into the safety of their care.

Then they could worry about the rest of whatever was happening between them.

He walked into her apartment, carrying two cups of coffee and croissants. Hopefully she was awake. If not, he didn't want to rouse her. She needed some reprieve, but they also needed to be ready to hit the road. The kidnappers could call anytime now. And they needed to come up with something that would help stall them until they could be found and they could get Joe.

As he rounded the corner, he found her sitting at the kitchen island bent over her phone and scribbling on a notepad. "Hey. Where were you? I didn't think you were coming back," she said, her words coming out in a flurry of syllables surprisingly devoid of anger.

And there he had been, worried about his rebuff and her feeling rejected.

"I hope you don't mind. I borrowed your car. I just wanted to get us some food and you are woefully lacking in the pantry department." He set the bag on the counter in front of her and she dug in, taking a sip of coffee and opening the wrapper without even looking up at him. She started to scribble again, but he couldn't read what she was writing. "What are you working on?"

"Huh?" she asked, taking a bite.

"What happened to light this fire?" he asked, motioning toward the notes.

"Oh," she said, swallowing her bite. "I woke up and I had this idea and I did a little digging." As she spoke there was a strange inflection, like she was hiding something, but he didn't press.

"About?"

"Well, last night we told the kidnappers the best formula was the one with the yellow lid from Costco. What if these guys actually listened and went there to get it?"

That seemed like a reach, but he didn't dare say that to her when she was feeling empowered in their hunt.

"I've been pulling security camera video—I got access from some contacts I have. I figure they have to have stayed in the area and there is only one Costco. The way I see it, even if they didn't get the formula there, at least it's a place to start. They're going to have to get baby food and diapers somewhere. Basically, everything. And we know we are looking for a man named Rico, could be short for Richard or Ricardo or Enrico. Or not." She shrugged and waved the thought off like it was of no matter. "If we can nab a photo of these guys, we could get to them in a matter of hours. *If* we get lucky."

If was the keyword in that statement. There were millions of things that could go wrong with her plan.

"Did you find anything on the video?" he asked, motioning to her computer as he took a long drink from his coffee.

"I have seen a few potential suspects. I've cleared about thirty individuals so far. We have three we are going to have to look into a little deeper." She stuffed the rest of her pastry into her mouth and stood. She stuck out her hand like she wanted the keys to the car.

He handed them over and, finishing off his croissant, followed her out. He chewed fast, swallowing the last bite as he got into the car and buckled in. He had a feeling today was going to be a wild-goose chase, but it was a hell of a lot better than sitting around and playing the waiting game.

Summer headed south, well over the speed limit and barely slowing at the stop signs. "The first one on my list is a man named Cody. I found his picture and info in a search of public records—he was picked up for a DUI a year or so ago. He is in his midfifties and isn't married. He lives alone and works for the power company. So far as I can tell, there is no reason that he would need formula and baby wipes."

He could think of quite a few reasons the man would need something like that, but if this made her feel better, so be it.

"Did you hear anything from the kidnappers?" he asked, holding on to the "oh shit" handle above the passenger-side window as she nearly flew around a corner.

"No." She shook her head. "But I did call the number

they contacted us from. Of course, it came back as busy and didn't go through. That was where I started when I couldn't find you." She glanced over at him and there was a strange guilty look in her eyes.

She was hiding something, but he had no idea what it could have been. Maybe she wasn't hiding anything and he was just seeing things that weren't really there. Maybe it was simply his own guilt for not being the man she needed that was leading him to read far too much into things with her. Or maybe he had lost some of his ability to look at her and know what she was thinking. It had been over a year since they had been this close.

"Anyhow, this Cody guy…" she continued, "he seems like the most promising of the leads I have so far. If we come up empty-handed, maybe our suspects just haven't hit the stores yet. But these guys will and, when they do, I'll be ready."

That was, unless they had actually been prepared to kidnap the baby and had gotten all their supplies in advance of taking any action. Any good team would have had everything planned out long before they'd taken any real action, and they'd have been overly prepared. But then again, the man they had spoken to last night had seemed at a loss when it came to babies.

"What are we going to do about the coding? What if we just hand it over?"

She looked at him like he'd lost his mind. "First of all, I don't have the code. Sure, I *had* it, but I don't keep that kind of information once I achieve my objective. I just pass it along to my team leader."

"Given the circumstances, don't you think they could work with us on this? Maybe give us some of the code and bury their own somewhere in it? We could use it to track them."

Summer nodded. "There isn't a chance. Besides, these guys are probably not the ones who want the code. In cases like these, when government secrets are involved, these kinds of ransom teams are normally only getting the information to sell it off to foreign governments or other bad guys. It would be stupid of them to use the codes for themselves."

He knew it was likely she was right, but they still needed some sort of leverage when it came to negotiations. If they didn't manage to get the drop on the men who held Joe, they needed to be ready to have something to trade. "What if we prepared some dummy code? Worst case, we don't use it."

She slowed the car, but only slightly. "Maybe I can get my team leader to help, but my crew would probably be starting from scratch. Who knows how long it would take." She sounded dejected, as if she already knew the idea wouldn't work.

He hated when she sounded like that, resigned to failing. "You never told me what the code was actually for."

"Does it matter?" she countered.

He pursed his lips. "Yeah. It could. I have a team we can turn to, as well. You know Zoey is amazing with tech. My teams at STEALTH, if given the information, can set to work. That way we have all of our bases covered. Consider it our contingency plan."

She nibbled at her bottom lip.

"You need to tell me the truth. If you want, it never has to leave this car, but I need to know why this is all so important to these people. If I don't know what is motivating them, then I can't know what they are willing to lose in order to get what they want. And the last thing I want is for them to get to a point in which they are so desperate that they are willing to hurt Joe. I would never be able to get over something like that."

She sighed. "How much do you know about Con-Flux?"

"All I know is what Zoey and my team at STEALTH have told me."

Summer scowled as she looked at him. "You can trust me, Mike. I hope you know that."

He hated the way she was making him feel right now. They both knew secrets weren't something that could be shared between them, not really. If he gave her sensitive information, it could end up with both of them being killed—possibly even by their own teams. If they told secrets, they were a liability. Whatever they said to one another, no one could ever know. It would be the greatest exercise in trust that either of them could ever participate in with one another—was he willing to take the leap of faith?

If he opened up to Summer, he would not only be putting himself at risk, but also his team—a team that contained his siblings. As much as he loved Summer, he could never put one of his siblings in that kind of position.

"You know I can't—"

She stopped him with a sideways glance. "I get it. But what I'm about to tell you could get me into a whole lot of trouble. I need you to be on the same page as me... and we need to get Joe back. No one outside of this car has to know what we say to one another. But you need to know some truths, and so do I. This is all about Joe."

He squirmed in his seat. If she told him something,

anything that put him in danger with his team… "I don't think—"

"Stop. I know what you are going to say," she said, her words coming out at a mile a minute. "But here's the deal. If I don't tell you who you are working for, and you continue on, you may find your guys get in deeper than you ever thought possible." She nibbled at her lip, like she was pausing to weigh the ramifications of what she wanted to tell him.

"What in hell are you talking about, Summer?"

She slowed her speed a little more. "ConFlux and its late CEO were working for the DOD."

He had known that the company had been taking military contracts, so her information wasn't much of a surprise. Yet her opening up to him made him clench. Something felt *off.* "Summer, stop."

"Don't worry, I already scanned my car for bugs. My phone is in a Faraday bag. Put yours in, too." She motioned toward the desert khaki bag between them. He did as she instructed. "Now, stop worrying. Just listen. You need to have an idea of what we are up against."

He set the Faraday bag back on the console between them. Of course, she would think about their safety. She'd likely had this conversation all planned out long before he had even gotten back with their coffees.

"Okay, but I don't want whatever it is you are going to tell me to—"

"Get you in trouble?" She finished his sentence, her words coming fast.

"That's one way to put it," he said.

"I'm trusting that whatever I tell you remains between us." She locked eyes with him. "Can I trust you?"

He paused, thinking about all the implications that

making such a promise would mean. If he agreed, he would be putting her before his family and before his team. "You know I care about you, that I want to know what you have to tell me, but you can't ask this of me."

"I am not asking you to compromise yourself, just to listen."

He wasn't sure she could have one without the other, but he didn't bother to argue. When Summer had her mind set on something, there was nothing that was going to stop her. The last thing he wanted to do was to be the one who would delay them from getting their son back. If she needed him to be on this team for the good of their spontaneous family, then he needed to get on board. Joe first, consequences second.

Mike gave a slight nod, motioning for her to continue.

"ConFlux doesn't just machine parts for the government. They also work in tech that is unknown by most of the public. In the early 2000s, they started working for the DOD, machining parts for fighter jets and then UAVs. But since then, those technology systems have started to take a back seat to other, more *dynamic* technologies."

Working overseas, he'd witnessed more than his fair share of dynamic technologies. When he'd been on patrol, he had seen everything from old car batteries used as bombs to tech that could sense vibrations on house windows and tell him what the people inside were saying. What, exactly, Summer was talking about could have a million different definitions, and he wasn't sure he wanted to know specifics. At least, he wasn't sure he wanted to ask and be drawn further into the web she was weaving.

He held his tongue.

She checked him, and her expression soured slightly

as though she knew exactly what he was thinking. "The code that was taken was for some of these dynamic technologies."

"What would the kidnappers within Rockwood want to do with it if they got their hands on the information?"

She looked away from him. "Well, that is where I'm a little foggy. I'm not sure whether or not this code would be kept by them or sold. And if it was to be sold, which I think is more likely, I don't know if it would be to foreign governments or traded domestically."

"Why would someone in the States want code for tech that was built for the US military?"

Summer smiled wickedly, like she was proud he had sniffed something out. "The DOD assigns governmental contracts to only a select handful of companies. These contracts can be extremely lucrative. In essence, this could be a case of corporate espionage—some other US company could be employing Rockwood to get the information so they can undercut ConFlux to gain control of the limited government contracts. But this is all just a hypothesis."

Holy crap. He'd had no idea. This information could change everything.

And he couldn't tell a single soul.

He dropped his head into his hands as he tried to make sense of everything she was saying. For now, the only certainty was that he had to know more about what Summer had gotten herself wrapped up in. "What kind of tech is this code actually for?" he asked, a sickening lump forming in his stomach.

She chewed on her bottom lip. "It is used in the making of IGS—Information Gathering Systems."

"Such as?"

She switched on her blinker, slowing as she turned down a side road leading to their primary suspect's residence. "They have been helping build nanotechnology the size of bugs and smaller, which can be deployed in a variety of mission settings from combat to civil unrest. Basically, it's used in building the proverbial flies on the wall. This tech can also be used, however, with whatever chemical weaponry they deem necessary."

He tried to control the shock that was undoubtedly marking his face. ConFlux had been profiting from the world of nano warfare. He'd heard whispers of tiny devices that were information collection bugs. There had been talks in Congress sometime in 2009 about such things, but he had yet to have heard of or seen them actually being built or deployed en masse.

The result of such devices being employed on the battlefield and in intelligence gathering was almost unimaginable. It was potentially as life-changing as bringing the internet to the public. Once this IGS technology was released, everything would change. There would no longer be any safe place. Everywhere and everyone could be compromised.

And now, the code to create the technology was at the center of their war to get their son back. They couldn't allow anyone to get their hands on the code—not when it had such potentially cataclysmic ramifications for the world—but they also had to do something to save their baby.

Chapter Twelve

Though Summer had promised herself she wouldn't compromise Mike by giving him information he shouldn't be privy to, she had done exactly that. But the DTRA and Kevin were doing little to help Joe, and she needed answers and she needed them fast. As far as she could tell, she would only get them by bringing Mike into her inner circle. Sure, she could potentially lose her job if they found out she had divulged government secrets, but right now she trusted Mike far more than anyone else.

No one cared about Joe as much as they did. No one would fight as hard as they would. Kevin had proved just that by blowing her off and telling her to just sit still when her son's life was at stake. If he found out about what she'd told Mike, he only had himself to blame.

She pulled her car to a stop about a half a block from their first suspect's house. The man was nowhere to be seen, but that didn't mean he wasn't inside with Joe, holed up like the criminal he potentially was while he waited for the ransom demands to be delivered. Well, he could keep waiting; she was done playing Rockwood's games. Right now, she was the one in control, hunting down the people who wished her and her loved ones harm.

This was her game now.

She glanced over at Mike; he looked at odds with everything. She didn't blame him.

He'd always had the power to bring her back to reality and make her feel like she was nineteen years old and completely adrift. Had she told him too much? Was he thinking she was a security liability to him? Was he thinking she was untrustworthy? Had she made a mistake in telling him anything?

Damn, she needed to get out of her head. But ever since she had dropped the info bomb, Mike had been silent. No doubt, he was thinking about all the things she'd said, piecing it all together with whatever his group already knew. He was also probably thinking about how he was going to tell Zoey and his teams at STEALTH about this newly acquired information.

She didn't want him to go to them with the details, but at the same time, she was almost sure it would be exactly what he would do.

"The nanotech they are working on right now at ConFlux is called Mayfly." She felt bad feeding him a fake code name, but if she heard it from another outside source, she would know if Mike and the STEALTH team used it.

Here was hoping she never heard the code name Mayfly again.

She hadn't wanted to bring Mike in this deep, but the people who had taken Joe had struck low and had left her with no other cards to play. She'd had to call him in; he was one of the only people she knew she could trust. At least with him, she could understand his motives and his driving forces. Understanding those meant she also understood his weaknesses—and his strengths. And right now, she needed every strength he bore as she was barely able to process a single thought. If he proved himself, she would tell him the whole truth. Maybe.

Though she understood that what was happening, and her inability to focus, was due to her emotional state, it didn't mean she could control their effects on her mental state. She had been trained to be mentally resilient and deal with stress, but no one had prepared her for a situation like this. Was she strong enough to do what needed to be done? What if she failed? What if Joe ended up getting hurt—or worse?

Her breathing quickened.

One step at a time. One task at a time. That's all she could focus on right now. Anything else and she would lose whatever ground she had managed to gain in her search.

Resilient. I have to be resilient.

This step was all about their suspect. If they got lucky, Joe would be inside the gray house with the white covered porch just down the street. Joe would be fine. He would be gurgling and cooing inside with this Cody guy and Rico, who would prove not to be monsters but merely instruments of the bosses who employed them to do their bidding.

Here was hoping. And here was hoping Mike didn't figure out she was still keeping things from him. If he did, he would likely never trust her again.

"Let's head over there, see if we can get a bead on Joe. If he is in there, we will bust down the door." She ran her hands over her face as she thought about calling Kevin again and telling him where she was and what they were doing. No. He didn't need to know she was going against orders. She was an agent for the DTRA and sometimes being an agent meant she had to go a little rogue.

Mike pulled out his phone from the Faraday bag and started to text someone. Was he already telling Zoey about the nano secrets she had shared? Was he telling her about Mayfly?

Summer stopped her thoughts before she let out a resigned and pained sigh. This, trusting Mike, would be a test.

"You ready?" she asked, grabbing her phone out from the Faraday bag.

By the time they got done here, it was likely that STEALTH would know all about the inner workings of ConFlux and their secret work for the Department of Defense.

He slipped his phone into his breast pocket as he looked over at her. "Let's stick together. No matter what happens, we can't split up. I don't want to lose sight of you. Got it?"

She nodded as she looked around. The neighborhood was quiet. It seemed as though everyone in the area was either at work or at school; there wasn't even a dog outside sniffing around. In fact, if she was forced to describe it, she would have said it was eerily devoid of any evidence of life. How was it possible that there wasn't even a bird fluttering around, picking at bugs?

The words "calm before the storm" came to mind.

Well, they were that storm.

She smiled to herself as she stepped out of the car and Mike followed. He walked beside her on the sidewalk. "Hold my hand," she said, extending it toward him.

If they wanted to be ignored, the best thing they could do was to look like a happy, normal couple.

He slipped his hand into hers and, as he did, she thought of the way his fingers had felt on her back as he had loved her last night. The memory made her want to sink into him, to let the warmth of his embrace lull her into a sense of comfort, but they weren't what they used to be and she would be foolish to think otherwise.

Without realizing it, she mirrored his walk and they moved in sync. Just another of the subtle body language cues that bespoke a happy couple. It was strange how their bodies had such incredible muscle memories when it came to each other—and especially their hearts.

She could so easily imagine falling back in love with him. And as she realized it, she wondered if she had ever really fallen out.

They moved toward the house, strolling along. The suspect's driveway was empty, but there could be a car parked in the garage.

The gray house sat back from the road, its yard in desperate need of a mow. Weedy flowers poked up through tall grasses as they angled for the sun. The blades of grass brushed against the cuff of her pants, making a scratching sound that she doubted she would have normally noticed, but now sounded as loud as a semitruck barreling down a dirt road.

Nearing the door, they could hear the sound of techno music playing inside, the noise thick with rhythm but devoid of anything Summer would have considered enjoyable. She sent Mike a glance. From the quirk of his brow, she could tell he was thinking something similar.

"Apparently, we are walking up on Studio 54 here," he joked.

"You think he has glow sticks and bottled water for us when we join the party?"

Mike chuckled. "Just the thought of what it must be

like in that house makes me worry about catching some kind of communicable disease."

"The only thing I think we are going to have to worry about catching from this guy is a case of being chronically single."

He started to laugh, the sound a bit too loud and out of place, and he clamped his mouth shut.

She stopped at the front door. The music rattled the windows and, from where she stood, she spotted a worn leather couch and a forest-green recliner perched in the man's living room. The floor was cluttered with spent candy wrappers and take-out boxes, but there was nothing to indicate their baby was inside.

"Let's walk around back," she said, making sure that they were still, as of yet, unnoticed.

Mike hopped down from the porch step, holding out his hand to help her. As she stepped down, she let go of his hand. She wanted to go for her gun, to be ready in case something went sideways here, but she talked herself off that ledge.

If the man inside saw them stalking around his house with their guns raised, there was no way she could talk herself out of the situation. Someone would undoubtedly get hurt, and the last thing she wanted to do was to put Joe into a situation in which he was in even more danger. Not to mention how things would play out with Kevin.

She needed to fly just under the radar here.

They moved quickly around the side of the house, slipping through the wooden fence's gate, silently clicking the lock open and making sure to keep it slightly ajar in case they needed to make a quick exit.

Her body tensed as they moved toward the back wall of the house, careful to stay out of sight from anyone who may have been inside. Hopefully the guy was alone or with only his accomplice, as she had assumed. While she was reasonably proficient with a gun, it wasn't typically her style to put herself into a situation where it could turn into a Wild West shootout. She was more of a "stick to the shadows and take them out at their proverbial knees" kind of woman.

Mike raised his fist in the air, motioning for her to stop. His body rested on the wall beside the sliding-glass door. His hand lowered to his weapon, readying for the threat, but as he peeked around, his hand moved off his gun and up to his face. Moving back to his position, hidden by the wall, he glanced over at her. His body was convulsing with silent laughter.

"What?" she asked, wondering what the hell had gotten into him.

"This is definitely not our dude."

"But…he was buying formula and diapers. And he had a history of working overseas and in the Sandbox. Are you sure?" She frowned. The hope she hadn't known she had been feeling twisted down her chest and pooled at her feet like spent tears.

"You have to see this. Seriously," he whispered. He stepped in her direction so they could switch positions on the wall and she could glance inside.

As she moved around him, she tried to remind herself that she'd known this was a thin lead from the moment she had discovered the man. She had been grasping at straws; she couldn't be disappointed now when it quite possibly would lead to nothing.

She leaned around the door frame and peered inside. It took her a minute to make sense of the scene in front of her. There, standing in the middle of what would have been a dining room in most homes, was a man in his mid-fifties. Around him was a series of white, lattice-style baby gates. The floor was covered with a zoo-animal-patterned blanket. The dining room had been transformed from the heart of the household, where most families had dinner chats and meetings, into a makeshift playpen.

Her gaze moved to the man. His chest was exposed; a pacifier was laced on a string around his neck. He wore an adult diaper and a pair of duck slippers. Sitting beside the man was a bottle and a can of the yellow-lidded baby formula.

What in the hell had they walked into?

She had always thought she was open-minded and relatively nonjudgmental, but standing there staring at this man-baby, she was utterly shocked. And angry. Angry because she'd wanted this to be a kidnapper, wanted to find Joe, and he wasn't there.

In her wildest dreams, she had never seen anything even remotely close to the scene in front of her. And though she was aware she should look away—that they should bug out and get as far from this as possible, and get back to their hunt for Joe—all she could do was stare.

The grown man dressed as a baby sat, blissfully unaware he was being watched. He reached to his left and picked up his cell phone like he was recording himself. He made gurgling sounds and popped the pacifier into his mouth.

Wow.

There was a tug on the back of her pants as Mike pulled her away from the door. "You agree this isn't our guy?"

She nodded, unable to put words to the flurry of thoughts and feelings she was experiencing.

Mike took her hand, a smile on his face. "If all your leads are this *interesting*, we are going to have one hell of a day."

Chapter Thirteen

Back in the car, all he could do was look down the road at the unassuming gray house and laugh. "Summer, that has to be one of the craziest things I have ever seen in my damned life." His words sputtered out from between guttural laughs.

Damn, it felt good.

She covered her mouth with her hands, seemingly embarrassed by the situation in which they had found themselves. "I swear, I had no idea. I just put the pieces together. Something was off." She started to giggle.

"Oh, I can totally understand how this guy would raise some red flags and how you would want to check him out, but *damn*." He roiled with laughter as he thought about the man standing in the middle of a baby-gate playpen dressed like an oversize baby.

He had heard of infantilism, but…just *wow*.

"I… That…" Summer giggled. "Did you…?"

"Oh, I saw what was going on in there. That was… wow." Their words filled the spaces between their laughter as they tried to make sense of exactly what they had stumbled upon.

Tears started to streak down Summer's face as her

giggles turned to full-blown roaring laughter. "That... is...the best...thing... I've ever seen...in my life."

For what must have been five minutes they sat in the car and laughed. Though it was one of the strangest things he had experienced, Mike was grateful. It had been so long since they had laughed together like this, and the tension of the kidnapping had seemed to push away the possibility of laughter until they got Joe back. This, these moments lost in the throes of joy, he wanted a life of with her.

He wiped the tears from the corners of his eyes then reached over and ran his thumb across Summer's cheek. "If nothing else, I feel like I need to thank you for that. Seriously," he said, gaining control over his aching gut, "I will never forget that as long as I live. That was amazing."

She dipped her head, moving her face deeper into his palm. "I aim to please."

"That, that right there, is something I know all about. You are by far the best woman I have ever met for that, and many other reasons." The words spilled out of him without his really thinking about it, but as they dripped from his lips, Mike suddenly felt embarrassed.

He shouldn't have said that, not right now, and maybe not ever. They were already treading on treacherous ground when it came to their feelings toward one another and any possible future they could have; he shouldn't be making it any more complicated by opening up to her like he just had. It was just, with levity filling the air had come the desire to be tender and honest. And Summer had opened up to him...she had trusted him with her secret. That had to mean *something*, didn't it?

She reached up and touched the hand that still rested on her face. "Before I had Joe, I always thought you were the greatest gift in my life. I was right, but then you ended up giving me a greater gift than I could have ever imagined. If that is all we ever get to have together, then I will consider my life blessed. You…you made me a mother."

His body drove him toward her and he took her lips with his.

Damn. He loved this woman so much. There were so many reasons not to kiss her, not to take this step or go down this road with her again, but he couldn't stop himself.

Besides, he could love a friend, and friends kissed… right?

She reached up and ran her fingers through his hair, pulling him closer to her, like she couldn't get enough. This. Her. It was all so *hot*.

But they couldn't. No.

Not right now. Possibly, not ever.

He removed his hand from her face as he leaned away, breaking their kiss. "I'm glad to have you back in my life. I don't know how I survived without you…and your friendship."

The light in her eyes flickered and dulled. "My friendship," she said, her words equal parts question and pain. "Yeah."

He didn't know what to do to make the light in her eyes reappear, but he wanted it back. She reached down and started the car, effectively putting an end to the moment, and it pained him. He put his hand on hers as she reached for the gearshift. "Summer, you know I never stopped caring about you."

She pulled her hand away. Putting it on her knee, she tweaked the fabric of her pants. "You can't do this to me." She sighed and looked down at her fingers.

"Do what?" he asked, not exactly sure which "this" she was referring to.

"I can't get my heart broken by you again. It hurt too much last time. I was stupid for thinking we could take things to the bedroom last night. I regret it. I shouldn't have even made that an option. At least, not yet." She sounded as if she was at odds with herself.

"Not yet? Does that mean you think there could potentially be something between us? Beyond co-parenting?" he asked, not sure if he should press her with questions.

"Our co-parenting arrangement needs to come first. Joe. He needs to come first." She pulled her hands into fists and then opened her fingers. "There are so many things going on right now... I'm afraid if we kiss again—if we do *whatever*—that we will both come to realize it was a mistake. And there is no going back. I don't want to relive the past."

He knew all too well about wanting to redo the choices he'd made in his past. His thoughts flashed to the agony on her face the moment he had told her that he couldn't marry her. If there was one moment he would want to take back, that was it.

Things could have been so different.

"You're right, Summer," he said, yielding to their complicated reality and the validity of her words. "I'm sorry. I shouldn't have kissed you."

"You didn't see me pushing you away." She smiled gently, looking over at him. "I—*we*—just have to both be strong and do what is right. At least, right now."

He had to find solace in the fact she had left the door slightly ajar, just enough for him to slip into her life and perhaps someday find a relationship. But he held no hope it would be the same as before, or that it would even really happen.

For now, he just needed to be in the moment.

"What other leads do you have?" he asked, trying to pull himself out of the heaviness of the air that surrounded them. "Please tell me that we have another diaper-wearing man to look into," he teased. "That was unforgettable."

She laughed, the sound sprinkled with stress. "I'm sorry. I never— Again, I had *no* idea."

"Oh, don't apologize for that. It was awesome." He laughed. "We need to find Joe, but part of me wants to go back and get pictures of that dude. Troy and AJ would get a kick out of that." He took his phone from his pocket, about to text his family.

"What are you doing?" All the laughter was stripped from Summer's voice, catching him off guard.

Why would she care who he was texting? Was she jealous?

"I was just going to tell the fam about the dude. They are going to laugh so hard."

She frowned, but nodded slightly. "Ah, okay."

Something was off, but he wasn't sure what he was picking up on—the weirdness of their relationship or something else.

"You want me not to tell them?"

She smiled, the action forced and false. "You know that if I see them again, they will tear into me for taking you there."

"Nah, they are cool like that. If anything, they're going to be jealous they didn't get to witness it firsthand." He laughed, the sound as off as her smile.

Her phone vibrated and she retrieved it. "Hello?" she said, answering.

He looked out the window as she put the car into gear and they started to slowly drive away from the man whom neither would forget.

"Any leads?" she asked, her sentence clipped.

He couldn't make out the words coming from the other end of the line; all he could hear was the timbre of a man's voice. It must have been someone she worked for. And then a thought struck him…she didn't work for STRIKE and she'd said she *had* worked for Rockwood, but who did she work for now? Who was on the other end of the phone, feeding her information and asking her questions?

He tried to check himself before he grew suspicious of Summer or read too much into what was happening. She had told him more than he could have asked for. If she hadn't told him something, it was for a reason. He didn't have to like it, but his life was also cloaked in secrecy, and he had to accept their reality. He, too, was limited in what information he could share, and with whom.

She glanced over as he looked at her, guilt flashing across her features.

Could she tell what he was thinking?

He turned, looking out the passenger-side window as they drove toward the highway.

He couldn't get sucked into the endless confusion of questions and second-guesses. He could be aware, but he couldn't force Summer to do anything or to tell him anything she wasn't ready to tell him.

In the meantime, he could wait—as long as it didn't interfere with their finding Joe.

"Sure," she said to the person on the other end of the line. "Thanks." There was a flatness to her voice.

She dropped her phone on top of the khaki bag sitting between them on the console.

He wanted to ask her who she had been talking to and what was going on, but he held back. She would open up to him when and if she wanted to. Until then he had to be patient.

"Who else did you want to look into?" he asked, trying to make the look of disappointment lift from her face.

"The next one on my list doesn't quite fit the profile we are looking for." She seemed to forget about the phone call on purpose, like she didn't want him to think anything about it.

Fine, two could play the ignore-the-obvious game.

"This time I have a lead on a man and a woman," she continued. "From the video I pulled, it appeared they were having a tense discussion in the formula aisle before getting the brand we recommended. They have no child on record and the man is on the federal watch list."

How would she know who was on the federal watch list? Was it possible that she was now working for the government?

Some of the pieces seemed to click into place.

"I'm sure your team has a pretty good idea of what they are doing and who they are looking for, but it seems to me that most new parents have probably had some kind of fight in the middle of Costco."

She laughed. "You have me there. You're probably right."

If he kissed her again, would she open up? They had put a pin in anything between them, but damn, he was tempted to try to make her forget herself again.

He thought of Troy and Kate. Kate worked for the FBI. Maybe he could make a call and she could get in touch with her people in the Bureau and they could look into Summer and find out who she worked for and maybe even why. And yet, the idea made an empty thud within him. He didn't want to have to do this kind of digging on the woman who had been such a big part of his life for so long.

Here Summer was, bringing him into her life with one open hand while pushing him away with the secrets she held in the other. Frustration filled him and a grumble slipped from his lips.

"What's the matter?" Summer asked.

He wanted to unleash the truth, to tell her all the things he was thinking, and then at the same time he wanted to rise above it all and not give in to the swirling mess of his thoughts and feelings.

"Summer, can I ask you something?" he said, glancing over at her.

"Sure," she said, but she didn't sound it.

"Something is bothering me about you, and I don't want you to get upset, but I need to make sense of a few things. Okay?" he asked, hating that he was going to have to take a roundabout to get to the truth of who she had become and why.

She slowed the car, but didn't stop driving. "Shoot."

He nodded, almost unconsciously. "So, you told me that things went south with STRIKE and you went to work for Rockwood. You don't work for them anymore. Yes?" he asked, treading lightly.

"Yep." She gripped the wheel tight, pulled the car over to the side of the road and put it in Park. Letting go of the wheel, she stared over at him. She opened her mouth like she was going to speak, but stopped. She motioned as if to speak three times before she made a sound. "I know what you are getting at. And I'm not as good at this as you are."

Had she meant for her words to be a jab? He wasn't sure what "this" she was talking about and he wasn't sure he would like it once he did, but he had to know.

"Good at what, Summer?"

She stared at her hands like they held the answers. "Did you tell your family about Mayfly? Did you tell anyone?" Her tone made him feel like he was the one on the spot and not her.

"I didn't. I wouldn't. You asked me not to. Why do you ask?" He made sure there was not a single twang of falseness in his voice; she didn't need to read anything into him that wasn't there. Right now, she had to be looking for anything to keep her feet out of the fire. "I wouldn't betray your trust, never again."

He could see her mouth form words and her eyes take on the storm that came with a fight, but just as quickly as the tempest started, it receded. She gave a resigned sigh. "I just needed to make sure you won't betray me, and that you know I will never betray you, Mike. I couldn't just run headfirst into this thing, whatever it is, without first doing some checking into you."

"Uh-huh." He crossed his arms over his chest and leaned back in the passenger's seat as he waited for the rest of her storm to play itself out. He tried not to be hurt by the fact she hadn't trusted him and she'd run a background check. If anything, he should have been flattered that she would go to that much work to have him in their lives. "And what did you find?"

"Nothing so far, but I'm still looking." She watched him as if she could find the answers she was looking for in his features.

"You mean *your team* is looking into things." His words sat sour on his tongue.

She cringed, the motion so subtle that if he hadn't been looking for it, he would have likely missed it.

"Yes, my team."

"You gonna tell me about who you are working for, or are you going to make me drag it out of you, Summer?" he asked.

She tapped her fingers on the steering wheel. "I'm not trying to be difficult, Mike. I swear." She paused, collecting herself. "You know if I tell you, I could be further compromising your safety and mine. Don't you think I've already compromised you enough, given the amount of information I've already shared?"

"I'm in the fray. You can't stop talking to me now."

"But will it make a difference if you know who I'm working for? Will it matter in getting Joe back?"

She had him there. "Based on this," he said, lifting the Faraday bag for her to see, "you must be working for a group made up of a lot of initials. I need to know how much trouble I'm going to be in if it comes out that I'm working with you. So, which alphabet soup organization is it? Please tell me that you are working for the government and not another group like Rockwood."

Her mouth fell open with shock. "No. No. I'm not working with the bad guys. It's nothing like that."

This woman was in deep. Only how deep was yet to be discovered.

"Did you come to Missoula just to meet up with me?"

She didn't meet his eye.

"So, yes?"

"I needed someone I could rely on." Her words were charged with emotion. "You were the only person I knew with connections to Rockwood who wouldn't know I had infiltrated the group. I needed information, but I also needed to stay in the shadows. My boss wants me to find out how much Rockwood had ended up pulling from ConFlux after I gave them the keys."

"Who are you working for, Summer? You have to tell me."

"The man on the phone was my boss at the DTRA. I've been an agent for them for the last twelve months. They have been great."

"The DTRA?" He was familiar with a lot of the acronyms within the federal government, but this wasn't one of them.

"The Defense Threat Reduction Agency. We are a part of DARPA. Technically, I'm working remotely out of an outpost connected to the New Mexico office."

DARPA, he had heard of; it had been created during the Manhattan Project. Did that mean she was working with weapons of mass destruction? "Holy hell, Summer. Are you working with nuclear weapons?"

"I'm not—at least, not right now." She shook her head. "Right now, I'm still working on low-level threat assessments and implementing effective neutralization strategies."

"So, let me get this straight…you are the one who finds 'threats' and then calls in teams to wipe them out?" He frowned as he tried to make sense of what she was saying.

"In layman terms, yes." She nodded. "And to answer your next question, yes, the DTRA is the reason I was working with Rockwood. Like I said, I had been infiltrating their company. Basically, Rockwood should have gotten nothing. It's why I needed you. Why I've been asking you about Rockwood. Do you know if they know my real identity? Have I been exposed?"

"Do you think they found out about your being a double agent and they connected the dots?"

"It's the only reason I can think of for why they are coming after *me* for the codes. I mean, why else would they target me—Joe?"

"Damn, Summer. Just… *Damn*…" He sounded breathless even to himself.

She put the car into Drive and merged back into traffic. "You can say that again. But I'm still not sure how they figured out that I was a double agent. There were a few times they might have found out, but the links would have been thin. I mean, how would they know I had access to any of the codes, codes I sent to my boss? For all Rockwood should have known, I only broke into the network. That was it. They shouldn't have known about any codes."

They sat in silence as she made her way onto the highway. He had no idea where they were going, but he didn't bother asking.

He chuckled as he watched her. "You do know how cool you are, right?"

She jerked slightly as she looked over at him. "What? What are you talking about?"

"Really. You may actually be one of the coolest chicks I know." He gave an amazed laugh. "Here I was, thinking that you had totally just screwed up your life and gotten yourself into major crap without intending to. And yet, I was wrong."

"No, you're not wrong. I definitely got myself into some major crap." She sent him a coquettish smile.

"Yeah, but what happened was entirely outside of your

control. You didn't know these people would infiltrate your family and steal Joe as a result of your work," he offered, hoping that his support would help rid her of any guilt she may have been feeling. She had only been doing her job. Nothing more. "So, explain the thing with Ben. Do you think it was him who sniffed out your identity?"

"He is smart, but I don't think he did. I was so careful around him. My team at DTRA ran strong cover for me. Like I said, I don't think he is the one behind the kidnapping or them asking for the ransom to be paid in the stolen code. I think he came to my apartment to win me back, and saw you. He was just hurt and angry. He is jealous."

Just because she didn't think Ben was behind Joe's disappearance, it didn't mean Mike would stop hating the dude. If anything, he wanted to punch him in the face more now than ever.

"Does Ben still work for them?" he asked.

She nodded.

Yep, he hated him. But sometimes two people didn't need to like each other to find common ground. "What if you called him? Do you think he could help lead us to Joe? Maybe he knows what they did with him."

She smiled. "I don't know...but that is a good idea, after all. I know I rejected it at first. Maybe he has someone he can go to. He loved Joe, too, you know."

The words burned at him, but he tried to cover them with the salve of possibly getting some much-needed answers. "I'm glad. Joe needs to have as many people in his corner in life as possible."

Yeah, being a parent was going to be one heck of a kick to the ass if these last few days were any kind of preview of what was to come. Underprepared and overwhelmed didn't even begin to encompass all the feelings he was having about becoming a father to this little boy. However, it came with the knowledge that when something involved his son, he would do whatever it took to make sure he was safe—even if that meant putting himself in dangerous and uncomfortable situations…with or without a grown man dressed up as a baby.

"Summer, you are having a hell of a big life." He smiled over at her. "I'm proud of you for making the best out of a bad situation. And again, I'm sorry I forced the change upon you."

She met his smile with her own. "I'd be lying if I said it has been easy, but at the same time, I have to admit that since we split, I have done a lot. I'm proud of how far I've come. How much I've learned. You forced me to grow in ways I never thought possible, and for that I can be grateful."

Chapter Fourteen

No wonder she had never done great as a spy. Sure, Summer had gone through a few months of training before the DTRA had put her into an active intelligence-gathering role, but when it came to Mike, he had unmatched skills in actually listening to her and picking her reality apart. Whenever she was around him, it was as if he stripped her naked and exposed her in a way that only he could see.

That inability to conceal anything from him for very long, and the desire to not want to hide any of her truths, had to mean something about them was unique, unprecedented and whispering of soul mates. Didn't it?

She chuffed at the thought. No, that's not what was going on here. This was all because she had been forced to bring him into her little world and reveal more than she had anticipated. Though she hadn't meant to give him breadcrumbs that led him to the truth, that was exactly what she had done. There was nothing ethereal or otherworldly about their bond, no. It had all been set up by her subconscious mind. She had wanted him to know the truth, to pull it from her. And more, to care.

Was her taking him down this path her subconscious

way of making sure that if he was going to be in their lives, he would be willing to work for it?

Gah... She had to stop picking this thing between them apart. They just needed to work together, find Joe, and then they could figure things out between them.

Pulling over at a gas station, Summer watched as Mike got out to begin filling up her car. "I'm gonna go make a phone call. I'll be right back," she said.

Mike answered with a tight nod. He definitely hated Ben, and she didn't blame him, but this phone call had been his idea and he could hardly be annoyed that she was doing as he had asked.

The justification for her actions did little to stop the pull at her gut that told her to hide what she was doing to protect his feelings. And yet, at the same time, she didn't want to hide, she wanted him to know and to be a part of everything.

This was all so confusing. It had to be the stress that was messing her up like this. Just the stress.

She walked to the side of the building, far enough from the gas station's car wash that she didn't pick up too much background noise, and far enough from the entrance that anyone coming and going from the little convenience store couldn't eavesdrop.

As she was about to speed-dial Ben, she stopped and hit the number just two down from it on her Contacts list. Kevin answered on the first ring. "Hey, how's it going?"

"Hi, Kev. It's going. Any word on Joe?" She silently begged for a miracle.

"Were your ears burning?" he asked, a smattering of excitement in his voice.

"What is that supposed to mean? Did you get him back?"

Kevin sighed. "You and I both have chatted about this

and you know that it is the US government's policy not
to negotiate with terrorists. In this case, that terrorist is
your son's kidnapper. However, I have finally gotten the
approvals required from top brass to *assist* in your son's
safe and rapid return."

Ah, the power that came with knowing the right people to call.

She rose on her tiptoes and put her free hand up
against the beige stucco wall of the store. "Thank you…
Kevin…thank you." Relief flooded through her, though
she hadn't even heard Kevin's idea. No matter what he
said, it had to be better than going to Ben and possibly
tipping their hand to whomever else Ben was working
with. As much as she had gone to bat for the man with
Mike, she still didn't truly trust Ben. Not in her world of
spies and counterspies.

"Don't thank me just yet, Summer," Kevin said, his
voice suddenly taking on a serious edge. "First, we don't
know if this is going to work, but it is what my team believes is the best option in this situation."

"And what is that? What are you guys thinking?" She
looked down at the dirt on the toes of her black boots.

"We have taken the code that you supplied us with
from ConFlux and have altered it enough that it looks
legitimate even to a proficient coder. Then we added in
a few little lines here and there, which should help us pin
down the IP address of whomever is trying to use it. Basically, once they run the program, we can swoop down
and take these guys into custody."

"How long will it take you to get the code ready?"
The kidnappers had only given her another twenty-four
hours. The people at the DTRA would have to work fast.

"Well, this is the part you are really going to like. We

are already done. We've been working on it ever since you told me about their demands."

"Kevin, you are amazing. No matter what the rest of the guys say."

"What? What are they saying?" Kevin said, laughter marking his words. "I will send you the code now through our encrypted server. Let me know when you put it into the kidnapper's hands."

"Will do," she said, smiling.

"And, Summer, give Joe a big hug from me." Kevin hung up.

She may possibly have the best boss ever. It took a special person to put his neck on the line to do what was right and go the extra mile to support his teams. And yet there was the little voice in the back of her head that screamed it was Kevin and her work as an agent within the DTRA that had really gotten her into this predicament.

Mike was just clicking the gas cap into place on her car when she made her way back out to the bay. "I have good news," she said, smiling over at him as she lifted her phone for him to see.

"Ben choked?" he joked.

"Better. I just got off the phone with my boss." She glanced around, looking for anyone or anything that was out of place. She motioned toward her car in the hope that if there was anyone following them or listening, she could thwart their attempts. "They have agreed to supply the fake code we need for the ransom. You are a smart guy with the idea for the code. Thanks to you and Kevin, we're going to get Joe back."

Mike flashed a smile but it was suddenly overtaken by a sour look.

Even to her own ears, the plan sounded simple…too simple. What was she missing?

"You know, kidnappers often kill—"

She cut him off with a raise of her hand. "I don't need to hear that. We don't even need to *think* about that happening to Joe. These people know the only chance they have to get the information they want is to give him to us. There would be no advantage in killing our son."

Mike nodded, but the look on his face didn't recede. "I just think we need to be prepared."

"There is being prepared and there is putting crap out into the universe that doesn't need to be put out into the universe." She was aware she sounded paranoid, but more times than she could count, when people put energy behind something, it tended to happen.

Losing Joe wasn't something she wanted to even imagine. Right now, they were just watching him…they would give him back. All she and Mike had to do was give them the information they wanted in exchange.

He put his hands up in surrender. "I hear what you are saying and I get it, but know that no matter what happens, I will be here for you."

She couldn't help but notice that for a split second Mike made it sound like Joe wasn't just as important to him as he was to her. Opening her mouth to argue, he stopped her with a glance.

"I know what you're going to say and you don't need to say it. If something happens to Joe, you know it will hurt me just as much as it may hurt you." His eyes shone. "I never thought I could instantly love anything or anyone like I love him. I know I've missed so much. And I wish I could have been there for all the milestones that I have already missed with him…" He hesitated, like he was attempting to collect himself, and it pulled at her heartstrings.

It was reassuring that he was just as invested. Though she hadn't been sure things would go this way when she had gone to see Mike, she was glad that he had so quickly embraced fatherhood. He had exceeded her expectations in his ability to be open and kind, generous of spirit and soul.

Since he'd left her at the altar, all she had done was focus on all the mistakes he had made in their relationship. She'd focused on the times he'd forgotten to text her back and had said the wrong things at dinner parties. She had spent all of her energy trying to stoke the fire that would burn away the love she had for him, and yet there standing with him, she was reminded that all it took was one spark to start a wildfire of passion. And damn, did this man know how to set her entire being ablaze.

"Nothing is going to happen to Joe," she said, choking on all the emotions that filled her.

"You know it," he said, wrapping his arm over her shoulders and walking her to the passenger side of the car. "Why don't you let me drive? Then you can work on getting the handoff scheduled."

She clicked on her seat belt as she waited for Mike to walk around and get into the driver seat. It was like the old days. They had slipped back into their habits so rapidly, and as much as she wanted to be annoyed—she had changed so much since they had been apart—she found solace in the familiar.

They had gotten answers. They were going to get Joe back, and yet she wasn't excited. If anything, she was terrified. What if something went wrong? What if Kevin didn't get her the information like he promised? What if the kidnappers didn't show?

She hated to get her hopes up.

She stared down at her phone, wondering what she should do next. Kevin was working on sending her the information she needed. There was only one thing she needed to do to get the ball rolling. She opened up her message app and tapped out a note to the number the kidnappers had used to contact them.

I have the code. Meet us at the Roadhouse. Half hour.

She waited for a reply as Mike fired up the engine and drove out of the bay and toward the road. He turned in the direction of her apartment, and she wanted to tell him not to, to go anywhere that would potentially lead them toward Joe, and yet she remained quiet. Just because they were driving, moving, it didn't mean they were moving in the correct direction.

Her phone's screen turned off.

What was taking them so long to get back to her?

Finally, after what seemed like an eternity, her phone beeped with a message.

They would meet them there in an hour, Joe in hand.

All they had to do was not screw this up. Get the code to the people, get Joe, and get out.

Doable. Very doable.

She raised her phone so that Mike could see the message. "The Roadhouse is only twenty minutes from here." She pointed for him to take the next left, leading them in the direction of the restaurant.

Mike smiled as he glanced over at the phone screen. "Good job."

She'd half expected him to say "here's hoping," but was glad when he didn't and instead let the air go still between them.

They rode in silence, the road noise filling the car. Her mind wandered to the restaurant, the layout. If they sat near the door, they would be in full view of everyone in the place. With witnesses came some level of additional safety. They could get Joe, get out.

Her phone pinged with a message from Kevin. The file was now in her hands and, with it, some of her fear lifted, just barely. So many things could go wrong, but she had to focus on getting everything just right.

The restaurant's parking lot was mostly full, but they found a spot not too far from the door. Her breath caught in her throat as she watched people walking in and out of the place, some getting in their cars while others chatted with friends before saying goodbye. Life was happening all around them.

No one knew about the terror and fear she had been feeling, only Mike. Was he feeling the same pressure, the clenching feeling, like everything in her future—and in Joe's—depended on this single meeting?

There was so much at stake, one wrong word or careless action could lead to her son's death, not to mention her own. Her life was of no consequence—she had chosen to put herself at risk thanks to her job—but Joe was innocent in all of this.

"Kevin sent the code," she said, forcing herself to focus on her phone in preparation for what she hoped would happen.

"If something goes wrong, and things come to guns, I want you to promise me that you will do everything you can to just get the hell out of there. I will take care of Joe—"

"I promise to get out of there, but only after I get Joe. I'm not letting him out of my sight ever again."

Mike smiled. "College is going to be really uncomfortable for him then."

She let out a laugh, the sound too sharp for the moment. "Think of all the things that I could save him from by always being there," she said, forcing a smile.

"He would be a chaste forty-year-old with a mommy complex for sure."

She laughed. "Oh, when you put it like that…"

Mike stepped out of the car, walked around and opened the door for her. He put out his hand. "Normal, happy couple. In and out. In ten minutes, Joe will be back in your arms and everything will be okay."

She smiled at the thought as she slipped her hand into Mike's. His hand was strong, just like the man.

This would all be okay.

Making their way inside, they chose a seat near the door so they could have full view of everyone who came and went from the restaurant. The eatery was busy, and the sounds of people talking and the smells of food cooking comforted her with their reminders of normalcy.

He took a seat next to her, sliding into the vinyl booth seat like they were out at just another dinner. Yes, she just had to fake it. Put a smile on her face and act like they weren't giving false information to a terrorist group to get an infant back from kidnappers.

Just another day. No big deal.

How had her life gotten to this point? At what moment had things taken this dark turn? And how could she avoid ever finding herself back in a moment like this?

She picked up a menu after a server brought them their drinks. She stared at the pictures of food and the letters that she knew spelled words, but she wasn't reading. All she could think about was how her hands were trembling and how she had to force them to stay as still as possible so as to not raise any sort of suspicion.

The front door of the restaurant opened and two men came in. In their arms was Joe's gray car seat.

What if they were playing a trick on her? What if Mike was right and they had hurt Joe?

Until now, she had thought waiting for the men and counting down the seconds until they arrived was the worst part. But now she was sure it was this moment that was the most painful. Being close enough to her son to almost see his smiling face and yet far enough away that he could be gone in an instant made her feel as if she was staring into an abyss.

The man closest to them looked over, spotted them and said something to the man carrying the baby. Their faces were tight and, as the second man looked over at them, a dark cloud rolled across his features. They walked like they were half dead with exhaustion.

They trudged toward them and, as they moved, she could make out the unmistakable bulges of guns tucked into the waistbands of their pants near their appendixes. Her throat tightened. She and Mike weren't the only ones ready and willing to fight.

Mike reached down, under the edge of the table, and put his hand on her knee like some kind of steadying force to remind her that everything was okay. "We got this," he said under his breath.

She didn't dare look away from the men approaching their table, but she answered Mike with a slight nod.

One way or another, they were going to do this thing. Here was hoping that the three of them made it out of this alive and the two men who had dared to steal their baby would end up paying for their actions.

"Evening," the man carrying the car seat said, but there was only falseness in his tone.

He and his friend slipped into the booth as a hostess brought over an antiquated wooden high chair and helped them set the car seat up at the end of the table. Summer stared at the car seat as the hostess lifted it into view, but she could only see the gray polka-dotted coverlet she used when Joe was sleeping.

"Thank you," she said, dipping her head toward the hostess as she turned to leave.

The woman smiled at her like she was just another customer on just another day.

Summer wrapped her foot around the base of the high chair and pulled the wooden stand closer to her.

"Hold up," the man across the table said, grabbing the high chair and stopping Summer from moving it any closer to her.

"Look, it's not like I'm going to pick Joe up and just go running out of here. We have a deal, but before I agree to anything, I have to know that my baby is all right." She scowled.

The man raised his hands in surrender, letting her pull the high chair over to her. "Just know that if you screw with us, we will hunt you down. Next time, we will kill the kid and you."

She could feel the blood rush from her features as she thought about the ruse she and her DTRA team were playing on the men, but she forced herself to focus on Joe.

She opened the coverlet. Joe was inside, his eyes

closed and a pacifier in his mouth. The pacifier was the cheap plastic kind found at any big-box store, not the usual blue silicone ones that he preferred. Reaching in, she ran her thumb across Joe's warm cheek. As she touched his soft skin, he let out a contented sigh and his lips pulled into a smile, the pacifier teetering on his lower lip.

Joe was fine. The men had kept their promise and kept her and Mike's baby safe.

The heaviness that had filled Summer ever since Joe had disappeared started to lift. They were all going to be okay as long as they could make it out of this restaurant without a problem.

"You've seen him," the man said, pulling the high chair away from her and forcing her hand from her baby. "Now, you need to give us the code."

"Look, I'm his mother, and I need to hold him. You can take those guns you're carrying and shoot us all, but then you won't get the code, and you probably won't make it out of here alive—or you don't know Montana."

"If you think you can touch that baby without first giving us what we are here for, then you don't value his life. You really think it's worth taking the risk?" the man asked, arching a brow.

She reached down and grabbed her phone, but she didn't take her gaze off of Joe. He looked so peaceful, so blithely unaware of the drama that had surrounded him and brought him to this moment.

"Before she gives you anything, we need to make sure you know that once we give it to you, that's it," Mike said. "We are out. No more harassing us or putting your hands on Joe. If you touch him again, I will kill you. Got it?"

He put his hand on hers before she had a chance to activate her phone to retrieve the information.

The man who had been carrying Joe chortled. "Man, if you think we want to babysit ever again, you are bat shit crazy." As the man peered over at them, she could make out the dark circles under his eyes, which were normally indicative of a new parent, or in this case, an underprepared kidnapper. "But first we gotta get what we came here for."

Whatever Joe had put them through, these jerks had had it coming.

Noticing the tiredness in their features, a sense of vindication filled her. At least Joe hadn't made it easy on them.

Good job, baby. She smiled in Joe's direction. Hopefully he would never lose that fighting spirit. Well, unless she was the one fighting him. Then she prayed he would take it just a little easy on her.

The man nearest the wall pulled out a small tablet she hadn't noticed him carrying and brushed aside a few crumbs the busser had neglected to wipe away.

"Rico here is going to check your code. If something is up, if it doesn't look exactly like it should, then we will kill the baby." The man nearest to Joe pointed at the car seat. "And believe me, we will be more than happy to do it. That little bastard kept us up all night and we haven't eaten in over twenty-four hours. I'm tired, I'm hungry, and I'm pissed...so don't screw with us."

No matter how uncomfortable and pissed off these guys were, it paled in comparison to everything they had put her through. If he thought he was scaring her, that he had any power over her now that Joe was so close, he was wrong. All she cared about was that baby.

But then, she wasn't going to get out of here if Kevin had screwed her on this. And Kevin and the DTRA had already made a mistake in failing to understand or to foresee the consequences in her data breach and theft. If they'd had their acts together, she, Mike and Joe wouldn't be in the position in which they now found themselves.

Could she really trust that Kevin had done everything in his power to make things right? Or had he and his IT team just phoned it in?

"Where do you want me to send the code?" she said, careful to keep her voice down.

The man pushed a slip of paper across the table with an email address. "Send it here."

She opened up her phone and clicked on the file Kevin had sent her. With a few more presses of buttons, the file was in cyber space and moving toward the kidnappers. "You should have it."

Her heart thrashed in her chest. This was the moment. The moment everything could go wrong. The moment Joe could be hurt, and it would all be her fault.

Had she been wrong to trust? Had she been wrong to come here? Had she been wrong to think that agreeing to lie to her enemy was the best course of action?

The man tapped a few keys on his tablet as Rico watched over his shoulder. They looked like two nervous schoolboys, which made her wonder exactly how high up in the ranks they were. Based on their fumbling of the kidnapping and this, it was easy to tell these two men were nothing more than the instruments of someone else's will…someone who didn't want their name or face to be known. The thought helped ease some of the tension Summer was feeling.

Hopefully these two didn't know good code from bad.

The man looking over the code turned to Rico and gave him a stiff nod, seemingly pleased with the information she had forwarded.

Without another word, the man slid out of the booth and stood. Rico gave her a vicious smile. "Here's hoping we never have to see you again. If we do, you and everyone you know will wind up dead."

Chapter Fifteen

To say things had gone unexpectedly was a bit of an understatement. In his wildest dreams, Mike would not have imagined that he and Summer would simply get Joe and be on their merry way within minutes. They had been fighting this so hard, and struggling to find work-arounds, that the answer and the handoff just seemed far too simple.

He didn't trust it.

Nothing of value was ever that easy. Especially not when it came to the safety of the people he cared about most.

Arriving back at Summer's apartment, he helped her bring Joe inside. Neither had said more than five words to each other since they had left the restaurant. From the worried expression on Summer's face, he wondered if she was feeling the same way. It surprised him that she had wanted to come back to her apartment at all. If he had been in her shoes, he would've bugged out and found himself on the next plane to South America.

She carried Joe in his car seat to her bedroom and he could hear her unclipping the seat belt and Joe gurgling as she must have lifted him out. She hummed as she set about working. Mike walked down the hall, stopping at her bedroom door and peering inside.

Joe was lying on the bed, kicking his feet in the air as he blissfully watched his mother take a suitcase down from her closet. After it was down, she grabbed a diaper to change her son, but Mike stepped in to take over.

"Thanks," she said. "He is acting pretty good, but I want him to be clean and dry when I hit the road."

So, she was planning on leaving. And Mike couldn't ignore the fact that she had only said *I*. Did that mean she had no intention of taking Joe with her, or was she planning on taking Joe but not him?

"Where do you think you are going to go?" Mike asked.

"If those guys are smart," she said with a dark laugh, "then by now they probably know that something is up with the code."

She hadn't answered his question.

"Do you really think they figured out it was bad code that fast?" He took the diaper she held, along with the bucket of baby wipes and the mat.

He glanced at Joe. They exchanged a look with one another like each knew exactly how poorly this diaper change was about to go. While he had changed a diaper in the past, it had been at least twenty years ago when he'd taken home a lifelike doll from his health class and put it through the ringer. And while the requirements for a good diaper change were probably the same, he wasn't sure whether diapers were or not. In fact, he couldn't remember or not if he actually used duct tape last time he'd been asked to do this.

"Rico and the other dude may not have figured it out, but whomever they are working for probably has...or is probably about to. All they have to do is run it on a big enough server and they are going to encounter errors."

"You are assuming the information they are looking for isn't buried deep." As much as he thought he understood IT and cyber security, he still felt out of his depths. "What exactly was the coding used for?"

"IGS," she snapped.

"That, I'm more than aware of. I know it's for the information gathering systems." How could he forget a bug that could infiltrate anyone's home and life? "I guess what I'm asking is why they couldn't just write this code themselves, or find someone who could?" he pressed, hoping for a real answer this time.

"Does it matter?" She raised her arms akimbo, giving him that cute look that used to make him forget what he was doing and sent them straight to the bed...the bed that was now hosting a wiggly baby.

Joe made a little raspberry sound as he stuffed the back of his fist into his wet mouth.

"Even you know she's being ridiculous, don't you, little guy?"

Joe kicked his feet as Mike went about stripping him down, making getting his little doll-size clothes off something closer to a rodeo event than the blissful moments he'd seen on television commercials.

"You want to put the extra diaper under his bum, and get a wipe ready for the splash zone." She motioned at her undercarriage.

Yep, this was definitely something he could imagine at the annual Arlee Rodeo. He could almost imagine the announcer talking through the tinny ring of an outdated sound system, his words coming faster and faster as he neared the eight-second mark.

He pulled out a wipe after slipping the clean, open diaper under Joe. Joe tried to roll, forcing Mike to hold him in place with one hand while trying to close the open lid of the container with the other. Apparently, juggling was also part of this rodeo act; and…well, he was quickly starting to feel as if he was playing the clown.

Summer put down a shirt that she was folding and stepped forward as if she was going to take over the operation.

"Nope," he said, putting his hand up to stop her. "You do your thing. Joe and I've got this." He smiled down at Joe. "If we are going to be buddies, then I'm going to have to figure this dad thing out."

Summer turned away from them, but not before he saw a pained expression flash across her face. She had brought him here and into their lives with all kinds of talk about him taking on an active role as Joe's father. But now that things were getting a bit more complicated, it felt like she was driving a wedge between them.

What else was there to say? What could he do to reassure her and make her see that he was going to be in their lives, and protecting them as long as he needed to?

"I know you're scared right now, but I told you before that I got you. If I need to get STEALTH on board for security or whatever…we can do it. We specialize in helping people in situations all too much like this."

She didn't turn to face him, just waved her hand in acknowledgment.

He opened Joe's sodden diaper and set about changing him, moving as rapidly as he could to keep from getting the mess anywhere it shouldn't be. Joe looked up at him with wide eyes, his lower lip starting to quiver as he grew chilled.

He let out a long wail, followed by a stream of warm liquid…hitting Mike's center mass. "Oh! Oh crap…" he said, covering Joe up with the clean diaper as fast as his hands would allow. Joe stopped wailing as Mike fastened the last strip over the baby's waist and slipped his pants back on over his flailing legs. Picking him up, he held him in one arm.

Joe's wail stopped and he went back to sucking on the back of his hand as Mike looked down at his soaked shirt.

The damage was done.

From beside him, Summer's laughter rang through the air. "I told you to watch out for the splash zone!" she said between laughs.

"A little splash zone I can deal with, but this—" he motioned toward his shirt "—was like sitting front row on Splash Mountain."

"No one said you weren't going to get your hands dirty," she teased. "I offered to take over, but no…someone was trying to be all cute and charming with his little fatherly act."

Mike wasn't sure if he should be offended or bemused, so he went with the latter. "Cute, huh? You think me getting peed on is cute?" He picked up the sodden diaper and wrapped it into a little ball.

"Don't you dare throw that at me, if you do…"

"What?" he taunted, holding it up a little higher in a mock threat. "What would you do to me?"

She stepped closer to him and they stood chest to chest, with her looking up at him. "You think you are real tough, don't you?" There was a look in her eyes that made him temporarily forget everything other than her and the boy in his arms.

That look. He loved that look; he had seen a flash of

it last night. But this time it was different. This time it didn't carry the pain of the past; instead it only spoke of the present and begged for a future.

"I'm always stronger when I'm with you," he whispered into her hair after leaning in.

She melded into him, Joe between them as she wrapped her arms around Mike and he took her with his free hand. This. This was his family. No matter if they were married or not married, in a relationship or not. These were the people he would happily lay down his life to protect and love.

There was nothing he wouldn't do for them.

"Babe, I hope you know how much I love you." The pressure that had been building in his chest from the first moment he had seen her in the parking lot released as he spoke the words.

There was a long silence. The only sound was of Joe making smacking noises as he sucked on his hand.

Summer didn't have to say anything back. He didn't care. He just couldn't hold those words in any longer. Not when they had already gone through so much, and not with her leaving without him.

She needed to know the truth—that his love for her hadn't gone anywhere and hadn't diminished with time. His love for her would be with him until his dying day, no matter the status of their relationship.

There was a bang on the apartment's front door and Summer jerked out of his arms. "What the hell?" Her voice sounded strangled by fear. "You don't think Rockwood found us already, do you?"

That was fast, but so was everything else in their lives.

"It's going to be okay," he said, handing her Joe. "You just take him and go into the bathroom. Get into the tub in case things move to guns. No matter what happens, I will deal with it."

"You can't go out there alone." She pulled Joe against her body, wrapping her arms around him like she was his shield.

"And we can't risk Joe getting hurt or taken again. If they get their hands on any of us, I have a feeling we aren't going to make it out of this alive."

Her eyes widened as his words struck home. "You… you have to be careful."

There was another series of bangs on the door, the sound reverberating through the apartment like church bells beckoning from their tower.

He nodded, motioning her to hide in the small en suite bathroom. "Go."

Watching to make sure the door clicked closed behind her, Mike made his way out of the bedroom and into the living room. He stared at the white door for a long moment. If he looked out through the peephole, he was the perfect target for anyone standing on the other side just waiting for the right moment to pull a trigger.

If there was a suppressor on the weapon, no one in the apartment complex would even know what was happening. The attackers could shoot him, come in and kill Joe and take Summer. Or, they could kill them all.

Summer was strong, capable, smart, and myriad wonderful things, but he was more practiced and physically stronger and, right now, he was their first line of defense. He couldn't just let an attacker get a bead on him, not when so many lives were at stake.

He rushed to the back door, silently closing and locking it as he slipped outside. The night air had the bite of coming frost and carried with it the unmistakable odor of danger.

The alley behind the apartment building was empty and he was careful to step lightly as he made his way down the potholed road and around the side of the building. Thankfully all the apartment blinds were closed. He made sure to remain concealed as he glanced around the side of the building. Standing in front of her door was a man, late fifties, gray hair, and he was wearing a suit jacket.

Though the man didn't look like either of the men who had taken Joe, Mike couldn't be sure that he wasn't their boss or someone else from the Rockwood organization. If anything, it was smart to send someone they didn't recognize, someone who could get in and get out without really being noticed.

Then again, if this guy was going for being unnoticed, what was he doing banging on the door? If the man was like Mike, he would have slipped in through the back of the apartment, done what needed to be done, and then slipped out into the darkness of the night.

Their murders would have gone unsolved forever.

It struck Mike how wrong it was that he was, in fact, planning their deaths.

He was warped. Yet it was this ability to think about the unthinkable and to plan for the worst that had made him effective as a military contractor. Death was inevitable; it was just how one got there that was up for grabs. And today, he would be pushing it away with both hands and maybe a foot to the ass.

The man banged on the door again, looking over his shoulder as if he could feel Mike watching him in the moonlight. It was odd how the human being had a sixth sense when it came to danger and yet rarely actually listened to it.

Yes, the man was right to be afraid. If he was smart, he should have listened to the fear and turned tail and gone back to where he had come from.

Tonight, he was playing with fire.

The man shifted slightly, his back to Mike as he looked out toward the main road. Mike slipped around the side of the building as he unholstered his gun and stalked forward. The man had pulled his phone out of his back pocket and was hitting buttons as Mike drew nearer.

He was so close that he could smell the man's expensive cologne and make out the faint red line on the back of the man's neck where he must have recently gotten a haircut. The guy put the phone up to his ear. "She's not here. Are you sure this is where you tracked her phone to?"

Oh crap.

Mike wished he could hear what the other person was saying, but all he could catch was a guttural moan escaping the man's throat. "I'm sure that she is going to go underground, given what happened to her son. We've trained her well enough."

Was this someone from the DTRA? Was her team swooping in to help her out? Something about the man's being there, even if he was someone from the DTRA, didn't quite sit right with Mike. Why wouldn't they have told Summer that they were coming? Why would they just roll up on her door in the middle of the night, especially knowing all that she had recently gone through?

"We need to get a bead on her. Use your resources," the man said, clicking off his phone and stuffing it back into his pocket.

The man moved as if about to turn around, but before

he could, Mike grabbed him by the neck, effectively pinning his head in a choke hold as he pushed his Glock's cold steel barrel against the guy's temple. "Who the hell are you? And what the hell are you doing here?"

The man gave a slight yelp, moving for what Mike was sure was a weapon at his waist.

He pressed the Glock harder against the man's temple, no doubt leaving a nice little ring on his flesh. "That's a bad idea. Just tell me who you are."

"My name's Kevin. Kevin Warble. I work with Summer. I'm here to help." The man spoke fast, brusquely.

"Help her with what?" Mike could give the man nothing, no clues he had any idea about what was going on or why.

"She is in danger. I can't tell you anything else." Kevin looked at him as Mike tightened his hold around the man's neck.

"Did they use the code? Are they coming for her?" Mike asked, giving the guy just enough information to make it clear that he wasn't completely in the dark.

Kevin said nothing but scowled and then moved to break out. Mike pulled tighter. "Dude, I don't want to hurt you. I just need to get some damned answers. Why are you making this harder on yourself than it needs to be?"

The man sighed. "I wasn't expecting Summer to have a security detail."

"You thought you could just come here and get the drop on her?" Mike countered.

"What?" Kevin stopped moving. "Why in the hell would I want to hurt Summer? She is a tremendous asset to our team."

Mike kept his gun firmly pointed at the man's head as he let go of his neck and allowed him to stand straight.

"You can't expect me to believe you are standing out here and banging on her door in the middle of the night for her own good. So why are you here? Are they coming for her?" he asked again.

"We have reason to believe so, yes. They ran the code." Kevin scowled. "I have to admit I'm disappointed you have any knowledge of what is happening here."

"Well, if you hadn't left Summer with her ass hanging out then maybe she wouldn't have had to come to me for help. If you are pissed, you need to look to yourself. As you said, Summer is a tremendous member of your team, and she has always been the same to me."

Kevin glanced away, like he, too, had known the DTRA had made a mistake when it came to the safety of one of their team members. "It wasn't our intention for anything to happen as it has. We didn't believe Rockwood had any knowledge as to what she had gained access to and had managed to send to us. If we had, you have to know we would have done everything in our power to keep her safe."

"You should have gotten out in front of this," Mike said.

"And you should lower that gun, but it seems like we are both a little bit jumpy when it comes to this situation."

This situation? The man talked about Summer's life like it was an afterthought. No wonder she had run to Mike for help.

He didn't like this man, not at all. But he lowered his weapon. For now, the only person who could find a way out of this muddied circumstance was the one person who Mike wanted to keep safe.

Hopefully he wasn't making a mistake in letting this man come close to the woman he loved.

Chapter Sixteen

Summer stared at Kevin like he had lost his mind. "You want me to do what?" she repeated.

Kevin smiled, the action saturated with remorse. "Your friend, Mike, was right in what he said out there. It was wrong of us to put you in this kind of situation. And I know that this solution is the best. It will keep you out of the line of fire for a while."

They stood in her living room, arguing. As soon as Mike had let Kevin in, he'd started to explain his plan. It was simple, straightforward, and unattractive. Be carted off to a safe spot. Alone.

"And what about Joe and Mike? Do you really expect me to just pack my bags and disappear? Leave my child behind?" She looked over at Mike. She didn't want to leave him; he seemed like the only person in her life who really had her best interests and her safety in mind. And she couldn't bear the thought of leaving Joe, who now slept peacefully in his crib in the back bedroom.

"I know that you are probably thinking this sounds crazy, but you need to keep your son safe. Mike can take him until we get a hold on these Rockwood people and can guarantee your safety. Then you can come back." Kevin paused. "You knew when you took this job that things weren't always going to be ideal when it came to having this career and a child. I'm sorry, but now it is time to follow through on your oath."

Her entire body clenched with resentment and anger. She had fallen into the "it won't happen to me" trap when she'd agreed to work for the DTRA. She had told herself that she was putting Joe first by taking the job with its financial security and eventual stability. She would only be a field agent for a short period of time and yet, here she was, paying the reaper for her hubris in thinking she had the world on a string.

It seemed like she would never be able to do the right thing.

She had promised that she wouldn't leave Joe again and here she was…

If she took Joe with her, he would be in danger—even on a military base. And what would she do with him while she went to work? They wouldn't let her take him into the field office, and she'd be damned if she'd leave him in the hands of a stranger. So that left her at odds again. Mike was her only option, but it still meant leaving Joe.

"Your son will be safer not being with you until we get this sorted. If you want, I can have him placed in a foster home if you don't feel good leaving him alone with him." Kevin motioned toward Mike.

"Oh hell no." She shook her head violently, nauseated by the mere thought of someone she didn't even know having physical custody of her baby after she had just gotten him back to safety. "Mike can take him. I will go with you."

"Perfect," Kevin said, his remorseful smile growing. "We have a private plane waiting on the tarmac just outside the air base. They will take us to Kirtland Air Force Base in New Mexico. You can hole up while we gain control over the situation."

Summer couldn't believe that this was what it had come down to: to save the people she loved, she had to leave them alone.

"Don't worry," Mike said, reaching over and touching her on the shoulder like she was nothing more than a friend. "I will take great care of Joe. If I need any help, I can always turn to Jess. You don't need to worry about us, you just need to get to a safe location before something else happens."

She just couldn't wrap her mind around this. She had made a promise to herself that she wouldn't leave Joe again; not when there were people out there who were willing and able to get their hands on him and put him in the ground to get to her.

Why did she have to make the choice between two men who had promised her the world, one out of love and the other with her career—but both central to her past, present and future? Mike had hurt her, deeply. Yet, there was no doubt in her mind that she could trust him with Joe. There were no safer hands.

Kevin's phone pinged with some kind of message. "I'll be right back," he said, turning away from them and stepping outside to answer.

"Are you really sure you can trust this man?" Mike murmured quietly, a look of total disgust marring his handsome face.

"Why do you ask?" Summer didn't want to tell Mike she didn't know if she could or she couldn't; she didn't know what to do or what the right answer was.

"Everything about him makes me want to tell you to run. I can keep you safe. I can keep both you and Joe safe."

"I have a feeling that you would say that about any man I have in my life. Ben as evidence."

He wrinkled his nose. "I don't like Ben and I don't like Kevin. And to my credit, I ended up being right about Ben." He gave her a long, studying look. "What are you not telling me about Kevin?"

There were many things she could have told Mike about Kevin, from how he took his coffee to how he had an odd penchant for liking to use Helvetica font in his emails. On the variety of field exercises and cases she had worked with him, she had started to pick up on some of his quirks. When he was nervous, Kevin always tapped his fingertips on his left thigh. He was rarely nervous, but when he was, it normally led to more trouble than she could handle.

"What do you want to know?"

The door opened and Kevin strode back into the apartment. "Our plane got delayed. There are heavy winds coming out of the north. Winter storm warnings tonight, and they are projecting at least a foot of snow in the overnight hours. Looks like we won't be traveling anywhere. However, the pilot says he thinks we can get out mid-morning tomorrow."

Summer let out a breath she hadn't realized she was holding. From the back room came the soft cries of Joe as he began to wake up. "I need to go take care of him. Just let me know what time you want me to meet up in the morning. In the meantime, I will make some arrangements for the night…anywhere but here."

Mike smirked. "Why don't you just go ahead and track her like you did earlier."

She twitched. "What are you talking about?"

"Your boss tracked you down thanks to your phone." Mike started to say something else but was cut off when Kevin moved between them.

"How else was I going to find you? You haven't been answering your phone. I needed to find you."

She felt violated. Sure, Kevin had the right and the permission to look into her whereabouts, but she couldn't remember actually ignoring any phone calls from him. Then again, she had been putting her phone in and out of the Faraday bag all day. Maybe she had missed some.

"I thought you were hurt. That Rockwood may have already gotten to you after the handoff," Kevin continued, "And I feel that it's absolutely ridiculous that I have to explain myself to you, Mike, or anyone else. You work for me."

Mike tried to say something, but Kevin shut him down with a backhanded wave. "Before things get even more out of hand here, I am going to leave. If you need help finding accommodations for the night, or if you want me to get you additional security, all you have to do is let me know. We are here for you." He walked out without another look in Mike's direction, closing the door behind him with a thump.

Joe let out a piercing wail from the bedroom and Summer rushed out of the room. What was she going to do? Should she just hit the road with Joe and not look back? And what about Mike? Should she take him with them? Or should she follow the rules and honor the oaths she had made to her job? She could just quit and hand over everything she had been working on. There were plenty of people who could do what she could do.

But Kevin really did seem to care. Sure, her boss had made mistakes in his handling of this situation, but he had personally come down to see her. He had set up a private jet to fly them somewhere he felt she could be safe. He had offered to be her escort to safety.

And so had Mike.

She ran her hands over her face as she walked into the bedroom. Joe was sitting up in his crib, looking out at her as tears welled in his eyes. "Baby…" she cooed. "Did we wake you up, sweetheart? Mama is so sorry." She reached in and scooped him up into her arms, pressing his warm, pudgy body against her chest like he was her security blanket and not the other way around.

She wished she could get him to her pediatrician for a quick checkup just to make sure those thugs hadn't done anything to him when they'd had him. She'd have to figure out how to do that soon. He looked healthy and well-fed, though, and she hadn't seen a bruise or a scratch on him.

Humming "Two Little Blackbirds," she rocked back and forth taking comfort in these stolen moments of presumed safety. She pulled the rich odor of baby deep into her lungs. He smelled so good. She would never forget that smell and the feeling in her chest it created.

This little being…this was her world. What else really mattered?

Her thoughts moved to Mike, to the day he had left her standing at the altar. In that moment, he had chosen to keep her safe in the only way he'd known how—by leaving her. Now, all of a sudden, standing here with a similar choice to make, she finally understood the level of love and pain he had to have been feeling to have made such a devastating choice.

Until now, she had thought that his actions had been out of some misguided fear and paranoia; that he had walked away out of cowardice. More, when he had broken her heart, he had dishonored the promises he had made to her.

She had been wrong.

Though she didn't believe he could love her in the same way she loved Joe, Summer could understand what Mike must have been feeling…the conflicting need to honor or to protect.

In their lines of work, to have the ability to do both was idealistic. They lived in a world of "either-or" but never "and."

What she could have was this one night.

She looked down at Joe, who had drifted off to sleep. Ever so gently, she placed him back in his crib, covering him up with her favorite elephant blanket. If only she could feel as safe and as loved, but also have the ability to forget the fear when he had disappeared.

Turning from the crib, she found Mike standing in the doorway of the bedroom. "I could watch that every night for the rest of my life."

"I hate to tell you this, but Joe won't stay a baby forever." She smiled, taking pleasure in this simple moment of them acting as a family, though it was edged with the sadness that came with growing children.

"What if Joe wasn't our only baby?" he asked.

But he had to have been teasing.

She stayed quiet as she tiptoed out of the room, having him move behind her.

"I mean, how many kids do you think you would want, if you could…" Mike added.

Just when she thought her life couldn't get any more complicated, there he went throwing this kind of talk at her. But maybe Mike was trying to help her take her mind off the danger that could be lurking just outside.

"I thought we talked about this," she said with a tired smile. "I always wanted a boy and a girl. If that didn't happen, I would want to keep trying until I had both sexes."

"I know you said that, but you know that isn't really an answer. According to that answer, we could end up having a dozen boys and still be trying for a girl."

"We?" She couldn't help the smile that spread on her face. "Are you saying you want to have more kids with me?"

He shrugged, suddenly taken with looking at the floor. "When and if things between us are right, I mean."

"Are you saying that you want to start over?" she pressed, excitement coursing through her as she spoke. Mike wasn't the kind who had been overly talkative when it came to his feelings, his wants, or the future.

Sure, they'd had a few conversations, but it had been years since the last one like this.

He finally looked up. "Summer, I told you how sorry I am for what happened."

She stopped him as she nodded and took his hand in hers. "Don't worry. For the first time, I think I understand. Truly. I don't envy the choices you've had to make and I never want you to have to make them again. From here on out, let's just be honest with one another. If you are afraid, if you feel like running, then tell me.

We can talk about it. If nothing else, we can run away together—as a family."

The fear that seemed to have permanently settled on his features lately lifted as he pulled her close. "Babe, I have loved you forever. I *will* love you forever. Do you remember the first time we met?" he asked, levity in his voice.

She laughed at the memory. It had been in Las Vegas, at a George Strait concert. For once, it had been raining in the desert city and everyone lined up outside was being drenched by the dust-laden droplets. Jess had been there with her, their annual girl's trip to the city. They had spent hours getting ready, curling their hair and styling their eyebrows on point. And with each torrent, their hair flattened and their makeup smeared farther and farther down their faces. She could still remember how Jessica's mascara had run down so far that it had made a black streak on her neck.

When Mike had first walked up, with his brother AJ, she and Jessica had been laughing about the state of themselves and trying to hide under their purses to no avail.

"You have always thought of yourself as quite the hero, haven't you?" she teased, thinking about how Mike had produced—out of seemingly nowhere—two ponchos for the women.

"I was definitely your hero that day." He laughed. "Not to mention, your hero when we poured you into the cab later that night."

"Oh yeah…" She had forgotten that part.

In truth, she hadn't planned on ever seeing Mike and AJ after that, but Jess had, at some point in the night, given the guys their phone numbers.

"If you hadn't badgered me," she continued, "you know I wouldn't have gone out with you again."

He laughed. "Yeah, but I could tell in the way you professed your love to me that night that you were the girl I wanted to spend the rest of my life with."

Summer covered her face in embarrassment. "Not one of my proudest moments. I told you then, and I think it begs repeating, but you know I'm not usually that kind of girl. I never cut loose like I did that night. I just…"

"Felt safe?" he said, finishing her sentence.

She nodded.

"You will always be safe with me. I will never hurt you again. Ever."

That wasn't a promise anyone in the world could make and keep, but she appreciated the thought. It was enough to know he would always be her guardian, the keeper of her heart, and the father of her child.

Not to mention that she loved him. She loved him so, so much.

And yet she didn't have time for that right now… They had to get out of here and away from this choke point before Rockwood's people came knocking.

She looked up at him and gave him a gentle kiss on his cheek. "I love you, too, Mike. But I won't make a promise I know I can't keep." She pulled out of his arms and turned away before he could see any of the pain she knew had to be registering on her face. It would have been the perfect moment to tell him she promised him the world too, but perfection was an illusion.

She'd rather have something that was real—and something she could keep forever.

"Do you mind grabbing my bag? I can make a hotel reservation once we hit the road." She didn't look back at him. Not yet, she needed a moment to get control of herself.

Safety had to come first. Then they could talk all he

wanted. In the morning, though, she would have to leave them…no matter what. With love came the responsibility to protect.

There was the creak of the bedroom door as he went for her things.

This was going to be their last night together, possibly forever. If something happened to her at Kirtland, this could be the last night she spent with Joe.

The thought made her feel as though her heart was being ripped from her chest.

How could she leave her son? But how could she justify putting him in harm's way just so that she could be a constant in his life?

From the very beginning of Mike's entrance back into their lives, she had told Mike he couldn't just come and go from Joe's life at the drop of a hat and according to his schedule. And yet she was doing exactly what she had told him not to. To say she felt like a hypocrite was a major understatement.

If she did get to see the boys again, there was no way she could ever draw lines in the sand. They would be equal…which maybe wasn't a bad thing. She had wanted Mike to be a co-parent. Cooperation and compromise. And maybe, someday, something more.

Mike came out of the bedroom, her bag and the diaper bag in one arm and Joe cradled in the other, his sleeping face lying on his daddy's shoulder. A lump swelled in her throat at the wholesome sight; a sight she couldn't have imagined just a few months ago.

How fast and how dramatically life had a way of changing.

"If you grab the door, I will take everything outside." He looked her in the eyes. "And don't worry, this time

I won't leave Joe alone. Not even for a second. We will meet you out there."

She answered with a dip of her head. "Just wait, let's go together," she said, opening the front door for them.

The apartment complex was quiet, but its peace was merely an illusion. Kevin and his team may well have been perched outside, watching and keeping guard. And on their heels could have been the Rockwood crew.

Would she ever really feel safe again?

Mike had his head on a swivel as he stepped out the door. She looked back, around her apartment. This was probably the last time she would be here. There wasn't much, a chair and a few boxes, and she wouldn't miss any of her things; but she would miss having a home.

Someday, maybe she would have stability in her life again. Until then, she'd say goodbye.

Chapter Seventeen

The snow had started to fall, coating the world in a silent blanket as they arrived at the hotel. After checking them in under a false name and acting like a happy little family of three, Mike got Joe and Summer into their room and then moved the car. He parked it two miles away, in front of another hotel, making sure to leave Summer's phone inside the glovebox, should anyone try to track her down again.

He expected they had been followed by Summer's people at the DTRA. That was exactly what he would have done—have a shadow surveillance team securing the perimeter at all times. If they didn't, and something happened, it would be even more of a black eye for the agency when they had to write up the reports. Congress would have a field day if they found out a baby had been put in danger, especially when it came time to allot funding for the program.

If Kevin was smart, he would be on his toes making sure that no further harm came to them.

Here was hoping. It was naive and idiotic to assume anyone was going to protect them. It was like the law enforcement adage about rural areas: "we aren't your first line of defense, we are merely the report takers after the fact."

More times than not, he had seen that sentiment in action. And he would be damned if he was going to be complacent and fall for the dupe of assumed safety.

Walking back to the hotel, he let the snowflakes land on his face. The chill felt good on his skin, invigorating. He had only been in Montana for less than a year; it had been a long time since he had been a part of a true winter. It was no secret that the place could be brutal, winds up to a hundred miles an hour sending snow sideways, blinding and freezing the world as it tore through the countryside.

If that was what they were in for tonight, it was no wonder the pilot had put a stop to them flying out. Truth be told, Mike was thankful she had been forced to stay for one more night. It was greedy and more than dangerous to keep Summer here, with her enemies possibly on the hunt for her, but he wanted as much time with her as he could get.

He quickened his pace, jogging toward the hotel as he carefully picked his way around icy patches on the sidewalks and the ever-growing snowdrifts starting to build alongside the road.

By the time he got back, he was breathing hard and the light layer of sweat that had started to accumulate on his skin just as quickly evaporated into the dry winter air. The blast of warmth hit him like a freight train as he entered the hotel lobby. The man behind the registration desk looked up and, recognizing him, sent him an acknowledging tip of the head.

Ah, small towns. They were part of the world in which

only a few things, things in the darkness of the night, went unnoticed or, at least, unspoken.

He hadn't missed that aspect of Montana. He had always loved the anonymity that came with being a member of STEALTH. But tonight, for once, he was just a man…at least as far as the people in this hotel needed to know. He didn't need them being suspicious if he acted outside of the norm. For now, the best thing he could do was to merely blend in and hope he had a forgettable face.

He tapped on their hotel room door before making his way inside. Joe must have been in the travel crib; a blanket was draped over the bars. Summer was perched on the bed, her knees up, as she watched some kind of true crime television show on the flat-screen.

She put her fingers to her lips as he walked in, then pointed at the crib, motioning that Joe was asleep.

There were so many things he wanted to talk to her about and so many questions that he wanted to ask— about what plans she had in mind, and how they would keep in touch when she went away. When Kevin had requested he take Joe, Mike's first reaction had been absolute and abject fear. He was in no way capable of taking care of a baby alone. The kid had peed on him; he could only imagine what else was in store. He didn't know much about taking care of a baby, and if he didn't have Summer standing over his shoulder and coaching him along, Mike wasn't sure he would really know what to do.

That being said, he would be more than happy to take his son. It was his duty as the father and, even if he wasn't Joe's dad, he would have done it for her.

Summer sat up and moved to the end of the bed. Standing, she made her way over to him and took him by the hand. Without a word, she led him into the bathroom, apparently wanting to talk somewhere that wouldn't bother Joe.

Good.

She pushed the door closed behind them with her foot. He rested against the marble counter and just as he opened his mouth to speak, she moved between his legs and took his face in her hands. He stopped as she stared into his eyes. His body responded; the hungry look she was giving him meant only one thing.

Leaning in, he took her lips and slipped his hands around her waist, pulling her hard against him so she could tell exactly how she made him feel. He wanted her, *had* wanted her from the moment she had come back into his life, but now she was on the cusp of walking back out.

Oh, the irony. It was an incredibly painful thing to have a life filled with contradictions.

As badly as he wanted to take this time and make every part of her body quake with ecstasy, he questioned it. Things were likely to change, permanently, between them if they opted for this road. If he chose to take her, here and now, it would be making the choice to keep her forever. But there was no way of knowing if she was in the same place or same frame of mind. Maybe she wanted to have one last night together.

He wanted to stop their kiss, to pull back and talk. But from her feverish pitch, if he pulled away now, it would only lead to a full stop. He couldn't run the risk of her thinking that his questioning their situation was any sort of rejection.

Summer was and had always been his everything, even when they hadn't been together.

She tasted like trepidation and excitement, mixed with

the sweet and salty flavor of her lips. He'd always loved the way she tasted.

Reaching up, she ran her fingers through his hair, guiding his mouth closer, savoring their kiss.

"Take me," she said, not even bothering to stray from their kiss.

Damn, she was so damn hot.

He flipped her around so that she was pressed against the counter and then lifted her onto the cold stone. She gasped as he slid down her pants and her warm flesh pressed against the marble. He smiled, taking a certain amount of joy in the fact that she was having such a medley of sensations. He couldn't have planned it better. She was the kind of woman who needed every sense thrumming to really enjoy lovemaking.

He got down on his knees in front of her and kissed her skin, starting at her ankle and slowly working all the way up her inner thigh to the soft, satiny fabric of her panties. She tasted just as good as her lips. As he gently ran his fingers under the edge of her underwear, she lifted her hips and he slipped them down her legs, exposing her fully to the air.

He pulled her closer to the edge of the counter as he gave her a greedy grin. Reaching up, he unbuttoned her shirt, pulling it off her shoulders as he kissed where the fabric had just rested. He slipped his hands behind her back and undid the clasp of her bra with two fingers. Thankfully, that part was easier than he had remembered. He smiled as he edged the black straps down and exposed her dark pink nipples to the air. They were as hard as he was and he pulled one into his mouth. She arched beneath his kiss, groaning as he made her nipple grow impossibly harder. He flicked his tongue against her hard nub.

He ached for her as she moved against him. "I hope I'm still as good at some things as you remember," he said, releasing her from his torturous kiss.

She answered with a lusting, seductive smile. "I'm sure you are. If anything, I bet it's like fine wine and it's gotten better with age, just like the rest of you."

He ran his hands along her thighs toward the point where they met. He grazed her most sensitive bit, making her shudder. "That's what I think of you calling me 'old.' You won't do it again, will you?" He pressed his fingers inside her as he spoke, eliciting only a nod as a moan rippled from her throat.

His mouth went to the place his fingers had been and her moan grew louder. This was one of those moments he wished he could make last forever. He loved watching her as she threw her head back, her glistening hair falling down her back. Her lips had grown pinker, the same shade as her nipples.

He took his time, savoring her sweetness and the way she writhed as he worked her over. Yes, if he spent his entire life in this position, he would have considered it a life well spent. It didn't take long until a series of quakes and shudders took over her body and she cried out.

He hadn't lost his touch. She held out her hands, motioning for him to stand, apparently unable to find the words.

Her eyes were glazed. This was just how he liked her—well sated, to the point that all she could do was smile and relax.

And yet, instead of relaxing, Summer reached down and opened his belt buckle, kissing his neck as she slowly unzipped his pants. With her mouth moving against his neck, he could barely register everything she was doing to him, but he soon found his pants on the floor and her putting on a condom and directing him into her.

She leaned back as he slowly moved inside her.

"Damnnnn..." he groaned, barely able to think about anything besides how she felt against him.

He had spent many nights since their breakup imagining moments and memory-makers like these, with her back pressed against the mirror and her ass on the countertop of a hotel bathroom, but they all paled in comparison to the reality.

Though she had been thoroughly satisfied once, Mike knew he held the power to send her there again. If this was going to be the last time they'd ever be together, he wanted to give her the best she could get. Maybe, if he was lucky, she would think about him after she left and use him in the same way he had spent so many nights thinking about and using her.

He pressed deep into her, hitting the depth of her but giving her more. She moaned, the sound full of pleasure and tipped with the sweetness he knew could bring her to the edge once again. Slowly, he worked in and out, until her nectar ran heavy...she was close.

Summer grabbed his hand and pressed it against her mouth as she finished. The sensation of her arching and quaking against him made it impossible to hold back. Together they found what they had both been missing.

Chapter Eighteen

There were perfect moments in her life, but last night had been one of the best. Mike had always been an incredible lover, but he was even better than she had remembered.

What was even sweeter was that after their lovemaking, they had gone to bed together. He had wrapped her in his arms and she had slept better than she had in years. Joe had even managed to sleep through the night, which was a miracle in and of itself.

But now came the time to say goodbye.

Every part of her hurt with the thought of leaving her boys. And there was nothing she hated more than goodbye. Hawaiians had it right, using only one word—*aloha*—interchangeably for both hello and goodbye. With only one word, you were reminded at the moment of parting of how good it had felt to say hello. It was almost a reminder that soon enough the person you loved so much would be coming back into your life. But maybe goodbye really was the better word here; she could make no promises of return. She could only hope.

Mike held Joe in his lap, rocking him gently as he fed him a bottle. Joe was gazing over at her as he guzzled the liquid, but she couldn't help but notice the way he refused to turn his head away from her. The look in his young, innocent eyes didn't make her leaving any easier.

"I'm sorry, little guy. Mama has to go. I love you." She looked at Mike and their eyes met. "And I love you too," she said, regretting that she hadn't said it before in the last few days.

She wished she had found a better moment to tell Mike how she was really feeling, but this would have to do. At least he wouldn't be left wondering if she felt the same as he did. Sure, they could only have a long-distance relationship right now, but hopefully the future brought something different.

She couldn't believe she was leaving.

But she had to go before this got any more difficult than it already was.

One more kiss. She walked over and ran her hand over Joe's soft, downy hair, trying to take this one last chance to memorize the way his hair felt, just like she was touching a passing cloud. Leaning in, she gave him a soft kiss and took in his baby smell.

She looked up at Mike. "I hope you know that you are going to do great. Since the beginning, I have always known you would be the world's greatest dad. And husband." Her voice cracked.

He took her hand, his warmed by the baby, and pulled her lips to his. "I love you, Summer. When things go back to normal, I would be honored if you would consider being my wife."

In her wildest dreams she wouldn't have thought something like that would happen—her walking out seconds after Mike promised her forever.

Though her thoughts briefly moved to the past, she really only cared about this moment and the hope that rested at her fingertips, fingertips that had just brushed against the clouds and now rested in the radiant warmth of Mike's sunny touch.

"And I would be thrilled if you would allow me the honor of taking you as my husband." She kissed him, lacing her lips against his with a delicate promise. "With or without a piece of paperwork, the ceremony, and a party... I thee wed."

"And I thee wed, Mrs. Spade."

She took his face in her hands. "Mr. Spade." She rested her forehead against his, letting this simple touch in this complicated moment be all that she needed to solidify the bond and promise that had been so long in coming between them.

"Forever, you will be mine and I will be yours." Mike put his hand on hers, cupping them together against the stubble on his face.

She gave him one last kiss, letting her lips linger on his for a moment too long, a moment that allowed the tears to start to well in her eyes. Instead of turning away, blocking him from seeing how she truly felt, she let him look upon her... let him see that this was harder than anything before.

"I'm sorry I have to do this. I'm sorry I have to leave," she said, trying to keep herself from sobbing.

"Baby, you know I understand. But you have to know that you are not leaving forever. Only for right now, and Joe and I will be waiting for you when you get back."

"Where are you going to take him?" she asked.

"Once I know you're safe, I'll take him back to the STEALTH compound. When you are ready, you can come there too. We can plan a real wedding. Get every kind of flower you can dream of and have a ceremony at the bottom of a rolling mountainscape. We could do it this month, have the world covered in snow. Do a winter wedding."

She knew he was talking of all this in an attempt to give her a moment to collect herself and to think about something other than the pain she was feeling, and she loved him more for it. He had always known how important it had been to her that she stay strong, and he also knew how it was a battle she often lost—and he loved her through it all.

"I'd love a winter wedding. Red flowers, gray mountains, white snow." She could see the landscape in her mind's eye. Yes, it would have been beautiful. "All I'd want is me, you, Joe and a witness. Something simple."

"All I want is you." He smiled.

"I'll start planning," she continued. "I have a feeling that I may have a great deal of free time on my hands when I get to Kirtland. They will probably have me doing a bit of training, but—"

Mike's phone buzzed, cutting her off.

He looked down, surprise registering on his features. "Kevin is outside. He is waiting."

She wouldn't even bother to wonder how or when Kevin had gotten Mike's number and tracked her down to this hotel, but he must have figured out that she didn't have hers with her and just as quickly gotten a bead on them.

There was no more time for softness, no more time for goodbyes. There was only the harsh, bitter, wintery reality that waited for her outside.

"Have a good flight." Mike let go of her and resettled Joe's bottle for him. "Let me know when you make it and that you got there safely. Okay?"

She nodded as she turned, grabbed her bags, and walked out. Looking back, she gave him one more wave as the door to her world closed behind her.

KEVIN WAS SITTING in a blue pickup outside the lobby's front doors. He was scowling at his phone, looking annoyed. This was going to be either the longest or the shortest trip ever. Only time would tell.

Summer knocked on the window. He looked up and motioned for her to get in, but the annoyed look on his face didn't lessen. Throwing her bags in the back seat, she climbed up into the front passenger seat of the truck and buckled in.

Kevin didn't say anything as he put the truck into gear and pulled away from the hotel. The air was heavy with angst, but she wasn't sure if it was coming from her or from Kevin. Though she wanted to ask him about the day's plans, she didn't dare speak. This was his show, and he had been kind enough to offer her a safe harbor.

They drove for five minutes before he finally cleared his throat. "What did you learn?"

She slid him a sideways look, trying to figure out exactly what kind of answer he was looking for from such a cold, no-lead question. "I'm sorry?" she asked. "What do you mean?"

"What has this exercise taught you?" He repeated the question in the same monotone voice.

"Exercise?" What was he talking about?

Kevin didn't say anything as he pulled up to the gates of Malmstrom Air Force Base, flashed the guard his ID and answered a few questions before the gates were opened and they were waved through.

He remained silent as her mind whirled, trying to

make sense of Kevin's question. Was he implying that what had happened to her—Joe's kidnapping...the code exchange—all of it had been some sort of training exercise?

She had to have heard him wrong. He couldn't have possibly put her and her child in danger in an attempt to teach her something... Or had it been to test her?

She didn't understand. She couldn't understand.

Her thoughts came in short, fast bursts.

If Kevin was using this to teach her something, he was a total jerk. Who would use her child? If that was what he was willing to do, then she wasn't sure this job and the people she worked for were the kinds of people she wanted to be associated with.

Anger oozed from her pores. She could kill the man sitting next to her. "How in the hell do you sleep at night?"

He frowned as he looked over at her. "What?"

"Are you telling me that all of this was your doing? That your people *took my son*? That you staged all this?" She tried to find the words threatening to melt together in her fiery rage. "How did you get Ben to go along with this nonsense?"

Kevin slowed as he drove through the base, toward the airfield. "First, I don't know who Ben is or what you think he's gone along with. Second, it wasn't my idea to do things this way. I have to answer to a boss, as well, and I was just told what to do and how to do it. I didn't agree to kidnapping Joe, but your friend Mike made it all too easy for our contractors to get their hands on your boy."

How dare he blame this on Mike. He hadn't done anything she wouldn't have done. "You had to have given them the okay. No one would just take a child."

"I don't have to answer your questions, but given the circumstances and how all of this has unfortunately played out, I will make an exception in telling you that those men—the contractors who took Joe—paid the price for coloring outside the lines. For this training exercise, they were given strict instructions to watch you and to learn your potential weaknesses while you dug into Mike for information about Rockwood. However, they jumped the gun. Both have been released from their contracts with DARPA."

"And that is all to say nothing about how you played me," she seethed. "You made me feel like I wasn't going to get Joe back. You manipulated me into playing their stupid game."

Oh crap. What have I done by bringing Mike into this?

"Is Mike in trouble?" she asked.

"Don't you think you should be more concerned about your own welfare, given the fact that you brought an unauthorized person into your work with the DTRA?" Kevin asked.

"If Ben hadn't threatened me, and if your people hadn't taken *our son*, I would have never gone to Mike for help. You forced me into a position where I had no allies. What little I told him was limited to what he needed to know. You can hardly hold that against me."

Kevin stared at her for a long moment. "Who is Ben and how did he threaten you, exactly? Are you talking about your ex from your days in Rockwood?"

She shrugged. Was this another of Kevin's sick, twisted games?

She should quit. Right here, right now. Then she should storm off in righteous indignation.

And yet she sat in the passenger side of his truck, unmoving. What did that mean? Was she just stunned so greatly that she was afraid to move? Did she love her job so much that she didn't want to walk away?

The thoughts rippled through her, creating an electric buzz that cascaded into her fingertips and down to her toes. The sad and beautiful truth was that she did…she loved this job. She loved being a part of something bigger than herself. Something that stopped the bad guys from getting their hands on the weapons that could and would hurt so many.

Summer didn't agree with the methods those above them had used to make her prove her worth and dedication, but if they had thought her unworthy based on their findings, she wouldn't be sitting where she now sat. "Did I pass? Are these stupid training exercises over?" she asked, wary but hopeful.

"We booked you on a private plane to take you back to the main office. What do you think?" Kevin asked, giving her a wink. "I seriously do hope you know that I am in your corner with all of this. I went to bat for you."

She couldn't bring herself to say thank you, but from the tired look in Kevin's eyes she didn't think he was looking for her gratitude. If anything, he looked apologetic. That response was something she could appreciate and understand.

She gave him a tight nod in simple recognition of his efforts.

"When we get to Kirtland," he continued, "we have set up a series of secondary training exercises with several other candidates."

"Candidates?" she asked, taken aback. "For what?"

"Thanks to your work, the DTRA has been working on a new program that focuses solely on worldwide IGS through nanotechnology. We would like you to take a lead role in the project and to help create a better training program so we never find ourselves in a similar situation."

"Am I being bought off?" she challenged. "Am I getting this opportunity because someone above you feels guilty or is it actually because of merit?"

Kevin chuckled. "I wish I had the answers for you, but you know as much as I do in this case. If I were you, though, I wouldn't look this gift horse in the mouth. This is the one chance you may get to advance and also get to be at home with Joe more often. After all this, do you really want to continue being a field agent?"

"No." There was no hesitation in her response, no need to think about her choices or about what she wanted. "I want to be with Joe. I can't put him into a situation like this ever again. And while I'm sure the DTRA would never intentionally put him into danger again, I can see now that, no matter what steps I take or don't take, being an agent will put him in harm's way. That's unacceptable. And as much as I love my job and I want to continue working with this group, I can't take that kind of risk with my child."

Kevin nodded understandingly. "If I'm being completely honest, I'm surprised you are still sitting here with me and are willing to go. I would get it if you turned in your ID and quit. What happened…was a cluster of mistakes and I'm embarrassed that it even happened like it did."

"From what you've said, none of this was your fault. You had a job. I had a job. We had to play our parts. I don't like it. I don't like what happened. It is unacceptable and I will be requesting that there be follow-up investigations and procedural changes, but what better way to do this than from a job inside? I can be the change so no one ever has to go through anything remotely close to what I've had to go through."

"That is one hell of a great perspective," Kevin said, nodding his head in appreciation. "I can tell you right now that it is that attitude and outlook on life that got you this job and is going to make you successful in years to come. I'm proud to be a part of your journey, but remember me and the benefits of this organization when you are looking down from your seat in Congress. Okay?"

Summer laughed. The last thing she wanted to do was to be involved even more deeply in politics than she already was. Even though she wasn't going to continue as a field agent and would instead move into more of a political sector role, it didn't mean that she wanted to become a dealmaker. And yet, who knew what the future would bring? Life had a way of throwing curveballs that were so strong and swift, no one could catch them; all they could do was try to get out of the way and hope for the best.

The plane's crew was standing out by the stairs, waiting.

This was her last chance to say no and walk away. But as quickly as the idea came to her mind, it disappeared. Summer's life was about to change in ways she struggled to imagine. To top things off, she could be the wife and the mother she had always wanted to be.

In this moment of change, she could have it all.

"Ready?" Kevin asked, motioning to the waiting aircraft.

She reached back and grabbed her bags, then opened the passenger-side door. "I'm as ready as I'm ever going to be."

Stepping out of the truck, she slung her bags over her

shoulder and closed the door. As the door slammed, there was a crack. That sound. She knew that sound. Without thinking, she hit the ground.

Someone was shooting at them.

As her body hit the cold, snow-laden tarmac, the bags she had been carrying rolled off her back. She felt heat radiate up from her core. Reaching down, her fingers prodded her side. There was something warm and wet. As she touched the spot, it felt as if a fire was racing through her, setting her nerves ablaze with pain.

There was a whizzing sound as another round pierced the air just above her head.

Someone wasn't just shooting at *them*; they were shooting at *her*.

Someone wanted her dead. And based on the fact that they were still shooting even though she'd been hit, they wouldn't stop until they were sure she was dead.

Chapter Nineteen

After having dropped off Joe with Jessica, Mike sat at the top of the offset from the airfield. He scoped from the hill and waited as Kevin and Summer sat in the truck. He could tell they were talking and as the minutes passed, some of the anger on Summer's face had started to diminish and was replaced with what he could best assume was relief.

His assault rifle with its long-range scope was perched on its bipod, concealed under the little makeshift tent he'd propped up around him using a borrowed sheet from the hotel. He'd also used all the white-and-black clothes he could find in an effort to blend into the snowy landscape.

She didn't need to know he was watching, that he couldn't stand by and just let her leave with a man and a team who had put them all in danger. Yeah, right.

If anything, given how much she knew him, it was a bit of a surprise that Summer hadn't been watching in the rearview mirror for him the entire way to the base. Sure, he'd had to borrow a late-model Buick from the hotel parking lot, but if things went right and she got on the plane without any sort of event, he would have the car and sheets back to the hotel before anyone even knew they were missing.

Getting onto the base had been more of a trick, but given his and STEALTH's levels of clearance, it had only taken a minute for the guard to make the necessary calls and for the gates of Malmstrom to open to him. Not for the first time, Mike found himself chuckling at the limited levels of security. Yes, he had a reason, the clearances, and a right to be on the base, but it struck him as darkly funny that he had to be there to provide cover and security for his fiancée.

He watched as the passenger door of the pickup opened and Summer stepped out, carrying her bags. As she closed the door, there was the rip of a round through the still Montana air.

What in the hell?

Using his rifle, he scoped the area around the base, looking for the shooter or shooters. Was there someone else, someone camouflaged like him, waiting just outside the perimeter of the airfield?

He looked over at Summer; she was lying on the ground. Her fingers came up from her side and, even from two hundred yards away, he could make out the distinct red color of fresh blood.

Someone had shot her.

How dare someone hurt the woman he loved.

Mike moved his sights in the direction in which he thought he'd heard the shot originate from. As he did, he caught a muzzle flash from the corner of his eye as the shooter fired off another round.

People on the base began to move quickly, like ants, as they started to make sense of what was happening and the reality that they were coming under fire from some unknown assailant.

There was another shot, but this time Mike spotted the

little orange blaze that appeared to erupt from a blanket of snow. Whoever was shooting at Summer was using cover, just like him. If the shooter had been just a little more careful in the planning, Mike might not have even seen the flash. He had gotten lucky.

Hopefully, he would continue to be.

Mike took aim, carefully making calculations for distance and wind speed as he lined up his target. He would likely only get one easy shot. If he missed, the shooter would be on the run at a distance, making it even more of a challenge to neutralize the threat.

He had to get this right.

Clear.

Take the shot.

He found his mark, a tiny black spot in the midst of white where he assumed the shooter's head would be. He aimed small, centering his sights on the tiny black spot. His finger moved inside the guard and he felt the steely, cold ridges of the trigger. He applied even, steady pressure, making sure not to engage the sympathetic movement in his hand and interfere with his shot.

Precision. This was all about precision.

This was the moment he had trained for his entire adult life. He was the protector, the keeper of hearts, the man in the shadows, and the hero no one could identify— if he did things right.

The shot didn't surprise him, he had known it was coming, but the pressure he'd applied to the trigger had been so steady and even that when the firing pin hit the primer, it nearly shocked him. The suppressor did its job as the round moved down the barrel and cut into the air. There was only the dull *pew* sound as the round left and sought its target.

He stared as the bit of copper found that little black dot in which he had been aiming.

Damn. Sometimes he was good.

He smiled at the shot.

But had he neutralized the threat?

The firing stopped. No more rounds filled the air from where the shooter had been lying and taking aim at Summer.

Just to be sure he'd done his job, Mike sent another round downrange, striking just a few millimeters to the right of his first aim. He wouldn't stop firing until he knew his target was no longer a threat.

Crimson blood started to seep out onto the ground near his target. The shooter moved to stand, pushing the cover he had been lying under up and off. The man was dressed in white-and-black camouflage of the more commercial type, like the kind someone would buy at a sporting goods store.

The camo outfit was unmarred, but as the man moved, blood poured from his neck, just below his ear. He reached up and put his hand to his neck, applying pressure. But it was too late and Mike watched as he sank to his knees, his blood pressure lowering and starting to fail as the life seeped from him.

If the dude thought he could attempt to hurt or kill the woman Mike loved…well then, the dude deserved to die. No one hurt Summer. Never again.

Mike grabbed his gear and slipped away, hoping to remain unseen and the man in the shadows.

He rushed back to the borrowed Buick and made to leave the air base. He didn't want to have to answer questions about the shooting and find himself in some kind of court battle. He wasn't that kind of man. No, he was the kind who snuck in, did his job, and snuck out. And, for all intents and purposes, that was exactly what he needed to do now, as well.

Except, he couldn't bear the thought of knowing Summer was wounded, bleeding, and he was about to start running in the other direction. No. He couldn't leave her. He had to get down there, make sure she was okay and help stabilize her until the medics arrived. This being a military base, it wouldn't take long.

He drove toward the airfield, stopping far enough away from the strip that he wouldn't get pulled over by the airmen starting to swarm the area. Getting out, he stepped into a snowdrift. A USAF Security Forces airman rushed toward him, his hands raised. "You need to stop right there, sir."

That was not going to work on him, not now, with Summer waiting. "The woman out there on the tarmac, she is my…" He paused for a half second as he thought of exactly what he should call her so that the airman would be most willing to let him go to her. "She's going to be my wife. I need to get to her. To make sure she's okay. She's been shot."

"I'm more than aware she has been shot, sir." The airman looked in the direction of Summer, where another airman was kneeling beside her. He had his hands on her stomach, applying what looked like a compress to stop the bleeding.

"Look, I need to get to her. Please. I'm begging you."

"Sir, we have an active shooter situation, I recommend that you get back into your car and leave the area before someone takes a shot at you."

Mike tried to cover his smirk. "I can guarantee that the

threat here is neutralized. I saw your shooter go down. If you let me go to her, I'll take you to the man's body."

The Security Force airman—known as an SF—turned away, clicking on his handset to likely call in to his fellow officers. Before the man could turn back, Mike sprinted past him toward Summer. The airman reached out and tried to grab him, but he swiveled around his grasp and charged away.

Mike slid to a stop on the icy tarmac next to her, the SF close at his heels. "Summer. Summer, I'm here. Are you okay?" he asked, taking her hand.

She looked up at him, shock in her eyes, but thankfully it looked as though it was only shock at seeing him as a smile crossed over her features. "Mike? What? How?"

He sent her a wicked smile in return and tipped his head in the direction of the shooter. "You couldn't believe that for one second I was going to let you get out of my sight. At least not until I knew you were safe and tucked away on the plane."

Her smile quaked as the airman holding the bandage moved. "Sir, you need to back up. The medics will be here at any moment, sir."

"I will leave as soon as she tells me to and not a second sooner."

"Sir, if you don't move away from this woman, I will be forced to place you under arrest."

The SF behind him piped up. "You should be under arrest already."

He had broken several laws and would be willing to break several more if it meant taking care of her, but for now he needed to get these guys to just back off. "I'm not trying to cause a scene. Really. I just—"

"Excuse me, gentlemen. Please leave my friend here

alone." There was the crunch of footsteps on the tarmac as Kevin walked toward them.

"But, sir—" the SF standing behind Mike said.

"Lieutenant, it would be in your best interest—should you wish to continue your career in the air force—if you simply busy yourself with finding out where the medics are. If they are not on-scene in the next minute, I will make sure all of you find yourselves in your CO's office getting the ass-chewing of a lifetime before the day is out. Do you understand me?"

Mike wasn't sure what had happened, or who was behind the pulling of the trigger, but it appeared as though the culprit wasn't Kevin. A certain amount of relief filled him; at least their enemy wasn't the man standing directly in front of them.

Before he made up his mind about their safety, Mike glanced at Summer, giving an inquisitive look between she and Kevin.

Summer dipped her head. "It's all good. I'll explain later though." She was breathing hard as though it hurt to take in too deep a breath. "Is the shooter down?"

Mike gave her a tight nod. "The threat has been neutralized. No other shooters in the area. But I haven't been able to make a positive ID on the trigger puller."

"I need to know," she said. She tried to move to standing, but the airman held his hands in place and she winced in pain.

"We will know who was behind this soon enough. For now, we just need to get you to the hospital and get you stitched up. We don't want you bleeding all over the place," he teased, trying to keep her from thinking about anything but taking care of herself.

"This is not going to make wedding dress fittings any easier, you know."

He laughed.

Behind him, the medics rolled up and, parking on the tarmac, rushed over. He was pushed out of the way as they took Summer's vitals. Her blood pressure was high, but her oxygen sat levels were normal and the bleeding appeared to be under control. From what he could see as they pulled up her shirt, the bullet had traveled clean through—entering from the back just to the side of where her kidney would be and exiting out of her side. He was no doctor, but based on the looks of the wound, she would be okay. Especially as the bleeding was no longer an issue.

"Sir, you said you would show us where to find the body of the shooter," the SF who had chased after him said, pulling him back to the world outside of Summer.

"Absolutely." Mike nodded. "Summer, babe, you going to be okay for a minute?" he asked over the sounds of the medics asking her questions and talking to each other.

Summer looked up at him and smiled. "I'll be fine. Nothing more than a little flesh wound."

He glanced at the medic, who gave him a slight nod, reaffirming her assessment. "She'll be okay. We just need to get her to the infirmary and get her fixed up."

"Don't take her anywhere without letting me know first. She is not going to the infirmary without me, understand?"

The medic gave him a glove-handed thumbs-up. "You got it, sir."

The SF put his hand on Mike's shoulder, the action too invasive, and Mike turned out of it. The airman was just doing his job, but he always hated to be touched—except when it came to Summer.

"The guy was up this way," Mike said, motioning toward the snowy patch where his victim had been. He started to pick his way through the airmen and medics milling around the area, some talking on handsets and others talking with one another as they all seemed to be trying to make sense of what had happened. He didn't envy their job.

"Did you see what happened to him?" the SF asked, following him off the tarmac and into the knee-deep mounds of snow shoveled off in preparation for a day of flights.

Mike shrugged, noncommittal. "I saw him take the shot that hit Summer. Then I saw a splatter of blood when a projectile hit him."

"Did you see who made the shot on the assailant?" the SF asked, his breathing heavy as he stumbled over a chunk of ice and was forced to recover.

Mike held back a chuckle; he felt bad for the kid, he really did. Here he was, trying to do his job and investigate a shooting and not look like a total idiot, and not only was Mike going to have to keep some key details from him, now the kid was tripping around in front of his main eyewitness.

"You all right there, Lieutenant?"

The soldier straightened his uniform and put his hand down to his sidearm as though afraid that somehow it would slip from its holster. "Yep, just fine." He cleared his throat uncomfortably. "You were saying…about the shooter?"

Mike smiled as he looked away and up toward the man

who lay dead in the snow. "I didn't see who shot him, or where it came from. Sorry."

"But you are sure the shooter was neutralized."

He nodded. He knew death. "Absolutely."

The young SF continued asking questions until Mike spotted the little knoll. "The guy is up there," he said, pointing just ahead of them. "You can make out his footsteps behind in the snow, just there."

The SF pressed by him, hurrying toward the body. He knelt as he reached the man and pulled back his balaclava. Even from where he stood, based on the chunk of missing flesh, Mike could tell the man was deceased. And yet the SF pressed his fingers to the man's neck. As he did, the man's head rolled slightly, exposing his face.

Mike knew that face. He had seen it outside Summer's apartment complex when the man had been sneering at him. It was Ben.

Mike had been right all along. Ben must have been stalking them, watching as they went around Great Falls together. If Mike had just trusted his gut from the first moment and kicked the guy's ass, this shooting would have never had to happen.

Now he was going to have to tell Summer she had been gunned down by her ex.

But why? Summer had told him that Ben had threatened them because of their being together, that he was just a crazy ex, but could this have also had something to do with Rockwood? Had they found out that she was, in fact, a double agent?

On the ground, by the tip of Mike's boot, lay a cell phone.

There was the crunch of footsteps in the snow behind them and Mike turned. Kevin was making his way next to him and, as he stopped, he looked down and also spotted the cell phone in the snow.

"Whoever made this shot was one hell of a marksman." Kevin winked in his direction.

What was that wink supposed to mean? Kevin couldn't have known that Mike had made the kill shot, and yet he definitely seemed to. Son of a…

"Yeah," the SF said, looking back at Mike from over his shoulder. "Considering I barely saw this dude until I walked right up on him, the shooter had to have known what he was doing."

"I'm sure it was probably one of your guards. You airmen are on the money when it comes to this kind of thing. You should be proud. I know I am," Kevin added.

"Well, sir, it will take a bit of investigative work, but I'm sure we will figure out exactly what happened here in just a few days. Either of you recognize this man?" the SF asked.

Kevin looked over at Mike then looked down at the cell phone, but not before Kevin gave him an understanding smirk. "I think ID'ing him shouldn't be too challenging. In fact, I would appreciate it if you could pull together as much about this incident as possible in the next day or two. I will talk to your superior officers and let them know that my team will be handling it from there."

"Yes, sir." The SF looked slightly excited at the prospect of working for someone as high up in the Pentagon as Kevin. He turned back to the body, snapping a few pictures with his cell phone as though he was trying to capture the entire scene.

Kevin had definitely just lit a fire under the lieutenant. Mike looked over at Summer's boss, who was still staring at him as though he was trying to read his mind. After a moment, Kevin knelt and pretended to tie his shoe. Checking to make sure the SF's back was turned to them, Kevin picked up the cell phone and stuffed it into his back pocket. He stood and gave Mike a tip of the head.

"Do you know this man?" Kevin asked, his voice barely above a whisper so that only Mike could hear.

He nodded. "It's Ben, Summer's ex."

Kevin sighed. "Good. Good. I'm glad he has been taken out of the situation. I have reason to believe he was feeding information to his organization about Summer."

"Well, he won't be anymore," Mike said with a devilish smile.

"Good job out here," Kevin said. "You handled this situation very well. I can only imagine what you've gone through, you know, with everything with your son."

Mike didn't know if he should admit his role to this man, but clearly there were to be no secrets between them when it came to this shooting. "Just doing my part."

As he looked over at the dead man and stared at Ben's lifeless eyes, Mike couldn't help but be the slightest bit pleased. He didn't like having to pull the trigger and take down a bad man, but he had told Ben that if he wasn't careful, he would put him in his grave. The man had been warned to not mess with Summer. Ben had made a choice to mess with the dragon, and he had called the flames.

"If there's anything I can do, as a token of my gratitude for your service to this country, all you have to do is let me know," Kevin said, extending his hand in gratitude.

Mike shook his hand as a sense of ease filled him. "Actually, there is something that Summer and I wanted, maybe when things cool off a bit, you can help…"

Chapter Twenty

It felt good to rest. A week had passed and she had been answering a flurry of phone calls with requests for interviews from a variety of newspapers and military journals, but as soon as she had mentioned their constant badgering to Kevin, all had come to a stop. In fact, besides hearing from Mike when he'd run to the commissary and a couple of messages from Kevin, she hadn't gotten any other phone calls. It had been pure bliss and she had finally just been able to enjoy her alone time with Joe and Mike. Things hadn't been this quiet in her life in a long time. Not saying she wanted to be shot again, but she was thoroughly enjoying the peace.

Mike was busying himself around the kitchen of their house in Kirtland, making her a sandwich. After she had been seen by the doctors at the infirmary and cleared, they had gotten on the plane and headed to New Mexico where Kevin had instructed them they were to stay until the things with Rockwood were cleared and she had finished up the training she needed for her new job—once she healed of course.

The house they had been assigned was far nicer, and larger, than her apartment in Great Falls. Everything had been prefurnished and all she and Mike had had to do was hang their clothes in the closets and set up a crib for Joe. Everything was nice, far nicer than she had expected to find on a military base. Thankfully, Kevin had gotten them into the officer's housing. Aside from seeing her friend Jessica, she had to admit that she held no desire to go back to Montana for a while.

Mike sauntered out of the kitchen, carrying a tray complete with two Tylenol and her antibiotics. Setting it down beside her on the couch, he made sure the blanket was wrapped neatly around her feet. "You need anything else? I'm gonna go check on Joe. He has got to be getting up from his nap soon." He motioned in the direction of the second bedroom.

"Kevin said he is going to stop by soon. I think he is worried about me." She smiled up at him. "He sounded *off,* maybe excited or something."

"Kevin's a good guy. You are lucky to have a boss like him," Mike offered. "If you want, I can give you guys a few minutes to talk without me around."

"No, he mentioned that he wanted to talk to you." She gave him a questioning glance.

Ever since the shooting, Mike and Kevin had been up to something, she could feel it, and yet both had kept their lips shut. She had to assume it was about his role in the shooting. No one had spoken of his killing Ben. It was almost as if it had been silently agreed upon by all involved that Ben's death would be one of those things swept under the rug.

No doubt, Kevin had had to pull a lot of strings for something like that to happen since the death had occurred on a military base. But the last thing DTRA would have wanted was additional scrutiny on their organization and what they had been doing on an airfield in the middle of a freezing Montana day.

Mike walked to the bedroom and there were the sounds of him talking to Joe as he obviously began a diaper change. After a few minutes, he came out to the living room with Joe cradled in his arm. When her son saw her, a giant grin erupted on his face and he threw out his arms, reaching for her.

"Oh, someone is happy to see Mama after his big nap," Mike said, bringing him over to her and placing him in her arms. He reached behind him and pulled out a bottle. "I made him this too. I bet he's hungry."

She took the bottle. Being a dad suited Mike more than she could have ever expected. Though he had struggled, putting the first diaper on and receiving a little shower, things since then had clicked into place between her two boys. They were made for one another. There was nothing better than watching them together, Mike talking to him and Joe laughing at his father.

Love filled her as Joe gripped the bottle, shoved it into his little mouth and started suckling. It had taken some major hardships and fighting to get here, but she finally had the life she had always wanted. The only thing that could have made it better was if she could have really and truly called Mike her husband.

It had been awkward when they had been shown the house and asked the status of their relationship. Neither had really known what to say until Mike had finally told the man they were engaged. Of course, the man had instinctively glanced at her naked ring finger, but had been gracious enough not to mention the lack of a ring.

There was a knock on the door.

She moved to stand, but Mike stopped her with a wave. "I got it."

He walked over to the door and opened it for Kevin. The warm desert air swept into the living room, with it came the scent of earth and dried grass.

"How are you feeling?" Kevin asked, walking inside and closing the door behind him. "All healed up and ready to hit the ground running?"

Summer put her hand to her side where the stitches were itching. "Maybe a few more days before I go for a run. But I should be ready to get back to training shortly. When were you thinking?"

Kevin glanced over at Mike and they exchanged looks, but she didn't understand why.

"I don't want you to worry about going back to work just yet. I'll let you know when we want you. In the meantime—" Kevin paused, walking over and sitting on the edge of the chair across the room from her "—I wanted to let you both know, in person, that we have analyzed Ben's phone. As it turns out, we found text messages and emails between him and his fellow members of Rockwood— one of which was a senator's son. He had been sent to take you out if he found that you were working for the feds."

"So, they didn't know anything about me stealing the codes from ConFlux?" she asked, silently begging for that fear to be unfounded.

"No," Kevin said, shaking his head. "You are in the clear. They had just feared that you were a double agent, as I said. When Ben learned the truth, he did tell his team. They ordered him to put you down."

"So, she is never going to be safe as long as Rockwood knows she was working for you?" Mike asked.

A lump rose in her throat.

Kevin rubbed his hands together. "Just for now. As such, we are going to keep you here until we can neutralize their organization. However, in the meantime, we will start building Summer an alternative identity. I have no doubts that we can make you, Summer—for all intents and purposes—disappear."

Disappearing and being safe at the expense of giving up her public identity was just fine. There was little to her life as it was, besides Joe and Mike.

"That's fine."

Kevin smiled and some of his nervousness evaporated. "Good. I was hoping you wouldn't find that to be too much of a problem."

Summer nodded. "I know we've had our issues, but you've gone above and beyond in making up for it. I appreciate all your hard work."

Kevin gave a slight dip of the head in acknowledgment. "You know how I feel about what happened, so I appreciate that you guys are taking all of this in stride."

Mike walked over and put his hand on her shoulder. "Here, let me take Joe." He lifted Joe from her as he kept feeding.

Kevin slapped his knees and smiled up at Mike. "Enough of that. Now, you said you weren't up for a run, but are you up for a small walk, Summer?" Kevin gave Mike a wink.

Mike held out his hand to help her to standing. Gently, she rose.

"What are you guys up to?" she asked, grinning.

"Well, no pressure or anything, but Kevin and I have been working on a bit of a surprise for you."

She cocked her head slightly. "And this would be?"

Mike smiled. "Come outside and see." He interlaced their fingers and pulled her toward the door. Opening it, she walked out.

There, along the road, someone had lined the sidewalk with red roses. The yard was covered in fake snow and at the end of the walk there was a string quartet playing "Ave Maria." The song brought tears to her eyes.

She really did love that song, and hearing it and knowing just how much work Mike must have gone through to make this happen in a place he had never been after changing his life basically overnight for her and Joe…it was all just *perfect*.

He walked her out into the middle of the fake snow and dropped down to one knee, Joe still in his arm. "Summer Daniels, I have loved you from the first moment we met. Our lives have been like our love and filled with ups and downs, but truly what they were meant to be. I want to be the best father and husband in the world and build a life with you that is filled with all the laughter and happiness that our lives will allow. Summer, will you marry me?" He reached into his back pocket and pulled out a gold band with a princess-cut solitaire at its center.

It was simple and beautiful as it gleamed in the New Mexico sun.

"Yes, Mike Spade." She covered her mouth with her hand and excitedly bounced from one foot to the other as he slipped the ring onto her finger.

But he didn't get up. "Now, since we are engaged…and before either of us can run, be chased, or slip away—" He looked over toward the quartet, where a man was standing with a Bible in his hand "I propose that we get married right here, right now."

He reached into his other back pocket and pulled out two rings, a simple gold band for each of them.

Summer squealed in agreement.

For once, everything was perfect. No more fear. No more running. They were safe and the stars had aligned. She and Mike would have their forever love and they could officially and legally become a family—the greatest gift she could have wished to receive.

For once in her life, she had everything—honor, love, and family.

* * * * *

COMING SOON!

We really hope you enjoyed reading this book.
If you're looking for more romance, be sure to
head to the shops when new books are
available on

Thursday 4th March

To see which titles are coming soon, please visit
millsandboon.co.uk/nextmonth

LET'S TALK

Romance

For exclusive extracts, competitions
and special offers, find us online:

MILLS & BOON

THE HEART OF ROMANCE

A ROMANCE FOR EVERY KIND OF READER

MODERN

Prepare to be swept off your feet by sophisticated, sexy and seductive heroes, in some of the world's most glamourous and romantic locations, where power and passion collide.
8 stories per month.

HISTORICAL

Escape with historical heroes from time gone by. Whether your passion is for wicked Regency Rakes, muscled Vikings or rugged Highlanders, awaken the romance of the past.
6 stories per month.

MEDICAL

Set your pulse racing with dedicated, delectable doctors in the high-pressure world of medicine, where emotions run high and passion, comfort and love are the best medicine.
6 stories per month.

True Love

Celebrate true love with tender stories of heartfelt romance, from the rush of falling in love to the joy a new baby can bring, and a focus on the emotional heart of a relationship.
8 stories per month.

Desire

Indulge in secrets and scandal, intense drama and plenty of sizzling hot action with powerful and passionate heroes who have it all: wealth, status, good looks…everything but the right woman.
6 stories per month.

HEROES

Experience all the excitement of a gripping thriller, with an intense romance at its heart. Resourceful, true-to-life women and strong, fearless men face danger and desire - a killer combination!
8 stories per month.

DARE

Sensual love stories featuring smart, sassy heroines you'd want as a best friend, and compelling intense heroes who are worthy of them.
4 stories per month.

To see which titles are coming soon, please visit

millsandboon.co.uk/nextmonth

MILLS & BOON
True Love

Romance from the Heart

Celebrate true love with tender stories of
heartfelt romance, from the rush of falling
in love to the joy a new baby can bring,
and a focus on the emotional
heart of a relationship.

MILLS & BOON
MEDICAL
Pulse-Racing Passion

Set your pulse racing with dedicated, delectable doctors in the high-pressure world of medicine, where emotions run high and passion, comfort and love are the best medicine.